Sign up for our newsletter to hear
about new and upcoming releases.

www.ylva-publishing.com

Other Books by Chris Zett

Irregular Heartbeat

Heart
FAILURE

CHRIS ZETT

Acknowledgments

Writing my second book was simultaneously easier and harder than the first. The knowledge that I could do it—that I had already successfully finished, edited, and published a novel—helped immensely. Unfortunately, my self-imposed expectations for perfection grew faster than my abilities, and I struggled in representing the characters on the page as I felt them in my heart. But even though writing might be a solitary experience, editing and publishing is a team effort.

I'm very grateful for everyone who helped me to transform this story from an okayish first draft to this novel I'm proud to share with readers.

My beta-readers—Trish and Bianca—gave me invaluable feedback in an amazingly short time. I promise to manage my deadlines better next time!

My publisher Astrid shuffled around deadlines and publication dates so I could rewrite the whole novel, taking out unnecessary secondary characters and adding new scenes on her advice.

My editors—Alissa, Miranda, and Amber—each improved different aspects of my writing. Special shout-out to Miranda for taking up the extra work last-minute and providing such insightful and detailed comments about my characters.

And an extra-big-thank-you-with-ice-cream-on-top to Sandra, who switched roles from senior editor to writing mentor to friend seamlessly and always encouraged and supported me.

And last but not least: Thank you, readers, for buying this book and maybe even my debut novel too. You help me sharing my stories around the globe.

Dedication

For Bianca—thank you for being courageous

Chapter One

"RILEY! WHAT THE HELL ARE you doing?"

Dr. Jess Riley wrenched her foot off the fluoro pedal to stop the X-ray and inspected the intruder.

Like a pit bull in green scrubs, Dr. Watts charged into the cath lab. He stopped only inches from her patient.

Her team, decked out in full sterile garb, froze.

Jess gave him an isn't-it-obvious look and pointed at the patient and the big, illuminated *X-ray in use* sign that should have stopped him. "Whatever it is, now is not the right time."

"You stole my patient! Are you so desperate for lab time you troll the surgical floor and poach my patients? You bitch!" Spittle flew from his mouth, as he hadn't even bothered to don the obligatory face mask.

Jess squared her shoulders and rose to her full five-ten. Not an easy feat, as the protective lead apron that covered her body seemed to weigh a ton after the two-hour intervention. Sweat slid down her shoulder blades and soaked her scrubs. She ignored her fatigue and discomfort and fixed her iciest glare on Watts. "I have no idea where your accusation is coming from. But I won't discuss this here in front of a patient during an intervention." She didn't remind him that as a senior attending in the cardiology department, she didn't owe him or any other cardiac surgeon an explanation.

He held her gaze, not backing down an inch. After what felt like an eternity, he growled. "Nothing to discuss. Your boss will hear from me. He'll regret the day he decided to cave in to HR and hire a woman to do a man's job." He stabbed the door button repeatedly as if the electronic door would bend to his will and open any faster. As soon as the opening was wide enough, he stomped out.

Was he trapped in the dark ages? Jess clenched her jaw shut beneath the mask. The threat he would talk to the head of the cardiology department didn't faze her in the least. She trusted her boss to have her back, and she intended to have a word with him about Watts's unacceptable behavior.

But the insinuation stung. Did more colleagues think she'd been hired because of her gender? She'd thought she left this shit behind years ago.

She shook her head to clear it from the emotional fog before tears started to rise. Recently, her protective barriers had been thin like early spring ice, ready to crack at any second. But she wouldn't allow her hormones to reign and encourage the idiots who still thought women didn't belong in medicine. Especially now.

"Are you upset? Do you want me to continue?" Scott's voice oozed with friendliness.

Of course, the boy-scout image was a façade, and he was as eager as the next cardiology fellow to pounce on her territory as soon as she showed any signs of weakness. Sharks. All of them.

Getting worked up over her young colleague helped her to pull herself together. "No." He wasn't so advanced in his training that she trusted him with her high-risk patient.

"Hey, I was just asking." Scott pouted. Not a cute look on him.

There wasn't a reason to be this short with him, but she wasn't in the mood to coddle another male ego.

Jess leaned over the sterile drape to check on her patient. He was still snoring softly from the sedative he'd received earlier. At least something was going according to plan.

She met Kayla's gaze over the face mask. The dark-brown eyes of the nurse showed support and not judgment. "Let's finish him up and get a cup of coffee."

The idea of coffee sounded heavenly. Jess pushed the residual traces of anger, frustration, and annoyance to the back of her mind and continued with the angioplasty. The most difficult part had been over before the interruption, and the rest she could do in her sleep.

Fifteen minutes later, Scott wheeled the patient to the recovery room.

Jess peeled off the sterile paper gown and gloves. The draft from the air conditioning sent a trail of goose bumps over her arms. She opened the lead apron to let even more air in and stretched. She couldn't wait to get off her feet for a short break.

Kayla sorted the instruments from the table, discarding the sharps in the safety container. "Will I see you this Saturday at the free clinic?"

"No, I swapped the shift. My mom's birthday is this weekend." And she couldn't miss that for the second year in a row. Besides, she was long overdue for a personal visit and talk.

"The patients will miss you, but your mom should come first." Kayla crunched the sterile wrap into a big ball and stuffed it into the trash. "What did Watts mean, you stole his patient?"

Jess shrugged. She honestly had no idea. She saw hundreds of patients each month and didn't need to search for more.

Before she could answer, Scott joined them, twirling his face mask in his hand. "We didn't steal him; he didn't want surgery. Really. Sheila said so."

"What? Who didn't want surgery?" Jess frowned. "And who the fuck is Sheila?"

"Um, Sheila is my girlfriend. She's a nurse on the cardiac surgery floor." Scott beamed at the mention of her name. "I guess Dr. Watts meant our last patient. He was scheduled for coronary surgery, but he was afraid. His son and the surgeons pressured him, and Sheila asked me to take a look at him. And I talked to him, and…" He trailed off as if he only now noticed the twin sets of glares on him.

"You mean, you really did poach on the surgery floor, and now Dr. Watts is blaming Jess?" Kayla's voice hardened, and she crossed her arms over her chest.

"Hey, I was right. Everything went well. No harm, no foul." Scott tried his best boyish grin.

That didn't help his case at all. Jess clenched her fists and fought the urge to yell. "Yes, everything went well. But you don't have a fucking clue what you did. You lied to me. You not only kept the backstory from me but told me an outright lie—that the cardiac surgeons had referred his case to us."

"But I just wanted—"

Jess held up her hand. She wasn't in the mood for whiny, entitled arguments. "No. I don't want to hear any of your shit. You think about what you've done and apologize to Dr. Watts." She held his gaze until he looked down.

Jess was about to turn on her heels and leave as a wave of nausea rolled through her. *Oh, fuck! Not now.* She tore off the vest and the restricting skirt of her lead apron and flung them on the stool in the corner, but even that didn't help.

As if chased by a bear, she sprinted to the bathroom. Jess made it in time to lose her breakfast as well as her dignity.

After retching for what felt like hours, she knelt on the cold tiles and tried to muster the energy to get back up again.

"Jess?" Kayla's voice came from outside the stall. "Are you okay?"

"Just a minute." Jess rose on weak knees and flushed. She wanted to pinch her cheeks for some color and straighten her hair, but she needed to wash her hands first. Ugh. Jess shook herself. Without intention, she had clutched the yucky toilet seat like a lifebelt.

Jess squared her shoulders, opened the stall, and brushed past Kayla to the sink. She washed her hands twice and disinfected them, then rinsed out her mouth. The tap water tasted horrible, but it was cool and fresh. Finally, she finger-combed her short hair and risked a glance in the mirror. Yup, she looked like death warmed over, and no amount of cold water could help her there.

Kayla's concerned gaze met her in the mirror. Her skin seemed even darker than usual next to Jess's unnatural paleness.

With a sigh, Jess faced her and leaned against the sink. "I'm fine."

"Nuh-uh." Kayla lifted the edge of her mouth in a half smile. "Didn't you just lecture your puppy about telling lies?"

Jess grinned against her will. "He's not my puppy. I only took him for a walk today."

"Not the point. What's wrong? Are you sick?" Her gaze raked Jess from head to toe. "Did the asshole surgeon and his comments get to you?"

She could say yes and leave it at that. But Kayla was one of the few friends she had at work, and she was right. Telling lies was out of the question. But Jess hadn't told the truth to anyone yet, not even her mom, and wasn't sure she was ready.

"If you were anyone else, I'd ask if you were pregnant. But I guess not." Kayla chuckled. "You're still a lesbian, right?"

"Yeah, the last time I checked. But that's got nothing to do with it." The words slipped out before Jess could censor herself. Oops. She held her breath, waiting for Kayla's reaction.

"No! Are you...? You can't be..." Kayla's eyes widened as her gaze swept over Jess's sweat-soaked scrub shirt that clung to her torso and revealed more curves than usual. "You're pregnant? How? No—scratch that. Why? Was it planned?" She pressed both hands to her mouth but couldn't hide the wide grin.

"Yeah. Thirteen weeks pregnant. I'm due in July." Saying it out loud was like coming out again. The weight lifting from her shoulders made her dizzy. "I thought it was past time. I turned thirty-seven last month. If I waited for the perfect relationship, I'd be too old." At least that was the reason she was willing to admit to right now.

"Congratulations!" Kayla enveloped her in a hug.

"Thank you." Jess soaked up the happiness emanating from her friend. All too soon, reality intruded, and Jess looked at Kayla. "Please don't tell anyone yet."

"Sure. I won't gossip. But sooner or later everyone will know." Kayla gestured to Jess's middle.

Jess sighed. "Yeah, but you know the cath lab policy: no lab time for pregnant employees. The studies and recommendations all say it's safe, but the chief of cardiology doesn't care about that."

"My lips are sealed." Kayla made a zipping motion. "But you better hope Scott isn't too clever and connects the dots. You looked really green."

Jess slumped back against the sink. Time was running out, but she was determined to make the best use of her skills for as long as she could.

┼┼┼┼┼┼┼

Jess clenched her teeth and swallowed a groan as another contraction tore through her. No, not a contraction. Braxton Hicks. Damn inconvenient, but nothing she couldn't handle. She'd been handling it all day.

"And that's why I called you." When the emergency medicine resident finished prattling on about the EKG and handed her the printout, she beamed like a preschooler who had painted her first rainbow. With her perky blonde ponytail, she looked not much older and not much smarter.

With one glance, Jess recognized the EKG pattern as a harmless atrial fibrillation with no sign of an acute heart attack. What a waste of time. She should have trusted her own resident to take this case, but she had always preferred her own judgment. Especially now since she had been banned from the cath lab for the last five months of her pregnancy—an eternity for an interventional cardiologist.

Jess addressed the patient. "Ever had an irregular heartbeat?"

"All the time. That's why I take those yellow and white pills. Doesn't bother me much." The wrinkles in the woman's face deepened. "What does this have to do with my pain?"

"Pain? Where?" Maybe this was getting interesting.

The woman pointed toward her lower abdomen. "Whenever I pee. Burns like hell."

Not interesting at all for a cardiologist. "Your irregular heartbeat has nothing to do with it." Jess smiled at the patient, but it probably seemed more as if she bared her teeth because in that moment, another wave of pain ripped through her.

The resident paled, and one of her eyelids twitched.

Jess could almost smell the fear. Good. She wouldn't dare to call the cardiology department for more of this nonsense without checking with her attending first. "Anything to add?" The question was rhetorical, but the resident didn't seem to know that.

It was comical to see her gather every ounce of courage she'd lost. She stood straighter, raised her chin, and balled her hands into fists until her knuckles whitened. "Um, Diana said she read a study that women were underdiagnosed because of atypical pain, and I thought—"

Okay. She had a point there, but Jess wasn't in the mood for a lecture from someone a dozen years younger who thought herself too smart to play by the rules. And besides, she had looked at the EKG. Her trip to the ED had been a waste of time. "Have you even been to med school? What is the most important rule? Horses! Look it up!" Another wave of pain robbed her breath. Jess shut her mouth with a snap.

The kid's upper lip trembled, and Jess regretted her words, especially in front of the patient.

She could only hope that the nice old woman wouldn't log a completely justifiable complaint about her.

Since when had she turned into one of those yelling types who intimidated residents with the same old sayings? *If you hear hoofbeats it's always horses not zebras* might have some truth in it, but that was no reason to attack the young doctor like this. Jess had been in the same position more than once during her residency, and the feeling of helplessness while someone undermined your authority was the worst.

But she couldn't handle an overly emotional resident on top of her pain at the moment. She would apologize or teach her something or do whatever to make it up to her—later. Much later.

Jess turned on her heel as fast as she could with the grace of a beached whale. She had to get out of here and find a spot to calm down, to breathe. She flung the door open and stormed out of the room.

And promptly collided with an obstacle. A living obstacle who touched her belly and arm.

"Keep your hands off me. What are you doing here, standing in the way?" Jess stared at the dark-haired woman in scrubs. She seemed vaguely familiar.

Whoever she was, she was clever enough to raise her hands in a peace offering and step out of the way.

Jess hurried past her but didn't go far before more pain stopped her. She pressed her hands to her middle as if that would help and panted until it was over.

"Dr. Riley, are you okay? Can I help you?" The woman had followed her.

"Okay? I haven't been okay for nine fucking months." Not since she'd had the clever idea of having a baby before she was too old. Her voice shook, and she clutched her belly again. "I don't have time for this today."

"Do you want to lie down? Should I call your obstetrician?" The woman looked around as if she expected someone from ob/gyn to come around the corner.

Jess shrugged in an effort to appear nonchalant. "Just Braxton Hicks. No need to call anyone. I've still got work to do." She fought to steady her voice. No one needed to know about the pain. She was in control and knew what she was doing.

The other woman studied her for a moment, then attempted a professional smile. "We could check you out real quick without signing you in. If you're right, you can return to work anytime."

That smile sparked a memory. Kayla had shown her pictures when she'd told Jess about the scandal in the emergency department. One of their residents was a former rock star, a drummer, which had drawn publicity when it all had come out. "You're the rock chick, right?" Jess pointed a finger at her. "What do you know?"

That seemed to shut her up. She looked as if she'd swallowed a lemon and didn't protest as Jess walked away.

Jess knew she should return to her department, lay her feet up in the staff lounge, and drink one of those terrible herbal teas her mom was so fond of. But she needed ten minutes for herself and some fresh air. So she detoured to the back entrance and the small yard.

She'd almost reached the bench when hurried footsteps caught up to her. "Dr. Riley, I'm sorry to disturb you out here, but I don't think you should be alone right now."

Jess frowned. She opened her mouth to tell the rock chick what she thought about this disturbance, but no sound came out. Her pulse pounded faster and faster, echoing in her ears. Stars danced through her field of vision, and she didn't know anymore where up and down were. She swayed, reaching out as if to balance on a log over a stream, then fell. Soft and fluffy darkness enveloped her, and finally, the pain in her abdomen was gone.

And then the pain roared back and chased the darkness away. It was even worse now, and her back and chest hurt too.

"Dr. Riley?" Someone shook her.

As Jess opened her eyes, the blue sky loomed above her. "What...what happened? Why am I on the ground?" She clutched her belly and moaned. After a moment, the pain passed, and she looked from one side to the other to reorient herself. A familiar figure leaned over her. Why couldn't the woman leave her alone? She needed a minute to breathe, and everything would be okay again. "You, Rock Chick! I said I didn't need help!"

A muscle twitched in the resident's cheek. "That was before you fainted. Now, shut up and let me help. And that's Dr. Rock Chick to you." Her tone was even, direct, and full of authority.

Before Jess knew what she was doing, she nodded. Maybe she had hit her head or something.

"Can you sit up?" The woman offered her hand.

The dizziness had receded, and she didn't need the help of the persistent resident. "I didn't faint," Jess mumbled, more to herself. She used both hands to push herself into a sitting position.

"Fainted, collapsed, call it what you want. You had a syncope and an irregular tachycardia." Rock Chick played doctor, pulled gloves and a stethoscope from her pocket, and worked through a physical exam before Jess could think about protesting. Maybe she did know what she was doing. She'd seemed competent enough the last few times she'd called cardiology for a consult. What was her name again? Diana something or other?

When Diana touched her belly, it hardened with another contraction.

Oh shit, were practice contractions supposed to be this painful? How much worse would the real ones be? Instinctively, Jess gripped the hand resting on her belly, never minding Diana's groan of protest. Served her right for barging in like this.

Once the contraction had passed, the wimp extricated her fingers and stretched them, wincing.

If she wasn't so pissed off at everything at that moment, Jess would have laughed at her pained expression.

Diana pressed her lips together and slung her stethoscope around her neck. "If I help, can you move to the bench?"

As she tried to get up, Jess noted two things: her pants were wet, and her knees had softened to jelly. Had she slipped and landed in a puddle? That might explain her fall. Another possible explanation flickered through her mind, but it wasn't something she wanted to consider now.

First, she had to get up, and then she had to get away from the obnoxious resident. As she couldn't do the latter without the former, she accepted Diana's help. It wasn't easy, and both gulped for air when Jess had settled onto the bench.

Diana hovered over her, much too close, rocking back and forth on the balls of her feet as if she was preparing for a tennis match. The intense stare matched a professional athlete too. "No way you can walk back now."

Thank you for stating the obvious. But Jess didn't want to give her the satisfaction of agreeing. "Just give me ten minutes, Rock Chick. I'll be fine." She lay down to rest and pushed her sweat-dampened hair from her forehead. She'd allow herself the short respite, and then she'd get up and face the rest of her workday.

"What kind of denial are you in? You're in labor, and I don't know if we have ten minutes."

Labor? Was this really labor? *It's too soon. I'm not ready!* First kids never came early. She was sure she'd heard that somewhere. She had meant to read up on the medical side of delivery but had thought she still had time. The C-section was scheduled in ten days.

"Could you unlock your phone so I can call for a stretcher? I don't have mine on me." Diana's voice barely broke through the thoughts that tumbled and crashed in Jess's mind like a washing machine filled with broken parts.

When and where had she gotten Jess's phone? She unlocked it and handed it back. Never mind.

How could she tell if she was in denial when the whole point of denial was to protect a mind from things it didn't need or want to know? And why was she thinking about psychological defense mechanisms when her body was being ripped apart by one wave of pain after another?

Whatever Diana said on the call, Jess couldn't hear a word.

Jess clutched her belly and tried to breathe the pain away as if that would suddenly work when it hadn't done her any good during the last several hours.

Heat shot to her cheeks. She had been too stubborn to accept the truth. Waves of pain. For hours. Dr. Rock Chick was right. This was happening. She was in labor, and her water had broken. Jess didn't know if she should laugh, cry, or kick herself. Since she'd decided she needed a baby in her life, everything had fallen apart. Her work, her relationship with her mom, her body. It was fitting that her body betrayed her today by going into labor instead of sticking to the plan—a nice, pain-free C-section with all the professional medical attention a person could ask for.

Instead, she got a dirty park bench and a former rock star turned emergency resident. Just perfect.

"Dr. Riley, I need to get you undressed to see how far you are."

Jess let her head fall back and nodded. What else was there to do?

Even though Diana's movements were careful, she couldn't help the fact that Jess's wet scrub pants stuck to her legs like a second skin and caught on her ugly, swollen ankles.

Jess bit her lip and looked away as Diana peeled them off the rest of the way. When another contraction started, much more painful than before, she couldn't help pulling up her legs and groan.

Diana looked back to the hospital entrance as if she'd rather flee than stay and help.

Jess could relate. If she could, she'd be out of here faster than she could say *delivery*. The reality of the situation hit her like a punch in the solar plexus and robbed her of her last breath. She was here with this resident, who wasn't even an obstetrician. Alone. Giving birth to her child. Her daughter. What if something happened to her baby? She gasped.

Think, Jess. You're a doctor too. What's the best plan to keep her safe? No doubt, the safest place for her baby was her womb, and she needed to do anything she could to keep her daughter inside as long as possible. *Delay until help arrives.* Not a sophisticated plan but the best she could come up with now.

Diana nodded with determination. But as she lowered her gaze between Jess's legs, she paled. "You need to push."

Was she crazy? "I can't. Not now. That's not the plan." Jess's eyes filled with tears.

"Are you kidding me? Fuck your plan. We don't have time for this. The head is crowning, and you need to push—now!" Despite her harsh words, Diana's movements were gentle. She pulled Jess's legs apart, holding eye contact all the time.

Jess wasn't convinced that pushing was the best option, but she couldn't come up with an alternative. Why hadn't she prepared for such a scenario? She always prepared for every fucking thing.

"Listen." Diana lowered her voice and squeezed Jess's knee. "I'm sorry that the birth is not going as you planned, but your child seems to be as stubborn as you are. We can do this but only with your help. So when the next contraction comes, you push. Okay?" Her expression was confident as if she'd done this a thousand times.

Another contraction came, and Jess was out of time. "Fuck!" She screamed the word like a war cry and pushed.

"Yeah, fuck!" Diana screamed back as if they were charging into battle together.

Jess's world reduced to a bloody fight, filled with pain, curses, and groans. She no longer knew or cared about the details. Her only clear thought was *push*, and so she did, until another cry pierced through the fog in her mind.

A shrill cry, full of anger at the unfairness of the world, full of need to belong, full of hope for a better future.

And when the crying bundle was placed in her arms, Jess's pain evaporated in a surge of hormones and pure love.

Chapter Two

LENA LEANED CLOSER TO STUDY the curve of the new-formed leaf, and the sweet floral scent of the rose enveloped her like her grandma's hugs. She hadn't been the type to wear perfume but had always kept a few dried petals in her closet. Taking a deep breath as if she could store the scent, Lena smiled at the memory. She missed her every day. Grandma would have loved this garden.

After another glance at the flower, Lena focused on her sketchbook and added a few fine black lines.

"Beautiful. I love the detailed depiction of the petals and sepals." Maggie's voice came from directly behind her.

If her pen had been on the paper, Lena would have ruined the sketch. She hadn't heard Maggie approach or noticed the rhythmic snipping of the garden shears had stopped. "Thank you. But what's a sepal?" Not used to compliments, her face flushed, probably as pink as the rose.

"The small, green, leaf-like parts beneath the petals." Maggie took a seat on the wooden chair next to the patch of grass Lena sat on. She removed her gardening gloves and wiped her forehead with a fabric handkerchief.

"Do you want some water or tea? I can get something from my kitchen." Lena gestured to the garden house.

"Water would be lovely. But I can get it. If you don't mind me rummaging around your kitchen." She rose from the chair with an agility that belied her age.

"No, stay, please. I feel bad enough that you won't let me help you with the gardening." Lena secured her sketchbook closed with a wide band and tucked the pen into one of the loops on the elastic. She placed the book on the side table next to Maggie's chair and hurried into the house.

It was just a few steps from front door to fridge, and she grabbed a large glass bottle she had filled earlier and left to chill. The fridge was pretty bare, but at the sight of the last bit of organic cheese, her stomach growled.

Had Maggie stopped for lunch? Probably not. She had been as immersed in her work as Lena.

Back outside, Lena placed two plates with cheese and apple slices on the small table and poured them both water. "Do you want something for the water? Mint?"

"Lemon balm, thanks."

Maggie had planted dozens of different herbs in all parts of the garden, but Lena was sure she remembered where the lemon balm was hidden. She found it a few steps away and rubbed a leaf between her fingers to release the citrusy scent. She plucked a few leaves and held them up. "Is this enough for you?"

Maggie nodded her approval and took half of the leaves into her glass. "Melissa officinalis."

Lena mentally repeated the name a few times. She'd sketch that one next and write down both names. "Is there anything I can help you with today? Carry something heavy?"

Smiling, Maggie shook her head. "I need to work to stay flexible. You have tai chi and youth on your side. I'm battling old age with the help of my plants."

And the workout was certainly effective. Maggie had to be in her late sixties—judging by the soft, wrinkly skin and hair that was mostly gray-and-white with only a hint of brown—but she moved like a much younger woman. Lena hoped she would be that fit in forty years.

They nibbled on their snack in companionable silence until a phone rang from the middle of the plant bed Maggie had been working in.

"Let me get it." Lena made her way between the roses, lavender, and half a dozen different green shrubs she couldn't name. She followed the ringtone until it stopped. Where was that phone? After a short break, the ringing started again. "Someone really wants to talk to you."

"They always call to sell me things I don't need. My name and number must be on a very gullible list somewhere." Maggie chuckled.

Lena snorted. Maggie might be the least gullible older woman she had ever met. "Ah, here it is." She snatched the phone from its hiding place under a rose bush in amazing shades of tangerine and burnt orange. "Oh, the hospital. I hope it's nothing serious." She hurried to bring the phone to its owner.

"It'll be Jess. It's Friday and time for her to cancel our monthly dinner. Again." The resignation in her voice was nothing new.

Lena pressed her lips together and swallowed a reply. She couldn't understand Maggie's daughter. If Lena had a mother as wonderful as Maggie, she wouldn't stay away all the time. As far as Maggie had told her, they didn't have any problems or disagreements; Jess was only too busy with work. Lena handed the phone over as it stopped ringing. "Oh, sorry."

Before Maggie could reply, it started again, and she answered it. "Riley. Yes. Oh. Oh." She paled, and the phone shook in her hand. "Okay. How is she? Can I...? Tell her I'll be with her as soon as possible. Emergency department. Thank you." She hung up and stared at the phone as if it could provide more information or guidance.

Lena reached over and took her hands, which trembled like a frightened bird. "Hey, what happened?"

"Jess...she..." Maggie looked at her with wide eyes, tears clinging to their corners.

Did she have an accident? "What happened?" She repeated the question in a soft tone.

"She had her baby. I'm a grandma." As if speaking the words out loud allowed Maggie to understand their meaning, her face transformed. A wide grin illuminated her face like the first rays of sunshine after a storm. "I'm a grandma!"

Lena couldn't help but grin with her. "Congratulations." She squeezed the still-trembling hands, but it wasn't enough to convey what she was feeling. Before she could question herself, she pulled Maggie in for a hug.

Maggie returned the embrace as if they were friends or family and not landlady and tenant. The scent of crushed herbs and warm soil, like summer, enveloped her, and Lena never wanted to let go.

Which was precisely why she retreated to a safe distance after another mumbled congratulations. She couldn't allow herself the illusion of being part of a happy family if the reality was just the opposite.

"Thank you." Maggie brushed at her dirt-stained jeans. "I need to change and drive to the hospital." But she remained rooted on the spot. "I don't have a present. The quilt isn't ready. Flowers? Maybe I should cut some flowers." She reached for the roses and pricked herself on a thorn. "Ouch."

"Careful. Why don't you go change, and I'll get the flowers?" Lena had thought nothing could faze Maggie, who had shown grace and composure even when her neighbor had had a heart attack right here in the garden. She'd taken care of her friend and called the ambulance as if she'd prepared for such an event.

Maggie hastened off toward the house, and Lena decided to pick the flowers quickly enough to have time to change herself. No way would she let Maggie drive herself to the hospital in Seattle and end up in a car crash.

To her surprise, Maggie handed her the car key without discussion.

Maggie's car was a cute Prius that drove so smooth and silent that Lena didn't even mind the afternoon traffic. Such a difference from her old, dying Ford.

Maggie looked at the small silver watch on her wrist. She didn't say anything about driving faster but fidgeted in her seat.

"You didn't tell me, is it a boy or girl?" Lena tried to distract her. "Did your daughter decide on a name yet?"

"A girl." She sighed. "Jess was still undecided about the name, last I knew." Maggie's tone was very neutral.

Lena glanced to her right.

Maggie smiled, but it was laced with tension

Uh-oh. She had wanted to redirect Maggie's thoughts in a positive direction. "Were you hoping for a girl when you had Jess?"

"When I was pregnant with Jess, I wished for a boy, not because I preferred boys but because I thought it would be easier for my husband to bond with a son." She chuckled. "But those two did all right. Actually, more than all right. She always trailed after him, and he encouraged her. She loved to hide in his office when he had patients in there. I will never know what age-inappropriate things she learned by listening in on those conversations."

"So your husband was a doctor too?"

"Yes, a cardiologist, same as Jess. He mainly worked in private practice, not in the hospital. More time for golf." She said the last bit in a tone that suggested she was teasing.

Lena had never met Maggie's husband; he had died a few years ago.

"What does Jess's partner do? Is he a doctor too?"

Maggie laughed. "No, there isn't a he in the picture. Or a girlfriend. Jess decided to have a child on her own. I don't know why she thinks that being a single mother is a wise decision with the work hours she keeps."

Lena agreed, but it wasn't her place to say so. She'd never known her father either, and the short time she'd lived with her mother alone hadn't been an advertisement for happy family life. For a moment, the reminder of what she'd missed itched like an old scar. But what was done was done.

"Oh?" was all she could answer without betraying her thoughts.

"I'm sorry, that was mean. But Jess is convinced that she can do anything she wants on her own. She's too stubborn and independent for her own good. For her sake, I hope she's right."

The more Lena learned about Jess, the more she wondered how she could be so different from her mother. But that wasn't fair. She probably had lots of redeeming qualities.

After twenty minutes, the fancy sat-nav in Maggie's car announced that they had to leave the highway, and Lena concentrated on the unfamiliar roads until they arrived at the hospital. She stopped in front of the main entrance.

"You go on in, and I'll park the car. I'll wait in the lobby until you're finished."

"Nonsense. Come with me. I'll introduce you. And who can resist a peek at a newborn baby?" Maggie talked rapidly in an uncharacteristically high voice.

Honestly, Lena wasn't eager to meet Jess, but she did love babies. And beneath the reasons Maggie had listed probably lurked the wish for backup. "You're right, I can't resist."

After lucking out with a parking spot close to the entrance, they made their way inside. The main hall was cool and empty, and their steps echoed on the stone floor. Lena followed Maggie to the admission desk, where a bored-looking young woman worked behind a glass wall.

"Hello, I'm Mrs. Riley. I'm here to see my daughter, Dr. Jessica Riley."

"Oh my God! Yes!" The woman's oversized bun wobbled as she nodded. "Diana…um, I mean Dr. Petrell delivered the baby all on her own in the garden. Half-naked! She tore off her scrub shirt to cover the baby, like a superhero. It was awesome! Come in!" She pressed a button, and a door opened. "They're in room seven."

Garden? Maggie hadn't said anything about that, and by the way she paled, maybe she hadn't known. She stood frozen in front of the admission desk.

"Room seven. Thank you," Lena said to the woman.

As Maggie hadn't moved yet, Lena took her arm and led her through the door. The smell of disinfectant and fear assaulted her as soon as they entered the ER proper, reminding her of her grandma's last day.

She leaned into the roses she carried and breathed against the knot in her stomach until it dissolved. *Concentrate!* Signs with numbers and arrows led her in the right direction. They reached room seven without meeting anyone. Lena was unsure of the protocol but decided knocking was the polite thing to do.

"What now?" A loud voice barked from the other side.

That seemed to rouse Maggie from her shock. She opened the door. "Jessica Eleanor Riley. Is that the way to answer a knocking?" Her tone was more exasperated than angry.

Suppressing a snicker, Lena followed Maggie inside. That was exactly the tone her grandma would have used on her. The last time she'd needed to, Lena hadn't been older than fourteen.

A woman in her late thirties rested on a gurney. The headrest was up so she was more sitting than lying, and she cradled a tightly wrapped bundle in her arms. Her dark-blue scrubs contrasted with her pale face. Short dark hair was curly where sweat had plastered it to the temples. Her frown faded as she recognized her visitor. "Oh. Mom. Hi."

And that sheepish tone was the same in which Lena would have answered fifteen years ago. Finally, something she could relate to.

"Here's Ella, your granddaughter." A proud smile spread on Jess's face, and she glowed with the joy of new motherhood. It transformed her completely. Now her natural attractiveness outshone her exhaustion, and the cornflower blue eyes sparkled with the same beauty as Maggie's.

Lena couldn't help but smile with her.

Carefully, Maggie hugged her daughter and grandchild at once. After a moment, she retreated and stroked Jess's face. "Oh, Jessi, you look tired. Are you okay?"

The love in her voice pricked Lena like the thorns of the roses she held. Her chest tightened until she had trouble breathing. She needed to get out of here. This was a private moment, and she had no right to intrude. She took a step back and collided with someone.

Strong hands grabbed her shoulders and steadied her. "Whoa. Careful. Beautiful roses."

Lena turned around.

The woman she had bumped into smiled down at her. She was clad in the same dark-blue scrubs as Jess. Her dark hair was fastened in a short ponytail, but several strands had escaped and gave her a slightly informal look. "Hi, I'm Dr. Petrell. You must be family."

Family? No amount of wishful thinking would make Lena part of a family again anytime soon. "No, no. I'm here as a friend to Maggie. She's the family."

Maggie witnessed the exchange with arched eyebrows.

"I have to leave now. Call me if you need anything. I'll take the bus home." Without meeting Maggie's gaze, Lena held the flowers and the car key out to her.

As soon as Maggie took them, Lena fled from the room. *This is not your family.* She was alone and that had been her decision. Now she needed to own it.

All the way outside, she balled her fists and bit the inside of her cheek to keep the tears from falling.

Chapter Three

Jess stumbled over a stuffed penguin in her kitchen and nearly lost her precious cargo. If she hadn't been so out of breath, she would have laughed at the absurdity of juggling half a dozen containers of breast milk.

Shouldn't it be easier to get ready for work now than during her pregnancy? She no longer resembled a whale about to beach, but instead of feeling rejuvenated, Jess was tired and weak like never before. Even in the worst times of her residency, she hadn't felt as sleep deprived as she did now.

Every time her mom had visited during the last four weeks, Jess had fallen asleep talking. She still hadn't decided if she was embarrassed or grateful her mom had taken to sending her to bed like an overtired toddler.

And that had made her too ashamed to even consider inviting Kayla.

Admittedly, the maternity leave hadn't helped with her circadian rhythm. Much like her residency, she was woken at all times of night and day to deal with emergencies. In this case, the emergency of her daughter believing she might die any second from starvation or loneliness. And the shift never ended and went on and on for a month.

When her boss had called to ask her to cut the leave short because they were short staffed, she'd been delighted. Getting out of the house and leaving Ella's care in professional hands for the day seemed like the perfect remedy for her exhaustion. In the last years, working as an attending had more fueled than drained her energy levels despite the long hours.

Only she wasn't ready. No professional help was in sight. The hospital daycare had changed their policy last month without warning and didn't accept kids younger than one year anymore. The only halfway acceptable daycare out of the dozen she'd visited in the city didn't have a free spot on short notice, no matter how much she offered to pay. If her mother hadn't offered to step in, she wouldn't be able to go to work. And that was the tip of the iceberg. She hadn't lost her weight. She hadn't read any of the articles she'd saved for her leave. She hadn't even managed the simple task of getting a haircut.

Jess picked up the penguin and set it on the kitchen counter next to her half-empty cup of coffee. She took a sip and winced. Tepid and bitter, it didn't help to calm her churning stomach. She hadn't felt so unprepared for her day since her first week of college.

Stroking the soft fur of the penguin, she went through her mental checklist. Milk. Check. Stuffed animal. Check. Baby's bag with diapers, wipes, and change of clothes. Check. Mom's bag with keycard, money, phone, and the latest edition of *Journal of Cardiology* in case she was awake enough to read more than two lines. Check. What was missing? *Just go. You're running late already. Stop with your stupid lists.*

At the elevator, the vague feeling of having lost something remained. What was missing?

When the doors opened with a ping, she entered and pressed the button for the parking deck.

Ella.

Jess jumped out through the closing doors and narrowly missed being squashed by the metal. *Fuck, how can you forget your own child?*

It took three attempts to enter the code to her condo. Her racing heart wouldn't slow down even when she'd reached the sleeping baby. She was dizzy with relief that Ella hadn't noticed her absence.

With shaking hands, Jess lifted her daughter from the cradle and held her close for a minute. The scent of freshness and innocence washed over her and calmed her nerves like magic, better than any checklist ever could.

Loaded with both bags and the baby carrier, she resumed her journey to the car. Even when she had stowed everyone and everything safely in her BMW X5 and was on her way to her mom's house, her heart rate was still elevated.

Ella cooed in that adorable way to signal she was awake.

Jess glanced in the mirror but couldn't see her daughter's expression. The thirty-minute drive to Shoreline passed in the blink of an eye, and Jess nearly missed her mom's driveway because an ugly lump of junk—that might have qualified as a car fifteen or twenty years ago—was blocking most of the garage. Her mom's tiny Prius might fit next to it, but there wasn't enough space for her own SUV. She ran through a list of her mom's friends, all of whom were either retired academics like her or old hippies or both. Neither group would drive such a piece of shit. Maybe someone was doing work at the house?

Not that it mattered. She parked on the street, not caring that she blocked the driveway. That thing didn't look as if it was able to go far anyway.

Before she had again succeeded in juggling Ella, her bag, and the car keys, her mom appeared.

"Jess, let me help." Her mom took the baby carrier and peered inside. "Oh, Ella, look at you. How you've grown. Aren't you sweet?"

"Growing is all she's doing for now." Jess covered her mouth to hide a yawn. "But, yeah, she's sweet."

Her mom looked up and studied Jess until she squirmed. "Do you want to come inside? You look tired. Have some coffee? Breakfast? You can meet Lena."

Who was Lena again? Jess looked at her watch and sighed. It wasn't important. As much as she could have killed for another coffee, she needed to get going. Morning traffic was always difficult to predict. "I better head off now. Thank you so much for taking her on short notice. I'll find a reliable babysitter or daycare soon." Jess swallowed and looked down at her oversized sneakers that were the only shoes that fit her pregnancy-ridden feet.

"Don't worry about it. We'll have much fun, Ella and I. Won't we?" With the last words, she stuck her head into the carrier and said something in that tone reserved for babies and kittens. Or, in her mom's case, more often than not, for rare plants. "Will you stay for dinner?" she added in her regular voice.

"I don't know yet. Let's see how the day goes, okay?" Jess wasn't looking forward to driving to her mom's again in the evening when all she wanted to do was sleep. But she wouldn't have gotten so far in her career with a habit of admitting weakness, not even to the person who should know her best.

"Sure. Say goodbye to Mommy." Her mom talked to Ella as if she expected her to do just that.

Ridiculous but cute. "Bye." Jess smiled and waved as she entered her car. No need to cuddle her daughter after she'd spent four weeks nonstop in her company. She should be happy to have some adult time, so why did her instincts make her want to cry or even grab the carrier from her mom? She clenched her jaw and forced herself to start the engine without hesitation. She gripped the steering wheel until her knuckles whitened. Missing her daughter might be normal, but this pain, as if she was stretched and stretched until something tore inside her, was absurd.

With a shake of her head, she drove to work as fast as she could.

Frantic beeping signaled an unnaturally high heartbeat. Some of her colleagues would mute the alarm in order to concentrate, but Jess flourished under the pressure. The monitor displaying the patient's vital signs was probably flashing with all kinds of alarms as the blood pressure fell. She didn't need to see it to know she had to act fast and finish the angioplasty to restore the oxygen supply to the heart.

Her vision stayed fixed on the X-ray monitor showing her attempts to place the catheter in the correct position. *Just a millimeter more.* That's it. She exhaled and gave the signal to inflate the balloon.

Scott pressed the device and counted to five. He had been hovering behind her shoulder all day. Now that he had finished his regular cardiology fellowship and started the interventional cardiology one, Jess should have let him perform the procedure. But she was too damn happy to be back in the cath lab to care.

As soon as he finished, Jess held out her hand.

Wordlessly, Kayla offered her the right stent without being asked.

With a grateful smile, Jess finished the procedure. She had missed working in perfect synchronicity with colleagues who read her mind.

The patient's heart rate dropped to normal levels, and the blood pressure rose again as blood flow in the most important coronary vessel was restored. Jess grinned. No matter how often she witnessed or performed the procedure, and no matter how well she understood the mechanism, this part still retained some of the magic she had felt the first time she'd seen it as a student. She had instantly decided that it would be her future.

The most important work was done, and the rest was routine: closing the puncture wound and applying a pressure bandage. That was Scott's job.

With the knowledge of a job well done, Jess relaxed and her adrenaline level plummeted.

Stars danced in her vision, and she blinked to remove them. She didn't need clear vision to pull at a catheter, but steady hands would be nice. Hers shook like a student's when they first drew blood. She attempted to take a deep breath but sucked the paper mask against her lips.

"Everything okay? Jess?" Kayla's voice was muffled as if through a thick wall.

Jess nodded, unable to speak as her tongue stuck to the roof of her mouth. She stepped away from the table and ripped the mask from her face to gulp in some air. Her heart raced as if she was the patient on the table. What the fuck was happening?

Maybe it had been a mistake to put on her prepregnancy lead vest that was too tight now. But she had been too proud and vain to ask for a larger size, and now she was paying the price for all those shallow breaths over the last few hours. Her breasts hurt like hell, especially her much-too-sensitive nipples.

Sweat ran down her temples, along her neck, and under the lead vest and the sterile paper gown covering it. It stung her eyes like acid. She was cold and hot at the same time, and an uncontrollable tremor ran through her. She took a breath—not a deep one since her movement was still restricted as if a boa constrictor held her in its grasp.

Out. I need to get out of this dammed vest.

She dug deep inside her training to project calmness and confidence. "Scott, finish here, please. I'll start on the report."

With her last shred of strength, she tore off her gloves and gown, then opened her vest. Each step was a struggle, but she held her head high, not losing sight of her destination, the door where she would be able to pull off the constricting vest and sit.

Only the door swayed from side to side until it vanished from her view. "Not again," she mumbled as the floor rushed up to meet her.

┼┼┼┼┼┼┼

The reassuring beep-beep-beep of a heartbeat monitor drifted in and out of her consciousness. Something grabbed her shoulder and shook her. A hand.

"Dr. Riley, wake up!" The woman's voice was warm and low but held so much authority that she wanted to comply.

But why? The heartbeat was steady. No reason for her to get up and look at it. She was as tired as if she'd run a marathon.

Marathon? No, she had been at work. Cath lab. But why was she lying somewhere in the hospital? Jess blinked, then squeezed her eyes shut as a glaring light blinded her. But the glimpse had been enough to recognize the room as part of the emergency department. *Why am I in the ED? Again? Is this a joke?* She tried to get up for a better view of her surroundings, but strong hands stopped her.

"Hey, Dr. Riley. Good to have you back. Stay down for a sec, okay?"

That voice. "Rock Chick?" She opened her eyes again, and this time the light wasn't unbearable. It was indeed the resident who had delivered Ella.

"Haven't we been over this already?" She chuckled. "It's Dr. Rock Chick or even Dr. Petrell, but you might as well call me Diana, as we've already seen each other half-naked."

Jess nodded. She would never admit this out loud, but Diana's presence alleviated her uneasiness. Jess trusted her, even though she barely knew her. "What happened?"

"What do you remember?" The mirth vanished from Diana's voice.

Jess considered the question for a moment. "I had finished an intervention and was a bit dizzy and sweating. I guess I got dehydrated wearing the lead apron and fainted."

"Mmh. That might be possible. But you didn't just faint." Diana rolled a stool from the side of the room and sat at eye level. A faint line between her brows spoke of her concern.

"What are you not telling me?" Had she hit her head? Broken something? Nothing hurt save for a faint ache in her breast and shoulder muscles, obviously from too many hours under the heavy protective garments.

Diana looked to the other end of the room. "Madison, please give us a minute."

A nurse Jess hadn't even noticed until now shrugged and left with a long glance back to her patient. It was rare that a doctor turned into a patient in her own hospital.

Jess frowned. Not exactly true in her case. She had managed to wind up on a gurney in the emergency department twice in four weeks.

After Madison had closed the door, Diana swiveled back to Jess. Her gaze bored into Jess as if she wanted to read her thoughts. "Your colleagues thought the same as you did. Just a bit of dehydration and low blood pressure. They elevated your legs, but when you remained unconscious and they couldn't find your pulse, they were clever enough to hook you up to the EKG." Diana paused as if waiting for her reaction.

Jess made a "go on" gesture. "Tell me. In medical, not in English." She didn't need to be coddled like a patient; she wanted to know the facts.

"You had a VT, and they shocked you. They—"

"VT?" Jess wasn't sure she'd heard correctly. Maybe she needed the English version after all.

"Yeah, a ventricular tachycardia. I saw the EKG printout myself. You had a heart rate around one eighty with wide ventricular complexes and…"

The rest of Diana's explanation got drowned out by a buzzing in Jess's ears. Why? She was healthy, had never had any serious illnesses, not even as a child. Why would she develop a dangerous cardiac rhythm? So dangerous that they'd had to shock her? That made no sense. Maybe they'd gotten it wrong. Maybe Kayla and Scott had misjudged the rhythm. Maybe the cable had been faulty and transmitted extra signals. Maybe…

"Dr. Riley?" Diana squeezed her forearm and pulled her out of her thoughts.

"Call me Jess." This was not the time to insist on decorum.

"Jess, I guess this comes as a surprise, but the EKG left no doubt. You had a VT, and electric cardioversion was the right choice of treatment. Now we've got to find the cause. Any prior events? Known conditions? Anything in your medical history?"

"Okay. Sounds like a plan." Jess relaxed back as far as lying on a gurney with barely a cushion could be called relaxing. If she had to trust anyone at work, it might as well be Diana who had proven herself already. "Nothing. I've always been healthy, and I've had more than a few EKGs and echoes during my residency, as we practiced on each other. I've never had a problem with endurance training—I'm a long-distance runner." She snorted and rolled her eyes. "Not so much in the last year. And since Ella's birth, I haven't been as fit as I wanted to be. But maybe I have unrealistic expectations."

"Maybe. But VTs are not an usual occurrence postpartum. And…" Diana ran her hand through her shoulder-length hair, tousling it even more than before. "Before the birth in the garden, you fainted too. Your pulse was racing. I had no way to time it, but it was way over the normal limit. As you recovered in seconds, I chalked it up to stress and pain. Maybe you had a VT then too, only self-limiting that time."

Her first instinct was to deny it and accuse Diana of a vivid imagination. Throw in a sarcastic comment or two, then jump up and stalk out. Only her bones were as heavy as the lead gown had been, and she was more tired than ever. She'd probably land on her face if she attempted to get up right now.

Jess rubbed the upper right side of her chest, which was still tender after the electric shock. Something wasn't okay. If she was honest with herself, it hadn't been for a while. But still, a VT? She couldn't believe it.

Ding! Ding! Ding! The heart monitor came to life with a familiar alarm that drowned out the other sounds. Her breath froze. Beep-beep-beep. The sound of her own heartbeat wasn't steady and reassuring anymore. She craned her neck to catch a glimpse of the monitor behind her left shoulder.

The spikes of the EKG came much too fast, were much too wide. She couldn't deny what she saw with her own eyes. Another VT. With each spike, fear stabbed her chest with razor-sharp icicles.

The lines jiggled as her vision blurred. Dizziness and nausea rose as if she'd been too long on a roller coaster. "Fuck." Her head fell back on the cushion, and she closed her eyes and waited for consciousness to fade.

Only it didn't.

As if a magical button had been pressed, her heart rate switched from highly elevated to normal, and the wailing alarm of the monitor stopped. The sound of her pulse pounded in her ears, echoing the faint beeps that again reassured medical personnel that everything was all right.

But it wasn't. Having seen it with her own eyes, Jess was no longer able to deny it. Something was seriously wrong.

She could have died.

Ella! The idea of leaving her daughter was unimaginable.

Bile rose in her throat. Jess swallowed it and pushed her fears to the back of her mind. She needed to function, not to feel.

She caught Diana's gaze and tried to project authority she didn't feel at the moment. "I want you to do an echo."

Diana nodded. "I've already ordered one. The tech should be here any minute. And then we can—"

"No, I don't want any fucking tech to know my business." Jess gestured to the portable ultrasound machine in the corner of the room. It wasn't the most modern or best equipment the hospital had to offer, but it would be enough for a glimpse at her heart. "I want you to do it while I interpret the pictures. And I want whatever we see on the screen to remain between us." It was bad enough that she had collapsed at work and that her colleagues had had to treat her arrhythmia in the cath lab. No way would she involve them further.

With a neutral expression, Diana studied her for a moment.

Years of not only surviving but thriving in the hierarchical world of medicine had taught Jess to withstand even the most heated glare. Never had she needed to suppress the instinct to squirm the way she did now.

After a few seconds that felt like an hour, Diana stood and got the machine. She positioned herself on a stool next to the gurney as the machine's computer booted up. "You know, I've no experience. But I'm willing to try."

"Lucky for you, I'm a cardiologist. I'll talk you through it." Almost giddy with relief she didn't have to face one of the techs or her colleagues, Jess pulled down the thin sheet that covered her.

She was naked underneath and didn't want to know when and how that had happened. She slightly rolled onto her left side and repositioned the sticker of an EKG lead that dug into her skin as her left breast came to rest on the gurney. Jess suppressed a sigh. Even half a year ago, her breasts had still been the perky almost-but-not-quite-Bs she'd had since high school. During the pregnancy, they had become these bursting bags of milk. She directed her gaze to the monitor. This wasn't the time to think about the price her body had paid for Ella. Anyway, her daughter was worth every pound she'd gained.

Diana shook the gel bottle with an ease that spoke of experience. Either she had done more than a few ultrasound examinations before, or she took ketchup to every meal. The gel glistened on the small ultrasound wand when Diana squirted a blob on it. "This might be cold."

Jess rolled her eyes. How often had she said the same thing?

"Sorry, I said that on autopilot. Where do you want me to start? I know how to check for pericardial tamponade, but we're not looking for a hematoma now, right?" Diana hovered with the wand at the swell of Jess's left breast.

It was obvious Diana knew more than she let on, but Jess appreciated that she let her have at least a little control over the situation. "Left parasternal, third intercostal space, index mark pointing to my right shoulder."

As the wand made contact with her skin, Jess flinched and held her breath. Hopefully Diana thought it was cold and not fear that produced the reaction.

She needn't have worried. Diana's gaze stayed on the monitor as she twisted and angled the wand. It wasn't hard to guess the exact moment she produced a clear picture. A proud smile lit up her face. Just as fast, it vanished again, replaced by a frown. "Oh." The sound that escaped Diana was the last thing a patient wanted to hear.

The monitor was filled with white lines on a black background showing barely any movement. For any other patient, the sight would mean nothing. But Jess had spent more years than she'd like to admit looking at similar pictures, and the diagnosis sprung to her mind: acute heart failure. Oh, fuck.

That couldn't be true. That wasn't her heart. No, no, no.

But the cold gel freezing her skin and the lines on the monitor moving in sync with her pounding heart left no doubt. Icy waves crashed over her head, and she fought to keep from drowning in fear.

She clenched her fists. *Ella, think of Ella. Fight this!*

"I'm not a cardiologist, but…" Diana looked at her with concern. "This isn't normal. The heart is hardly moving."

"Yes. Freeze that picture for a second." Jess leaned up and brushed Diana's hand away from the console of the ultrasound machine. "Let me measure the EF." With practiced movements, she confirmed what her trained gaze had already guesstimated. An absurdly low number stared back at her. She hesitated over the save button but eventually pushed it. This was too serious to pretend it would go away on its own.

Jess let herself fall back on the gurney with a sigh. What had caused this? She tried to take a mental step back as if the lines and numbers on the screen belonged to another patient. "Myocarditis? Coronary ischemia? Both are unlikely." What else? There was something, but she was so tired that her thoughts faded away as if shrouded by thick winter fog.

Diana studied her for a second. "I know it's rare, but—"

"If it's rare, you can forget about it. All residents want to capture the elusive zebra, but all we ever see are plain horses." Jess grimaced. If she had a dollar for every suggestion of a rare disease from a student or resident that had turned out to be another routine case, she wouldn't ever have to work another day.

"Indulge me for a second, just like I indulged in your secret examination here." Diana's tone was gently teasing, something Jess had never experienced at work.

Jess couldn't summon the energy to protest. She nodded and gestured for Diana to go on.

"I recently read an article about peripartum cardiomyopathy and how it's a severely underdiagnosed disease. Most women have a mild case, and the symptoms are similar to ordinary exhaustion and lack of sleep, but some develop an acute heart failure. What do you think?"

"PPCM?" The idea sliced through the fog in her mind like a signal fire. It was rare, but everything fit. She was a healthy woman without prior history of heart disease who had delivered a child not long ago. Maybe Diana was on to something. "We can't test for it. We'd have to rule out everything else first. Let's call a colleague of mine, and you present the facts. If he agrees with your conclusion, I'm willing to entertain the idea."

"Who do you want me to call?" Diana fished her phone from her scrub pocket.

Jess considered this for a second. Whoever she called, the news would spread faster than a wildfire. If she had to face her department, she might as well start from the top and involve her boss right away. "Call Dr. Huong."

30

The angry vibration of her phone woke Jess from the first deep sleep she'd had in weeks. She reached for it, going more by feel than sight in the dark and unfamiliar hospital room that was illuminated by the monitor next to her bed.

Two past nine. Shit. She had intended to close her eyes for half an hour before calling her mom to let her know she'd have to stay the night, but that had been more than four hours ago.

She swiped to answer. "Hi, Mom."

"Jess, are you still at work? I don't know if I should be angry or concerned." Her mom didn't sound angry, so maybe she hadn't fucked up too much.

"Yeah, but…" How could she tell her mom on the phone that everything had changed this afternoon and her life had come tumbling down like a house of cards? "Something happened."

"Are you okay?" The concern in her mom's voice nearly broke her.

Jess swallowed and balled her hands into fists. The pain of the nails digging into the soft flesh kept the tears at bay. Barely. "Yes. No, not really. But I will be. It turns out I have PPCM and have to stay here. Can you watch Ella overnight?"

"Of course I'll take care of her, don't worry. But what is PPCM? Is this a kind of overnight shift?"

Oh, right. Her mom had her own PhD and had been married to a cardiologist for over forty years, but how could she expect her to know what this acronym meant? "No, It's a medical condition. Peripartum cardiomyopathy. It means my heart is temporarily damaged and I have to be careful for the next few weeks." *Or months.* But that wasn't something she wanted to think about or admit out loud. "The recovery rate is very good. It'll sort itself out when I take some medication." Or not, but she didn't want to think about that either.

"Oh my God, honey. What happened? Do you want me to come to the hospital?"

Yes. Her inner child she thought she'd outgrown over twenty years ago wanted her mom to come and hold her while they cried together. But that would be selfish. Her mom shouldn't have to drive here in the evening, lugging Ella around. They both needed their sleep. "No. I'm fine. If you take care of Ella, I can get a bit of sleep and come and get her in the morning." It took all the acting skills she had learned during med school to keep the neediness from her voice.

"Are you sure? But let me at least come and get you. Let me take care of you. I can stay with you in your condo, or you can come home with me."

The way her mom insisted would have been annoying any other day. It reminded Jess that she was weak and helpless like Ella. She sighed. "Can we talk about it tomorrow? I'm too tired to think."

"Oh, Jess, I'm so sorry, honey. What do you need right now?" The compassion was worse than the concern, and it tugged at Jess's composure until it threatened to unravel.

I won't cry. I won't cry in a fucking hospital bed. In my own fucking department. Where anyone can come and see me and blab about it to the whole fucking staff. "Just…nothing. Please." She choked on the last word.

"Okay. We'll sort it all out later. Tomorrow morning I'll pick you up, and we'll plan the next steps together. When do you want me to come?" Here was the mom she needed. No fussing, just practical reassurance.

"Thanks." The paperwork should be ready early, even if Jess had to do it herself. If she set her alarm to six, she could even get a couple of hours of paperwork in. "Could you come around eight?"

"I'll be there. Sleep well. I love you."

"Love you too." Jess voice shook. When had she said this last to her mom?

She rubbed her eyes. Sleep. She needed to get back to sleep.

As if she could with all the problems looming ahead like the ascent of a mountain. She'd have to plan every step and handhold carefully so she wouldn't fall.

Chapter Four

LENA PLUCKED THE MINT LEAVES from her tea and stirred a dollop of honey into it. She cradled her favorite ceramic mug against her chest and breathed in deeply. Nothing was as good as fresh herbs. Some days she couldn't believe how lucky she was to live in Maggie's garden.

The door swung open and nearly hit her in the face.

Lena jumped back, and tea splashed all over her front and soaked her top. Hot, burning tea. Ouch. She pulled the thin cotton from her skin and looked up.

The disheveled woman with dark circles beneath her eyes looked familiar. She glared at Lena from beneath unkempt hair. "What are you doing in my house?"

Wait? Her house? Oh. Was that Jess? Nothing of the beautiful afterglow of giving birth remained.

"Shouldn't I ask you that?" The skin on Lena's chest burned, and she tried to cool it by flapping her top, but it was too tight to give real comfort.

"I don't have to explain anything to you. This is my family's house. What are you doing here?" Jess stepped closer and towered over Lena by at least a couple of inches.

"I live here." Lena snarled right back. She wanted to kick the intruder out, but then it clicked. Jess obviously didn't know she had been living in the garden house for the last ten months. Lena's anger deflated. "You're Jess, right? I'm Lena. Maggie rented the house to me." She held out her hand.

"Dr. Riley." Jess ignored her hand and stepped past Lena, looking around the room with a frown. "My name is Dr. Riley, as is my mother's."

"Um…come in." Lena didn't know how to react, so she went with her default setting: politeness. Even if Jess had already entered the house. "If you insist, I'll call you by your last name, but how I address Maggie is between her and me. Can I help you?"

"I don't remember the furniture, so it must be yours. It'll take a bit of time to move all that, so you can take until the end of tomorrow to remove everything."

Lena blinked. Was she joking? But the tone didn't hold even a trace of humor. "There must be a misunderstanding. Let's go talk to Maggie and clear everything up. I'll change my top, and then we can go to the main house."

Jess's icy blue eyes moved up and down as she studied her. "What are you doing with your top?"

"I burned myself when you stormed inside." Lena held up the empty mug.

"Oh, um, I'm sorry." Red spots bloomed on Jess's cheeks. "You don't need to come. You can start packing." Without waiting for Lena's reply, Jess stalked off.

Lena followed her to the door. "Hey, wait a minute…"

Either Jess didn't hear or didn't care as she stormed away. The dramatic effect of her exit was diminished by the fact that she stopped halfway to the house, clutched her side, and gasped for air.

Shaking her head, Lena closed the door and went into her bathroom to change. As she peeled off her bra, the cotton brushed her skin, and she winced. A glance in the mirror confirmed what she had suspected. An angry stripe ran down her chest, as if she'd smeared herself with raspberries, from the valley between her breasts to her navel. Fortunately, she didn't detect any blisters. She rinsed the stained top, then pressed the cold, wet cloth to her skin.

The relief was instant, and she sat on the toilet seat as her knees grew weak. *What happens now?* Maggie had promised her the use of the garden house for at least the next year, but now her daughter intended to live here. They hadn't signed a lease because she had trusted Maggie when she'd said her word was worth more than any paper. Just as Lena's own word was worth more than a credit report. Maybe that had been foolish. When would she learn not to trust anymore?

With a sigh, she placed the top back into the sink and stood. Time to find out if she would be living in her car tomorrow. Quickly, she spread some aloe lotion on the burn and went into her bedroom to dress in a loose shirt.

As she got closer to the main house, she hesitated.

Jess's voice drifted through the half-open French doors, and the tone suggested she wasn't happy with whatever her mother answered.

Instead of interrupting them, Lena took a seat on a chair on the far side of the patio. The large wooden structure spanned the length of the house and extended into the garden with a curved edge. Terra-cotta planters filled with plants in in all sizes and shapes, from evergreens to herbs to exotic blooms, lined the edge and blurred the border to the garden. She would miss this peaceful oasis, not only the calming design but her daily contact with Maggie. She'd thought the older woman had become her friend, not just her landlady, but maybe that had been wishful thinking. The burn on her breast started again, this time from within, not just skin deep.

A shrill cry interrupted the fight. The baby didn't seem to like the raised voices either.

The door opened fully, and Lena jumped up, afraid she wasn't welcome.

Maggie stepped out onto the deck, a frown carving deep lines into her face. But when she looked up at Lena, the lines softened. Smiling, she walked over.

That smile promised everything would work out fine, but Lena had been disappointed too often to relax now. "Would you…?" She swallowed. "Would you like me to leave?"

"No, honey, not at all." Maggie shook her head. "I don't know what Jess said, but this is a misunderstanding. The house is yours for as long as you want it."

"Thank you." The pain that had gripped Lena the moment she feared she might be on her own again slowly abated. "Are you sure? She is your daughter, after all."

Maggie reached over and took Lena's hand. "I've told her you live here now and if she wants to stay, she is welcome to live in the main house. I've already converted Jess's childhood room into a nursery for Ella, and she can stay in the guest room next to it." She glanced back at the house; the baby's crying had subsided. "To be honest, even if you didn't live in the garden house, I'd like her to stay close. She's…" She opened and closed her hands a few times, letting go of Lena's. "She's not as fit as she should be. She needs help, whether she wants to admit it or not."

Lena nodded. Jess had looked pale and tired. "Is she sick?"

"Yes. It was quite a scare. It's all very new and…" Maggie's shoulders slumped. "But she's optimistic she'll be fine soon." The smile that accompanied the last words was weak.

That sounded serious. Lena didn't want to pry, but it was difficult to hold back the half dozen questions tumbling in her mind. "I'm sorry to hear that. Can I do anything to help?"

"Please be patient. She shouldn't stress herself. That's bad for her condition. Maybe give her some time to get adjusted? My daughter has always had difficulty being spontaneous." Maggie shrugged apologetically. "She'll come around to you. I'm sure by this time next week, she'll be embarrassed about her behavior and apologize."

An illness wasn't an excuse to be rude in Lena's book, but she was willing to give Jess a second chance for Maggie's sake. "I hope you're right." Lena stood. "I'll leave you to it and head back to the garden house. I have to work soon." And she wanted to put an ice pack on her chest, but Maggie didn't need to know that.

"You take care, and let me know if Jess troubles you. I'll talk to her." Maggie hugged her.

Lena managed not to wince when her shirt was pressed against her skin. The pain was worth knowing Maggie wasn't kicking her out.

Chapter Five

THE CLOCK ON LENA'S CAR had given up long ago, and its perpetual five-to-twelve status was more a comment on the general state of the vehicle and maybe even Lena's life. The urge to dig out the cell phone from her bag was strong, but Lena resisted. She couldn't drive any faster anyway because she couldn't risk a ticket. That wasn't in her budget for this month. Or any month.

As she didn't plan to stop for long, she parked in front of the driveway instead of maneuvering into her spot. She jumped out of the car, clutching her backpack in one hand and the keys in the other. Her mind was already three steps ahead. Shower and change before she hurried off to her next job.

"What do you think you're doing?" The harsh voice interrupted her thoughts.

Lena flinched and froze.

Jess stood in front of the gate with both hands on her hips, blocking her entrance. She scowled at Lena with those bright eyes that were still beautiful despite the icy glare. In black jeans and a slate-gray sweater, she made an imposing figure next to the sleek gray-and-white stroller.

For four days she had been able to avoid Jess, but today her streak of bad luck continued. It had started with a visitor at the farmers market knocking over her display of preserves. Only two glasses had broken, but she'd been covered in sticky fruit and sugar. Then she must have given someone the wrong change, because she'd ended up ten dollars short at the end of the day. Counting everything thrice had made her late, and she didn't have time to accommodate Jess's mood. "Just parking for a moment."

"You can't park that piece of garbage here." Jess pointed to her car.

Garbage? That was a harsh assessment. True, the car had doors in two different colors, neither matching the faded beige of the body, and rust spots that looked like a contagious disease. But it worked fine most days. But that wasn't the point here.

"Do you need to leave now?" Lena raised her hand with the key in an apologetic gesture. "I'm sorry, but I only need twenty minutes. I'm home to change for my other job and—"

"I don't care about the organizational deficits of your day. You can't park there. If you leave the car there, I'll call a tow service to have it removed." Red blotches appeared on Jess's cheeks, and a drop of sweat formed on her temple, but her hard gaze was unwavering.

"Tow service?" The nerve of this woman! Lena clenched her jaws to stop herself from blurting out what she really thought. Jess made it difficult for her to honor her promise to Maggie to be patient. "Okay, if you insist, I'll park on the other side of the street." Lena didn't want to believe her threat was serious, but she didn't intend to test the theory.

"I insist." Jess's lips were pressed into a thin line, and a muscle in her jaw twitched.

Back in her car, Lena risked a glance at the cell phone. She had lost more minutes than anticipated; there was barely enough time to shower and change. Washing her hair would be out of the question. A granola bar in the car would have to be enough to get her through the afternoon shift at the café.

She sincerely hoped her patience helped Jess on her way to recovery. The sooner she got well, the sooner she would be able to return to her own home.

✝✝✝✝✝✝✝

"Tammy!" Lena woke and almost fell in her haste to get out of bed. In the precious seconds it took to untangle her legs from the sheets, her baby sister's cries urged her to hurry as her heart nearly burst out of her chest.

Then reality hit her with the force of a car accident.

Tammy wasn't here. Tammy would never be here again. Tammy didn't need her anymore. *Don't go there!*

38

Freed of the sheets, Lena fell back onto the bed. "Just a dream." Her voice was hoarse. And why did she whisper? She was alone, as she had been for the last ten years.

She tossed and turned but couldn't find a comfortable position to fall back asleep. The bed was softer and wider than the cot in Tammy's room had been, but she would exchange all the comfort in the world to hear the soft breathing of her baby sister.

No way would she be able to sleep anytime soon with the memory of Tammy buzzing through her mind like a swarm of bees.

She glanced at the alarm on her nightstand. Three. Ugh, way too early to start the day. Maybe tea would help her relax again. She got up without bothering with the light. The smooth hardwood floor beneath her bare feet was solid and reminded her of her grandma's house.

As she filled the kettle, another cry pierced the silence. Not a dream but a real baby's cry had woken her. Oh, of course. Jess's daughter. But why could Ella be heard all the way through the garden? During the last week, she had barely noticed the presence of a newborn baby in the main house.

She left the half-filled kettle in the sink and stepped closer to the kitchen window. A cool breeze had replaced the warmth of the evening and carried scents of summer flowers through the open window.

The light of a full moon cast long shadows between the trees and flowerbeds and transformed the night into a magical black-and-white world. Someone moved on the far side of the garden, the direction the cries came from.

As the bulky figure got closer, Lena could discern Jess and her daughter in a baby carrier she had fastened to her front. In pajama bottoms and a loose T-shirt, Jess looked much younger and less imposing than the last time Lena had seen her.

Ella continued to cry, interrupted by hiccups.

"I know, honey, I know. I hate bloating too. It's fucking annoying." Jess's voice was deep and low, and the cadence of her speech was a soothing singsong that belied the curse words. She continued to talk, but most words were incomprehensible.

The intimacy between mother and daughter bound Lena to her place with invisible cords. She wanted to leave, wanted to respect Jess's privacy, but the soft mumbling mesmerized her.

"I'm sorry my milk had to be replaced with this shitty formula, but this is all I got tonight. I miss it too, but you don't want to get any traces of my meds. Terrible stuff. I never thought I would miss breastfeeding, but I get it now." Moonlight lit her face as she paced the lawn in front of the garden house. Something glittered on her cheeks. Tears? But her expression was full of love as she gazed down.

Lena would have never expected the intimidating and infuriating Dr. Riley to have a vulnerable and sensitive side. Why couldn't she show basic decency in her interactions with Lena, then? She shook herself as if she could dislodge the negativity that way. Concentrating on the soporific mumblings helped, though. The words of love and comfort banished some of her own loneliness.

After a while, Ella calmed down, and Jess's voice drifted off on her way to the main house.

Memories of her time with Tammy rose. Good memories. The special cuddling time in the morning when Tammy was waking up, the joy of holding her during feeding, Tammy's delight in simple things like colorful scarves.

Lena stared into the summer night until her legs grew heavy and she had difficulty keeping her eyes open. When she returned to her bedroom, she had again stored the memories in the depths of her mind where they wouldn't interrupt her daily life.

Chapter Six

For once, the alarm on her phone and not Ella's cries woke Jess. She quickly switched it off so as not to rouse Ella. She hadn't quite figured out what would disturb her. Most of the time, nothing but a heavy metal concert during a tornado would wake her. Jess blinked and rolled to her side to look outside. The sun had barely risen, and cheerful pink clouds dotted the sky. She groaned. Whose genius idea had it been to get up with the chickens? But she couldn't blame anyone but herself.

Bone-deep weariness was nothing new to her. Sheer determination had propelled her through med school, residency, and fellowship, all the way to the top of her profession. She was determined to get back to her former fitness level, and starting the day with a workout was the first step.

Well, the second step. First she had to take her medication. She shook one pill out of each of the four bottles, then broke the diuretic in half. She didn't need as much as she had in the beginning of her treatment a week ago. A good sign. She swallowed them all at once with a bit of tepid water from the bottle on her bedside table. Ugh. She shook herself. Getting a taste of her own medicine had taken on a completely new meaning.

She stood and threw on her prepregnancy workout tights and a sports bra. Both cut deeper into her skin than she wanted to acknowledge. "Ouch!"

Ella made a sound and moved her tiny head a bit to the side.

Oops. Jess held her breath and waited to see if Ella would wake up. She hadn't meant to speak out loud.

Noiselessly, she fastened the chest strap of her heart rate monitor. She hadn't worn one for her workout in years, as she knew her body well, but she had ordered a new one as a concession to her condition.

Ella's eyelids fluttered once, twice, then her features relaxed and she was deep asleep again.

With a sigh, just internal this time, Jess threw on one of the oversized, washed-out T-shirts from her teenage years that her mom had kept for gardening. She switched on the baby monitor that was sitting on the nightstand between her bed and Ella's cradle, bent down to kiss her, and left the room without looking in the mirror. She played with the monitor's receiver as she tiptoed down the stairs, avoiding the creaking ones with muscle memory formed as a teenager. Her mom wouldn't mind if she knocked and deposited the device in her bedroom, but she'd have to face questions or, even worse, encouragement. Jess didn't need anyone cheering her on. Or watching her fail.

Outside, the crisp morning air was laced with humidity. Dew drops sparkled on her mom's flowers like tiny diamonds, and birds sang with an enthusiasm she couldn't quite share.

She used the steps from the patio to the garden to stretch. At least she hadn't lost all of her limberness and was still able to reach her toes now that most of the baby bump had disappeared.

Due to the baby monitor, she would limit her morning exercise to the garden. She started with a light jog, but before she even reached the far end, she was breathing hard.

Instead of slowing down, she ran faster. She wasn't a quitter.

One hundred and seventy-nine steps until the end of the garden. One hundred and seventy-nine back again. Fourteen steps up to the patio. Her lungs burned, and her heart raced so fast she thought it might trigger another arrhythmia. But no dizziness. She looked at her watch. Her heart rate was still acceptable. She ran down again.

Counting kept her focus from the pain in her lungs as they tried to get more oxygen into her system, but something wasn't right. Her second round had two hundred and three steps. In the third, she was at two hundred and fifty-two before she had to stop.

Panting, she rested her arms on her shaking legs. She didn't want to sit. Any second, she would start to run again. Her lungs protested; it hurt as if shards of glass were stuck between her ribs. And her heart. She didn't want to think of her heart, but she had to. She checked her watch for her heart rate.

Fuck. Maybe she needed a longer break after all.

"Are you okay?" Lena was standing much too close. How had she snuck up? What the fuck was her mom's tenant doing here at this time of day anyway?

For a second, Jess was tempted to say no and fall down on the lawn. Instead, she straightened to her full height, using the extra inches to glare down on the intruder.

Lena wore loose black yoga pants and a bright pink top proclaiming she had taken part in a charity race. Without staring at her breasts, Jess couldn't tell which run. She wrenched her gaze upward and used her best scowl, honed through years of intimidating residents. "What are you doing in the garden? Now?"

The stare seemed to work. Lena took a step backward. "Um…I live here, remember?" She tilted her head, and the fine lines around her hazel eyes crinkled in concern. "I was about to start my morning tai chi routine. Do you need any help? Are you okay?"

Did she look as bad as she felt? Why did Lena keep asking that? Heat that had nothing to do with exertion shot to her cheeks, and Jess gritted her teeth. She'd rather fall flat on her face than accept assistance. Another lesson she'd learned in med school was to never show weakness. Jess turned on her heel and walked back toward the main house. Every step was a struggle as if she'd exercised wearing her lead apron in addition to a heavy backpack, but she made it without stopping.

Lena couldn't keep her gaze from Jess as she dragged herself back to the main house. She watched because Jess looked exhausted, not because her running tights fit like a glove and revealed feminine curves that provided a direct contrast to her prickly demeanor. She was only making sure Jess didn't collapse. Jess looked as if she had been training for hours despite the very early morning. Maybe she had. Who knew what that woman considered normal hours?

When Jess reached the patio, Lena shrugged and faced the rising sun. She was behind schedule but needed at least thirty minutes to focus and gather her strength for the coming day.

Afterward Lena showered and dressed in layers. Today she was working at the farmers market, and the weather was supposed to change frequently.

As she was about to cut some fruit for breakfast, a knock sounded on the door.

To her surprise, Maggie stood on her porch with a plate full of scones. They were still warm, judging by the steam rising from them, and smelled heavenly.

"Hi, come in." Lena's stomach growled. "I hope you want to share. Otherwise this is just cruel torture."

Maggie chuckled. "I made them for us. Do you have time to eat with me?"

"About thirty minutes until I need to leave. I have some preserves I made last week and some fruit. Is that okay?" She didn't have much more to offer since today was her shopping day. She always exchanged some of her preserves for vegetables and cheese. The sellers at the farmers market looked after each other.

"That sounds perfect." Maggie carried the plate to the small semicircular table beneath the kitchen window and sat on one of the chairs.

"You want coffee or tea?" Lena set the table, then checked the water kettle. Still hot.

"Is the coffee Rachel's? I can't resist her roasts."

"What else?" Her friend often gave Lena her leftovers, and Lena appreciated the quality, even if she seldom drank the stuff herself.

"Will you get me some today? I'm almost out."

"Sure." Lena inhaled the fresh scent of ground coffee as she measured a generous portion into the French press. "Do you want me to pick up anything else?" She carried the coffee to the table and took her seat opposite of Maggie.

"No, thank you. I put an order in at the cooperative, and they'll deliver later. Jess never learned to cook and lives on takeout or crackers and cheese. I want to reintroduce that girl to healthy eating so she can store up a few vitamins that don't come from a pill."

Lena took one of the scones and buttered it before adding a spoonful of her strawberry peppermint preserve. "She doesn't look unhealthy to me, just exhausted. This morning I saw her running."

"What? Where?" Maggie paled, and her scone fell to her plate. "Oh, sorry, but…she shouldn't be working out alone."

"Why? I saw her in the garden when I got up for tai chi." It was the safest neighborhood Lena had ever lived in, and she had never heard anyone say you shouldn't jog alone.

"She had… Before she came to live here… I shouldn't tell you, but…" Maggie's lip trembled, and tears sprang to her eyes.

Lena took the older woman's hand. "Is it because of her illness?"

Maggie swallowed and wiped her eyes with her free hand. "It's so unexpected. It's not that I don't trust you, but Jess is extremely private and it's not my place to tell. Let me just say, she needs rest and to get away from all the stress."

"Let me know if I can help in any way." Lena was no fan of getting sneered at, but she wanted to support Maggie. And her daughter obviously did need some help. Lena wouldn't say so aloud, but Jess Riley didn't appear to be someone who had taken rest and stress-free living to heart. Every time they met, she could feel waves of annoyance and anger emanating from her.

"Thank you. I think it would be enough if you keep an open mind about her. I know she sometimes comes across as abrupt and a bit rude, but when you get to know her, you see that she isn't like that at all. I think she could use a friend." Maggie picked up her scone again and bit into it with renewed appetite.

Lena closed her mouth with a snap when she noticed it hanging open. A bit rude was the understatement of the day, probably the year. She swallowed her reply. She wouldn't get between mother and daughter, especially if Maggie was blinded by maternal instinct. She would keep her distance, and if a miracle happened and penguins could fly, she might end up being friends with Jess.

††††††††

"I'm no better than a spy. Or a stalker." Jess hid behind the shades in Ella's room as her mom and Lena walked arm in arm to the stonier section of the garden.

Ella burped. That might translate as "Yes, Mom, you are. Why are you doing this?"

She held Ella up to her left shoulder and patted her back. "I don't know, but something is wrong with that Lena. Why would she spend her free time with a woman twice her age?"

Now her mom was showing Lena several green plants, not even blooming ones. "Is she really interested in gardening, or is this a kind of game to gain access to a rich old woman?"

Her mom was far from frail or forgetful, but maybe the intruder didn't know that.

Without warning, her mom straightened up and looked at the house; it seemed as if her gaze bored right into Jess.

She took a step back. "Whoa, that was close. Do you think she saw me?"

Ella squirmed on her shoulder for a few seconds, then cried once.

"Okay, okay. I'm finding something else to do." She sniffed at Ella's behind. "Maybe clean you up?"

Jess went to the dresser on the other side of the room. The wooden surface had once displayed her collection of track trophies, but now it served as a changing table. A soft towel was spread on the top, and her mom had decorated the board above it with a mobile. Plush animals in oversized, striped swimsuits danced around a wide, grinning sun. Silly. Who thought of these things?

Everything she needed was stored in the topmost drawer: wipes, lotion, diapers, and Ella's clothes. It wasn't convenient, unlike the cleverly designed changing station she had at her condo, but it wasn't her intention to use it any longer than necessary.

She gave the mobile a push so it twirled, and Ella tried to follow with her gaze. Those light-blue baby eyes were so huge and full of wonder that these animals danced only for her. *Maybe they aren't that silly after all.*

She cleaned and changed Ella, then picked her up to pace the room again.

Eight steps from door to window, ten steps from bed to closet. How often had she walked the same path in her teenage years? She had been a trapped tiger, waiting to jump the cage and explore the world. Posters of models and actresses had stirred in her a longing she couldn't name. She had thought she wanted to be like them, look like them. A goal unachievable for a lanky, dark-haired teenager who more closely resembled the androgynous guys accompanying the women in some of those pictures.

Now she knew she had wanted to be *with* the women.

But that hadn't worked out so well. At all. She'd never had problems meeting women or even getting second or third dates. The problems always started when they demanded more of her time than she was able to give. No one understood medicine had to come first.

Well, now that Ella came first and medicine a close second, her chances of finding a wife weren't improving. She'd be forever alone and have to turn to her mother for help like a teenager. Would she ever be fit enough to return to her condo? What if her heart failure wouldn't improve? Then she'd always have to depend on help.

Heat shot through her, and her breath caught. Trapped. She was trapped in this weak body and this tiny room.

Ella squirmed in her arms and cried.

Jess took a few deep breaths to calm herself. Her chances were very good for a full recovery even if nothing in medicine was ever one-hundred percent. She needed to find ways to relax soon. She shouldn't project her stress onto Ella.

Her gaze went back to the window. The roof of the garden house and part of the patio were visible, but trees and shrubs hid the rest. That was an oasis, with several rooms and enough space to pace. Jess's place was out there and not in this tiny room.

Everything came back to Lena. Jess didn't share her mom's trust in Lena at all. She needed more information, and the first step would be to talk to her mom and see what she knew. If something wasn't right, she would prove it. She owed it to her mom to protect her.

Having a plan settled her, and Ella calmed down as if she agreed.

After the woman had moved out, she'd redecorate the garden house, and it would feel like a home, something she'd been searching for since she left med school.

"Perfect solution." Jess grinned. "Don't you agree, honey?"

Ella only yawned. But what did she know?

The minute her mom returned from the garden, Jess went downstairs, baby monitor tucked into her waistband. Had her mom been baking again? Scones had tempted her yesterday, and today cinnamon filled the air. Her stomach growled. But whatever it was, she'd better stay far, far away from it. Carbs weren't her friend right now.

Unfortunately, she found her mom in the kitchen, arranging cinnamon buns in a container. A couple didn't fit, and she placed them on a plate. "Good morning. Have you eaten breakfast yet?"

"Morning. Not yet. I'll have a yogurt." Her mouth watered at the sight of the fresh buns, but she opened the fridge and took out a container of natural yogurt. Boring stuff, but she wouldn't get her figure back by indulging every time something smelled delicious.

"Do you want some tea? I picked some fresh mint."

"Thanks." If her mom was in the mood for pampering, it could only help her cause. Even if she could kill for a cup of decent coffee. But living without caffeine was supposed to be good for her heart. At least if she believed what she told her patients.

While her mom prepared the tea, Jess sat at the wooden table in the window bay and ate a spoonful of yogurt. Ugh. Maybe a bit of honey? Honey wasn't like sugar, right?

She rolled her eyes and put the spoon down. Carbs were carbs. Maybe she wasn't hungry enough if she was still so picky. And she hadn't come to the kitchen for breakfast anyway. "Mom, I ran into your tenant yesterday. She was up early."

Her mom raised her eyebrows. "Why don't you say Lena? Tenant sounds so impersonal." She placed a steaming mug of tea in front of Jess, then sat down opposite with her own. She added a teaspoon of honey and offered the jar to Jess.

Sighing, she shook her head. Had her mom read her thoughts? *Focus on the conversation, Jess.* "Yeah, fine, Lena. Don't you think it's strange she's out early every day?"

"Like you were? She told me you met, and you had exercised. Should you be alone while doing it?" She managed to sound nonaccusatory, just concerned, but she still induced an immediate guilty conscience in the way only mothers could.

Jess winced. She should take notes to learn the skill herself before Ella reached puberty. "I wasn't doing anything strenuous." Not a complete lie— it wouldn't have been strenuous if she'd retained a fifth of her old fitness level. Best to leave this topic and seek another way to learn more about Lena. "Has she been living here for long?"

"Almost a year, maybe ten months or so. Since I renovated the garden house." Her mom blew over her mint tea and took a small sip.

Now she mentioned it, Jess remembered her saying something about renovating and renting the garden house. But Jess's mind had been on her midlife crisis and the idea she needed a baby, a family of her own, someone to love and cherish. She had avoided really talking to her mother ever since because she'd been afraid she wouldn't understand or approve. No wonder she had missed the news about someone living here.

Again, guilt scratched on the door, but Jess refused to let it in. This talk wasn't about her failures as a daughter. The purpose was to gather information.

Jess leaned back in her chair. "How did you find Lena?"

"I shop at her stall at the farmers market, and she had put up a sign that she was looking for a place to live as soon as possible. She told me she couldn't stay at her old apartment any longer."

Now they were getting to the good stuff. "What happened at her last apartment? Why did she have to leave?"

"Oh, that was bad. Her roommate wanted her to pay extra because she didn't like Lena's job, so she couldn't afford the place anymore."

That story seemed highly suspicious. Jess stared into her tea as she thought about her next question. Her mom had left the leaves on the stalk, and it looked like limp seaweed. Not very appealing. She preferred her drinks from a reliable source, not homegrown. It smelled refreshing, though. She took a sip. Not too bad. "Why is a job at the farmers market offensive? Does she sell fish?"

"Oh, no, not that job. She teaches relaxation techniques too. She takes clients at home several evenings during the week. Her roommate knew about it beforehand but changed her mind later. Now that Lena lives in the garden house alone, that isn't a problem anymore."

Relaxation techniques? What did that even mean? And strangers were coming and going through the garden in the evenings? That didn't sound like a great idea. Jess could almost feel her blood pressure rise as she thought about it. Her mom was too trusting. "Why does she have two jobs?" Was working at the market a cover for shady activities in the evening?

"She actually has three." She held up her hand and counted them on her fingers. "Farmers market Thursday and Saturday, teaching on various evenings, and she works at a cute organic café almost every day."

Her mom went on about the virtues of the café, but Jess wasn't listening anymore. It sounded like a bunch of hippies had opened a place to hang out, nowhere she intended to visit.

The answer to what was wrong with Lena was obvious. Money must be a major problem. Did her mother even get a security deposit? Did she check the woman's credit status? Probably not. She had seen a friendly face and someone in need and had reacted. The next thing Jess knew, Maggie would be paying Lena's bills and writing checks for special projects.

Jess needed to find out more about the activities at the garden house and Lena's financial situation before her mother got drawn in too deep.

Chapter Seven

LENA PEDALED THE LAST FEW yards up the drive, then swung down and stretched. Finally. Her legs felt every one of the three miles from the bus after the long day at the café. But when the car wouldn't start this morning, she'd had no other choice.

She pushed the bike through the gate and behind the garage. As she turned the corner, the sight of Jess nearly made her groan. She was too tired for this.

For once, the woman didn't appear imposing. Her upper half had disappeared behind the paper bin. She wore jeans that hugged her curves.

Lena stumbled and caught herself before falling headfirst into the compost bin; she'd grazed one of the stones bordering the narrow lane. "Shit." She should have watched where she was going instead of ogling her rude neighbor.

Jess jerked her head out of the paper bin with a crimson face.

They stared at each other. What was happening? It wasn't as if she had disturbed Jess doing something embarrassing. "Um, hi."

Jess looked at her and at the paper she was clutching in her hand. "Hi." She stuffed whatever she had rescued from the bin into her pocket. "I, ah, I lost a phone number I noted on an envelope. From…from a friend."

If Jess had said that without the blush and the panicked expression, it would have been a valid explanation. But something was off. Maybe it was something she wanted to keep hidden from her mother. Or a date. Not something that should concern Lena.

"Okay. Glad you found it." Lena walked past Jess, leaned her bike on the fence, and locked it with both chains. The thirty-year-old bike had been a yard sale find and wasn't valuable, but it was the only one she had and her backup for the days her car acted up. At least during the summer.

"Yeah. I, um, need to go." Jess hurried up the path that led to the main house. After a few steps, she stopped and looked over her shoulder. "Where did you come from? Work? Do you always work that late?"

Since when did Jess show an interest in her day? But Lena had nothing to hide, and the flustered version of the usually overconfident Dr. Riley was oddly endearing. "I picked up a double shift at the café today. The other waitress flaked out." Even though she was so tired she could fall asleep on the spot, she was still happy to have put in the hours. Now she could afford to get her car checked out.

"Oh, you're waitressing? Where are you working?" Jess's blush had receded, and she studied Lena through narrowed eyes.

"Cashew Cult. It's an organic café close to the farmers market." Lena shifted from one foot to the other under Jess's intense gaze. When she didn't say anything and seemed to be waiting, Lena talked on. "They use local produce, and the food is delicious. Especially the cakes. But the evening food is great as well, a lot of Mediterranean and Middle Eastern stuff. You should check it out."

Oh no. Why had she invited Jess? The last thing she needed at work was a critical customer. But she believed in the quality of the food, even if serving it was far from her dream job.

"Maybe I'll have to see for myself. Sooner or later I have to go out in public with Ella." When she mentioned her daughter's name, Jess's face softened. A hint of the attractiveness Lena had seen in the hospital popped up like the first shoots of green after a long winter.

"Good idea. You wouldn't be the only mother with a stroller. Is Ella doing better?" Maybe Lena could get her to warm up a little if they talked about her daughter.

"What do you mean?" Jess tensed like a cat about to pounce.

"I saw you two a few nights ago in the garden. She seemed to be having difficulty going back to sleep. The poor girl sounded unhappy about something."

"Oh, that." Jess relaxed again. "She's better now. I switched to a different formula. She seems to love it."

"Glad to hear it." Lena wanted to prolong the conversation now she'd found a topic that didn't lead to immediate antagonism, but she was ready for a hot shower. And she had to hurry because she expected her clients soon. She freed her bag from the bicycle rack. "I'm sorry, but I need to go. See you around."

Jess nodded and strode off toward the main house without a backward glance.

Lena followed more slowly, feeling every stone dig into her soles as if she was walking barefoot on the gravel. She so wanted to rest her feet for a few minutes, but she had bills to pay.

Ella was finally fed, changed, and cuddled back to sleep. Jess hadn't had a minute for herself since she'd returned to her room. She wanted nothing more than to curl up and sleep like her daughter, but she still had work to do.

She fetched her laptop from her desk and carried it to the window seat overlooking the garden. As a teenager, she had spent most evenings here, planning her future. Before she sat down, she pulled the crumpled envelope from her pocket. A ridiculous lampshade with penguins juggling balls in all colors of the rainbow cast a soft light. It wasn't so bright as to disturb Ella, but it provided enough light to read.

She straightened the paper with her hand. It was addressed to Lena Walker at a different address in Seattle. She guessed this was the apartment she'd had to move out of. What was more interesting, however, was the part of the return address that was still legible. Someone had written to her from a women's correctional institute in Illinois. The name of the sender had been damaged by the opening. No matter how she held the paper or squinted, the lower halves of the letters didn't make any sense to her.

Jess typed the name of the prison into the search bar on her browser and clicked the link that appeared. The website looked professional, with nicely done pictures. They even had a page where you could look up current and former inmates and their crimes by name, number, or date of birth. She hadn't known something like that existed. She typed in *Walker* but hesitated before pressing *send*. Did she really want to know if Lena was registered there?

Even if the information was public, it felt like a violation of privacy. But Lena could be a con artist or thief who preyed on old widows like her mother. If she was honest with herself, Jess doubted that theory, though. What criminal worked three jobs?

She looked out the window to the garden house and moved a bit on the seat, trying to find a more comfortable position. Had the window seat always been this narrow, or had her mom changed it during the remodeling of the house?

Darkness had fallen since she'd come inside, and the lights in the garden house were on. They shone golden, a warm contrast to the pale light provided by the waning moon. It looked harmless, cozy, and inviting.

The door of the garden house opened, and the lights on the porch shone on a man and a woman in jeans and sweatshirts. They seemed to be talking to Lena, but Jess couldn't make out their features.

After a moment of hesitation, she hastened downstairs to her mom's study to get the binoculars. On her return, she had to pause halfway up the stairs for a couple of breaths. When would her stupid heart improve?

She held the binoculars to her eyes, but it was too late. The people had left, and the porch was dark again. Her hand trembled as she lowered the binoculars. Was she taking things too far?

Maybe Lena had friends over. Normal people did that.

Her gaze returned to her laptop, which still showed the prison's website with Lena's last name typed into the search field. She closed the lid with a snap.

Time to go to sleep.

The first rays of sunshine barely sneaked over the horizon, as Lena breathed deeply to center herself for her tai chi routine. She began with circular movements of her arms and went through a series of easy qi gong exercises. Icy dew prickled the soles of her bare feet and made her feel alive. Soon her muscles warmed up despite the early morning. As she was about to start the form, loud steps and heavy breathing interrupted her concentration.

A sweaty and flushed Jess approached through the back gate. She wore the same training clothes as last time. She rested both her arms on the gate and tried to catch her breath for quite a long time. At last, she straightened and wiped her face with the hem of her T-shirt. The color of her cheeks was slowly fading to normal.

Lena didn't want to continue watching from afar without Jess knowing she was there. That would be creepy. But she didn't want to ignore her either, as Jess didn't look all that well. Maybe Maggie's concerns about her exercising alone were justified. She walked over.

"Good morning."

Jess twirled around and glared. "What are you doing here? Spying on me?"

Not this conversation again. But Lena remembered Maggie asking her to show a bit of patience and refrained from rolling her eyes. Instead, she smiled. Or at least pulled up the corners of her mouth in a resemblance of a smile. "No spying going on here this morning. I was doing my tai chi routine. Best way to wake up."

"The Chinese thing where you move super slow, like a snail?" Jess tilted her head to her side. "Isn't that for old people?"

Don't let her provoke you. Jess was probably embarrassed that Lena had seen her breathless. "It's Chinese, yes. And everything is slow because the movements should strengthen your core muscles. It has all sorts of health benefits, and even elderly people can do it. Or maybe they get so old by doing it?"

Jess snorted with laughter. The sound was one of the first genuine friendly reactions she'd shown Lena. "Touché. I haven't seen anyone doing it outside of TV documentaries about China."

"Then you haven't been to the right places. People all over the world do it. Everyone can benefit from core strength." *And relaxation and inner harmony. Especially you.* Lena pressed her lips together. Instinct urged her to invite Jess to join her, but her mind held her back. She wasn't so stupid as to want to spend more time with someone who didn't care for her company.

"Not everyone. I don't think tai chi is what I need." Jess shrugged.

"What do you need?" Whatever form of exercise Jess was doing, she didn't seem to be getting what she needed from it.

Jess's brows furrowed as she contemplated the question and she dropped her gaze to the ground. "If I only knew…" Without another word, she went past Lena toward the house.

+++++++

As soon as Jess was out of sight behind the vegetation, she slowed down. No need to stress her heart again.

At the end of her short run, she had been out of breath and dizzy. Actually, it had been more fast walking than running, but that was even worse.

Her method of training wasn't working. Maybe she needed to try something else. Like tai chi? She laughed. Um, no. That didn't sound like her at all.

After checking on Ella, who still slept, she went to her room to shower and change. As she walked past the dresser, the blood pressure monitor drew her gaze.

She'd somehow managed to ignore it since the day she'd moved in with her mother. Doctors really were the worst patients—not because they thought their bodies worked differently from other humans, but because they knew they didn't.

Sticking her head in the sand hadn't got her anywhere before, and it wouldn't help her now. Jess grabbed the device, shook it with a little more force than necessary, and blew on it to remove some of the dust. She closed the cuff over her left upper arm, then pressed the start button. The machine inflated until it seemed ready to burst. Or squash her arm. She wasn't so sure that wasn't the more likely outcome.

Jess clenched her teeth. No wonder everyone had high blood pressure these days if the process hurt so much. The pain might even add another twenty or so to the count. She sighed when the cuff deflated and the numbers appeared on the screen.

One eighteen over sixty-five. Pulse ninety-eight. Good enough. So her meds were working fine.

She couldn't get the thing off fast enough and shoved it on the dresser again.

After she had showered and dressed in something that fit her current size better, she pondered her next move. She could search for Lena on the inmate list, which felt wrong, or she could go to the café and talk to some people there who knew her. That might still count as stalking but was slightly better. She'd pick a day when Lena was at the farmers market and go then. But who would go with her?

She mentally went through her list of friends. Or rather, acquaintances. Most of them were colleagues she didn't want to see right now because she couldn't trust them to refrain from gossiping about her. Kayla would be the obvious choice, but she was busy with her day shifts and volunteering at the free clinic this week.

Maybe Diana? They weren't friends, but she was certainly funny enough to spend an afternoon with. Where had Jess put her number? She took her work bag from the closet and opened the outside pocket. Here it was. Right where she had left it.

She took her phone out and was about to call when she saw the time. Half past six. She texted instead.

Hey, Dr. Rock Chick. Got time for a chat?

Not one minute later, the phone rang.

"Didn't we settle on first names after seeing each other naked?" The amusement was clear in Diana's voice. "How are you?"

"Fine. But recuperating is boring as hell." Jess paced in the small room, wondering how to phrase an invitation. Why hadn't she thought this through?

"I can imagine. You don't seem like the type to be happy about unpaid vacations and forced rest."

They both laughed, and Jess remembered her manners. "Sorry to bother you this early."

"Don't worry about it. I'm on my last night shift. In about an hour, I'll be off work for the next three days."

What a perfect coincidence. "Would you like to hang out with me one of those days? I've heard about a nice café I wanted to try out."

"Oh. Hold on a second." Diana voice was muffled as she talked to someone in her vicinity.

Jess suppressed a snort. Asking the girlfriend for permission?

"Okay, sure. Not today, though. I need to catch up on sleep first. Tomorrow? Or the day after?"

"Let's say tomorrow. The weather is supposed to be fine and we can sit outside." And Lena would be at the farmers market.

Chapter Eight

Lena sat on one of the strategically placed chairs between the flower beds. She wished she had more time to enjoy Maggie's ample opportunities to sit and relax in her garden. With her sketchbook balanced on her thighs, she outlined the foxglove. If she was lucky, she would be able to color this sketch before her shift at Cashew Cult. She hummed as her favorite extra-fine pen flew over the paper. It had been over a week since she'd last been home and awake enough to try to sketch.

The sound of her phone made her flinch. She wanted to ignore it, but it might be another client. She pulled the phone from her pocket.

Unknown caller. Her pen slipped from her fingers and fell to the ground. Had her mother somehow gotten her new number? "Lena Walker."

"Hi, Lena, this is Rachel."

"Oh, hi." Lena let out a shaky breath. "How are you?"

"I'm fine." But her tone belied her words; her friend sounded far from her usual cheery self. "I'm calling from my mom's place. She had an accident. A car hit her when she was crossing the street. Broken hip and wrist. The idiot of a driver ran and left her there."

"Oh no, how is she?" Lena closed her sketchbook and clutched it against her chest.

"Okay now, but she had to have an operation and a lot of physiotherapy." Rachel sighed. "Her insurance is minimal. Now the bills are stacking up."

"I'm so sorry." Lena could understand where Rachel was coming from. When her mother had broken both wrists in a drunken fall down the stairs, she hadn't had insurance either. And Lena was still paying off the debt. Debt. Lena shuddered. "You're calling about the loan, right?"

"Yeah. I'm sorry. I know we have the rates and everything in writing, but I need to help my mom, and..." To her credit, she sounded genuinely sorry. Not that it helped Lena in any way.

"It's okay." She had hoped to take on fewer clients in the evenings now she had all the regular bills under control. But not paying back the loan wasn't an option. Rachel had helped Lena to start her business selling preserves at the farmers market.

She swallowed. Twice. "Do you need everything at once?" She wouldn't be able to make the payment, but maybe she could get another loan somewhere. The thought of the interest she would have to pay made her dizzy.

"No, but maybe we can renegotiate the rates. How much can you pay?"

Lena tried to calculate, but the numbers fled her mind like a swarm of frightened sparrows. "I need to check my bills. Can I call you back?"

"Let's talk on the next market day. I'm living with my mom again and can't always pick up the phone." Rachel sighed and didn't elaborate. She didn't have to. More than once, they'd talked about Rachel's concern for her aging mother, who lived alone.

"I'll talk to you tomorrow, okay? I need to check in with work first, pick up a few extra shifts."

"Thanks. Talk to you later." Relief replaced the trepidation in Rachel's voice as she said goodbye.

Lena pushed the phone into her pocket, picked up her pen, and opened her sketchbook. She wanted to immerse herself in the sketch, where everything was beautiful and blooming and brilliant. But her fingers shook.

Before she could draw another line, wet spots dotted the paper. She wiped the tears from her cheeks and packed up her sketching supplies.

Striding back to the house, she bit the inside of her cheek to keep from crying. But it was no use. Her vision blurred, and she walked blindly down the path.

Until she ran into a soft obstacle that immediately started cursing. "Can't you watch where you're going?" Jess pushed her away and held her at arm's length. "Are you...are you crying? Did I hurt you? I'm sorry." The last words were a whisper.

"No. Yes. No." Lena shook her head to clear it. "I'm sorry. Let me go. Please."

Without discussion, Jess let go of her arm and took a step back. Lena fled before she could embarrass herself even more.

The café was nicer than expected but lacked organization. The outside seating was scattered around a couple of trees, and Jess clearly saw a more efficient placement of the tables and chairs to maximize space and serve more customers. But at least she had enough room next to the table to park Ella's stroller.

It was their first outing as mother and daughter, but Jess had no time to stress about that as she concentrated on keeping up a conversation with Diana as well as thinking of ways to find out more about Lena.

She rolled the little cookie that had come with her decaf coconut latte between her fingers.

Coconut. She couldn't believe that neither her mom nor Lena had mentioned the café was vegan. And the waitress had reassured her that the cookie was gluten-free, not that she had asked. She usually enjoyed her gluten-filled pleasures with real milk.

Was Lena vegan too? Could vegans be criminals? As long as they didn't use a horse to flee, they could probably still rob a bank. Or old widows like her mother.

A waving hand appeared between her eyes. "Hey, Jess. You haven't heard a word I've said, have you?"

Oops. Maybe she hadn't been as successful as she'd thought in keeping up with the conversation. She set the cookie on the saucer again. Gluten-free or not, she was on a diet. "Sorry. Just… It's the first time I'm out with Ella." Good. Babies were a wonderful excuse.

"It's fine. I told you work was boring, but you asked about it anyway." Diana smiled and gestured to the stroller. "She's super cute. Isn't it nice to have some extra weeks at home with her, no matter the reason?"

That was a very glass-half-full approach to her cardiac situation. One she hadn't even considered. "I like your way of thinking. It's not what I had planned, though."

Diana took a bite of her vegan carrot cake and nodded. "You said the same thing before she was born. What were your plans?"

Did she want to go there with Diana, someone from work? Maybe the short version would do. "Usually, I'm very organized, and even before I got pregnant, I had a schedule worked out and dates set for the C-section and when I would return to work afterward."

"You returned early, didn't you?"

Jess shrugged. "My boss was desperate to get me back. And I never expected this illness to throw a wrench in my plans and ruin my fitness." She grinned. "But you're right. It does have some unexpected positive side effects. The time with Ella is wonderful."

"And you're looking great. How are you doing?"

The waitress showed superb timing in interrupting them before Jess needed to come up with an answer. "Is everything okay? Can I bring you anything else?" She smiled encouragingly.

Jess was tempted to order one of the many baked goods that smelled so delicious, but the tight fit of her jeans reminded her why she needed to remain strong. She was about to send the waitress away but then remembered her mission. "Everything is great. But...I was wondering about the other woman I saw working here recently. Her name is Lena? Is she here today?"

"Lena? No. Did you have a problem?" The waitress frowned and swiped a few of her long braids behind her ear.

"No, no problem. We were talking about, um, a recipe. For, um, jam." Wasn't that what her mom had said Lena made for the market?

"Oh, her preserves are excellent. We even sell them in the café. She works here most days. Maybe you can come back tomorrow. That's typical of Lena, promising you the recipe instead of selling you her product. She is much too nice and has absolutely no business sense." She said the last bit as if it were a compliment.

Maybe it was in a hippie vegan café. "So she's nice to everyone?"

"Oh, yeah." The waitress warmed to the topic and nodded vigorously. "Last week, we had an awful customer, super demanding. She made Ethan cry. Lena comforted him, talked to her, and solved the problem. I have no idea what she said. Ethan couldn't hear her because she never raised her voice, not like the customer did. But the woman seemed to be happy in the end. She left a big tip. Lena took over his tables for the rest of the shift because he was too distressed to work, but she gave him all of the tips, and he said it was a lot."

No business sense seemed like a correct description. If Ethan were her resident, she'd have told him to suck it up and get back to work. But she guessed her opinion wouldn't be valued here. "That's nice."

Before she could ask more questions, another customer caught the gaze of the young woman and she excused herself.

Diana chuckled. "You said this was the first time you were here?"

Busted. "Yeah, well…"

"Don't worry. Your secret is safe with me. You're obviously a bad liar with a crush on this Lena."

Better to let Diana believe that than to explain. Apart from wanting to protect her mother, Jess couldn't give a good reason why she was snooping. Maybe it had been a mistake to come here. Jess stared at her fingers, coated with cookie crumbs. She wiped them on her napkin, taking more time than necessary. The queasiness of her stomach made her glad she hadn't ordered anything to eat.

Ella pierced the uncomfortable silence with a cry, and Jess reached inside the stroller to put a steadying hand on her. "Shush, honey, everything is fine."

Ella didn't believe this lie for a second and cried harder.

With her other hand, Jess moved the stroller back and forth. The motion didn't help either. She stood and took Ella out, holding her to her shoulder.

"What do you need? Fresh diapers? Food?" She could provide the first without problem but had forgotten to pack formula. It wasn't Ella's usual feeding time anyway. Jess held her up closer to her face but smelled nothing suspicious. What else could a baby need? Attention and cuddles?

Jess tried different positions, but no matter how she held Ella, the crying persisted. From the corner of her eye, she looked at Diana to see if she was annoyed.

To Jess's surprise, she grinned. "She sounds just like her mother."

Was that a dig at her temper? Jess stiffened but then thought about it for a second. Okay, maybe Diana had a point. Jess was known for being unafraid to voice her opinions. She had zero tolerance for stupidity, and the hospital was mainly staffed by idiots. Diana had proven to be the exception—plus she had a good sense of humor.

Jess tried to relax, mostly for Ella's sake. Not that it worked. "Unlike her mother, she doesn't have a valid reason to complain right now. The day is sunny with perfect temperature, she has a cozy mobile bed to sleep in, and someone who waits on her every second of the day."

Diana chuckled. "Is that your definition of happiness? A bed and someone to wait on you?"

"Hell, no." Jess had to laugh herself. "I'm currently living at my mom's. We are still negotiating the line between helpful support and smothering spoiling."

A spark of interest shone in Diana's eyes, but Ella intervened with another bout of crying before she could ask for details.

Jess switched Ella around again so she rested with her head on Jess's shoulder, looking backward.

"Hey, Ella. What are you complaining about? Didn't get any cake?" The soothing voice came from behind her.

Surprisingly, Ella quieted for a moment.

Lena? Wasn't this supposed to be her day off? Jess swiveled around. "What are you doing here, Lena?"

She arched her eyebrows and the corner of her mouth twitched. "I work here, *Jess*. I could ask you the same."

Embarrassment mixed with anger at herself was a volatile combination. Ella's cries started again and shortened her fuse. Jess didn't know how to explain her visit, and she wasn't about to defend herself. This woman had no right to judge where she was going, no right to laugh at her, no right to…

"But I won't." Her shoulder-length brown curls bounced as she shook her head, and her hazel eyes twinkled with delight. "If I had the time, I would prefer to sit here and drink coffee too."

Lena's smile disarmed her, and Jess didn't know how to answer. She couldn't insist on being called Dr. Riley if she called Lena by her first name. For the first time in ages, she didn't feel the need to have the last word. A weird feeling. But not exactly unwelcome.

Lena walked around to Jess's side and addressed her daughter. "Ella, I know life is hard and unfair. Something is always wrong, and you don't even know what or why." She didn't talk in the usual baby speak everyone, Jess included, tended to fall into automatically.

For a few hiccups, Ella paused her cries, and Jess stroked her back.

Lena started singing in a low, warm voice. Her words didn't make any sense, like a fantasy language she had made up, almost magical.

Jess listened, spellbound. That voice, that melody wrapped her in a cozy blanket and hugged her until her unrest dissolved into a warm pool of honey and milk.

The moment Ella succumbed to the song's lure, her little body softened, and she molded herself onto Jess shoulder as if she belonged there.

And she did. A powerful wave of belonging and love ran through Jess's veins, and she clutched Ella tighter.

She should lay her back into the stroller so Ella could get more rest, but she was reluctant to let go, to stretch the band that connected them for even those few inches.

Lena's song came to an end, and Jess blinked as if waking from a dream.

"Oh, it worked. That song was beautiful. What language was that?" Diana whispered.

Jess appreciated her consideration in trying not to wake Ella again.

"My grandma always sang it to me," Lena whispered back. It was oddly intimate to hear her voice from behind, so close to Jess's head. "It's Croatian, but I have no idea what it's about. She had learned it from her grandma but knew nothing else of the language."

Jess knew she should say something, thank Lena, but words eluded her. She bowed her head down to Ella's, closing her eyes. The clean baby scent mixed with lotion filled her with elation. She wanted to stay like this forever but was unable to ignore her surroundings for too long.

Diana and Lena were talking as if they had known each other for ages, smiling and nodding at each other. Being friendly seemed to be a default setting for both of them.

Unlike Jess, who had always feared friendliness would be confused with weakness, especially as a woman in a male-dominated specialty. Since when had that spilled over in her private life? Jess's emotions shifted in yet another direction as if she was blindfolded on a roller coaster; the queasiness made her stomach roll.

She quickly laid Ella in her stroller before she sensed her tension and woke up again.

Lena glanced at her with a smile. "Do you need anything for her? I can heat formula in the kitchen."

Jess didn't want to admit she hadn't brought anything. "No, thanks. We should go home." Oh great, now she had turned into one of those mothers who talked in plural form.

"Sure. I'll send my colleague over with your bill. I need to start my shift anyway." Lena waved goodbye to Diana. "It was nice talking to you. Maybe we'll see each other at Jess's place someday."

She walked away, weaving between the tables with an elegant swing of her hips.

Jess tore her gaze away. *You can't stand the woman, and now you're ogling her? Just because she has a nice singing voice. You're pathetic, Jess.*

"So that was Lena." Diana watched her with a knowing grin.

Jess ignored her.

✛✛✛✛✛✛

That evening, Jess pushed the stroller up the steep slope to her mom's driveway. Okay, maybe not steep, but it felt like going up Mount Everest rather than the gentle incline it actually was.

"Hey!" The surprised greeting was accompanied by shuffling steps.

Jess looked up. In the semidarkness she had almost barreled into the person standing there. And not any person. Lena. Why was that woman everywhere she went? Was she stalking her? Jess dismissed the thought as fast as it popped up. That was more her guilty conscience talking. She hadn't gotten over the fact she had been caught snooping at the café.

By now, the other waitress had probably told Lena all about her questions. Heat flooded her cheeks, and she stifled a groan. Since when was she the blushing type?

"What are you doing here?" Frustration at her body's betrayal colored her voice rougher than intended. Even as she said the words, she regretted them. Lena lived here, for fuck's sake, and she had to get over asking that every time they met.

"Still living here." Instead of snarling back, as Jess would have done, Lena spoke softly. Her tone might even convey a gentle teasing, but Jess couldn't be sure without seeing her expression.

65

Her anger deflated like an air mattress with an open valve. She wasn't used to teasing. Apart from Kayla and Diana, who had only started recently, no one had attempted that for a long time.

Lena bowed over the stroller, peeking inside. "And how is Ella doing? Sleeping already?" She hummed a few notes.

The memory of the lullaby rose with unexpected force. The warmth that had flooded Jess during the song enveloped her like a bubble bath. "Fine. She's fine. But I needed to walk her, as she had problems falling asleep tonight. That's unusual for her. Maybe the day out was too much excitement." *Shut up! Maybe you had too much excitement too, Jess.* She straightened her shoulders and took a step back. She must be even more exhausted than she'd thought. Or hormonal. "I better get her to her own bed."

"Sure. That's where I'm heading too." Lena yawned.

"Good night." See? Jess could be polite if she wanted to. It was sad she needed to remind herself of that fact.

She started to push the stroller but nearly doubled over when a spasm ran through her back. "Ouch." She let go to clutch her back but had to put a foot forward to stop the stroller from rolling down the drive. The unnatural position worsened her pain.

"What happened?" Lena hastened around and took the handle. She engaged the foot brake. "Did you hurt yourself?"

Jess clenched her teeth and massaged her back with both hands. It was an awkward position, but the pressure of her fingers lessened the stiffness enough that she could breathe and talk again. "Just a twinge in my back. Nothing serious."

Lena extended a hand. "Do you want me—?"

"No." Jess took a step backward. She barely knew the woman, hadn't decided yet if she liked her, and definitely didn't trust her to massage her back. Even with her few friends, she had never been a touchy-feely person. "It's nothing unusual."

"Okay." Lena raised her hand in a consolatory manner. "Why don't you join me for tai chi in the morning? It's great for back pain because it trains every core muscle. Plus, it helps to replenish your energy levels and soothe your emotions. Sometimes when I need strength or calm, I close my eyes and do the form in my mind. I had back pain too. That's one of the reasons I started years ago." Her voice caught at the end.

What were the other reasons? Jess was more interested in Lena's past than in the virtues of tai chi. And doing something mentally sounded downright weird. "Um...I don't know." She wasn't good at doing anything in slow motion; she had spent most of her life in the fast lane for a reason.

"I try to get in a session most mornings at six before work. You can join me whenever you feel like it. Can I help with the stroller? Let me push it to the house."

Jess might be exhausted and temporarily unfit, but she was still capable of caring for her child. "I can do that. Night." She loosened the brake and pushed, this time more carefully, hoping her back would grant her a dignified exit.

It did. Barely. Maybe she should find a method to loosen her back muscles. A professional massage, a real bubble bath, anything but taking lessons from Lena.

Chapter Nine

JESS STRETCHED HER LEGS OUT along the window seat. With a couple of extra cushions, it was almost as comfortable as in her teenage years. She pulled off her socks, glad to see they hadn't left an indentation on her skin. The swelling was under control with the right medication, and her tiredness was improving too. During the day, she didn't notice her heart failure anymore if she didn't attempt to work out or carry heavy loads. Yes, much better than two weeks ago.

She stared out at the garden. The warm evening light cast shadows from behind the house and enhanced the colors of the flowers. Her mom had outdone herself in building an oasis. No wonder Lena loved living here.

Someone walked down the path from the driveway to the garden. Not Lena. This woman was much shorter and curvier. She rubbed both hands on the sides of her slacks, shook them out, and then rubbed them again.

Lena met her halfway down the path. She was dressed much more informally in yoga pants and a short-sleeved wrap top in multiple shades of pink and purple. Her curls were up in a loose bun.

The two women shook hands, and from a distance it appeared businesslike, not like a greeting between friends or lovers. They talked for a minute, and the woman's words were accompanied by gestures with both hands. She was nervous, but why?

After they came to some sort of agreement, Lena laid a hand on her arm and they disappeared into the garden house.

Something didn't add up. Was the woman a friend or one of the so-called clients? What were they doing in there? Curiosity had simmered inside Jess like a badly buried fire since she'd first heard about Lena teaching relaxation techniques. Now it flared as if stoked by a gust of wind. Relaxation? What did that even mean?

Was this a code word for prostitution? Her stomach clenched at the thought. Jess didn't think of herself as a prude, and she'd been involved in a few one-night stands of her own when she was younger, but she couldn't imagine having sex for money. How could you summon desire on demand?

She grimaced. That wasn't the most likely scenario. Maybe they were meditating or doing tai chi or whatever. She could take a walk through the garden to see if she noticed anything. Just to be on the safe side.

She checked that Ella was still sleeping, then tucked the baby monitor into the pocket of her sweats. It took only a moment to sneak down the stairs, slip into her shoes, and leave the house without being seen by her mom. She hastened through the garden, but instead of keeping to the main path, she detoured to the trees that grew on the backside of the garden house.

She stepped on a branch. It broke with a snap.

Jess froze. That had been as loud as a whip. Could they hear that in the house?

She walked on more carefully, keeping her eyes on the ground until she was close enough to look into the back windows.

The bedroom curtains were drawn. The bathroom had frosted glass that ensured privacy, so Lena hadn't bothered with curtains or blinds. And why should she even suspect someone was peering inside her bathroom on private property?

Maybe this wasn't Jess's brightest moment. She hung her head and was about to retreat when the light in the bathroom came on.

Laughter and two female voices pierced the quiet. The blurred figure that entered the room was much too curvy to be Lena.

Spying on a stranger using the bathroom wasn't okay.

The woman raised her arms and slipped off her shirt.

Why was she undressing? Against her better judgment, Jess's gaze stayed glued on the woman's movements as she pulled down her pants.

Acid burned in Jess's stomach, making her sick. What did this mean? She closed her eyes to concentrate. Had her wildest speculation been accurate? Was Lena a prostitute? How dare she do this on her mom's property! How could she trample all over her mom's generosity?

There might be a different explanation, but Jess couldn't think of one. They had neither greeted like girlfriends nor lovers when they'd met on the path. No, they had seemed like strangers.

She had to find out. It was only fair to know what was happening in her mom's house. She tiptoed to the front. Maybe they were occupied enough by whatever they were doing that she could peek into the window or even listen in on their conversation.

When she reached the side of the porch, she crouched low and crept beneath the kitchen window. The light was off, and Jess risked raising her head to look inside. Nothing. Soft, flickering light shone from the other side of the main room.

Jess crept on, past the door, to the other window. The candlelight cast irregular shadows over the wooden porch. She couldn't hear anything.

Could she risk another peek? She had to if she wanted to know what was happening. She raised herself in an awkward half squat she couldn't hold for long and tried to look between the thick off-white candles on the inside windowsill. She caught a glimpse of the curvy woman in a white, fluffy dressing gown with her back to the window. More burning candles were scattered all over the room. Lena was nowhere in sight.

"Jess?"

Shit. Jess tried to turn around and stand up at the same time and promptly lost her balance.

She reached for the windowsill, but her clammy hands slipped.

With a booming thud, she fell on her ass. The wooden boards beneath her vibrated when she braced herself to regain balance.

When she looked up, it wasn't just Lena staring at her.

Her mom towered over her, eyes wide and mouth open. Slowly, her expression hardened from disbelief to disgust. Something she had never, ever seen on her mom's face before, at least not directed at her.

Oh fuck.

Jess's face burned hot with embarrassment and anger at her own stupidity. How could she ever explain getting caught snooping in a window?

She swallowed the rising bile and held her mother's gaze. If she had learned one lesson working with highly competitive colleagues, it was that offense is the best defense.

╫╫╫╫╫╫

Lena opened and closed her mouth like a fish on the pier. Had Jess been spying through the window? What on earth had she been thinking?

"Jessica Eleanor Riley!" Maggie hissed next to her. By the tone of her voice, she was feeling as incredulous as Lena. "What are you doing?"

Slowly, Jess stood. She squared her shoulders and raised her chin as if she was about to enter a battle.

"Mom." She locked her gaze with her mother's, completely unapologetic. "You don't know what she's doing in there. I think she's a prostitute. Here. In our garden house."

The words hit Lena like a punch in the stomach. Had she just said…? Her vision blurred like a watercolor sketch in the rain. She reached out to the side of the house to steady herself.

"Jess, what makes you say such a horrible thing?" Maggie put her arm around Lena's shoulder as if to show her daughter on whose side she stood.

The warmth and steadiness helped Lena to fight her dizziness and nausea, but she was still unable to say anything to defend herself.

Jess gestured to the house. "She is meeting the strangest people in the evenings for this so-called relaxation technique. The woman undressed. You told me yourself she has financial problems and would do anything to earn money. This all adds up. She is a prostitute, and we can't have her stay here."

Her voice droned in Lena's ears, and she couldn't make sense of why Jess was saying these awful things. But she didn't need to understand. Anger sliced through the shock paralyzing her, burning away the fog slowing her thoughts. How dared Jess to accuse her of such a thing? Had Heather heard her? How could she explain this scene to a client?

Lena pushed away from the wall. She hissed to Jess in the iciest tone she could muster, "Get away from me and my house. Now." She took a deep breath and looked at Maggie. "Are you still willing to help me?"

Maggie nodded with a grim expression and squeezed her shoulder before letting go. "Of course."

"Help? Mom, you can't go in there! Do you even know what she's asking of you?" Jess moved as if to place herself between her mother and the door.

"Don't be ridiculous. I know exactly what's going on, and I don't go around making assumptions like you do." Maggie gripped Jess's shoulder with one hand and shook her. "Jessica, what you did and said is not acceptable. This is not the way I raised you. I have no idea why you made such a terrible accusation, and I don't care. You need to apologize. And keep your voice down."

Jess pressed her mouth together, and a muscle twitched in her cheeks, which had flushed bright red.

Lena couldn't tell if she colored out of anger or embarrassment. She hoped for the latter. "I don't have time for this now. I need to get back to my client."

"Just a second." Maggie stroked her thumb over Jess's cheek. "Jessi, nothing illegal or illicit is going on here. If you don't trust Lena, trust me." Her voice was warm and laced with conviction.

Jess's stiff stance deflated. She lowered her head. "Okay."

"Okay is not enough. To make up for your appalling behavior, you will shut up now, accompany Lena inside, and do as she says. I've been her assistant more than once, and now you can take my place. Don't worry, I'll watch Ella tonight. Afterward, you'll apologize, and tomorrow we three can talk about this at length."

Lena recognized the mom-voice. Her grandma had been able to summon the same loving fierceness at will.

"You can't make me…" Jess looked up with wide eyes and blinked.

Lena wasn't so sure it was a good idea either. Did she want to bring Jess's negativity and distrust into a client session?

"Mom." The word was drawn out in a whiny tone that reminded Lena of every teenager she had ever witnessed in a disagreement with their parent.

Maggie stared at her daughter and crossed her arms in front of her chest.

For a long moment, Jess held her gaze, unblinking, as if she searched for answers. She swallowed visibly and nodded, then shifted her gaze to Lena. "I'm sorry. I'll do what Mom wants."

It wasn't a sincere apology, but Lena had no time to insist on anything more. Maybe Jess needed to see with her own eyes what was happening inside, or she might never completely leave her suspicions behind. "Okay. Let's do this."

Maggie kissed Lena's cheek and whispered. "Everything will be all right." With a stern "Behave yourself, young lady," to Jess, she left before either of them could answer.

Lena opened the door to her home and hoped Jess would follow without further discussion.

Jess wanted nothing more than to disappear in the darkness that had swallowed the garden. Something wasn't adding up, and she had miscalculated badly. She had no idea what her mom had sent her into. But no matter what, she did trust her.

She had to blink when she entered the little house. Warm air engulfed her like a tropical holiday. Candles flickered on every available surface, and the scent of vanilla and something spicier she couldn't name eased her frayed senses.

The woman she had seen earlier sat in an armchair and sipped a steaming drink from a small bowl. She greeted Jess with a smile as if she had expected her.

Jess automatically smiled back, then studied the main room of the house, which had changed dramatically since Jess had last lived here. A small but fully equipped kitchen with a breakfast nook was to her left, and to her right a two-seater couch and an armchair took up most of the living area. A wooden desk stood on one side stacked with notebooks. Everything was neat and uncluttered but still comfortable and cozy. Jess had no idea how Lena achieved the effect, and now wasn't the time to contemplate that. She had already missed most of what Lena was saying.

"And this is Jess, my neighbor. She'll be our victim tonight." Lena finished her explanation with a smile.

Victim? Jess raised her eyebrows. The playful tone of Lena's voice was meant to tease, but it still wasn't a word she liked to hear in this context.

"This is Heather, my client. She wants to surprise her fiancée with a new skill on their honeymoon." Now Lena was grinning even wider. She seemed to enjoy yanking Jess's expectations around.

Jess deserved this. And much more. Lena approached the whole situation with more class and humor than Jess would have in her place. If anyone had called Jess a prostitute, she wouldn't have stopped yelling by now. How could she ever apologize to Lena for that?

Lena picked up a neatly folded dressing gown and handed it to Jess. "You can undress in the bathroom. You're not allergic to anything?"

"No allergies. But what...?" Undress? Lena wanted her to wear nothing but a dressing gown? The warm air and the lulling scent slowed her thoughts to a crawl.

"Great. I'll let Heather choose her favorite oil. Go and get changed." She grinned, and the flickering light made her eyes sparkle as she winked. "You may keep your panties on."

Jess was still hung up on the naked part, and her expression must have shouted out her confusion. Before she could ask another question, Lena opened the door to the small room they had always used to store the extra deck chairs.

Now it was empty except for a massage table. A colorful sheet in a mandala-like pattern covered the mattress. More candles burned on the windowsill.

Jess's muscles weakened, and she nearly stumbled. This was about a massage? Lena was doing massages in their garden house? What had she gotten herself into?

"Heather, take a look at these while I show Jess to the bathroom." Lena pointed to a collection of small brown bottles with handwritten labels, then steered Jess toward the back of the house.

Jess knew damned well where the bath was, and she guessed Lena was aware of the fact. But the warm hand on the small of her back was oddly reassuring, something real and solid in this confusing evening.

The bathroom door shut behind Lena with a click, and she let go of Jess, took a step back, and stood straight with her hands pressed against the door. She studied Jess with a frown. "As you've probably guessed, these appointments are about massages, nothing else." Her tone was matter of fact as if they were discussing the weather. "I actually don't do them myself. I teach them. Mostly couples, rarely single persons. When that is the case, Maggie helps out by getting massaged, and that's what she volunteered you for tonight. Nothing more."

Not knowing what to say, Jess nodded. It might be a first for her, that she didn't have a quick and sarcastic reply on the tip of her tongue. Were her wits failing her like her body had done?

"If you don't want to, you don't have to do this. I wouldn't hold it against you. Not everyone is comfortable being touched by complete strangers." Lena smiled but didn't relax her tense stance. "I can call Maggie and tell her I changed my mind."

Jess winced at the thought of facing her mom again right now. She had felt five years old again when her mom had scolded her on the porch, like the last time she had been lectured about privacy and snooping at doors. It was a lesson she'd thought she'd never forget. Obviously, she had.

Sneaking around someone's house and peeking through the windows was stalkerish, creepy, and plain wrong. She owed Lena an apology, and she would start with whatever task was required of her.

"No, don't call her. I'll do whatever you need me to." Jess held up her hands. "I'm sorry, I—"

"Stop. I can't do this now." Lena's voice quivered, and she blinked a few times. "Let's get this evening over with, okay?"

"Okay. I can do that." Jess attempted a smile to reduce the tension crackling between them like the electric charge of a summer storm. "So I undress, go in there, and get a massage? That hardly seems like a punishment."

The corner of Lena's mouth twitched. "Maybe I'll stick my hands in ice water or something." She pushed off the door behind her and left.

As soon as she was alone, Jess let out a sigh. Before she lost her courage, she shed her clothes, folded them, and stacked them on the washing machine next to what she assumed were Heather's. With her back to the mirror, she wrapped herself in the dressing gown and left the bathroom to face whatever Lena had in store for her.

She found Lena and Heather bowed over a tray of dark glass bottles on the coffee table.

Heather held one up, sniffing. "This one."

"Great choice." Lena screwed the tops on the other bottles. "It's a combination of ylang ylang, vanilla, tangerine, and a hint of lavender. Very soothing." Without looking at Jess, Lena pointed to the small room. "Jess, why don't you make yourself comfortable on the massage table? Just open the dressing gown and we'll take care of the rest."

Grateful no one was watching, Jess opened the gown and clambered onto the table. With her face in the soft ring of the headrest, she could only see a small part of the wooden floor and her hearing was dimmed.

The twin sets of footsteps approaching drowned out her increasing heartbeat. They stopped next to her.

"We'll pull the gown down now to bare her back. If you're doing this in a hotel, you can leave the gown in place over her lower half, but if you're at home and mind getting oil on it, replace it with a towel. You can do this part as sensually as you want to." Lena's voice was teasing again.

Jess's gown was pulled down in a quick and efficient movement that barely touched her skin. Even though it was more than warm enough in the room, her skin pebbled when it was exposed to the air. Or with anticipation.

Why was she nervous about this? Jess swallowed. She'd had professional massages before, spa days even.

"Watch her skin. I'll show you something." Lena touched her with ice-cold fingers.

Jess yelped and flinched. "Hey!"

Lena laughed, a warm and mellow sound that appeased her again. "Sorry, but I couldn't resist. Heather, you touch her now."

Heather's hands were warm, and Jess's tension receded. The touch was tentative but not uncomfortable.

"See? That's why I had you cradle the cup of tea for a while. And I placed the bottle of oil on the stove for a minute just now. This should all be about relaxation and sensual experiences, and we don't want to cause more tension." Lena continued to explain something technical about the oil, but Jess stopped listening.

A hand on her shoulder caught her attention. Lena had stepped to the front and crouched to look at Jess's face from below. "Everything okay? Are you comfortable? May we start?" Her gaze and voice were bare of teasing now and full of warmth.

Jess nodded, afraid her voice would betray her uneasiness with the whole situation. She didn't mind professional touch, and she didn't care what Heather, a complete stranger, thought, but lying half-naked under Lena's eyes was different.

Lena held her gaze for a second, then rose but left her hand on Jess's shoulder. She had warmed it somehow since she'd touched her before.

"Heather, pour the oil on Jess's back, here in the middle. Just a few drops. We can always use more if it's not enough."

Jess concentrated on the sensual flow of the oil on her skin, anticipating the next step. It had been a while since someone had touched her in a nonmedical context. She tried to remember when she'd had sex last but came up blank. Not during her pregnancy, and she hadn't been on a date for several months before that. Had it really been over a year?

Warm hands spread the oil, their touch light as a feather and hesitant. Not exactly unpleasant but not very relaxing either.

"You can use your whole hand. The distribution of the oil is as much for your skin as hers," Lena said, and more hands touched her. The second pair, Lena's, was stronger, more decisive, painting wide arcs and circles on her back.

That was more like it. Jess sighed and relaxed into the movement. The experience was similar enough to the professional massages she'd had in the past that she could switch her brain off.

All too soon, they moved on to something else. Lena demonstrated a certain stroke, and Heather tried to emulate her. The back and forth between the two sets of hands was confusing at first. Jess had never noticed the strength lurking in Lena's hands.

The general stroking and kneading paused. "After the warm-up, we'll search for knots and areas of tension in the muscles and tendons. Follow the lines of the muscles with your fingertips, and soon you'll notice little differences, bumps."

Heather did so, hesitating here and there. "Is this one?"

Ouch. Not quite. Jess wanted to tell her it was her scapula, but Lena beat her to it.

"This is part of the shoulder plate. Move farther to the middle and take care not to press too hard on the bones, especially the spine."

Heather did as instructed, and Jess groaned.

Oh yeah, that was definitely a tense spot.

Lena chuckled. "I guess we found one. Now we'll work on loosening it." She demonstrated something that felt as if she was trying to push an iron rod through Jess's skin.

Before Jess could complain, the pressure disappeared. She groaned again, this time from relief.

"Pressure is one way of relieving the tension, but only temporary. I'll show you some other tricks."

As Lena proceeded to work the spot between her left shoulder blade and her spine, Jess wanted to melt into the table. She hadn't even realized how much her muscles had suffered in the last months. It had been ages since she'd last felt able to move freely.

Closing her eyes, Jess gave herself over to the massage. She could almost visualize wave after wave of endorphins bubbling from the spring in her mind and floating through her body. The low tones of Lena's explanation muted to white noise as she sank deeper into the bliss.

Heather found a different spot to test her newfound knowledge. It wasn't as effective as Lena's touch but still felt wonderful.

No wonder her mom loved to participate as Lena's assistant. Who would say no to a free massage?

Movement next to her head alerted Jess someone had changed positions. She opened her eyes. Bare feet had entered her field of vision, and she recognized the black yoga pants as Lena's. Her feet were slender, and muscles played under her skin as she rose on her toes for a moment. Purple polish, so dark it was almost black, shone on immaculately groomed nails.

It wasn't as if Jess had a foot fetish or anything, but she appreciated beautiful feet. She'd always loved to give her girlfriends foot massages when they'd come home after a day of walking around in too-high heels.

The urge to stretch out her arms and touch Lena's instep popped up out of nowhere. She could almost see herself caressing Lena's feet. She'd start with a massage of the soles, then she'd stroke along the inside. Lena would shudder and moan, and Jess would push the cuffs of the yoga pants up and trace a finger over her shin. Goosebumps would erupt all over the soft skin, and she'd kiss them away and—whoa!

Don't get carried away here, Jess! She licked her dry lips. What the fuck had just happened? She was warm and tingly all over, and her breasts were too tight, squished beneath her.

"Are you still okay?" Lena's face appeared again in her field of vision. "You tensed up."

Oh, great. Jess wanted to bury her face in the table, but the hole that allowed her to breathe made it impossible to hide. "Fine. I'm fine." She swallowed and willed her croaking voice to behave. "Just a cramp in my foot."

"Right or left? Let me have a look at it." Lena stood and started to move toward the end of the table.

Oh fuck. Why had she said that? If Lena gave her a foot massage now, she'd die of embarrassment. "No, no." She quickly wiggled her toes. "All good now."

"Sure?" Lena was back at her head. She touched Jess's shoulder. "Let me know if it returns."

"Mhm." Jess's agreement morphed into a moan as Lena's hand slid to her neck and traced with thumb and one finger up and down next to her spine.

Lena explained something to Heather, but Jess didn't listen as thoughts swirled in her head.

Had Lena noticed? Since when did she fantasize about feet? Or Lena? She couldn't stand her and wasn't attracted to her. Or was she? Why had her libido chosen this moment to wake up?

This was the fault of all the endorphins altering her brain chemistry. Nothing to worry about, a completely normal reaction for anyone. She suppressed a snort. *Right, blame it on hormones. Like everything else that's happened in your life recently.*

An eternity—or at least what felt like one—later, they finished with the same circular motions as in the beginning.

Lena pulled the dressing gown up over Jess's back and placed a large, fluffy towel over her legs like a blanket. "Jess, rest a little bit and relax while Heather dresses. Then you can take a shower if you want so you don't stain your clothes."

Relaxing wasn't possible for Jess right now. The thought of lying here—naked—and showering—still naked—in Lena's house sent all the wrong signals to her body. *Hormones. Just hormones.* A normal reaction to a massage. Okay, that had never happened before, but it was still normal. Just because she felt that way didn't mean she was going to act on it or anything.

Quick steps announced Heather's return from the bathroom. "Thank you, Jess."

She raised her head as far as she could. "You're welcome. Have fun on your honeymoon."

As soon as the door closed behind Heather and Lena, Jess climbed from the table.

Dizziness claimed her, and she had to lean against the table for a second until her vision cleared. Then she hastened to the bathroom to dress. Oil stains were the least of her concerns. She wanted to be gone from the house before Lena returned.

Chapter Ten

WHEN LENA LEFT THE HOUSE at ten to six, Jess was already in the garden. She wore loose sweats and a long-sleeved T-shirt. With her back to the garden house, she showed no sign of noticing Lena's approach.

Last night, Jess had been gone from the house when Lena came back. She had expected her to stay and apologize, to explain her behavior. Sneaking away under the cover of darkness didn't seem like Jess's style at all. But a part of Lena—the tired and emotionally wrung out part—had been grateful to avoid the confrontation after a long day.

For Jess to show up this morning was a surprise. It was too soon to tell if it was a good or bad one.

An idea popped up. Should she? Lena usually wasn't the teasing type, but something in Jess's demeanor pushed her to provoke as if poking a stick in a hornet's nest. Not that she would do that to hornets, because she was neither stupid nor cruel to animals.

"What are you doing here?" Lena said, loud enough to startle Jess, who flinched. Good.

She spun around with a frown. The fire Lena had hoped to stoke flared in her eyes. Jess opened her mouth as if to berate her but closed it again as the angry lines transformed into a half smile. "I live here." There was slight irony in her tone as she acknowledged Lena's joke.

"What a coincidence." Lena decided to let her off the hook for now. She hadn't had her daily dose of tai chi and she wasn't in the mood for an apology if that was why Jess was here. And she wasn't up for more discussion. Maybe tai chi would have the same calming influence on Jess as it had on her? It was worth a try.

"Join me?" Lena took a few steps into the middle of the yard and kicked off her shoes. "You can leave them on if it's too cold for you." The dew on the short grass woke her up better than Rachel's coffee. She positioned herself and wriggled her toes to connect to the earth beneath her.

When she sensed Jess had positioned herself next to her, Lena started her ritual, explaining as she performed it. "I'm not a tai chi instructor, but I can share with you what I've learned. We start with a warm-up to develop internal focus and strengthen the core. Standing with legs as far apart as your hips, we turn to the east and greet the sun three times." She opened her arms and lifted them outward and upward in a wide circle, bringing them together over her head. She pressed her palms together with fingers pointing upward, then pushed them down toward her navel, exhaling slowly. "Again. Inhale going upward, exhale coming down. Send the warm breath from your middle through your legs and arms, pushing it to the tips of your toes and fingers."

She had no idea if Jess was following her instructions, but she could hear breathing that matched her own. "Once more."

When she had finished the third round, Lena raised her arms again. "Now we stand here, rooted to the earth like trees. Hold your arms as if you'd hug a tree or hold a giant ball. Concentrate on the flow of your breath. There is no right or wrong pace, but just feel it flowing through you." There was so much more to this exercise, but she didn't want to overwhelm Jess in the first few minutes.

When Jess's breathing had settled into a comfortable rhythm, Lena twisted her head to look at her. Jess had closed her eyes, and her expression was calm, but her body was still stiff, her arms already shaking a little, pulled down by gravity.

"May I show you something that can help you hold this position more easily?" Lena asked in a low voice.

Jess opened her eyes, and her arms fell to her sides. She nodded, and her eyes sparkled with interest.

"To let the energy flow and to gain the strength from your connection to the earth, it's important to stand straight but not ramrod straight. You want to relax your lower back and lengthen the spine, and that's best achieved by tilting your pelvis forward." She demonstrated by shifting her pelvis a few times, then turned sideways so Jess could see her profile.

"Like this? It's…um…awkward." Jess blushed and angled her pelvis to the front. "Are you making fun of me?"

"No. I promise. It takes a while to feel natural." Lena demonstrated again. "Look at the rest of my body. If you bend your knees a little, your center of gravity is perfectly aligned to keep you standing upright without effort. And if you pull back your shoulders, your arms automatically rise a bit." She showed her. "Again, it's all about finding your center, your middle. It shifted a lot during pregnancy and is probably still not where it was."

Jess had begun to mimic her, but at the last comment she stopped and glared. "What are you saying? I'm fat?"

"What? No!" Lena raised her hands, palms outward. Why would Jess think that? "I'm sorry if I said something offensive, but I wasn't talking about your weight. At all. I was talking about an internal sense of balance, your center of gravity. And not that it matters, but I don't think you're fat."

Jess snorted and looked down. Some internal battle was going on, but after a few seconds she squared her shoulders. "So what did you mean?"

Lena smiled, relieved Jess had worked through another confrontation instead of letting her temper flare. "Let me show you. If I stand as I would normally, I'm not really steady. My center isn't stable." She stood like Jess had a minute ago, reasonably straight but not at all well balanced. "Shove me at the shoulder."

Jess did after a short hesitation, so light the touch barely registered.

Laughing, Lena made a come-on motion with her hand. "A bit harder. I'm not made of glass."

The second shove was better. Lena swayed a bit but regained her balance in no time. "Did you see that? It wasn't too hard, but I had to work to remain in my position. My balance was off." She repositioned herself in the correct pose. "Now shove me again."

Jess did, and this time Lena had no difficulty holding her balance.

"Again, much stronger."

Jess lifted her eyebrows. "Really?"

"Really. I promise, I'll survive."

This time, the contact would have been sufficient to tumble her had she not anchored herself with her center to the earth. "That's it. Did you see? If you're a master, no one can push you over, not even with all your strength." She laughed. "I'm not, so please spare me."

Grinning, Jess raised her hands, palms outward. "I won't. That was amazing. So this is a kind of fighting stance?"

"Tai chi is based on the same principles as kung fu, but this is not about fighting. This is about finding your inner strength and holding on to it." Lena swallowed. The last sentence echoed in her mind in the voice of her grandma, who had shown her this technique to help her handle the changes puberty had thrown at her. At first, she had thought it was all about physical aspects. Only years later had she understood that her mind had been shaped as much as her body.

Jess positioned herself again, trying to emulate what Lena had taught her. It was far from perfect but a massive improvement.

"Looks much better. Does it feel different?"

Jess closed her eyes and shifted her weight a bit by rolling back and forth on her feet. "Yeah." Her voice was full of wonder. "Yeah, it does."

"Wonderful. You won't master this in one day, but the key is practicing regularly. We'll do this now for the next ten minutes."

"Ten?" Jess opened her eyes, and all her poise vanished. "Isn't that boring?"

Lena laughed. "No. Concentration. Breathing. Inner strength. Remember? But I'll go easy on you, and we'll only do five minutes today. And you can lower your arms any time you need to. Mainly concentrate on your breathing and your center."

Snorting, Jess closed her eyes again. "I have a pretty precise inner clock. I'll hold you to it."

++++++++

From her position a few feet behind Lena, Jess had ample time to study her during tai chi. Lena hadn't spoken much. She seemed to be into all the inner peace and focus stuff. And why not? It was a good feeling to concentrate on simple things for a while, like where to put your hands and feet next.

Jess had chosen this time and place to meet Lena because her mom would still be asleep. She hadn't expected to get drawn into a tai chi lesson before she could apologize. And she hadn't expected to enjoy it. Yes, it was much too slow and tame compared to her usual exercise. Nothing like the endorphins she got from running or the adrenaline of competing against others. But somehow it had helped to reduce the pain in her lower back that had been her constant companion during the pregnancy. The sick feeling in her stomach persisted, but that had nothing to do with her body and everything to do with her recent behavior.

With a seriousness Jess couldn't quite share, Lena bowed to the ground and ended the lesson. She smiled at Jess. "How did you like it?"

"It was not what I expected." Jess wiped her palms on her sweatpants.

"Is that good?" Lena removed her hairband, and her curls tumbled down to her shoulders. She combed her fingers through them once, not that it made much difference. They seemed to have a will of their own.

"Yeah." It would be so easy to keep up the small talk and ignore everything that had happened in recent weeks, especially yesterday evening, but that wasn't Jess's style. "I, um… Can we talk for a minute?"

Lena raised her eyebrows. "Aren't we talking now?"

None of her planned introductions fit. Jess took a deep breath as if she intended to jump in icy water and held Lena's gaze. "I'm sorry."

Lena's eyes widened, but the smile didn't leave her lips.

"I'm really, really sorry for my behavior since I moved here." Before she lost her courage, Jess continued without waiting for a reaction. "I shouldn't have acted like an ass when I found out my mom rented the house to you, and I shouldn't have tried to snoop around to gather incriminating information."

"Incriminating? What did you think I was up to?" Lena's smile dimmed, and a deep line appeared between her brows. "Wait? Did you think I was a prostitute all that time? That wasn't just something outrageous you said to provoke me?"

"No, I mean…" Jess swallowed. "I only thought that last night…when I spied on you. Before that I didn't have a theory about you, just a stupid suspicion something was wrong. I thought you might want to scam my mom or something."

Lena paled. "Scam? No! I would never… I'm not like…" She pressed a hand to her mouth as if she was sick, and tears glittered in her eyes.

"I know." Jess stepped closer and reached out a hand but was reluctant to touch her. "As I said, my assumptions were stupid, and I apologize. For everything."

Lena's gaze swept over her for a moment, then she wiped her tears away. "I accept your apology. Let's start over." She grasped Jess's hand, which she hadn't withdrawn, and shook it. "Hi, I'm Lena, your neighbor. Nice to meet you."

Jess exhaled, and the sickness she'd felt since she admitted to herself how wrong she'd been slowly dissolved. "Hi, I'm Jess." She searched Lena's eyes for her emotions. Was it that easy for her to forgive?

Hurt still glittered in the hazel eyes like raindrops on leaves after a storm, but nothing was masked or blurred. Lena regarded her with an openness and inner calm that put Jess to shame.

"I...I better go and see if Ella's awake." Using her daughter as an excuse to flee was a cowardly move, but Jess needed a moment to process what had happened.

A wide smile swept over Lena's face. "Say hi to the little one for me."

Jess nodded. "I will."

Chapter Eleven

"Sheila totally freaked out when she found them in the on-call room. She grabbed Scott and Courtney's clothes from the floor and locked the door from the outside." Kayla doubled over from laughter. "They had to pound on the door and call for help because both their phones were still in their scrubs."

"Who is Courtney again?" Jess smiled, even though she couldn't care less. Most residents and fellows messed around. Even she had done it once or twice when she was younger. A lifetime ago.

"ED resident. Haughty bitch. Doesn't respect the nurses." Kayla pushed her sunglasses up in her hair and wiped tears from the corners of her eyes, then leaned back on the desk chair. "Nice place your mother's got here."

As if she'd heard, Jess's mom chose this moment to appear on the patio. She carried a tray with freshly baked chocolate chip cookies and milk.

Jess rolled her eyes. Milk? Really?

"I have a snack for you, girls." She put everything on the table and smiled at Kayla. "It's so nice of you to visit my Jess out here."

"Thank you, ma'am. This smells wonderful. Your garden is beautiful."

"Isn't it? I recently rearranged the perennials over there and—"

"Thank you, Mom. But we were just talking about work." Jess needed to curb this before her mom offered Kayla the extended tour and Kayla was too polite to decline.

"Oh, I see. Then I'll leave you girls to it. It was nice meeting you." With a nod to Kayla, she left again.

Jess buried her head in her hands and groaned. What had she done to deserve this? Had her mom just called them girls? She was thirty-fucking-seven, and her mom served milk. She glanced at Kayla. "I'm sorry."

Chuckling, Kayla picked up a cookie, tore off a piece, and dipped it in the milk. "Why? I think she's super nice." She stuffed the soggy cookie in her mouth and moaned appreciatively.

"She's great. But sometimes she seems to forget I grew up."

"As my daddy is happy to remind me anytime I visit, we'll always be their children. You'll see with Ella one day."

"I guess." Jess snatched a cookie before she could control herself. Maybe just half? It would be impolite to let her guest eat alone, right? With a sigh, she put it down next to the glass of milk she didn't intend to drink. Lying to herself wouldn't get her figure back.

"They are delicious," Kayla said around cookie number two. "Don't you like them?"

"I love them, but I need to watch what I eat. My heart can't afford to carry around the extra pounds I gained during pregnancy." Jess wasn't so sure if her heart or her vanity suffered more, but that was the only reason she would say out loud. "I'm not making good progress with working out. I still don't have the strength to run, and the drive to my gym is too far."

"What are you always telling your patients at the free clinic? Exercise doesn't mean you need an expensive gym or fancy equipment. What did you advise Mrs. Jameson last year?"

Jess grimaced. "To go walking? But that's something for old people!"

"Yeah, face it, you're old." Kayla grinned. "Hey, why don't we go somewhere together now? I saw a park a few blocks away. Is it nice?"

"No idea. I haven't been there for years." Jess couldn't even remember the last time. "Okay, let's check it out. I'll ask my mom to watch Ella."

As they walked down the driveway, Lena's old car came to a sputtering halt in front of the house. Jess frowned. That didn't sound healthy at all. She had no clue about cars, but she wouldn't trust her life to a vehicle like that.

Lena was about to get out, but she stopped with one leg on the ground and the other still inside. "Oh, hey, Jess. I'm sorry. I forgot. I'll park around the corner." She let herself fall back on the seat, closed the door, and started the car.

Jess guessed the wheezing sounds were supposed to be attempts to start the motor. She had almost forgotten about the stupid incident when she had yelled at Lena because of the car. Ella had been colicky all day and had just fallen asleep when the car had woken her. But that hadn't been Lena's fault, and Jess had behaved like a selfish ass.

She couldn't take back her words, but she needed to rectify the situation. Jess hurried over and knocked on Lena's window.

Lena swiveled around, her eyes wide. She pressed her lips together and rolled down the window—manually. How old was this car?

How on earth could she have been so hostile that Lena seemed afraid to even talk to her? Jess's cheeks burned again, as they had in too many interactions with Lena. "Um, Lena. Don't go. Leave the car here. I'm sorry about…" She swallowed against the sudden dryness of her throat and forced herself to be honest. "I'm sorry about being an asshole before. You can park here anytime you want. You live here, and I'm just the guest."

Lena's mouth hung open for what felt like an eternity. Ever so slowly, her astonishment faded and transformed into a beautiful smile. "Thank you."

"Yeah, well, it needed to be said." Jess needed to get away before she embarrassed herself any further. She pointed at Kayla. "We're on our way to the park. See you later."

She waved at Kayla to follow and started down the driveway again.

Kayla caught up to her before she even reached the street. "Do you want to tell me what that was about?"

"No. I'd rather forget it ever happened." Jess couldn't possibly outrun her, as she was already short of breath. She slowed to a much more prudent pace.

Their friendship wasn't so deep that Jess would feel comfortable talking about her idiotic behavior. So she did what she always did when life got too complicated. She reverted to work. "How's the situation at the free clinic? How is my star patient? I miss Mrs. Jameson and her cookies, even if I wouldn't be able to eat them now."

As the sun dipped behind the tall trees next to the main house, the shadows on the flower bed lengthened and Lena had difficulty seeing the minute details of the leaf she wanted to include in her drawing. Should she get a light or resume her sketch whenever she could next steal an hour of time?

She stood and sighed as her knees and spine protested. Okay, no more sketching tonight. She raised her arms in a stretch.

"Um…hi." Jess's voice came from behind her. When had she gotten so close?

Lena turned around, and Jess's gaze shot upward to her face. Had Jess been looking at her ass? She probably had some grass clinging to her. She shifted her pens and sketchbook into one hand and brushed over her wide pants with the other. The linen was wrinkled from sitting too long in one position, but whatever had distracted Jess must have fallen off already. "Hi."

Jess gently rocked Ella's stroller. "What are you drawing?"

"Nothing special, just some flowers." Lena clutched her book to her chest and hoped Jess would leave the topic alone. She was out of practice and didn't intend to give Jess a reason to make fun of her.

"I was about to start a walk. Do you want to join me?" Jess looked down at the handle of the stroller and no longer at Lena.

Did that mean she was asking to be polite? But polite wasn't really Jess's style. She would have just said nothing if she didn't mean it. And Lena's stiff legs would definitely enjoy the movement. "Sure. I'll grab a jacket and leave my sketchbook inside. Are you going down the road?"

Jess nodded. "I wanted to go to the park."

"Then I'll cut through the garden and meet you at the back gate."

"See you in a minute." Jess flashed a genuine smile.

Lena knew she had made the right decision. She hastened back to the house, placed her sketching supplies on the kitchen table, and grabbed her olive-green wrap jacket from the back of a chair. The well-used cotton was soft as she slipped inside, and she left the sides hanging open for now. It wasn't that cold yet.

When she emerged from the small gate at the end of the garden, Jess was still a few yards away. She pushed the stroller and mumbled something to Ella that Lena couldn't understand.

"Which way are we going?"

Jess looked up and shrugged. "I don't have a specific route, just toward the park. Ella seems to like the movement. I think it helps her fall asleep."

"She's still awake? May I say hello?" When Jess nodded, Lena leaned over and peered into the stroller.

Brilliant cornflower blue eyes stared back at her, full of innocence and happiness.

Lena wiggled her fingers in greeting and grinned when Ella gurgled back. "Hi, cutie. How are you? Enjoying your walk so far?" She reached out with her finger and lightly touched one of the tiny hands.

Ella opened and closed it around her finger, holding as tight as she could.

"Sorry. Your adorable daughter won't let me go." Lena couldn't stop smiling.

"Adorable? Hm." Jess smiled back.

For the first time, Lena saw the resemblance between mother and daughter, especially as Jess's eyes shone in the same shade as Ella's.

The soft grip around her finger loosened, as Ella let go in order to move her hand to her face. She yawned and almost swallowed her fist in the process.

Lena and Jess both chuckled.

With a sigh, Lena drew back her hand and straightened. "We better start our walk. She seems ready for bed."

Jess nodded and began walking at a brisk pace, wordlessly pushing the stroller.

It wasn't what Lena had expected from a relaxing evening stroll, but she enjoyed the chance to stretch her legs.

All too soon, Jess slowed. She was breathing deeply in an overly controlled way. Was she out of breath already?

They hadn't walked that fast and hadn't gone far at all. Maybe her illness had something to do with it? Lena wanted to ask if she was okay, but experience had shown that Jess wasn't open to concerned questions.

They walked at a slower pace until Jess's breathing had settled again. As they were still in a residential area, most of the houses had lights blazing in at least one or two rooms. A woman walking her dog on the other side of the road held her hand up in greeting, and Lena reciprocated. Kids' laughter came from behind a hedge, and a few houses down a man talked behind a fence. The voices blended into indiscernible background noise.

The peaceful atmosphere washed away Lena's stressful day. "This is nice. I've never taken a walk out here in the evening."

"I never used to either. Usually, I wouldn't even be home from work at this time. And where I live, you wouldn't go out on the streets to walk around without a destination," Jess said in a low voice.

"Do you miss your own house?" Lena couldn't imagine living anywhere other than Maggie's garden.

"Condo. Yeah, sometimes. I love my mother, but I've lived on my own for so long that it's difficult to share my space again. Plus, having more than two rooms for myself and Ella would be nice too."

"I've never lived in my own house before, always with roommates. And I get what you're saying about having your own space, but sometimes I miss the familiarity of sharing with people you care for. Like my last roommate." She groaned. "Maybe not so much sharing a bathroom with her obnoxious boyfriend, but still."

"Did you move out because of the boyfriend?" Jess's voice was wary.

"No, she didn't like that she couldn't play her music super loud while I had my massage clients. Are we back to the interrogation?" She didn't mind talking about that part of her past, but the judgment in Jess's tone irked her.

Jess stopped walking and looked at her. The low evening light broke through trees and softened her features. "No, no, I'm sorry. If you want to, we can talk about me instead." She grinned. "You know, I'm a doctor, and we tend to be self-absorbed and egotistical. I love talking about myself."

Lena laughed. She doubted that, but they could test the theory. "Are you sure?"

"At least, that's what my dates think of me." A hint of bitterness clung to the statement. "Ask me anything."

"Are you such a bad date? Are you seeing someone right now?" Lena expected Jess to deflect the questions but wanted to give her a taste of her own medicine.

"No, I haven't for a while. Not since before I got pregnant. Too occupied with work, and whenever I tried, it fizzled out after a few dates." Jess shrugged. "I don't intend to be a bad date, but nothing much is going on in my life but work, so I can't talk about anything else."

"I can relate. Some weeks all I do is work and sleep. I haven't had the energy to date either." And Lena didn't want to think about how long it had been. "But isn't there always something else to talk about? Dreams? Hopes? Favorite movies?"

"Maybe if I had time to actually watch movies. And recently my dreams have been about starting a family. Not such a good topic for the first couple of dates. I might have chased the women off before dessert." Jess laughed in an awkward way that was adorable.

"Yeah, lesbian dating isn't what it's supposed to be. I haven't had the U-Haul on the second date experience either." And that was how Lena had wanted it. Her no-commitment vibes had always helped to protect her heart.

"Oh, you're a lesbian too?" Jess looked over to at her with a grin. "I guess my gaydar is a bit rusty."

"See, now we have found something in common. Mine has been gathering dust for a while too." Lena grinned back, and they continued their walk in companionable silence.

At the next crossing, Jess stopped. "It's getting dark. Do you want to turn around?"

"No, not at all. This is nice." She could walk for hours. This new side of Jess wasn't something she'd expected to find. Had Jess really meant it when she'd told Lena to ask her anything? Time to test her commitment to that statement. "Was it a difficult decision to have Ella on your own?"

"Wow, you don't play around with easy questions." Jess stopped walking to adjust Ella's blanket even though her daughter hadn't moved. She continued with her gaze on the street, "I guess the answer is yes and no. The wish of having a child had always been there but quiet in the shadows of whatever I was doing at the moment. There was always a good reason to postpone. Since I started high school, I've always had this plan for my life. I had mapped out the steps I needed to take to succeed professionally and even personally. But I realized there weren't many years left to find a wife, settle down, and get pregnant, and I didn't want to waste them on searching for the perfect partner. So I skipped a few steps, and here we are."

Lena wasn't sure how to answer. She had never met someone who planned their life like that. Most people she knew, herself included, tried to keep from drowning as life's tides and currents threw them from one direction to the other.

Silence stretched between them like an empty ocean until Jess said, "I'm sorry. That was maybe more than you wanted to know, right?"

"No, that's fine. Thank you for sharing. It totally changes my perception of you."

"Now you see me as a sad thirty-something who is overly concerned with the ticking alarm in her ovaries?"

"Um…" Lena would never say that, but she couldn't deny it either.

Jess snorted. "You don't have to answer that."

The rustling of trees from the nearby park and muted music from one of the houses accompanied their walk as Lena thought about Jess's words. Having a dream and a plan for her life and following them was something Lena had abandoned long ago before she even left high school. Jess's tenacity was admirable.

"What's your dream?" Jess asked quietly.

"Not starving?" Lena laughed, but it sounded hollow to her own ears. "That's not really true, but I haven't had much time to think about dreams and goals in the last few years. I was busy paying my bills."

"I'm sorry. You're right. Being able to follow your dreams is a privilege, even if dreaming doesn't cost anything."

Lena hummed noncommittally. In her experience, that wasn't true. You paid for dreaming with tears and heartbreak. But she didn't want to go into that right now. That was much too depressing for the first talk between not-even-friends. Lena needed to steer the conversation back to safer ground. "Are you up for a little round in the park?" She pointed to the entrance.

"Sure. I think we can make the short loop before it's too late." Jess navigated the stroller past a narrow segment of the path.

As they walked on, Lena mulled over what Jess had said. She had been flung into adulthood much too young and tucked her dreams away for later like toys packed in boxes in dark and dusty basements. Until now, she had forgotten those boxes even existed. Maybe she should search for them and see if their contents were still relevant today. But later.

Now she would make a conscious effort to stay in the present, to enjoy the walk beneath the tall pine trees and the sense of peace and stability they offered by being there, always the same.

Jess quickened her steps at the sight of Lena waiting for her on the patio. The last few times she'd asked Lena to join her, she had needed to work in the evenings. This would be their third walk together in the last couple of weeks.

Usually, she didn't rely on others for entertainment. After a long day in the hospital, surrounded by people who constantly wanted to talk about one thing or another, Jess had always relished her alone time in the evenings. But now she had only her mom and Ella for company, she missed spending time with someone closer to her age.

"Hi, Jess." Lena stood and grabbed her olive jacket from the table. Today she wore a wide, asymmetrical gray skirt that ended just below her knees and a loose navy tank top.

Jess had been on more dates than she'd like to admit with women who talked, lived, and breathed fashion twenty-four-seven, but she'd never met someone like Lena who effortlessly combined clothes in all shapes and colors. She clearly cared more for comfort than showing off her body, even if she had nothing to hide. The self-confidence she carried herself with was sexier than a plunging neckline or high heels.

"Hi, Ella. How was dinner?" As Lena bent over to look into the stroller, the skirt molded itself around her backside.

Jess averted her gaze so as not to stare. Okay, maybe Lena didn't hide all her assets.

"Ready to go?" Lena's question was still directed at Ella. She always talked to Ella with her normal voice.

Of course, Ella wasn't impressed and yawned instead.

"I guess that means it was plenty but now start this walk so I can get to sleep." Lena chuckled and straightened, smiling at Jess.

Jess couldn't help but smile back as they started walking down the driveway. "How was your day?"

"Fine. The market was busy, which means I need to make more preserves soon. The owners of the café let me use their kitchen on Mondays when they're closed."

"Can't you do it at home or in my mom's kitchen?" Jess had no idea of the amount of preserves they were talking about, but her mom's six-burner-stove was large enough.

"I could, but for health permit reasons, it's easier if I do it in a professional kitchen. And I can do several batches there at once, which saves time. I just need to buy the glasses and print the labels beforehand. And I need to pick apples in my friend's orchard." Lena's shoulders dropped, and she looked at her feet. "I hope my car starts. It's been acting up lately. The drive is over an hour."

"I could drive you." Jess was ready to jump at any excuse to get out of the house for a few hours.

"No, that's not why I said that. I'll find a way. I can always barter with someone at the market for a few hours' work."

"I know you didn't say it to make me do it. But I offered. I have nothing to do all day but heat baby food and change diapers. You would be doing me a favor by letting me drive you somewhere."

They walked on for a couple of minutes without talking. For once, Jess didn't mind that someone didn't immediately agree with her. She loved that Lena took time to think over her decisions but then stuck to them.

"Okay, I would love your help."

"Great. When?"

"Could we pick the apples next Sunday? That's my only day off."

Since she'd been on sick leave, the days blurred into one another, and Jess needed a moment to remember what day it was today. Tuesday. "Sunday is fine. And when will we pick up the jars?"

"Maybe Monday before I go to the café? I'll call the shops and order what I need so we can pick it up and deliver everything to the café in one go."

"Oh, I have a doctor's appointment on Monday. But I'll reschedule it. No problem."

"No, don't. Seeing your doctor is more important."

"No, really, it's fine. I can move it to Tuesday. One of the perks of working in a hospital is getting easy access to appointments." Jess wasn't keen on discovering her heart failure hadn't improved. It could wait a day. "So Sunday apples and Monday café?" Jess held out her hand.

Lena shook it. "But you let me bring lunch."

"Deal." Jess smiled. Watching someone make preserves sounded far more interesting than getting an echocardiogram.

"The doctor's appointment? Is it about Ella?" Lena glanced in the stroller with a concerned expression. "Is she okay?"

"No, this is about my heart failure." Jess would rather not talk about it, but she had no reason to hide anything from Lena.

Lena stopped walking. "Heart failure! Oh, wow, I had no idea it was that serious." Her eyes were wide, and she clutched the bar of the stroller.

"Didn't my mother tell you about it?" Jess winced. It had never occurred to her Lena wouldn't know.

"No, she wouldn't give any details. She just said it was something unexpected." Lena's gaze swept over Jess. It held the same concern she'd shown for Ella seconds earlier. "I'm sorry. I don't know anything about heart failure. Is it okay to ask some questions about it?"

"Absolutely." Questions about the disease she could handle. "I'm a cardiologist. Ask me anything you want to know."

"The first question that pops in my head is: Isn't it something that old people get?" Lena blushed.

Jess had to laugh. "Yes and no. It's not common at my age but not unheard of. The kind I have is very rare. It's called PPCM, peripartum cardiomyopathy, which means I got it because of my pregnancy. The specific cause is unknown, but it's probably a combination of unlucky genetics and high levels of oxytocin at the end of pregnancy and during nursing." Talking about it theoretically, as if explaining any other cardiac disease to anyone else, wasn't as uncomfortable as Jess had expected.

Lena tilted her head to the side. "And what does that mean for you?"

"I take some medication, and if you look at statistics, I'm very likely to recover." And Jess had decided she believed in the numbers. They wouldn't let her down. "I didn't want to stay away from work so long, but I haven't been fit enough to go back. And that's why I need to get back in shape." Jess pushed the stroller and took the turn to the park.

After a few steps, Lena still hadn't caught up to her. Jess looked back.

Lena hurried after her, then touched her arm lightly, ready for immediate retreat. "But what does it really mean? Inside?"

"Inside?" Did Lena want to know about the structural damage?

"Emotionally. I can't even begin to imagine being in your shoes. Are you afraid?"

"Oh." Afraid didn't even begin to cover it; terrified was more like it. Jess shivered as if a sudden blizzard had wiped away all warmth. Only Lena's hand on her arm provided a sliver of heat. "Yeah. What if my heart doesn't recover? I might not be able to take care of Ella on my own." Her throat constricted, and she swallowed once, twice, as if she could get rid of her fear that way.

"Is there anything you can do to improve it? Can I help in any way?" The warm voice held none of the pity Jess had expected.

Focus! Jess had learned long ago to push her fear and doubts aside to concentrate on what had to be done. Somehow, under Lena's supportive gaze, the ballast that had to be shifted seemed lighter than before. "I guess you're doing it already. You keep me company on my walks. I love Ella, but interesting conversation isn't her forte. Talking to you stops me from brooding and wallowing in self-pity." Plus, she enjoyed getting to know Lena but wasn't sure how to express that particular feeling.

"If you want, we could do this more often. Whenever I'm home in the evening and you're up to it, I'll take a walk with you."

"Thank you." The idea of walking with Lena every evening brought a smile to Jess's face. The promise was like the scent of a good wine, making her head buzz with anticipation and warming her from within.

"You could join me for tai chi in the morning too. It's supposed to be good for your health." The enthusiasm in Lena's voice was infectious.

"Great idea." Jess nodded. "You've been right about tai chi and core muscles. I read up about it after your lesson and found some scientific studies that show a positive benefit in cardiac diseases."

A smile played on Lena's lips at the mention of studies. "So you'll join me tomorrow?"

"If you'll let me know when it's getting to much. I don't want to occupy all your free time. I'm sure you have better things to do." Jess walked on, even if it meant Lena's hand slipped from her arm. But she didn't want to appear too eager, too needy.

Lena laughed. "You would think so, but really, you're much better for me than falling asleep on the couch while trying to read something. That's what I usually do."

"I saw you sketching several times in the garden. Don't you do that in the evenings?"

"Sometimes, yes. But most evenings I'm too tired to concentrate after working all day."

Jess could relate. After twelve or fourteen hours at the hospital, she often felt the same. More evenings than not, she'd fallen asleep on the couch in her apartment while her friends went out. And now that she had Ella, she didn't expect her tiredness to leave her for the foreseeable future. She shook her head and chuckled.

"What? Do you think my work isn't tiring?" The hint of defensiveness in Lena's voice wiped the grin from Jess's face.

"No, no. That's not it! I was just laughing about my own delusions. What you described sounds exactly like what I did in the evenings before I moved here. When I wasn't on call on the weekends, I might have gone out to dinner maybe every couple of months when my friends remembered I was still alive. The rest of my evenings, I spent on the uncomfortable couch. Why I thought this situation would improve when I had a baby in the house is beyond me." Jess groaned. "Stupid."

"Stupid is a bit strong. Expectations and hope can cloud anyone's judgment. Sometimes, when you want something enough, you don't heed the warning signs." Lena's voice wavered at the last words. She swallowed audibly. Was Lena still talking about her?

Jess had promised not to pry for more information, but the pain in Lena's voice stirred something in her. Protectiveness? Whatever it was, it helped to keep her curiosity at bay. If Lena wanted to tell her what had hurt her in the past, she would at her own pace.

"Whenever I bore you to death with my poor-me stories, just say the word and stop me," Jess said. "Or kick me."

"You're not that bad. And that's what friends are for." Lena's voice was lighter now.

Friends? Regular steps in perfect synchronicity filled the silence as Jess tried on the fit of that word. Her old friends had fallen to the wayside as she'd focused on her chosen path through med school and residency. Were they still her friends? She hadn't even thought about calling one of them when she'd fallen ill. And she couldn't imagine an honest conversation like today with any of them. Kayla was more of a work friend. When they did meet outside of the hospital, it was to vent about colleagues. Maybe Diana might count as a friend, even if their relationship was in the early stages.

But Jess had shared more with her than anyone else in recent years; she had even admitted to being afraid.

And now Lena offered her this gift, even though she had treated her like shit at first. Jess wanted to thank her, to apologize again, to tell her how much the offer meant, but the right words eluded her. *Keep it simple.*

"I like that. Friends." Jess took a deep breath to push the stroller up the hill. To her surprise, her lungs burned less than expected and she even had a little air left to talk. Maybe her doctor's appointment would be something to look forward to after all.

Chapter Twelve

"Oh, here's the crossing where the cute cat crossed the road two years ago. You have to turn left." Lena waved toward the side street.

Cute cat, really? But Jess had stopped asking questions thirty minutes ago. The answers were just too confusing. Lena's internal map was like a collage, a collection of mental pictures, fun facts, and memories of unique trees.

All too soon after leaving the highway east of Seattle, Jess was lost. She'd followed Lena's directions and turned more times than she could count onto increasingly worse roads.

She wasn't completely lost, of course. If she looked at the sun and the time, she could calculate the cardinal points. She'd always prided herself on her sense of direction, which also helped her navigate twisted coronaries with a thin wire and transformed the black-on-white X-ray into a three-dimensional map in her mind. But her mental road map included street names and clear directions.

She needed to trust Lena to return her to safety after their fruit forage expedition in the Washington wilderness. At least Lena seemed confident in her instructions.

"Stop here and I'll open the gate," Lena said and pointed to a grassy spot next to the road.

Gate? Maybe she didn't know what she was doing after all. Jess saw only clusters of trees and shrubs overgrown with weeds and vines. But she did as instructed.

Lena jumped out of the car and approached the hedge, if you could call something that was a mixture of at least half a dozen plants a hedge. She reached between the green leaves and pushed.

Slowly the hedge, or at least a part that was more than wide enough for her car, moved. An overgrown dirt road led around a bend.

Jess followed Lena, who shut the gate behind her car.

Smiling, Lena returned to her seat and motioned Jess forward. "Only another mile. The road won't get worse."

As promised, they soon reached their destination. The old wooden farmhouse didn't look too bad from a distance, but when Jess stopped between the house and the barn, it became obvious no one had lived here for quite some time.

"Are your friends still using the house?" Jess doubted it was safe.

"No. When they come here, they hike down to the river and camp. They use the place not more than three or four times a year but are reluctant to sell. They have a vague plan to renovate sometime in the future and retire here."

The paint was flaking and had faded to an indistinct pale gray in most places; the windows were boarded shut, and weeds, grass, and moss grew everywhere—the yard, the porch, and even parts of the roof. The barn was in similar condition.

Jess couldn't imagine the work it would take to make it inhabitable again. "Might be cheaper to tear it down and build a new house."

"I guess. I suppose it's mostly nostalgia and not a real plan." Lena stretched her arms over her head, and her T-shirt rode up to reveal a toned stomach. She had dressed differently for today's expedition. Instead of her usual layers of loose linen and cotton, she wore jeans and a T-shirt. Both were faded and frayed at the seams but looked soft and comfortable despite the tight fit. "Are you ready to stretch your legs a little bit? The orchard is behind the kitchen garden, or rather, what's left of it."

Jess opened the trunk to get the buckets. "Lead the way."

The walk through the overgrown garden didn't take long. The sun shone, and a light breeze carried a mixture of scents Jess couldn't identify. Everything smelled fresh and full of life. Bees and birds buzzed around them, not minding the intrusion into their territory. As they followed the almost unrecognizable path, Jess looked around for the vegetables that must have grown here years ago, but she couldn't identify anything. "Mom would love it here."

"Oh, she does. She came with me last year to collect some seeds. It was difficult to get her to leave. Only when darkness fell was I able to tear her away. I wonder why she volunteered to stay home with Ella today."

"She's taking her to meet some friends. I think she wants to show off her perfect granddaughter." Jess laughed. "I can see her staying here for hours. I didn't know you'd known her for so long."

"She bought one of my preserves last year, and we started talking about heirloom tomatoes and old types of vegetables. I mentioned this place to her, and she asked to go together. Her knowledge is amazing, I learned so much from her on that trip. She doesn't just know the facts, but she can also relate them to you in such an interesting way. I think she might miss teaching."

Jess blinked at the open admiration in Lena's tone. Intellectually, she knew her mom was an accomplished botanist who had published several papers and books and had been a popular professor at the university. But for Jess, botany had never seemed as interesting or important as her father's work. She'd never thought anyone besides other botanists would value her mom's knowledge. Maybe it was time she asked her mom about her work and listened as an adult and not a know-it-all teenager with preconceived judgment.

"You might be on to something. She always loved teaching and never complained about her teaching requirements like some of her friends did and always tried to improve her courses. I'm sorry I never showed the slightest interest in plants. She'd have been all too happy to teach me everything she knows."

"It's never too late to show some interest." Lena's statement lacked the reproach Jess mentally gave herself.

"That's what I just thought." Jess's mood lifted even further. They exchanged a smile, and Jess nearly stumbled over a pothole. *Careful here, Jess.* She swiveled her head to the front.

At the sight in front of her, Jess's mouth fell open. "Wow." She had imagined the orchard as neat rows of trees, all roughly the same size. The grove was made up of old trees in all sizes and shapes. The gnarled branches twisted in every way possible. Some had been more successful and had overgrown the neighboring trees, creating a thick canopy of leaves. One apple tree had branches that grew in large boughs down to the ground, creating a shady dome that would have been the perfect place for a kid to build a fort. "I would have loved to hide in this private cave and read all summer."

"Me too. Or I would have climbed them all and built a crow's nest somewhere." Lena smiled wistfully. "I always loved to find places to scan the horizon."

"Oh? What were you looking for? Pirates? Dragons?" Jess put the buckets down and looked around for a good place to start.

"My mother." Lena's smile vanished. "If I had spent more time in a cave reading, my life would have been much better." She took a deep breath and squared her shoulders. "Let's start over here. This kind of apple is good for cooking, and the branches aren't too high. Just pick whatever you can reach, never mind the size or shape." She strode to the tree and started picking without looking back.

This was the first time Lena had mentioned her mother. If she hadn't grown up with her, did that mean she had died? It seemed to be a difficult topic for Lena, so Jess respected her silence.

They picked their way around the tree in opposite directions. Jess waited for the usual signs of exhaustion to kick in, but neither her heart rate nor her breathing quickened. After twenty minutes, she was still fine. A wide grin broke out she couldn't hold back if she wanted. Maybe she could return to work soon.

Work. Jess trailed her hand over the solid tree trunk. The rough bark grazing her fingertips and the scents of summer were so far removed from her day-to-day life in the city. It was nearly impossible to imagine herself back in the sterile hospital. She closed her eyes and let the peace of the orchard wash over her.

When she opened them again, Lena stood a foot away, pulling a branch to her with one arm. The other was stretched out to reach an especially big and red apple, but she couldn't get a hold on it. She had to balance on her toes, making the jeans hug her ass as if they'd been tailored to captivate Jess's attention.

Stop staring. Jess pulled her gaze upward and used all her willpower not to linger on the swell of Lena's breast. Whoa. Since when had her libido woken up like this? Today was about friends collecting apples together, nothing else.

Apples. Right. She put down her basket and waded through the soft, knee-high grass to Lena's side. "Let me. Just hold the branch down."

But Jess had underestimated her reach. To grab the prize, she needed to get even closer. A floral scent enticed her senses. Her side pressed into Lena's, and no amount of willpower could erase the sensation of the soft breast next to her own. Sparks shot through her, igniting a fire in inappropriate parts of her body. She suppressed a groan.

She wanted to prolong the touch. Instead, she propelled herself upward on her toes and grabbed the apple with more force than was strictly necessary.

It tore from the branch, and the flexible wood vibrated, raining leaves and tiny pieces of bark on both of them.

Lena sneezed and let go, stumbling into Jess.

In an attempt to regain her balance, Jess reached around Lena with her free arm, but it was too late.

They tumbled to the ground, Jess on her back and Lena on top of her, the precious apple clutched between them.

Jess exhaled and took stock of her situation. The grass had cushioned her fall, so nothing hurt but her pride. When she experimentally wiggled her toes, everything moved as it should. She opened her eyes to see how Lena was doing.

Lena's brown curls fell like a mane around her, and several leaves, twigs, and pieces of bark were stuck in her hair. Wide hazel eyes, a shade lighter than the leaves with brown flecks like the bark, stared at Jess in shock. "I'm so sorry. Are you hurt?" Lena scrambled to get up but lost her balance and fell onto the grass.

"I'm okay." When Lena still looked concerned, Jess hastened to reassure her. "Really. Don't worry. The ground is surprisingly comfortable as if we were lying in bed at home." Bed? Why had she mentioned bed?

Lena raised one sexy eyebrow. "Okay. If you say so." With a smile as if nothing had happened, she jumped to her feet and held her hand out to help Jess up.

Jess accepted the offer but let go of the hand as fast as possible before the sparks started again.

When they both patted their clothes to loosen the leaves, bark, and grass clinging to them, Jess noticed she was still clutching the apple and offered it to Lena with a flourish.

Laughing, Lena clutched it to her chest. "I hadn't figured you for an Eve, but you keep surprising me." She winked and put it carefully into her almost full bucket. "Come on, we need some of those pears over there before we can fight the blackberries."

Fight? That sounded exactly like what she needed to get her mind off her sudden attraction.

Lena placed the last two pears into her bucket. Full again. She carried it to the next tree, where Jess had wandered in search of fruit that was easier to reach.

It was safer to work on separate trees after what had happened earlier.

At the memory of the tumble in the grass, her cheeks heated. Jess's steady arm had held her while they went down, and the soft curves of her body had cushioned the fall. Even if Jess appeared soft on the outside, she had emanated a strength that Lena enjoyed a little too much.

She had to step back to clear her head. This way led only to heartache.

Jess had stopped picking pears. She raised her arms over her head and twisted her upper body from right to left as if she wanted to remove some kinks.

The way her shirt stretched over her front didn't help Lena's good intentions, and she diverted her gaze to the buckets full of pears and apples. "I think we have enough. I'll carry these to the car, and we can have a snack before we tackle the blackberries."

"Snack? That's a great idea. And I need to drink something too. Is there somewhere we can...you know...get rid of our drinks later?" Jess's head hung down, and she looked anywhere but at Lena.

Lena wrinkled her brow. What did she mean? Oh! "There's an old outhouse that's still fairly okay. But I usually just wait until I'm back home."

"That's what I would have done last year. But these fucking meds don't allow me the luxury anymore. I feel like an old woman, always on the lookout for the next bathroom." Jess grimaced.

Now that she knew her a little better, Lena recognized the embarrassment in Jess's voice, even though the tone was snarky. "I guess that's annoying. At least they help, right?"

"Yeah." Jess sighed. "I guess they do. Last month I wouldn't have been any help out here. Carrying a couple of apples would have been too hard, never mind a bucket full." She hefted her bucket and stalked toward the car.

Lena pointed out the location of the outhouse, and Jess handed over her bucket and took a detour. She returned after Lena had stowed the apples in the trunk.

Lena fetched the cooler from the back. "Could you grab the blanket? We can have a picnic."

"Great idea. How far is the river you mentioned?" Jess rinsed her hands with disinfectant, then picked up the large woolen blanket with one arm and closed the car with the other.

"At least a thirty-minute walk downhill. Uphill takes even longer." Lena tried to keep the question from her voice. Would Jess be able to make it?

Jess sighed. "Too far for me."

"I know a closer place where we'll have a great view of the water." Lena led them back to the orchard. "You said your medication was working but did your heart improve? You look much better than a few weeks ago."

"Thanks." Jess snorted. "Better doesn't mean good."

"Sorry, I didn't want to imply you didn't look good." Lena winked. "Who knew that you were so vain?"

"Touché." Jess laughed. "Do you want to picnic at the apple trees?"

"No, over here." The apple trees reminded her too much of Jess's soft curves under her and Jess's scent all around her. No, the other side of the orchard was much safer.

They reached a part where huge cherry trees bordered on what used to be a meadow that swept downhill until it reached the river. Lena sat in the shade of an older tree that barely produced anymore. She placed the cooler next to her but didn't unpack it. Her concern for Jess tied her stomach into knots. "Are you worried?"

"Worried?" Jess looked at anything but her.

Lena waited. She wouldn't dig if Jess didn't want to talk.

With a sigh, Jess pulled one knee up to her chest and hugged it with both arms. "Yeah. Of so many things."

"Tell me?" Lena shifted to sit cross-legged. One knee brushed against Jess's leg, and the warmth was comforting. Hopefully for Jess too.

"If my heart hasn't improved, I know all the terrible things that can happen. And not just theoretically, from a book or the internet, I've seen them at work more times than I can count." Jess ran one hand through her hair. "I want to stay strong and positive for Ella, for Mom, but it's hard. I tried but can't shut off my inner doctor."

"You don't need to be strong now." Lena's instinct was to hug her, but she wasn't sure it would be welcome.

"Yeah, I do. I'm afraid if I just give in a little, all that anxiety and anger will burst out, and I'll lose control." Jess stared down at the river for a few minutes. "My world collapsed a couple of months ago, and I have no idea if I'm strong enough to rebuild it."

"I think you are. And you have your mom to support you." Lena swallowed. "And me." A couple of weeks ago she wouldn't have said it, but she did mean it.

"Thank you. Could we talk about something else?" Jess let go of her knee and stretched her leg out.

It came to rest next to Lena's leg. She didn't retreat, because that's what friends did, right? Sitting with their legs touching. "Of course. What are you thinking of?"

"Food." Jess pointed at the cooler and grinned. "You promised to feed me."

Lena accepted the change of topic and unpacked the cooler. She took out two refillable water bottles and the snacks. She unwrapped the beeswax papers. "What sandwich would you like? I have Swiss cheese with apple-cranberry chutney or feta with tomato-walnut pesto. The carrots and cucumber sticks are for the guacamole." Lena unscrewed the lid of the glass container she'd stored the dip in.

"Wow. When you said you'd bring something to eat, I thought you meant some muesli bars or plain sandwiches. Um…can we share? I'd like to try both spreads."

"Sure." Lena waited until Jess had taken a piece, then took the other half of the sandwich.

Jess moaned after the first bite. She chewed with her eyes closed. After she'd swallowed, she opened them again and gazed at Lena. "Wow. I know

I'm repeating myself, but I can't adequately describe how delicious this is. Where did you get the chutney?"

The compliment made her grin. "Thank you. I made it."

Jess picked up a couple of carrot sticks and offered one to Lena. "Okay. I take it back. You can have some carrot sticks, and I'll take all the sandwiches."

Laughing, Lena dipped hers into the avocado dip. "Can I maybe bribe you with the promise of a jar of chutney at home?"

"Mmh..." Jess rubbed her chin and pretended to think hard. "Delayed gratification. I'm not so sure I'm into that."

"Maybe you didn't have the right motivation until now." Lena bit her lip. Oops, she hadn't meant to lower her voice quite like that. It had slipped out before she could censor herself.

Jess held Lena's gaze for a few heartbeats, then took her time to choose a piece of cucumber.

Oh shit. Lena didn't want to lead Jess on. Flirting wasn't fair when she wasn't available for anything more. She had neither time nor emotional strength for romance at the moment. Awkward silence hung between them as she searched for a neutral topic to redirect the conversation, but Jess beat her to it.

She rubbed her finger over the beeswax wrapping, then smelled it. "Is this wax? On fabric? Is it washable?"

Lena leaned back against the tree and stretched her legs. "Sure, you can use water or a mild soap if you need it. You can reuse it for a long time. A friend of mine made them in exchange for some preserves."

"That's cool. You seem to have a friend for everything. How come they're never at your house?" Jess tilted her head and nibbled on a carrot stick.

"I don't have really close friends, more a loose circle of like-minded people who exchange products and favors. If you work at the farmers market long enough, you get to know a lot of wonderful people. But I don't have time to hang out with them."

"And dating? Do you have time for that?" Jess's tone and expression were neutral, but her eyes held an intensity that excited and frightened Lena at the same time.

Was Jess asking if she was available? Or was this a general question, small talk between new friends? Either way, the answer was the same. "I don't have time for dating between all of my jobs. When I was younger, I tried the casual dating, friends-with-benefits thing a few times, but…I'm not good at keeping things casual. It's easier to just not date."

Jess's eyes widened slightly, but Lena didn't know her well enough to guess what that meant.

With a sigh, Lena took the easy way out and ended the eye contact. She picked up half of the other sandwich and for the next few minutes, concentrated on chewing.

After they finished lunch, Jess stretched out next to her, folded her arms beneath her head, and closed her eyes. She yawned. "I'm not at all motivated to pick blackberries next. You never mentioned blackberries when you asked me to drive you." A slight smile around her lips belied her grumpy tone.

"I asked you?" Lena plucked a blade of grass and tickled Jess's nose. "I remember a completely different conversation. You begged me to let you drive me."

Jess rubbed her nose and opened her eyes. When she saw the grass, she caught it with her hand. "Hey! I'm old and sick. I need my rest." She closed her eyes again.

Lena studied Jess's face to see how serious the remark was. Fine lines around her eyes showed the few years she had on Lena, but the ever-present dark shadows from the first weeks of their acquaintance were gone. Her initial paleness had turned to a light gold complexion that seemed much healthier than even last week. Jess looked great now, and during their daily tai chi sessions and evening walks she hadn't seemed out of breath, but it wasn't Lena's place to judge how she felt. *When in doubt, ask a question. Or five.* Her grandma's motto had always proven to be helpful.

"How are you really feeling? Do you want to sit it out? I can handle the rest on my own. That's what I would have done anyway if my car was working." Lena smiled when Jess's eyes flew open.

"No, I was just joking." Jess sat up and flicked the blade of grass away. "Let's pack this up, and I won't stop working until all the blackberries are picked."

"Don't make promises you can't keep." Laughing, Lena stowed her wrappers and the nearly empty guacamole container in the cooler and stood. "But seriously, thank you. Blackberries are the most important part of our excursion today. Without them, I can't make my preserves tomorrow and I'll have nothing to sell."

"Don't mention it. I love picking blackberries." Jess shook out the blanket and folded it neatly over her arm. "As long as I can eat some of them."

At the car, they exchanged the picnic stuff for some smaller buckets, then Lena led Jess around the house to the edge of the property where blackberries had taken over the length of what had been a nice fence years or probably decades ago.

Only as they got closer, it didn't look at all like a healthy growth. Most leaves were brown, and the branches were a lifeless gray and shriveled in some places, broken in others. And the blackberries were tiny remnants, hard and dry, nothing like the big, juicy fruits she remembered from last year.

Lena touched one of the leaves, and it crumbled like the plans she'd had. Tears burned in her eyes. She wanted to curse, to cry, to fling the bucket into the damned tangle of branches. She clutched the bucket harder to ward off the impulse.

Take a deep breath. Focus on the positive.

But as much as she tried, she couldn't find even the tiniest ray of sunshine in the bleak storm her life had developed into.

"What the fuck?" In a move that surprised no one, Jess showed no restraint and kicked a branch. "Hey! Some idiot has cut the roots."

"Oh. The neighbors must have done it." Maybe that was the positive side of this. Someone else was getting their fence back. It wasn't so easy to feel happy for them when unpaid bills were stacking up and she needed the blackberries to replenish her preserves or she would be sold out soon.

"Is there another place we can get them here?" Jess rose and brushed dried leaves and dirt from her jeans.

"No. It's all private property. Let's go home, and I'll think of something. Make a few calls." But she didn't move. She couldn't yet.

Jess stopped to rub a stain above her knee, then walked over to Lena. Her eyes reflected the clear azure sky and held a rare warmth. Tentatively, she put her arm around Lena's shoulder as if she expected resistance. "We'll find you some other blackberries. They grow like weeds. The whole state must be full of them."

Lena leaned against her, allowing herself to soak up the solid strength for a moment. She didn't need Jess's support; since she'd been a teenager, she had learned to rely on herself and her own resourcefulness. But it felt good. If only for a moment, she'd relish the feeling of having someone on her side.

†††††††

Just as they were about to cross Lake Washington, Jess's phone rang through the speakers of her car. Lena hadn't even seen her hook up the phone, but she guessed a fancy car like that had Bluetooth.

Jess never even took her eyes off the road as she pushed a button on the steering wheel to accept the call. "Riley."

"Hi, it's Diana. Sorry to bother you when you're on sick leave, but I saw a patient who had a note in her file to call you anytime she's admitted." Diana's voice was different from the last time they'd met at Cashew Cult, more serious, more professional.

Lena glanced out of the side window, wanting to give Jess the illusion of privacy. Gray clouds covered the sun, but it didn't seem to deter the boats out on the water, enjoying the afternoon.

"That's okay. Who is it?"

"Alberta Jameson."

"Oh."

That one syllable carried so much emotion that Lena had to look at Jess. She'd paled, and her right hand clutched the wheel with white knuckles.

"She's eighty-four, has a history of congestive heart failure due to aortic stenosis, and—"

"I know." Jess interrupted with an impatient gesture as if they were speaking face to face. "Why is Mrs. Jameson in the ED?"

"She was out of breath in the supermarket, collapsed, and they called an ambulance. She's..." Diana let out a sigh. "Her heart failure is decompensated, and she has pulmonary edema. She's refusing intubation or intensive care treatment. She's a little better now with diuretics and morphine, but I called her daughter to come and see her. I'm not very optimistic."

"Her daughter lives in Portland. It'll take a while. I'm coming over." A muscle in Jess's jaw twitched.

"You don't need to. I've got everything covered. I just wanted to let you know."

"That's not why I'm coming. I'm not far—maybe ten, fifteen minutes." She quickly looked over her shoulder, then accelerated and changed lanes.

"Okay. See you soon." Diana hung up.

The speaker crackled with static for a few seconds before the Bluetooth realized nothing further was coming.

"Are you okay?" Lena had no idea who Mrs. Jameson was, but she obviously meant a lot to Jess.

Jess kept her gaze glued to the road. Her jaws worked, but she didn't say anything. They were going faster and faster.

"Jess?"

Seventy. Seventy-five. Lena grabbed the handle of the door. A sign for a park and ride appeared like an oasis. "Jess. Get off the highway here. Now!"

That seemed to break through her trance. "What? No. I don't have time to stop."

"We're not stopping for long. Just to change seats. I'll drive." Lena put all the authority she didn't feel into her voice. "Think of Ella."

That seemed to do the trick. Jess decelerated to a reasonable speed and signaled to get off the highway. At the first opportunity, she stopped the car, jumped out, and stalked around the front.

Lena met her halfway. "Thank you for letting me drive."

"Please hurry." Jess nodded once and pressed her lips together.

The SUV drove smoothly, with much more power under the hood than either Lena's old Ford or Maggie's cute Prius. Lena remembered the general location of the hospital from her last visit, but she wanted to make sure she was driving the best route. "Will you tell me where to get off the highway?"

"Yeah. I have staff parking, so we don't need to look for a free space." Jess's voice was clipped.

Lena didn't dare to look at her as she concentrated on driving. "Do you want to tell me about Mrs. Jameson?"

"She's the unofficial helper, motivational speaker, and cookie supplier to the team at the free clinic. All the staff and the patients love her; she has a way of setting everyone at ease."

"She sounds like a wonderful person." Lena took the exit to merge onto I-5 North. "Have you known her for long?"

"Three years or so. She was my first patient at the free clinic, and I might have been a bit nervous." Jess chuckled. "It was her first time too, and we kind of bonded over it. Afterward, she always insisted on coming when I was there." Jess hit her thigh with her fist. "Oh fuck!"

"What?" Lena had wanted to distract Jess with her questions, not distress her even more.

"I haven't been at the clinic for weeks. She was doing so good when I last saw her a couple of months ago. What if she didn't see anyone and has been waiting for me to return?" Jess groaned. "I let her down."

"You can't know that." Lena risked taking one hand off the wheel to squeeze Jess's thigh. The muscles were like steel. "From what you told me about her, it seems as if she has a great relationship with everyone at the clinic. Don't you think someone would have noticed if she wasn't okay?"

"Maybe. I don't know." Jess exhaled.

"What is this free clinic anyway? Is this part of your job at the hospital?" Lena asked to keep Jess talking.

"No, the hospital has nothing to do with it. It's for people who have neither insurance nor any other means but need regular treatment. They offer everything you need for basic care. Medical appointments with doctors and PAs, nurses who do outpatient visits, physiotherapy treatments. I know some people from my hospital who volunteer their time, but most work somewhere else. And we have several retired or disabled staff, especially former military. They couldn't work full-time anywhere else but fill in a few hours at the clinic when they're able to."

Lena wouldn't have expected to see Jess in such a setting, but maybe she had underestimated her. "How often do you go?"

"Depends on my schedule. Once or twice a month." Jess pointed to a sign. "Take the next exit. We're almost at the hospital."

Parking wasn't too difficult, as most of the staff garage was empty on a late Sunday afternoon. Lena sighed with relief after she'd maneuvered the oversized SUV into Jess's slot.

As soon as the wheels stopped turning, Jess jumped out and strode to the exit. At the steel door, she waited for Lena, rolling back and forth on her toes. Wordlessly, she held the door open, then caught up after Lena passed her, led the way to a back entrance, and opened it with a card fished from her wallet.

Behind the unmarked door, they stepped directly into the emergency room with the unmistakable smell of disinfectant and background beeps and voices.

Jess didn't stop until she reached a counter where a couple of women in blue scrubs worked at two computers. "Mrs. Jameson. Which room?"

If the two were surprised to see Jess in dirt-stained jeans and a T-shirt, they didn't show it. The older one glanced at the computer. "Room five, Dr. Riley."

"Thanks." Jess strode deeper into the department, past an area with curtained stalls to a quieter side corridor.

Lena tried not to look right or left. She wasn't squeamish when it came to her own blood, but she didn't want to know what lurked behind those curtains.

As they rounded one more corner, Jess almost collided with Diana. In blue scrubs and tied-back hair, she looked older and more serious than she had at the café. "Hey, Jess. Lena. Good to see you." She smiled at both of them.

"How is she?" Jess's grimace might have been her attempt to smile back.

"Much better. The diuretics are working." Diana shrugged. "Maybe I called you too soon."

"No, absolutely not. Aortic stenosis is like that. I'll go and see her now." Jess wiped her hands on her jeans, then looked down as if she only now noticed how she was dressed.

"She's in room five. Maybe you can convince her to stay at least overnight."

Jess nodded. "I'll see what I can do. But she's pretty independent."

"That's an understatement." Chuckling, Diana shook her head. "I hope I'm that feisty when I'm in my eighties." The admiration in her voice was obvious. "Call me if you need anything. Or want any tests done."

"I will. Thanks." Jess turned to Lena. Her gaze flickered over Lena's face like clouds chasing over a sky. The care and fear Jess had shown in the car seemed muted now as if she was slowly gaining back her control. "Do you want to wait in the coffee shop? Or drive home?"

Her expression was difficult to read, and Lena had no idea what Jess preferred. "If you think it's okay, I'll tag along." And to be honest with herself, she was interested to see Jess's interaction with Mrs. Jameson.

With a nod, Jess strode toward the room. She mumbled something that might have been "thanks," but Lena wasn't sure.

Room five was tiny, with barely space for a gurney, a desk, and a couple of stools. Only the desk light shone, bathing the room in a warm, golden light.

The woman beneath the sheets was frail, and even though an oxygen mask covered her mouth and nose, her complexion was grayish. But her smile was wide and genuine when she recognized her visitor. "Dr. Jess. What are you doing here? Shouldn't you be with your little one?"

"Hey, Mrs. Jameson." Jess wheeled one of the stools over and sat at her side. Her voice shook a little. "And shouldn't you be at home scolding the neighborhood kids? What if they play ball in your yard again?"

"As long as they don't trample my flowers." She chuckled, but it sounded a bit breathless. "Who is your lovely companion?"

"This is my neighbor and, um, friend, Lena. We were on our way home from picking apples together when Dr. Petrell called me."

"It's good to meet you, Mrs. Jameson." Lena stepped closer and stretched out her hand.

The older woman's grip belied her frail appearance. "Take a seat, my dear. Friends of Dr. Jess are my friends too."

As Lena arranged the second stool next to Jess, she glanced at her from the corner of her eye. Jess's posture was more relaxed than in the car, but worry lines were still visible around her eyes as she studied the monitor above the bed.

A green EKG was all Lena recognized, but she guessed the other colorful numbers meant much more to Jess.

"Mrs. Jameson, Dr. Petrell told me you want to go home tonight." Jess's voice was careful, with a hint of a question.

"I'm sure I'll sleep much better at home."

"Home is always best." Jess tilted her head to the side. "But maybe, just for tonight, you'll sleep better with oxygen. And wouldn't it be nice to have some assistance from the nurses if you need to get up in the night?"

"Ah, you're as bad as all the doctors. You always want to lock people in your hospital." Mrs. Jameson shook her head, but her voice held no real conviction.

"How about you do me a favor and stay one night, and tomorrow I'll come back to sign you out if you insist on leaving." Jess held out her hand. "Deal?"

"You got a deal. But only if you throw in a few pictures of your little girl. I heard she's called Ella, right?"

Jess laughed. "Yes. Ella."

Mrs. Jameson shook the offered hand, then kept hold of it and placed it on her bed. "Tell me about her. Is she keeping you up all night? I've knitted a few caps and socks, but I don't have them with me."

The last of the tension receded from Jess's shoulders as she held the older woman's hand and told her about the day Ella had decided to spit at least half her formula over Jess's shirts with each meal. At the end of the day, she'd run out of fresh clothes to wear.

In the cozily lit room with Jess's soothing voice, Lena almost forgot they were in a hospital.

Chapter Thirteen

FOR THE FIRST TIME IN too long, Jess woke up eager to start the day before any alarm sounded. When the dawn twilight transformed the shadows into recognizable shapes, Jess allowed herself to get up. She barely recognized this feeling from when she was younger and used to look forward to work every day. Even before she'd gotten pregnant, anticipation had been rare. She'd thought starting a family would help to regain that, but so far it hadn't worked out as planned.

Snippets from the last couple of days played on auto-repeat in her head. She had enjoyed her time with Lena more than she'd thought possible, and with all the flirting and sparks and accidental touches, it had felt as if they were on a date. But both of them had equally pushed forward and pulled back, and Jess wasn't even sure what she wanted anymore.

And the only thoughts that could push that confusion to the back of her mind were worries about Mrs. Jameson and her own impending checkup.

Diana soon set her at ease with a text. Mrs. Jameson had improved further overnight and would be discharged later that morning.

Her own health was another matter. Since Lena didn't need her to drive to the café today, she had rescheduled again while at the hospital. She didn't need another day of not knowing. Her heart had improved somewhat, but would it be enough to return to work? Would she be able to withstand hours of physical and mental stress for days?

When Jess arrived in the lower garden, it was still empty. She had beaten Lena for once. She waited for a minute, but when she didn't detect any movement, she bowed to the ground, even if it was silly, and took up a meditative stance, facing east, arms raised as if she was hugging a tree.

Hugging. A. Tree. She didn't think she'd get over that description anytime soon.

At first, worries about her heart raced through her mind. Instead of chasing them, she tried something new. She concentrated on her breathing, in and out, the wakening birds, the first rays of sunshine painting the gray leaves in brilliant green. In and out. She closed her eyes. In and out.

"We can add another move to your form today if you want." Lena's voice was close and soft.

Jess opened her eyes and blinked twice against the sunlight. When had Lena joined her? She lowered her arms, only now noticing how heavy they'd become. She'd never before managed to last the full time with her arms up. "Sure. Um, hi. Didn't hear you coming."

Lena smiled brightly. "I know. But you had the perfect posture and seemed so...centered? I didn't want to interrupt."

Centered. Not a bad word to describe the mixture of calm and energy that glowed somewhere deep inside. Maybe there was something to this finding-your-middle stuff after all. "I could use some of that today."

Lena held her gaze for a moment, then nodded. "Let's practice the new move." She fell into the position where the last movement Jess had learned ended. "I'll show you once how it's supposed to look in the normal tempo, then we'll do it movement by movement."

"Okay." Jess watched in awe as Lena's arms and legs flowed in a complex half-circling movement from right to left and back to center. If she'd blinked, she would have missed most of it. That was more complex than anything they'd done before. If this wouldn't keep her mind off the rest of the day, nothing would.

"Repeat it after me." Lena started again at the beginning, this time in slow motion. "And don't forget to breathe."

Jess inhaled deeply and let her hand follow Lena's example as she exhaled. With each new breath, they continued the movement until they'd made it through the whole sequence.

Lena led her through it a second time, then a third. The fourth time she did it all on her own, and the thrill of achievement flushed her cheeks after she'd finished without tying a knot in her arms.

"Great. Now repeat the form from the beginning, adding the new movement." Lena smiled and adjusted position so she could do her own form, much longer than Jess's.

When they finished, sweat had soaked Jess's shirt, and she sensed her muscles where they'd stretched in unfamiliar ways. But she wasn't tired or out of breath. Instead, the weird ball of energy still buzzed, filling her with confidence. What had Lena called it? Centered?

The high lasted through her shower, through changing a particularly nasty diaper, and through the drive to the hospital.

But as the automatic doors opened to her almost-home for the last several years, the smell of fear assaulted her, muting the glow. She dragged herself to the cardiology wing to meet up with Wendy, her favorite technician.

"Good morning, Dr. Riley." Wendy nodded politely and entered data into the ultrasound machine without bothering to tell her to undress or how to lie down. The fifty-something woman with the short, no-nonsense hair was Jess's favorite exactly because she didn't waste time trying to fill silences.

As Jess positioned herself on her left side, goosebumps erupted on her skin that had nothing to do with the fact that she'd ignored the paper gown that would have to be removed in another minute anyway. Her heartbeat accelerated in anticipation of the exam. Shit. That wouldn't do. The picture quality worsened with tachycardia, plus it sent the signal she wasn't back to her old self again. If only the calm from this morning could be harnessed and brought into the exam room. But if she got up to perform tai chi, Wendy would probably call for a psych consult.

Sometimes when I need strength or calm, I close my eyes and do the form in my mind. Jess had dismissed Lena's statement as a weird, new-age, pseudo-hippie thing, but what did she have to lose?

As Wendy stuck the EKG leads to her chest to synchronize the pictures with her heartbeat, Jess closed her eyes and took a deep breath. She pictured raising her hands in front of her body and pushing downward with the exhale. In and out. With each breath, she led herself through the short form she'd learned so far.

"Ready?" When Wendy's voice pulled her from her mental exercise, Jess fixed her gaze on the monitor and the display of her heart rate.

Sixty-eight beats per minute. Normal. Phew. "I'm ready."

┼┼┼┼┼┼┼

"Hey, Jess!" The greeting stopped her as she was leaving the hospital.

She stepped back from the automatic door to keep it from opening. Dr. Rock Chick, of course. She smiled. "Diana, hi. Good to see you."

"You too. You look great." Diana nodded in the direction of the cardiology ward. "Did you visit Mrs. Jameson?"

"Yeah. Thank you for keeping me updated. Her daughter is driving her home now."

"That's nice of you to come and visit her again this morning."

"I promised." Jess was sure she could leave it at that, and Diana would skip to a new topic. Jess had never shared personal details at work. But Diana was becoming a friend. "Actually, I wasn't just here to visit. I had my checkup, and everything has improved. I'm almost back to normal."

"Wow. Congratulations." Diana enveloped her in a hug that was over before Jess could decide whether she liked the display of friendship in the hospital's main entrance hall or not. "Does this mean you'll be back at work soon?"

"Yeah. I had a talk with my boss, and we decided to play it safe and give me another couple of weeks to recuperate. But then I'll be back to torture residents again."

"I'm looking forward to that." Diana grinned and pointed to Jess's cheek. "And who did you fight in your free time?"

Jess's hand rose to cover the faint scratch she'd discovered as she looked in the mirror this morning. It must have happened during the fall. Heat flooded her face as she thought of Lena in her arms. "When we came here yesterday, we were on our way home. I, uh, I picked apples with Lena…um, to make jam. Lena was planning to do a new batch to sell. She sells them at the farmers market. Only the blackberries are missing. The blackberries we found were brown and dry, and she was really devastated she had to reschedule and look for another good place to pick." Whoa. Why was she babbling all of a sudden? That had never, ever been her problem. Maybe the relief that she got a clean bill of health had addled her brain.

Diana's eyebrows had slowly risen, and now the corners of her mouth twitched. "So you picked apples, but now she needs some blackberries to make jam?"

That's what she should have said. "Basically, yes."

Diana grinned. "I have the perfect solution. Emily inherited this beach house, and we have way more berries than we can ever use this summer. It would be a shame if it all went to waste. You could even make a weekend vacation out of it. Stay a night or two."

Jess couldn't picture it. She'd have to take Ella, of course, with all her stuff to change and feed. Sharing a cozy cabin with Lena? Her mouth was dry, and she had to swallow twice before she could get a word out. "Overnight?"

"Yeah. It's a nice house with two bedrooms. We can't get away at all next month because of our work schedules, so you can take the keys and go whenever you want."

Oh, two bedrooms. Jess didn't know if she should be relieved or disappointed. "Thanks, but…I don't know." Going to a beach house sounded nice. She'd been off work for over two months, but that was nothing like a vacation. Her mom's garden was lovely, but a change of scenery sounded like the perfect getaway before she started work again. "Maybe."

"Let's go and get the key from Emily, and you can decide later." Diana briskly walked toward her partner's office, who was a senior attending in the ED.

Jess followed, grateful Diana had chosen the back route. She wasn't in the mood for the curious gazes of the staff.

After knocking twice, Diana hesitated for a fraction of a second before opening the door. Emily Barnes sat ramrod straight behind her desk and looked up with a stern expression. When she saw Diana, a smile softened her features.

Jess marveled at the transformation of her usually icy colleague. How these two had ever kept their relationship a secret for even a minute was beyond her. "Dr. Barnes."

Dr. Barnes's eyes widened as she realized Diana hadn't entered alone. She cleared her throat. "Dr. Riley, good morning."

"Oh, no." Diana sighed. "This is a strictly private visit, so you two should shed your alpha doctor routines and call each other by first names like all other mortals."

Jess would have never talked to her senior attending this way when she was a resident, but then, she'd never been so stupid as to enter a workplace relationship, especially with someone higher in the hierarchy. She usually was all for maintaining a healthy distance from her colleagues since most of them annoyed her. Meeting Diana privately had been one step, but should she take the next? She glanced at Dr. Barnes to judge her stance on this and met a gaze that contained the same mixture of puzzlement and annoyance she was feeling.

But why not? Jess grinned. "I wouldn't call it alpha routine, but okay." She walked over to the desk and offered her hand. "Jess."

"Emily." The other woman rose and shook her hand with an even grip. "What can I do for you both?"

"I've found the perfect solution for our blackberry problem. Her friend needs a lot of them, and I offered the beach house for the weekend."

Emily blinked twice and looked from Jess to Diana. She held the gaze of her partner for a moment before she nodded and smiled at Jess. "That's a great idea. I'd hate for them all to go to waste, and we can't find a free moment to drive up there." She walked around the desk to open a locker, removed a set of keys from her bag, and separated one from the rest. "Here's the key. We have tons of sheets and towels at the house and some nonperishable food, coffee, wine. Help yourselves to anything you want. When we decided to keep the place, we'd planned to open it for friends, but everyone is working these days. It's a shame to have such a beautiful house when no one gets to use it."

Jess grinned and put the key in her pocket. This was the longest not strictly work-related statement she'd ever heard from Emily. She was obviously as uncomfortable as Jess was with Diana's let's-all-be-friends approach but was working hard to overcome it. "Thank you."

Emily stopped fiddling with the rest of the keys and looked up. "You're welcome. Really."

"And when you're back and we have survived the next month, let's meet for dinner or something. You could bring Lena too." Diana took Emily's hand while she talked in the casual way couples did without conscious thought.

Jess had never been a touchy-feely person, but she had to admit it looked kind of nice. "I can't answer for Lena, but I'll tell her. Dinner is a great idea, and it'll be on me. As a thank you." And the idea of sharing dinner with Lena and another couple sounded nice too. Wait, not *another* couple, just *a* couple and a pair of friends.

She'd better leave before they planted any more of these mushy thoughts in her head.

Chapter Fourteen

"WHAT ARE YOU DOING HERE?" Although lacking any malice, Jess's gentle teasing still pushed the wrong button today.

Tears burned in Lena's eyes before she could prevent them. She jumped up from the bench between the garage and the main house and pressed half of the mail into Jess's hands. "For your mother." Then she strode as fast as she could without running toward the garden house.

"Hey, Lena." Jess was next to her in a few seconds. "What's happened?"

Shaking her head, Lena looked down and walked on. "Nothing."

"Okay," Jess said doubtfully, keeping pace with her. "I wanted to thank you."

"What for?"

"Your mental tai chi trick helped me find some calm when I sorely needed it."

"I'm glad for you." Lena attempted a smile but failed miserably. "I don't think tai chi will pay my bills or… Never mind."

"Bad news? Can I help?" Jess pointed to the crumpled letters Lena still clutched in her fist.

"I don't want your money." Borrowing money from someone to repay a loan was a vicious circle.

"Maybe I can help you find another solution. Or at least listen to you complain about it. God knows you've listened to too many of my problems already." The care in Jess's voice almost broke her will.

How long had it been since she'd shared her burden with someone? Even as a teenager, she'd often kept her own counsel; she hadn't wanted to burden her grandma, and her mother hadn't cared enough to ask.

"One letter is about a loan. I think I can handle that if I pick up some extra massage work in the evenings."

"More work? Don't you earn enough money with all the double shifts at the café?"

Lena held up the letters. Creases marred both, but her attempt to smooth them proved futile. "Obviously not. At minimum wage it takes ages to pay anything back."

"Oh. I hadn't thought of that."

"I guess you haven't had to work for minimum wage."

"No, you're right. I'm sorry."

"Nothing to be sorry about. You had the brains and the opportunity and got the right education. I chose to support my fucked-up mother instead of going to college, and now she's writing to me from prison, demanding even more money." *Oh shit.* Had she just said that out loud? She swallowed. By the raw burning in her throat, she must have screamed it. *Shit, shit, shit.*

"Prison?" Jess whispered the word as if it was some dirty secret.

Yeah, she had said it. Lena squared her shoulders and met Jess's gaze. If she had to face Jess's disdain, she would do it head on. "Yes. My mother is in prison for theft and fraud."

"I'm so sorry for you. That must be hard." Jess lightly squeezed her arm. Her hand lingered, and Lena soaked up the warmth like a freezing person who had stumbled in from a snowstorm.

Disarmed, Lena didn't know how to answer. She had been prepared for contempt, for rejection, for being shunned out of this new life she'd started. Not for the compassion softening Jess's expression. She nodded, and tears welled up again. No one had ever acknowledged it was difficult for her too.

Before Lena could explain anything, Jess pulled her into an embrace.

Lena breathed in the faint scent of baby lotion clinging to Jess's shirt as strong arms enveloped her like a comforting blanket.

She couldn't hold back any longer. And she didn't even know if she wanted to. Tears streamed from her eyes, and a sob broke from her depths.

"It's okay." Jess pressed her closer. "Let go."

And she did. As if a dam had broken, she couldn't contain her pain any longer. She sobbed until everything washed away. The only reason she wasn't carried away with the flood was Jess, whose calm presence anchored her. Even if Lena did get swept away, she knew Jess would come after her.

An eternity later, her tears had run dry, and she slowly regained awareness of her surroundings. She had soaked Jess's shirt. And crumpled it. "I'm sorry." She tried to remove the creases with her hand.

Jess stopped her futile movements, pressing Lena's captured hand against the area she'd been rubbing. Beneath Jess's right shoulder. At the swell of her breast.

Oh. Lena had been rubbing her breast.

Heat shot to her cheeks, and the embarrassment she'd felt after crying escalated to mortification. "I'm sorry," Lena said again. It still wasn't enough.

"Hey, don't be. I'm glad I could be there for you, even if I only provided a shoulder." Jess gently squeezed her hand before letting go. "Do you want to talk about any of it? The loan? Your mother?"

Lena shook her head, not trusting her voice. She pulled back her hand and reluctantly severed the connection to Jess.

"But please tell me if I can do anything for you." Jess's gaze searched Lena's eyes. The brilliant blue held no hint of disdain or reluctance.

This time, Lena forced herself to speak. "Thank you. Really. But I need to do this on my own."

"Okay. But whenever you want to talk, I'm here for you." A grin broke through Jess's concern like the first hints of color after a bleak night. "Do you want to hear some good news?"

"Oh, yes, your checkup! Is your heart doing better? And how's Mrs. Jameson?" As if it was infectious, Lena couldn't help grinning with her.

"Mrs. Jameson is fine. At least for now. And, yes, my heart's much better, but that's not what I meant. I ran into Diana at the hospital, and she told me the blackberries at her vacation house are overflowing and she needs someone to pick them all. We can go anytime." Jess beamed proudly.

"Oh." Not one but three pieces of good news. Great even. "Thank you." Maybe the universe was still working on its balance and everything would even out eventually.

"May I sit with you for a bit?" Maggie carried a tray that held two glasses and a pitcher of tea with large ice cubes and mint leaves.

Lena hastily gathered the pencils and pens that had taken over most of the surface of the small wooden table. "Please. It's your garden."

"I didn't want to interrupt your sketching, but you looked as if you could use some refreshment." Maggie put down the tray with a sigh and poured them each a glass. Then she sat down, took off the giant straw hat she always wore in the garden, and fanned herself with it.

The slight movement of the air was welcome, even if it barely reached Lena's side. When had the temperature risen? At least the walnut tree still provided enough shade for the table and both chairs.

"Thank you. That looks perfect." The tall glass was cool, and Lena held it against her cheek before she took a sip. "Ah, this is delicious. And you didn't interrupt anything important. I just had some unexpected time on my hands. The café rescheduled my shift." She sighed. "They mixed up the schedule and don't need me today."

"Again?" Maggie's brows wrinkled. "That doesn't seem fair. Are they at least paying you? You kept the day free for them."

"Pay? Why would they?" Lena snorted at the idea. "And even if they wanted to, they couldn't. They barely make ends meet as it is." She suspected there hadn't been a scheduling conflict but the owners had decided to either do some extra shifts themselves or had found someone willing to work for even less than she did. "I guess I have to look for another job soon."

"Oh!" Maggie grinned and clapped her hands together. "That's wonderful!"

"Wonderful?" Had Lena missed the sarcasm in her voice? She couldn't see anything wonderful apart from the fact she had the morning off. And she'd rather be working on reducing her debt.

"Of course I'm sorry they treat you like that at the café, but I have to admit I had another reason for coming out here apart from the tea. I heard back from my publisher, and I have the go-ahead for the next book: *History of Gardening in the Pacific Northwest*." A proud smile appeared on Maggie's face. "They already paid me an advance."

"Congratulations." Lena smiled with her. She didn't see how that related to her news, but she was happy for Maggie. "What do you want to do for a celebration? Should I bake a cake?"

"Oh, no. It's much too hot to bake. But I have a proposition for you."

Lena smiled at the phrasing. Maggie probably needed help carrying a big bag of mulch or some decorative stones. She took another large gulp of the tea, then packed her sketching equipment into the soft leather roll her grandma had given her. "What can I do for you?"

"To include everything I want in the book, I need help. I can't do it all on my own: gardening, research, typing, sorting my notes."

Lena thought about it. Not *if* she would help—that was a given—but when. She had time today, and she was sure she could squeeze in a couple of hours here and there. As much as she liked their evening walks, maybe she would have to let Jess go alone for a few weeks. "Of course I'll help you garden so you have time for the rest. But I might have to do some work in the evenings after I've finished my shifts. Or I could start now." She looked at her watch. "I have until six, when I have my next massage appointment."

"No, I don't need your help gardening." Maggie grinned. "Well, I sometimes do, but I thought you could work with me on all of it. As my assistant. I can pay you with my advance, and you would have steady income and a reliable job for at least a year, maybe longer. I have no idea what the café pays, but I'd offer you the same rate I paid my assistants when I was teaching at the university."

Lena stared at her. Assistant? With regular work hours? "But I don't have any experience." Her mouth was parched as if she hadn't had a drink a moment ago. With shaking hands, she refilled her glass. A drop of tea splashed on her sketch of the flower bed, blurring the lines. She was too confused to care. "And I would help you anyway. You don't need to pay me." The moment she said it, Lena wanted to take it back. She could use the extra money. But what she'd said was true, and she'd help in any way she could.

"Well, I know I don't have to…but I'd love to. My main requirements for an assistant are that we get along well, that they love to learn, and that they have a good work ethic. You are more than qualified on all points. I love your enthusiasm when you learn something new about a plant and how much you concentrate to get every detail of each drawing just right, even if it takes you several attempts. You don't cut corners to get the work done, and that's what I need most. We'll figure out the rest together. Okay?"

"Okay." Half a dozen questions about the details popped up in her mind, but none were a deal breaker. And she'd rather work with Maggie on whatever project she needed than run around the café all day. But following her heart and not her brain had led her to where she was today: no education to speak of, working three jobs, and struggling with debt. So this time she'd proceed a little cautiously. "I'd love to work with you. Would it be okay if I kept on selling my preserves at the farmers market? I would make the hours up to you in the afternoon and evening."

Maggie sipped her tea and smiled. "Certainly. It pains me to see you stretching yourself thin in every direction, but I won't keep you from it. But you don't need to work in the evening to make up for anything. We'll plan around your schedule."

Lena blinked. Was there a catch? Or worse, was this some kind of charity project? Had Jess told Maggie about Lena's financial problems? She studied Maggie's expression. Open, relaxed, friendly. Not at all judgmental, condescending, or pitying. Even if Maggie knew about her financial problems, this offer was too good not to accept. She smiled reluctantly. "Thank you. I'm really looking forward to working with you. When do we start?"

"Tomorrow? Wait, no, tomorrow is a market day. See how easy this is?" Maggie winked. "Friday morning? You take today off to relax and sketch or do whatever you want to do." Maggie finished the last of her tea and started to get up.

That Maggie remembered her schedule filled Lena with gratitude. "Friday it is. But I think I've sketched enough for today. Can I help you with the garden? What are you working on today?"

That wasn't strictly true; she'd never get tired of sketching. But she needed time to think, and planting or watering the garden was the perfect task to let her mind wander.

The sight of Lena sitting on the wall behind the garage brought a smile to Jess's face. She pushed the stroller faster. "Hey, what are you doing here?"

Laughing, Lena hopped down to join her. "Waiting for a cute girl to come and pick me up."

Whoa. Had Lena called her cute? Grateful for the twilight that hid her confusion, Jess searched for a comeback.

"Hi, Ella, how is my cutest girl?" Lena stepped closer and leaned over Jess's shoulder to peer inside the stroller even though it was too dark to make out Ella's features.

Ella cooed and gurgled. Lena seemed satisfied with the response and looked up at Jess. "And hi to you too."

A faint floral scent drifted over, and Jess smiled. She had missed this. For two evenings in a row, Lena hadn't been able to accompany Jess on her walks. She'd kept to her usual route and tried to soak up the peace and quiet of the neighborhood and the park. As always, the birds had sung, and the flowers had scented the evening air, but Jess hadn't enjoyed it quite as much without company. Maybe because she wasn't too happy alone with her thoughts and the doubts that snuck in from time to time.

"You're so quiet. Is it okay for me to join you on your walk?"

"Oh, sorry. Of course it is. I was just thinking about that actually. It's been kind of boring the last two nights without you."

"I would have preferred to be with you too. But I had already scheduled massage clients. At least they were both couples so I didn't have to work as much myself."

A warm tingling ran down Jess's spine as she remembered Lena's hands on her. *Don't go there. Think about something unsexy. Like work.* "Um… Mom said she offered you a job?"

Lena elbowed her in the side. "As if you didn't know. I'm still undecided if I should be mad at you or grateful."

"What?" Jess stopped. "Why would you be mad at me?"

"I'm not mad. I'm just…" Lena frowned and looked down. Her fingers played with one of the long strings that hung down from the open neck of her blouse. The neckline revealed skin that glowed golden in the evening light. Just a hint of collarbone peeked out.

Jess directed her eyes back to Lena's face. That was safer.

Lena hadn't noticed. She was still regarding her feet with a thoughtful expression.

"It's okay. If I did something stupid or aggravating or whatever, please tell me. I'm past the point where I want to intentionally annoy you, and I'm sorry if I did." Jess continued walking, keeping her eyes to the front. Sometimes talking about something emotional was easier if you didn't have to face the other person. Jess had never felt the need to hide; she usually didn't care what the other person thought. But Lena seemed to care, sometimes too much.

"No, it's my fault. I didn't ask you not to tell Maggie. And you're under no obligation to keep secrets for me." Lena was still talking in riddles, but at least she was talking.

"I'm sorry, but what secret did I reveal?" She couldn't think of any, and when she talked to her mom about Lena, she was careful to let her do most of the talking so she didn't get a hint about Jess's feelings. The last thing she needed was her mom noticing she found Lena attractive. She would only start to meddle in her well-intentioned mom way.

"About my financial problems. Maggie knew some already, but she didn't offer me a job before. I guess it's her way of helping me. And I am grateful, but still…I would have liked to remain her friend and not her charity case."

"Whoa. Stop right here." Jess engaged the brake so the stroller wouldn't move on its own. She reached for Lena's hands with both of hers. "I didn't talk to my mom about what happened on Monday. Apart from a conversation weeks ago when I first started living here, we haven't talked about your financial situation or any jobs. And I can't believe she offered you the job as a charity situation. That's not like her at all. She takes her books seriously. Didn't she say why she offered it to you?"

Lena squirmed but didn't pull her hands away. Tears glittered in her eyes. "She said she trusted my work ethic and likes to spend time with me. That's why she wants to have me as her assistant. But I don't have a degree or any experience and—"

"No. If my mom says she hired you because she trusts you, that's the main reason. Are you taking the job because of the money?"

"No!" Lena's curls flew from side to side. "I even offered to help her for free. I love helping Maggie with her work. She's taught me so much already, and I enjoy spending time with her."

"See, that's the reason she offered it to you." Jess squeezed the hands that still rested in hers. The contact was meant to soothe and reassure Lena, but somehow it did the same for her, and Jess didn't even know why she should be anxious.

"I'm sorry I was mad at you," Lena whispered.

"You don't have to apologize. It was a misunderstanding. No harm done." With a stroke of her thumbs, Jess let go of Lena's hands before she could follow the impulse to hug her. Since when had she become so touchy-feely? Could she still blame the hormones two months after giving birth?

She loosened the brake and started walking again.

If that had been Lena when she was mad, Jess didn't wonder anymore why people described her as too nice. She was much too concerned with everybody else's feelings to express her own. They couldn't be more different if they tried. But maybe Lena's way wasn't so wrong. At least it had resulted in a conversation that cleared up the misunderstanding. Whenever Jess was mad, she let the other person know without a possibility of doubt. Loud and clear. More often than not, her temper ran away with her and she never even heard explanations or apologies. When she looked at it with a clear head, this behavior was immature and not acceptable at all.

Damn, this walk was turning into another introspective session. So much for Lena's company stopping her from pondering too much.

"How about we drive up to Diana's beach house on Saturday afternoon after you finish work and stay overnight? We can pick the blackberries on Sunday and then drive back."

"Do you want to sacrifice two more days to help me pick berries?"

"Sacrifice?" Jess laughed. "I had so much fun picking apples. And the way Diana talked about the house, it sounds like a nice weekend trip, like a vacation. When was your last vacation? Mine's been ages ago."

"Vacation? I can't remember. I guess when I was little, when my grandfather was still alive, before I started school. We did a road trip and ended up at some lake in a rental cabin. But I can't remember where or when that was."

"Oh, wow. I wanted to complain that mine was four years ago, but I guess I better shut up."

"No, no, tell me," Lena said in a lightly teasing tone. "Where did you go? What did you do? Caribbean Islands? Paris? Hawaii?"

"New York. Sightseeing and shopping for a long weekend after a conference." Jess mumbled. Yeah, that didn't sound spoiled at all.

"Shopping? Is this something you love to do?" Lena's question lacked the expected judgment.

"Not really, no. But I was dating someone at the time who enjoyed it very much." Jess grimaced at the memory. "We didn't last much longer than the weekend. It's kind of sad it was my last vacation."

"Why has it been so long for you?"

"Work." Jess sighed. "To get to the position I now have, I never dared take time off. But that's probably all ruined. After what's happened, I guess I have to climb up the ladder once again and fight on each rung with someone five years younger and single. Or at least without kids." Another depressing topic she had wanted to avoid. "But we're getting off track. So do you want to go with me, or rather us," she pointed to Ella, "on a mini vacation to a beach house and pick some blackberries?"

"If you ask me that way, how can I say no? I'd love to." Lena squeezed Jess's arm. Before the touch fully registered, it was over, and only traces of warmth remained. "Thank you."

"Great. Wonderful. No need to thank me. I'll pack everything we need, and when you come back from the market on Saturday, you can take a nap in the car, like Ella does."

Chapter Fifteen

THE RADIO SCREECHED AS THEY moved out of the station's reach. Jess quickly switched it off before it could wake her passengers. For most of the two-hour drive, Lena and Ella had both slept soundly. Jess didn't mind; traffic had kept her busy but never stressed her enough to temper her good mood.

"Oh, sorry. I didn't mean to sleep that long." Lena yawned and half-turned in the passenger seat to face Jess. Her eyes were still adorably small and sleepy, and her smile was more relaxed than Jess had ever seen.

She pulled her gaze away from Lena and back to the road. Was that how Lena looked when she woke up in the mornings? The urge to find out leapt at her like a deer crossing the road. From one moment to the next, she wanted to wake up next to her. Wanted those hazel eyes to be the first thing she saw in the morning.

What's wrong with you? The couple of hours of soft rock and lovely views must have switched her brain to a sappy setting. "That's okay. You seemed to need it. Could you do me a favor and see if Ella's still asleep? I haven't heard her for a while."

Lena unhooked her seatbelt to completely turn around. "Her eyes are open, but she's busy studying the fish." She let herself fall back into the seat and buckled the belt again. "I think she likes them." Her tone was filled with pride.

And she should be proud. For at least fifteen minutes, Ella hadn't stopped reaching for the string of handmade wooden fish in rainbow colors Lena had brought home from the farmers market. Another of her long list of friends had made them. "Maybe she'll take after her grandma and study biology but specialize in marine life instead of botany."

"Or maybe she'll move to Alaska and work on a fishing trawler."

"Uh...I hope not. I don't want to have a smelly daughter."

Lena sniffed. "I didn't want to say anything, but...you already do have a smelly daughter. She needs a pit stop soon."

Laughing, Jess nearly missed her turn when the GPS announced it. She looked at the display. "Five more minutes. I'll open the window."

A warm breeze carried salty air and the scent of pines.

"Oh. I can smell the ocean." Lena opened her window and held out her hand.

When they reached their destination, Jess parked in the well-kept space next to the small bungalow and shut off the SUV.

Ella protested the end of their journey. Before Jess could reassure her, Lena got out and opened the door next to the baby carrier.

"Don't worry. We'll move you around again in a second. We'll clean you up and feed you and walk around this amazing place." Lena's singsong voice caught Ella's attention.

Smiling, she fixed her gaze on Lena's lips and reached for her with both arms.

Jess was as mesmerized as her daughter. With an internal sigh, she tore herself away. "Could you take her while I get our bags?"

"Sure." Lena waited with Ella at the front door until Jess came with the bags and key.

The entrance opened directly into the living room. An oversized couch dominated the room and stood with its back to them, facing the large window and the inviting seat beneath it that was built into the wall. To both sides, a pair of mismatched but comfortable-looking armchairs rounded out the seating arrangement.

To their right, beyond the armchair, an open door revealed dark-red kitchen cabinets and a sturdy table. Jess set their duffle bags down near the door and reached for the carrier. "I'll use the table to change Ella, and you can go ahead and pick a room."

Lena neither moved nor answered. She had taken a few steps inside the house and then stopped, staring out the window.

Following her gaze, Jess could see a patch of grass and several old pines on the plot behind the house. Between them, a few pink clouds streaked over a dark azure sky, and the low-hanging sun reflected off the blue-gray waves of the Pacific Ocean like strands of molten gold.

"Do you think we can get close to the water?" Lena whispered in awe.

Jess grinned. "Sure. Diana said something about cliffs, but she texted me directions on how to get down to the beach. It involves a staircase, so maybe we shouldn't risk it in the dark."

"Oh, right. But can we go tomorrow morning? I've always wanted to touch the ocean." Wonder and excitement colored Lena's voice as if she was about to visit the Mona Lisa.

"But Seattle is right next to the water. Puget Sound isn't the ocean, but surely you've been on one of the islands or somewhere up and down the coast?"

Lena shrugged. "I only moved here four years ago and haven't had the chance."

"And before?"

"I lived in the middle of the country, nowhere near a coast."

Jess couldn't imagine living to her age without having seen the ocean. Okay, the list of places in the US she'd visited was much smaller than most people's, but she'd always taken the ocean for granted.

Ella's protest saved her from finding a response. Jess slung the bag with Ella's stuff over one shoulder.

"Let me take her. Maybe one of the rooms has the same view?"

After Jess changed Ella, safely stored the dirty diaper in an airtight container, and heated a bottle with formula, she went looking for the best place to feed her.

Lena had removed their bags, probably to their respective rooms, and had carried the cooler and the empty containers for the blackberries inside. A door that led out to the porch stood open.

Outside, Lena was nowhere to be seen, but a wooden swing seemed like the perfect place to enjoy the sunset while giving Ella her dinner.

When the bottle was nearly empty, Lena reappeared from her exploration between the trees. Her cheeks glowed in a healthy pink that rivaled the sky. "The cliffs are close, and you can see water for miles and miles." She gestured in the direction she had come from. "It's so beautiful. I can't wait to go down there."

"Why don't you go? I'll stay with Ella."

"What? No!" Lena's hair flew in the light breeze as she shook her head. "We'll go down tomorrow. But come to the fence and look at the water. We'll carry her. I'll get the wrap."

Ella finished the bottle, and Jess held her up to her shoulder. Wrap? Before she could decide if it was a good idea or not, Lena returned with what looked like an extremely long shawl made of a light material in all the colors of the rainbow.

Jess stared at it. "I have no idea how to use something like that. I have a carrier at home, like a backpack."

"Oh, it's super easy once you've done it a few times. I always carried Tammy like this." Her face fell, and her mouth opened as if she was surprised by her own words. "My little sister."

The sadness in her words tugged at Jess's heart. She burned to know what had happened to Tammy and why she was no longer a part of Lena's life, but even more than that, she wanted to bring back Lena's smile. "Okay, why don't you take her and show me next time. We should go now before it's too late. I don't want you to fall down the cliff in the dark."

Ella didn't seem to mind in the least as Lena held her to her front and wrapped the shawl around herself in a complex crisscross pattern. She rested her head on Lena's cleavage.

Lucky baby. Jess forced her gaze away.

"Do you want to check her before we go?"

"No, she looks happy enough, and I trust you." Even though she mostly said it to lighten Lena's mood, Jess did mean it. She hadn't thought it possible she would trust anyone so soon with Ella, apart from her mother.

Lena led her down a path between the mature pines. It was shady and cool, and with each step heavenly scents rose as they crushed old pine needles.

Almost without warning, they emerged from the tree line. Tall grass and several hardy plants she couldn't name clung to the stones and almost hid the fence made of wire and wooden posts slanted at precarious angles. To one side, a much sturdier wooden bench stood facing west, showing Lena wasn't the only one interested in watching the sun set over the water.

"Wow." Jess sat down to enjoy the view. The sky was more indigo than blue, and the sun had already dipped partly into the ocean.

"Yeah. I've got no words..." Lena wrapped both arms around Ella.

She stood at the fence, and even though it was still a good distance from the edge, Jess's stomach dropped at the sight of them.

"Come here." Jess had never been afraid of heights, but looking at Lena, with her enraptured profile glowing in pink and orange, caused her insides to flutter like a swarm of drunk butterflies. "Sit down."

Lena regarded her with a raised eyebrow.

Oops, her tone might have been harsher than intended. "Um, please?"

"Everything okay?" Lena sat down next to her on the small bench, close enough that their sides touched.

The swarm settled down and buzzed contentedly. Much better. "Yeah, sorry, seeing you that close to the fence..." She gestured at the drooping wire. "I didn't want to endanger Ella."

"Sure." Lena rolled her eyes but softened the gesture with a grin before she faced the setting sun as the ball of fire dissolved into the ocean.

All too soon, the spectacle was over, and the light breeze carried in a coolness as if the water had doused the heat of the sun. Only Jess's left side was still warm, and she had to resist the urge to snuggle closer. Why was she having these thoughts all of a sudden? Maybe it was a kind of nesting instinct. Was it some residue left from her pregnancy? But she hadn't felt this snuggly with anyone but Ella in the last year, more like a prickly cactus on speed.

She reached out to caress the bare head of her daughter, carefully avoiding any contact with Lena's skin. "I forgot to put a cap on her. It's getting colder."

"I think she's still fine. But let's go back. And have something to eat."

Jess's stomach grumbled at the mention of dinner. Maybe that weird sensation had been hunger?

‡‡‡‡‡‡‡

While Jess readied Ella for bed, Lena cut the cheese and vegetables she'd bought at the farmers market. She filled two low glasses with carrot, cucumber, and celery sticks and transferred the roasted pepper hummus from its reusable takeaway container into a ceramic bowl. The orange and red hues reminded her of the perfect sunset she'd just witnessed.

Humming to herself, she placed cheese cubes and apple slices on matching plates and stacked everything on the serving tray she'd found on the counter.

Jess's anxiety about the fence had been cute, and Lena hadn't minded the gruffness in her voice. It was too easy to read the true intentions in Jess's eyes. She was so damned attractive when she focused intently on something or someone.

Were Lena's thoughts and feelings as easy to read? It wouldn't be good if Jess saw Lena's interest in her eyes. Not at all.

Lena carried the tray to the main room and studied the seating arrangements. In the warm glow from the two small lights on the side tables, everything looked extra comfy and romantic. But she didn't want to switch on the bright overhead fixtures. The sensible choice would be to sit in one of the armchairs, but then it would be uncomfortable for one of them to reach the food. She sat on the couch with a sigh and placed the tray in front of her on the wooden table.

"Mmh, that looks delicious." Jess's low voice came from directly behind her. She walked around the couch on fluffy blue socks and sat next to Lena.

"You look comfortable." The sight of Jess in a gray hoodie that had been washed so often the name of the college was illegible tempted Lena to change out of her shorts into something warmer too, but her stomach demanded she wait until after dinner.

Jess shrugged. "Ella slobbered all over my T-shirt, so I had to change anyway." She looked around. "What do you want to drink?"

"Oh sorry, I forgot about that. What did we bring?"

"Nothing. Diana said we can drink anything we find. I think I saw water, soda, and beer in the fridge. And some wine on the counter."

"Oh, I haven't had wine for ages."

"I haven't had alcohol since before I got pregnant with Ella, but I've heard a glass of wine is supposed to be good for the heart."

"Don't you need to ask your doctor about that?"

Jess laughed. "This cardiologist approves."

"I'll get us some." Lena started to rise.

"No, stay. It'll just take a minute." With her socks, Jess slid more than walked to the kitchen. "Red okay?"

"Sure." Lena should limit her intake to one glass too. She wasn't used to it, so the wine would make her tipsy. A stupid idea if she wanted to avoid revealing her budding attraction to Jess.

After a minute, Jess returned carrying two wine glasses in one hand and an open bottle of Pinot Noir in the other. Two bottles of water stuck out of the pocket of her hoodie. She placed everything on the table, then poured them each a glass.

Grateful for the water, Lena sipped that first. For the help in keeping her wits, she would forgive the use of plastic for once.

"Thank you for dinner." Jess raised her wine glass. "To our mini vacation."

"Thank you for bringing me here." Lena touched her glass to Jess's and looked in her eyes.

The cornflower blue wasn't as bright as in the sunlight, but the dim lighting erased the fine lines around her eyes and gave her an ageless look, warm and inviting.

When Jess closed her eyes to twirl and sniff the wine, her dark eyelashes fluttered.

Before she had even had a sip of wine, Lena was already dizzy. She closed her eyes and breathed in. Oh, yeah. Diana and her partner weren't skimpy when it came to wine. The first sip flooded her senses with something tart and fruity like cranberry or blackberry before it warmed her with a softer flavor, almost like vanilla. "Mmh. I think it's the best wine I've ever had."

Jess hummed in agreement. "I love it too. It will be so hard to limit myself to one glass." She took a carrot and dipped it in the hummus. After finishing it off in two bites, she dipped two more and sighed. "I think this is the best hummus I've ever had. So we're even."

"Hey, you didn't bring the wine."

"Did too. From the kitchen."

Lena laughed. "Oh, I'm so looking forward to the first time Ella uses that line on you."

"Nah, she won't. She'll forever stay a cuddly and sweet baby."

"Really? You'd want that?"

Jess nibbled on a slice of cucumber. "Actually, I can't wait for her to talk, to express her thoughts, to show me she's a person with her own will." She chuckled. "Even though I'm afraid our tempers will clash more than once if she takes after me. At least that's what my mom told me. She said my first word was *no*."

Up. Tammy's first word had been up, and she'd said it to Lena. She had wanted to be up in Lena's arms, not their mother's; her heart had nearly burst at the trust and love in Tammy's eyes. Her mother hadn't liked that show of free will at all and had given them both the cold shoulder for a day. "I think you'll be a wonderful mom."

"I don't know." Jess swirled the wine in her glass without drinking. "Sometimes I doubt if I made the right decision or if I was egotistical. I'm a single mother with little time to give."

"That might be true, but you're not the first woman to ever face this problem. And you have a great mom to help. But you give something else that's important, not just time and love, but you respect her as a person, even now."

"Thank you for saying so, but I'm not so sure it'll be enough." Jess sipped her wine slowly as if she relished every little drop. "My heart failure scared me. Not only because of what it could mean for me, but for Ella too. When you're young and healthy, you think you're immortal." She snorted. "I should've known better. I've treated patients much younger than me. But somehow..."

"Somehow you never thought it applied to you?" Lena leaned forward and put one hand on Jess's thigh. The muscles were hard as if she was ready to jump up at any second.

"Exactly. Stupid."

"Or human? If you worried about every little thing, you wouldn't be a good mother either or a good role model." The tension under Lena's fingers eased, and she reluctantly pulled her hand away.

"Good point." Jess stretched out her legs and shifted so her right side rested against the back of the couch. "Enough about my sad, sad life. Do you want kids?"

Why did everything today poke into the same wound? Lena shuddered and placed her wine glass on the table before she spilled it on the couch. "Yeah. Someday." She sighed.

"Why not now?"

"Apart from being single, broke, and working too many jobs?" Lena pulled one leg up and hugged it to her chest.

"Apart from that. Say you won the lottery or a millionaire rode in on a white stallion and swept you off your feet or something. Would you want kids now?"

Lena considered the question. It had been years since she'd allowed herself those kinds of dreams. Ella's smile, her tiny fists when they clutched Lena's little finger, her sister's tears when her father had taken her away—they all flicked through her mind like a trailer for a sappy movie. "I'd love to have two or three kids. I always wanted to grow up with a sister and brother and would want the same for my kids. A wife, two or three kids, a cat. Not necessarily a white picket fence." She laughed to lighten the mood, but it sounded false to her own ears.

"It seems we're not so different. I always wanted a sister too. And a cat someday." Jess reached out and lightly stroked down Lena's shin. "You're cold. Goosebumps everywhere." She pulled a quilt from the back of the couch and covered Lena's legs with it.

"Thank you." Lena snuggled into the old blanket. "Do you mind being alone?"

"Alone?"

"Without a partner. Would you rather share this evening with a girlfriend? A romantic weekend at a friend's beach house?"

Jess's brows wrinkled as she chewed a slice of apple. Finally, a smile tugged at the corner of her mouth. "No, not at all. I probably wouldn't be here with a girlfriend. Whenever I dated, I wasn't into too much proximity. Even staying over on the weekends was usually too intimate for me. Maybe I'm too independent. Or maybe I've never been in love before."

"Never?" Lena didn't know if she should envy Jess or feel sorry for her. She used to fall head over heels all the time when she was younger. That was one of the reasons she'd stepped back from dating.

"I thought I was, but I guess it was mostly lust. And that's been ages ago. Since I held Ella in my arms for the first time, I have a completely different definition of love. She's part of me, lives in my heart as no one ever did before."

Tears burned in Lena's eyes, and she quickly blinked them away. Jess's words stirred something deep inside and tugged at corners of her own heart. That was exactly what she wanted in her life, someone to live inside her heart and in turn to be part of theirs. She wasn't sure her mother had ever thought of her like that, and her grandma had taken her feelings with her to the grave. She'd have to find her own family one day.

"Hey, why are you crying? Did I say something? I'm sorry." Jess brushed her thumb over Lena's cheek. Heat bloomed under Jess's fingertips and seared the cold in her heart away.

She couldn't find the right words, so she shook her head and leaned forward into the touch.

Jess moved closer and cupped Lena's face with both hands, and it was the most natural feeling in the world to sink into them.

Lena got lost in the sea of blue as Jess's eyes searched hers. For what, she wasn't sure.

Their breaths mingled, and the heady scent of the Pinot Noir dazed Lena. She licked her dry lips.

Jess moaned, and her eyes darkened like the sky before a storm.

Lena couldn't say who moved first, but suddenly they were kissing.

The brush of Jess's lips was tentative, almost shy. Asking, not taking. Offering, not imposing.

The sweetness in the gesture was Lena's undoing, and she responded with the most enthusiastic *oh, yes* she could convey without words. As she deepened the kiss, she bumped her nose against Jess's and quickly angled her face until they fit. Perfect.

The tip of her tongue darted out to explore the inside of Jess's upper lip. So soft.

Moaning, Jess opened her mouth and let Lena in. She tasted of tart wine, sweet apple, and something all her own.

Pleasure shot through Lena with every stroke of Jess's tongue against hers, weakening her spine. She raised her hands to hold onto Jess. To get closer to her. To get drunk on this dazzling heat and forget everything else. She clutched the thick sweater on both sides, and the hint of the firm body underneath was all the support she needed.

143

Jess's hands slid upward until they tangled in her hair. Sparks shot from the fingertips on Lena's scalp through the length of her body. They ignited a fire deep inside her that hadn't burned in such a long, long time.

Without warning, Jess stiffened and drew back. She cocked her head to one side and frowned. Her rosy lips were swollen, and her pupils were wide.

"Sorry." And with that, she jumped up and left the room.

What just happened? Panting, Lena tried to organize her jumbled thoughts and emotions. One second they were kissing like...like what? Lovers? Teenagers in heat? Nothing she'd ever done compared to this. And the next second, Jess had run away. From her? From herself?

A faint cry filtered through the pulse pounding in her ears. *Ella.* So maybe Jess hadn't run from someone but to someone.

But what would they do when she came back? Talk about it? Ignore it? Continue as if nothing had interrupted them? At the thought of another kiss, anticipation swirled in her middle like a ball of liquid heat.

She took a large sip of water to cool off, then reached for the vegetable sticks and the bowl of hummus. She'd need to keep up her strength for the emotional roller coaster this weekend.

When she'd finished off her food and the lone glass of wine, Jess still hadn't come back, even though Ella had been quiet for some time. Lena gathered the dishes and cleaned them to give her time to show up.

Had it been thirty minutes? Forty? Lena locked the front and back entrance and switched off the lights.

In front of Jess's door, she paused. Nothing. Not even the sound of breathing.

With a sigh, she went to her own room. Sleep would take a long time to come, but experience had taught her it would find her eventually. It wasn't the first time she'd gone to bed with disappointment as her only companion, and it wouldn't be the last.

Chapter Sixteen

JESS TIPTOED TO THE KITCHEN so as not to wake Lena. The predawn light was enough to see both the living room and the kitchen were empty. Lena had cleared away last night's dishes. Jess swallowed against the sudden dryness of her throat. How would she explain why she hadn't returned?

But first things first. Even though she wasn't allowing herself caffeine yet, she still liked to start the day with a hot drink. When she reached for the water kettle, it was warm. Her stomach dropped. Lena was already up and about.

She opened a few cupboards until she found mugs and a dozen colorful teas, then picked a yellow package that looked as optimistic as she'd like to feel. The scent of something fresh and sharp rose as she poured water in the cup. Ginger, nice. Maybe it would help settle her queasy stomach.

Yeah, right. Who are you kidding? Only a talk would do that. And an apology. Again. She squared her shoulders and opened the door to the porch in search of Lena.

And there she was, standing on the patch of grass in front of the porch, facing east where the sun peeked through the pines and cast long shadows. Her features were relaxed, and a serene smile played around her lips. Lips that had kissed Jess until she'd lost all sense of time and direction.

Jess took in a sharp breath. Stupid idea. She wasn't ready to talk.

But before she could run away again, Lena opened her eyes and focused on her. She held one finger to her lips and beckoned Jess closer with the other hand.

The unease settled like leaves after the wind calmed down. Jess pulled the baby monitor from the waistband of her sweatpants and placed it and her steaming mug on the wooden railing, next to a small collection of shells and driftwood. The grass was cold but soft under her bare feet as she took her usual place at Lena's side and greeted the sun.

An hour later, the sun had climbed above the trees and warmed Jess sufficiently that she looked forward to her now cold drink.

When they stepped onto the porch, Jess couldn't avoid it any longer. But between their morning routine and Lena's calm presence, her embarrassment had faded enough that she found it easier to talk. "About yesterday evening…I'm sorry."

"Okay." Lena went into the kitchen before Jess had a chance to read her expression.

That was all she had to say? Wasn't she mad or disappointed or maybe even glad they'd stopped when they had? Jess picked up her stuff and followed. "Okay? Are we good?"

For a second, something other than her usual calm flashed in Lena's eyes, then her shoulders drooped and she looked down. "It was just a kiss. No big deal. I'm sorry too for crying and being needy."

Wait, what? "Do you think that was a pity kiss?"

"Wasn't it?" Lena's voice was so low she was difficult to understand.

"Hell, no. I'm sorry I ran, not sorry I kissed you."

Her eyelids fluttered minimally as Lena studied Jess for a long moment. Then she nodded. "Apology accepted. But why did you run?"

Now it was Jess's turn to look down. "That wasn't planned. My attraction just flared, and I acted without thinking. And it kind of overwhelmed me." She pressed a hand to her middle as her stomach somersaulted. Usually, Jess would take back control with a sarcastic remark and a change of topic. But she didn't want to treat Lena that way. "I…um…I'm not ready for a relationship and sex—not that I want to be presumptuous—but I'm not ready for sex right now. And yesterday I didn't trust myself not to act on my emotions. That's why I stayed away."

"Thank you for explaining. And maybe it's for the best." Lena shrugged halfheartedly. "As much fun as sex would have been, I don't think it would have been the wisest choice either."

Fun. That word jumpstarted her imagination in a totally inappropriate way. Jess bit her lower lip to counter the tactile memory of Lena's kiss.

She should be happy they were on the same page. Jess didn't need another complication in her life right now, and Lena wasn't playing games with her but offered her the option to move on.

A sudden urge to tackle the day filled Jess with energy. "Why don't I make us a quick breakfast. Afterward, we can head down to the ocean before we pick your blackberries."

"That would be perfect." Lena smiled.

A soft sound came from the baby monitor as if Ella wanted to remind them she was here too.

"Someone else wants her breakfast. I'll go and get Ella." Lena pointed at the monitor. "If you want, I can feed her while you cook."

"Um…I don't know. Have you done something like that before?" Not that she thought feeding a baby was difficult; she was just unsure if she wanted someone else to take over for her. This was her time with Ella, the intimate moments where she watched her daughter enjoy her meal. Something she didn't even like to share with her mom when she was around to do it herself. But as she thought about it, the idea of sharing with Lena didn't raise any feelings of resistance. Maybe because of the longing she'd shown yesterday as she'd talked about her baby sister, or maybe because of the genuine care she expressed for Ella.

Whatever it was, Jess didn't mind. *Huh.*

"Countless times with Tammy." Lena's sadness from yesterday resurfaced with this one name.

Jess wanted to kick herself for bringing it up again. "Great. Fine. Sure, you can give her the bottle. I'll get it for you." She hastened inside.

Lena went straight to Ella's room, and Jess could hear her talking through the baby monitor. She said nothing important, but it made Jess all warm and tingly just the same.

She shut off the monitor to concentrate on the task at hand, heating the bottle of readymade formula in the electric heater she'd brought.

Before she could check the temperature, Lena came in with Ella, removed the bottle, and sprinkled a few drops on the inside of her arm.

"Perfect. You mind if we go outside?" Lena balanced the wriggling Ella, the warm bottle, and a cushion without seeming fazed in the least.

"Go ahead." What else was there to say?

It took all her willpower not to sneak peeks outside.

She'd better start their own breakfast before Lena noticed. They hadn't brought much. Scrambled eggs and the rest of the delicious cheese from the farmers market would have to be enough, together with the bread Lena had gotten for sandwiches. It looked suspiciously healthy, with whole grains or something, but it wouldn't kill her for one day.

Lena's indistinguishable mumblings accompanied Ella's happy sucking noises through the open door to the porch.

Jess couldn't stop smiling as she scrambled and cooked the eggs. Family. This morning was exactly like she had always imagined a family of her own should feel.

Jess, get a grip. One kiss and you're playing happy family in your head. Amazing kiss, but still… With a shake of her head, Jess switched off the stove and plated the eggs.

During breakfast, Jess kept her gaze on the food and the conversation to the weather. If Lena stared at her strangely, so what? She couldn't take any deep conversation with her thoughts and feelings all mixed up as if a tornado had picked everything up and shaken it before tossing it out again.

After they'd eaten, Jess clad Ella in a floppy hat and smothered sunscreen all over her.

Lena held up the wrap. "Do you want to carry her to the beach?"

As much as she wanted to, Jess wasn't sure she actually could. Sure, her heart had improved, but she'd never taken such a long walk carrying Ella instead of pushing the stroller. "Nah, you take her."

Ella seemed to enjoy the wrapping procedure as much as Jess liked watching Lena handle the cloth with strong hands and nimble fingers.

The path through the pines seemed shorter than last night. When they reached the bench, they followed another path on their left at the top of the cliffs until they reached a wooden staircase that seemed sturdy enough.

Lena didn't hesitate and descended toward the water with one hand on the railing and the other wrapped protectively around Ella.

Jess followed slowly. She didn't want to think about the way back up, which she was afraid would hurt. It had been the right decision not to carry Ella; she wasn't up to her old standards. Even while pregnant, she'd always taken the stairs to the cardiology unit on the fourth floor. At least until the last month.

At the foot of the stairs, Lena waited for her, gaze fixed on the water. "Isn't it beautiful?" Her voice was hushed as if they stood in a museum in front of a masterpiece.

The sight of her slightly opened lips and wide eyes was irresistible, and Jess didn't even try to look away. Lena was gorgeous, maybe even more so than yesterday. If only her gaze would turn to Jess with the same adoration.

"Beautiful, yes." Jess didn't know why she whispered too.

Lena removed her sandals. "Ooh, the sand is warm." She took a few steps toward the water. When she reached the curvy border between the dry and wet parts of the beach, she hesitated.

"It'll be cold." Jess grimaced. With all the stones, shells, and driftwood littering the beach, she wasn't getting out of her shoes.

"I don't care." Lena took another step and shivered as her foot touched the wet sand. A wave lapped at the shore and lazily flowed over her feet. "Ouch. You're right, that really is cold." Laughing, she waded into the waves until her ankles were submerged. "Hey, Ella, look at that. The ocean." She bent forward so Ella's gaze was angled to the water.

Ella's enthusiastic gurgling was most likely a response to the enthusiasm in Lena's voice and her twisting movements, but Lena appeared to take it as confirmation. She squatted and submerged her hands in the water, then softly touched Ella's nose with the tip of her finger.

Jess couldn't help but laugh as Ella wrinkled her nose. Would it be like this as Ella grew up and they got to share more and more first times? That was what she'd always wanted, to show a child all the great things life had to offer. Recently, she'd been more occupied with recuperating and taking care of the basic necessities of life than with the beautiful discoveries they could make together.

Lena fished a shell out of the water and dried it on her shirt. She held it out to Ella, helping her little hand to glide over the smooth inside and rough outside.

The sight of Lena sharing her first moment at the ocean with Ella warmed Jess more than the rays of the sun could. Instead of considering the baby a disturbance or at best a necessary evil, Lena actively involved Ella in her own exploration and shared her joy freely.

Jess's eyes started to burn. The reflection of the light must be even worse so close to the water. She pulled her sunglasses down from her head. There, much better.

She chanced another glance at Lena, who shielded her eyes and studied the horizon, laughing as a flock of seagulls swooped down to fish. She had obviously forgotten to bring her own sunglasses.

"Here," Jess removed hers and held them out. "Take mine."

"No, you'll see less."

"But you have Ella, and I would prefer if you didn't stumble over a rock and fall face down in the water or something."

"If you put it that way…" Lena took the glasses and put them on. They slid down to the tip of her nose, and she had to adjust the fit a bit. "I always thought your head was too big… Now I have proof."

Jess laughed. "I would make you pay for that comment, but you're hiding behind a tiny human shield. Not fair."

"Let's walk along the shore for a bit. I promise not to drown Ella."

Jess looked down at Lena, who was still squatting, digging with one hand in the wet sand. "Do you need help getting up?" Jess gestured to Ella. "Is she too heavy?"

"No, she's fine." Lena stood without assistance even though the muscles in her legs quivered slightly.

Her long, well-formed legs Jess couldn't look away from. She'd noticed them before, of course, as Lena often wore shorts in the garden or one of her asymmetrical knee-length skirts, like today. But now she knew how soft that skin was even covered in goosebumps like yesterday. Lena's naked feet dug into the wet sand, and she was wearing the sexy dark-purple nail polish again.

Jess's feet were sensibly clad in trainers, with long jeans covering her ankles. They hadn't been swollen for a couple of weeks, but she hadn't lost the habit of hiding them. Well, cold water was supposed to be good for circulation. She toed off her shoes and bent down to remove her socks and cuff her jeans.

"I can't remember when I last took the time to actually walk on the beach. I mostly saw the ocean from afar." Jess kept her gaze on the ground as they walked. Just so she wouldn't tread on anything sharp. Not because she didn't trust her eyes to stay away from Lena's legs or Ella's head resting contently on Lena's cleavage or Lena's smile as she took in everything the ocean had to offer.

"That's sad." They had reached a stonier part, and Lena slowed to pick her way. "And now?"

"I wouldn't want to be anywhere else." Jess held her breath and stepped into the surf. The first contact with the cold water stabbed her toes with a thousand icy needles, but after a few seconds, a not-so-uncomfortable tingling replaced the pain.

This was real. Like Lena.

The blackberry bushes were hidden at the western end of the lot and as loaded as Diana had promised. In a wind-sheltered area, the hedge grew higher than Lena could reach, and many long branches were pulled down to the ground by the weight of the berries.

Jess stared open-mouthed. "That's more than enough to feed an army."

"Even if we only pick the ones that are easy to reach, we should get plenty." Lena grinned and lightly elbowed Jess. "Don't worry. We don't need to pick all of them."

"Whew." Jess exaggeratedly wiped her brow. "I thought we'd spend the next couple of weeks here."

"Nah, I don't want to get on the wrong side of Maggie by kidnapping her family."

Jess spread a blanket in the shade of a pine and placed Ella's carrier on it. "She's asleep again. Lazy girl doesn't want to help us." She bent down to drape a white cotton cloth over the opening to shield Ella from the sun. Her faded jeans looked as soft as the cloth. A loose navy T-shirt hid the rest of her figure, but Lena remembered the feel of her body all too well.

Her fingertips itched with the desire to go over and explore again. Instead, she drank deeply from the water bottle she'd brought. It was still cool but didn't help to douse the heat that had simmered inside since their kiss. *Stop it.*

Unlike her own mother, she knew better than to follow every impulse, no matter how pleasurable it was. Ever since Jess had admitted to being attracted to her, Lena had been playing the what-ifs in her mind. If Lena messed this up, she would jeopardize her living situation and the job with

Jess's mom. Or worse, if Lena gave in to her attraction and fell for Jess, she would surely break Lena's heart. Jess had said it herself—she wasn't ready for a relationship. But what if they managed to have amazing sex and stay friends?

Before her libido could win the argument, she forced herself to look away. *Concentrate on the blackberries. That's why you're here, not for a romantic weekend at the sea.*

Jess joined her a minute later and picked up her own bucket. She either sensed Lena's need to work uninterrupted or was busy with her own thoughts. Wordlessly, they picked side by side and had soon filled all but two containers.

"Wait." Jess put her hand on Lena's arm to stop her from placing a berry in her empty bucket. "What do you think about a competition?"

"Competition?"

"Let's race. Whoever finishes her bucket first gets a prize."

"Oh, what would that be?"

Jess plucked the berry Lena still held between her fingers and popped it in her mouth. "Mmmh. What would you want?" A tiny drop of purple juice stained her lip.

The urge to wipe it away was strong, and Lena clutched her bucket with both hands to stop them from reaching out. What did she want? *Another kiss.* No! That was not an appropriate price. Something innocent, like food? "Dinner?"

Jess pushed her sunglasses up into her hair and studied Lena for a moment. "Like a date?"

Whoa, that wasn't innocent at all. Lena wanted to say yes and no at the same time, so she made a joke instead. "Just a dinner. Two friends, maybe the loser's daughter…"

Jess laughed, and her eyes twinkled with mischief. "You mean the winner's daughter." She pushed her sunglasses down as if to ready herself for the race. "On the count of three. One, two…" She lightly pushed Lena out of the way and reached for the branch full of ripe berries she had been working on. "Three!"

Lena reached around Jess and stole the berry she had just picked, then fled a few feet away to another good spot.

She worked methodically along the hedge until the bucket was nearly full. Once she had picked everything within easy reach, she was still a few berries short. A branch arched above her, taunting her with ripe berries. But even on her toes, it was too high. Lena placed her bucket on the ground and jumped up to grab a few leaves and pull the branch down. Perfect.

One by one, she plucked the berries and let them fall into the bucket. To get the last few, she needed to change hands. The branch strained to snap back into its natural form, and when she tried to find a grip with her other hand, it did just that. Instinctively, she moved to hold it in place, not looking where she placed her fingers.

With all her might, she grasped the branch in her fist. And poked a couple of thorns right into her palm and thumb.

She let go, and the branch tore upward, raining ripe berries everywhere.

"Ouch! Shit." Lena balled her hand into a fist to stave off the pain. How could she have been so stupid? Hadn't she learned anything from the apple-picking incident last week?

Jess ran over to her. "Lena? What happened?"

"Nothing. I scratched my hand." Lena spoke through gritted teeth.

"Let me see." Jess's voice was calm and strangely compelling.

Before she could think about it, Lena opened her hand and held it out. A thin red line followed the lifeline like an evil twin, and the inside of her thumb bled profusely. A drop fell on the ground. "Uh, sorry." Lena pulled her hand back.

Jess stopped her with a gentle grip around her wrist. With her other hand, she pulled a package of tissues from her pocket. "Hold this."

"But..." Lena could do this herself.

"Do me a favor and let me." Jess grinned. "I'm a highly trained professional after all. And I need the practice as a mom. If Ella takes after me, even a little bit, I'll have to take care of a lot of scratches in the future." She let go of Lena's wrist.

"Okay, *Doctor* Riley." Lena smiled and took the package of tissues with her free hand.

Jess cringed. "Um...about that..." She looked everywhere but at Lena's face. With a sigh, she took a tissue and soaked up the blood on the palm and the thumb, then inspected the scratches. She took Lena's bottle from the ground and poured some water over her hand, then blotted it dry. Her fingers were warm where she cradled Lena's hand in her own. "I think everything came out," she mumbled, probably more to herself.

"Feels like it." Lena couldn't see Jess's expression since she kept her head down, but a slight blush was visible on the tips of her ears. Or was it sunburn?

Jess pulled out another a tissue, opened it, folded it again into a narrower but thicker bandage, and wrapped it around the bleeding thumb. She pressed her hand around it. "Let's wait a couple of minutes, and that should do the trick. When was your last tetanus shot?"

About the time she'd last had a job that came with health insurance. But she wasn't about to say that out loud. "Maybe four years ago? Five?"

"That's fine." Jess shifted on her feet and sighed again. Then she squared her shoulders and raised her head, gaze steady and open. "I apologize for my arrogant behavior when we first met. I could say I was cranky because of my recent diagnosis and hormonal imbalance, but there is no justification for treating you that way."

Lena searched her expression for her intentions but found only honesty and regret. "Are you saying this because we're friends, and now that you know me you're sorry you behaved like that? Or are you genuinely sorry you treated another human being like shit?"

"Oh." Jess's brow wrinkled. "I've never thought about that. Maybe both? If I'd never seen you again, I don't know if I'd have reevaluated my behavior, but if I had thought about it, I would've regretted it. I was full of anger and frustration and poured it out over everyone who crossed my path. That's not who I want to be." As she talked, the grip on Lena's thumb tightened until it was almost painful. "What I do know is I'm genuinely sorry."

"Okay. Apology accepted." Lena smiled and softly squeezed the hand that held hers. Maybe she lingered longer than was strictly necessary to convey the message, but the warm flesh under her fingers felt right.

Relief softened Jess's features as the tension receded. A tentative smile bloomed on her lips.

Her very attractive lips. Considerate and charming Jess was a serious distraction.

Lena wiggled her thumb in Jess's grasp. "Do you think it's stopped bleeding?"

"Impatient?" Grinning, Jess unwrapped the thumb and inspected it for a second. When no blood welled up, she blew over it. "There. All better now."

The warm air tingled on her skin, but Lena chose to ignore it. "You're going to be a great mom. But what's your professional opinion, Doctor? Will I live?"

Jess groaned. "I guess I've earned the teasing. Yes, you'll live, at least until you've sampled my cooking skills." She pointed at the bucket she'd dropped when she'd raced over to Lena. Blackberries had spilled everywhere. "And if you keep on teasing me, you'll get the same as I cook every evening, a bottle of lukewarm formula."

Chapter Seventeen

A CAR HONKED TWICE, AND the motor roared as it overtook Jess's BMW on the highway. She checked her speedometer. Yeah, okay, she was driving just under limit, but that was no reason to behave like an idiot. She opened her mouth to let everyone know in explicit terms what she thought about guys like that when Lena chuckled next to her.

"I hope the five minutes he gains will be worth the anger eating at him."

Jess snapped her mouth shut. Right. If she cursed now, she wouldn't be any better. And hadn't she decided to let go of her anger? She glanced back at Ella. Still sleeping. That girl really liked to be moved around, whether in a car or a stroller.

At the sight of her daughter peacefully enjoying the ride, Jess's anger evaporated as fast as it had risen. Lena was right; it wasn't worth it. She drove on until they reached the café, not caring how slow she was.

"If you go down this alley, you can park at the back entrance. No one will be here today." Lena pointed to a narrow road.

Jess maneuvered her BMW right, hoping her mirrors survived the walls on both sides. A few seconds later, they arrived at the parking space for the café that seemed big enough for a couple of vans. She reversed the car into it to give them better access to the trunk.

"I'll unlock the door. If you want, you can wait inside with Ella while I unload everything." Lena jumped out of the car and went to the large metal door. The blue paint was sun-bleached and flaky, but the area was clean, and the little patch of green next to the concrete was free of weeds.

Since Ella was still sleeping, Jess decided to help with the boxes before moving her. They had bought small preserving jars and an obscenely large bag of sugar. The buckets of fruit and berries rested in the back of the trunk, and the scent enveloped Jess as she opened the lid. It conjured up a picture of Lena, with adorably stained blue lips, fingers, and even a colored strand of hair. Her own lips prickled at the memory of the taste of the berries, and her mind involuntarily leapt to the tart taste of the wine and the kiss.

The creak of the door pulled her out of her thoughts. She stacked three of the boxes on top of each other and carried them inside, which may have been a bit ambitious.

"Where do you want me to put them?" Jess fought to keep the strain from her voice. No need to embarrass herself even more in front of Lena, who had seen enough of her weakness in recent weeks.

"Next to the dishwasher, over there."

Good thing she pointed it out. It didn't look like any dishwasher she'd seen before. Jess set the boxes on the counter and took a shaky breath. Under the pretense of looking more closely at the stainless steel contraption, she stretched her back. "Why do you want to clean them? They're brand new."

"I always run them through a special cleaning and sterilizing cycle. You never know how they've been stored."

"Good idea." Jess hadn't expected that kind of effort for homemade preserves, but Lena seemed to take her business seriously.

They emptied the trunk in no time, and soon the kitchen was stacked with everything Lena needed. On the last trip, Jess carted the still-sleeping Ella inside, and Lena brought a coarse linen bag.

When Jess placed the carrier on a small wooden table at one end of the room, Ella opened her eyes with an unfocused gaze. Jess leaned closer into Ella's field of vision and whispered, "Sleep on. I'm here."

Ella yawned, blinked twice, then fell back asleep.

"Will it be okay if I use the dishwasher?" Lena tied her hair into a bun and put on an apron.

"Probably." Jess walked over to join her. "I haven't found out what wakes her. Most of the time she sleeps through the most terrible noise, like last week when Mom's neighbor used a chainsaw in the garden. Sometimes a whisper on the wind seems to wake her. We'll give it a try. What can I do to help?"

Lena lifted the biggest bowl Jess had ever seen from a rack and put it in the sink, poured the blackberries into it, and covered them with water.

"You don't need to help. This is how I earn my living, after all. You don't even need to stay. This will take a while." She gestured to the buckets of apples and pears on the counter.

"Haven't we had this discussion before?" Jess rolled her eyes but grinned. She held up her hand to tick off the points she wanted to make with her fingers. "I offered to help; you didn't ask me to. I have nothing else to do but watch my daughter sleep. I'm going crazy inside the house. And I need to practice working more than an hour at a time. You can view it as helping me rehabilitate."

Laughing, Lena handed her another apron. "Okay, okay. Thank you. Do you want to wash the blackberries or peel the apples and pears? Or stack the jars into the dishwasher?"

Jess groaned as she put the apron on. "We need to peel them all ourselves? Isn't there a fancy machine we can use?"

"No, that's why it'll take all day. Still willing to help?" Lena's eyes twinkled with mischief.

Jess had never enjoyed cooking or the preparations that came with it, but she actually looked forward to spending an afternoon in this kitchen in Lena's company. "Let me start the dishwasher. Maybe you'll have finished most of the apples by the time I'm done."

"You wish." Lena walked over to her. "Let me show you how this works."

By the time Jess had stacked everything in the large plastic racks and started the wash cycle, Lena had peeled a surprisingly large number, but more than enough apples were left for her. She checked on Ella to see if she minded the noise, but she was still out.

Smiling, Lena looked up and beckoned Jess over without stopping her peeling. Her hands flew over the apple, removing the complete skin in one go. Circular strips fell to the counter, releasing a fresh, tart aroma. After she finished peeling, Lena threw the apple into a pot of water where it bobbed on the surface.

"Lemon water. To avoid brown stains."

"Clever. Citric acid is an antioxidant."

"If you say so. I only know that my grandma taught me what she learned from her mother."

"Seems like sound advice." Jess smiled and held her hand out. "Can I give it a try?"

"Sure. Peel what you can easily reach, and don't worry about the area around the stem. We'll cut that out later."

Jess took the peeler and tried to remember how Lena had held it. She didn't want to admit she'd never done this before. Her first attempt got stuck in the apple after an inch and removed a short and uneven piece of skin. She adjusted the angle and tried again. A few more inches before she got stuck this time. It shouldn't be so difficult—people all over the world did this every day! But with Lena's gaze resting on her, heat crawled from Jess's neck to her cheeks.

"May I?" Lena reached out but didn't touch.

Jess looked up, expecting a smirk or frown, but Lena smiled encouragingly. Jess wanted to hand the peeler over, but Lena pressed her hand around Jess's and angled the tool into the right position. When their fingers touched, a light tingling ran up Jess's arm again. Oh great, the sparks were back while they played with sharp instruments. She needed to be careful she wasn't the one bleeding today.

Lena quickly let go. "Try it again."

Her voice was hoarse and low, and it had the same effect as her touch. Jess had to take a calming breath before she trusted her hands to move without trembling. To her surprise, she managed to almost peel the complete apple before she lost the correct angle again.

"Good job. You'll get the hang of it soon after a couple more apples." Lena stepped back and opened a drawer to get another peeler.

"A couple or a dozen, but who's counting?" Jess needed to lighten the mood. The repeated surges of tingling and heat confused her. Since when did women affect her like this, so uncontrollably? Usually she was the one who seduced and unnerved her partner, rarely the other way around. A change of topic was in order. "Did you do a lot of cooking with your grandma?"

Lena took her place on the other side of the pot. "I always helped—peeling, cutting, stirring. Grandpa often worked late shifts, and we spent most of our evenings in the kitchen, preparing meals for the next day or preserving food. Grandma grew up in a rural region without much money and believed in preparing for the worst, even though they both had stable enough incomes and a supermarket on the corner."

Chris Zett

"Are you using her recipes?" Jess threw her apple into the pot and picked another. She wasn't as fast as Lena, but she was slowly getting the hang of it.

"Not really." Lena laughed. "She believed in the magic of sugar and thought her preserves should last at least fifty years, just in case another war started or something. I cut a lot of sugar from the recipes and use more apples to thicken the preserves. They're a natural source of pectin. But I learned the basics from her."

Lena's voice was soft and warm like a summer evening when she talked about her grandmother. Her love for her family was obvious. Yet she seldom mentioned her mother, and Jess was reluctant to ask. From the bits and pieces she had mentioned, Jess got the impression Lena hadn't grown up with her. And now she was in prison, but Lena hadn't said for how long. Jess curbed her curiosity, not wanting to dampen the mood. Lena would tell her when she was ready.

Working side by side, they'd soon worked through the pile of apples while Lena talked vividly about her grandma and their favorite meals. Jess could picture her as a kid sitting at the kitchen table, talking about her day.

Would Jess share that with Ella when she got older? Who would talk to Ella while she was in the hospital? Going back to twelve- to fourteen-hour days didn't sound so appealing when she thought of that.

"Can you finish peeling the rest? I'll cut them and start cooking the first batch." Lena took out a cutting board and one of those chef's knives Jess associated more with crime TV shows than real cooking.

She shuddered at the thought of the knife coming close to her hands. "Be careful. My sewing skills are rusty."

"Don't worry. It's not my first time." Lena expertly used the knife, turning the apples into chunks faster than Jess would have thought possible. "Could you wash the mint, please?"

"Mint? Didn't you want to do blackberry jam?" Jess looked around for the herbs.

"I brought it from Maggie's garden." Lena pointed to the linen bag. "And I'm always adding something special. It's what makes my preserves different from what you can get at the supermarket."

"What are your most popular flavors?"

"Strawberry-jalapeño and apricot-vanilla-Earl Grey tea. But I have enough of those still in storage. And I vary my preserves with the season.

160

In the fall and winter, I sell a lot of chutneys too. Today we start with blackberry-mint-apple, and later we'll do some rosemary-pear-blackberry."

Jess took the bundle of mint—complete with stalks and leaves—from the bag and washed it. "I only ever buy strawberry or blueberry jam. The most exotic one might have been a combination with vanilla. I guess I'm a bit boring." She shook out the herbs and placed them next to Lena's cutting board.

Without glancing at Jess, Lena took the mint, removed the stalks, and cut the leaves into fine strips. "Oh, there's nothing wrong with those flavors, but not everyone is always into vanilla. Sometimes it's fun to add something spicier."

Heat shot through Jess and dried her mouth as if she had taken a bite of the jalapeño Lena had been talking about. Was Lena flirting with her or just casually throwing out statements Jess's reawakening libido was latching onto?

"Want me to rinse the blackberries?" Maybe submerging her hands in cold water would douse the simmering in other parts of her body.

Lena couldn't help watching Jess hasten away. Her expression when Lena had teased her was too funny. With difficulty, Lena averted her gaze and put one of the huge stainless steel pots on the stove.

She should stop doing that. Her excuse was she liked to rattle the composure of the too-stern, too-tense woman she'd met a few weeks ago to get back at her for her arrogant behavior and remove the mask for a few seconds. But since they'd become friends, that wasn't necessary anymore. Jess had let her in and offered her more than a passing glimpse beneath the surface. And she wasn't even thinking of the kiss that had elevated their relationship to another level. Or rather, balanced it precariously on some precipice. So why was she still doing it? Did she want to tip into more-than-friends territory?

With a sigh, Lena grabbed the kitchen scale, weighed the apples, and placed them in the pot. After a quick calculation, she added some sugar and closed the lid, then went to see how Jess was doing.

She had removed the leaves and debris floating on the water and was now placing the blackberries in a sieve. Carefully, by hand. Her brows wrinkled, and she bit her lip in concentration as she sifted through, looking for spoiled berries.

Lena stepped next to her to wash her hands in the other sink.

"How am I doing, chef?" Jess grinned. "Everything up to your standards?"

"Fine. Kitchen helper could be a new career for you." Lena dried her hands on a clean towel. "Would you mind weighing them for me? I need to look at my notes to see how much I used last time."

"Sure."

Jess continued sorting the berries as Lena retrieved a notebook and pen from her backpack. She glanced at Ella, who still slept soundly. "You're lucky she loves to sleep so much. How is it at night?"

"In the beginning, when I was home with her alone, I had the feeling she never slept at all. Whenever I closed my eyes for a second, she opened hers and cried. But now she seems to be in a more relaxed phase. I'm hoping it will last a while." Jess finished washing the blackberries and poured half of them into the bowl. "How much do you need?"

Lena skimmed through the book until she found the right page. She glanced at the scale. "Add another handful. That should be fine."

Turning her head to look at Lena, Jess raised one eyebrow. "Another handful? What kind of measuring system is that?"

"My grandma's. She always cooked and baked with handfuls and pinches. Adding this and that until her gut said it was right. I try to at least stick to approximately the same ratios every time I reproduce a recipe."

"Well, it's your name on the jam. As a scientist, this is very unsettling for me." Jess exaggeratedly shuddered, then added a handful of blackberries to the bowl. "How does your gut feel now?"

"Perfect." Chuckling, Lena opened the pot to stir the apples. They had started to break down, and a heavenly aroma rose up in the steam. "You can add the blackberries now."

"Mmmh."

Jess was leaning over her shoulder, and her moan vibrated on the sensitive skin behind Lena's ear.

The wooded spoon fell from her hand.

Hot applesauce splashed upward.

Lena jumped back and collided with Jess, who steadied her with one arm around her waist.

"Careful," Jess mumbled, reaching over to retrieve the spoon with her free hand. "Don't burn yourself."

Even though no drop of the hot liquid had touched Lena's skin, it might be too late for the warning.

Jess let go to pour the blackberries into the pot. "And now?"

"Now we wait. Close the lid and let it simmer." Would that work for their attraction too? If she waited long enough, would the different ingredients mix well enough to turn into something new, something delicious?

Lena stepped away. *Don't be silly.* That had never worked for her. Each and every one of her previous romantic affairs had turned inedible after stewing too long. She didn't have the time and energy to invest in a girlfriend as long as her debt was piled up over her head and she needed every second of her day to keep from being buried alive.

And she was here to work today, not to flirt. She reached for her notebook again. "I'll note the amounts for next time."

Adding the numbers didn't take long enough to gain the emotional distance she needed, so she stalled by sketching a few blackberries next to it.

Jess had gone to the far side of the room and was talking to Ella in that low, comforting tone. Ella made some bubbly noises in response to whatever her mother mumbled.

"Is it okay to heat some formula here?" Jess straightened and looked over to Lena.

"Sure. No problem." Lena filled a smaller pot with water and put it on the stove to heat.

Jess wandered over to her, carrying Ella on one arm and her baby bag in the other. "Would you mind holding her for a second?"

"Mind?" Lena eagerly reached for Ella and cradled her in her arms. "I'd love it. Hi, cutie." She smiled.

To her delight, Ella answered with an adorable smile of her own.

"Did you see that? She's smiling!"

Jess transferred the formula to a bottle and placed it in the water. "She knows she's in good hands. Return her if you need to work on something again."

"The pears can wait."

Jess's gaze fell on the open book Lena had been working on. "May I look at the other recipes?"

"Sure."

Jess skimmed a few pages, then stopped at a sketch Lena had done for one of her preserve labels and whistled. "Did you draw this? This is amazing."

"Um, yeah. I was just testing out some ideas for my labels."

"Wait, you do your own labels? I thought you hired a designer or got them off the internet or something."

"No, I could never afford a designer."

"And you certainly don't need one. They look professional. You should do this for a living."

"Thanks, but...doing it for a living involves investing time and money I don't have right now. I have no formal education. And sketching is something I can always do as a hobby." Lena hoped Jess would let it go. She was happy right now to have Ella in her arms and didn't want to taint the moment with thoughts about her financial situation.

Jess regarded her skeptically but accepted her answer and shifted her attention back to the warming formula. She removed the bottle and dried it on a towel. "Do you want to feed her again?"

Lena swallowed and hoped her voice wouldn't break. "Yeah. I'd love to."

Ella grabbed a strand of her hair and clutched it in her tiny fist. Her eyes were so open and trusting. To her, Lena was a safe human, providing warm arms to hold her, a soft voice to calm her, and the promise of milk to feed her. Neither her history nor her present problems were important.

Yesterday she had struggled to stay in the moment as memories of feeding Tammy for the first time rose. Tammy had been out of the hospital for a week and was only supposed to get formula when their mom wasn't home. But their mom had been drinking and was sleeping it off, oblivious to Tammy's crying. Lena had prepared the formula, meticulously following the instructions on the package. She'd babysat neighborhood kids before, but never in her seventeen years had she needed to give anyone the bottle. She'd been a nervous wreck, but the second Tammy took her first sip and smacked her lips, she'd lost her heart. And like all meaningful relationships in her life, even that simple bond with her sister hadn't lasted. In the eyes of their mother and Tammy's father, she'd only been the babysitter. Tammy's father had made that clear, even when Lena had distanced herself from her mother and her destructive behavior years later. When her sister was taken from her, she'd lost a part of her heart she could never get back

She bowed her head over Ella and breathed in her fresh baby scent. Nothing was as calming. Swallowing her self-pity, Lena blew a raspberry on Ella's stomach and looked up again.

Jess didn't seem to have noticed anything. She tested the bottle against the skin on her arm. "Perfect." She held it out to Lena.

"Thanks." Lena concentrated on the baby in front of her. She wasn't Tammy but Ella, a wonderful, tiny person. They'd forge their own connection, as long as she got the chance to be part of her life. "Hi, Ella, I've got something for you."

╬╬╬╬╬╬

Wednesday afternoon, Jess returned from her midday walk to excited voices coming from somewhere on the first floor. She removed Ella from the stroller, hoisted her on her hip, and searched for her mom and Lena. She found them in the large formal dining room at the table for twelve.

Her mom looked up from the papers she and Lena were huddled over. "How are my girls?"

"Mom." Jess rolled her eyes. "Don't call me that."

Grinning, she pushed her reading glasses up into her gray locks. "Just wait and see when Ella's older if you can stop calling her your little girl. See, at least I omitted the little."

Jess groaned and barely stopped herself from stomping her foot. Okay, if she wanted to protest being called a girl, she shouldn't behave like an adolescent. But her mom knew how to push her buttons.

"Here, fuss over your granddaughter." She passed Ella on and smiled as her mom's attention fixated on the baby.

Jess walked over to Lena, who was watching their interaction with a grin. "What are you working on?"

"We're sorting her notes and working on an outline." Lena's eyes sparkled as she gestured at the stacks of paper. "Maggie has several years' worth of notes and so many ideas."

165

Pages full of her mom's handwriting were strewn over the length of the oversized table, interspersed with crude drawings of what Jess guessed to be parts of plants. Sticky notes in several colors were stuck to them, labeled in Lena's neat hand. Someone had hung a giant piece of paper to her great-grandmother's china cabinet, and the same colorful sticky notes, with lines drawn between them, adorned it in a pattern that hopefully meant more to Lena than to her.

"You mean you're fighting the chaos? My mom has brought many assistants to tears with her unscientific approach." Jess grinned as she remembered discussions between her parents at this very dinner table about her mom's work style. Her father had been like Jess: meticulous, organized, and linear. Her mother believed in creativity, chaos, and the organic growth of ideas. But seeing as she'd retired as a respected professor after a long career at the university, it must have worked for her.

"I can't judge the scientific content of the book, but I'm assisting her in visualizing with a mind map, and we're color coding the different topics." Lena pointed from the stacks of papers to the sticky notes. "As soon as she's decided what goes into the book, I'll start typing up the notes. It's so exciting to learn more about what's growing outside right under our noses." Her cheeks were flushed, and she had leaned forward as she spoke, into Jess's personal space.

Close enough that her scent—fresh soap with a hint of mint—invaded Jess's senses and sent her thoughts scattering. Holding her breath, she stepped over to the mind map.

The longer Jess regarded it, the more she could see the logical structure. Amazing. Lena not only tolerated working with her mom, she actually seemed to like it. And was good at it.

A phone beeped, and Lena sighed.

Jess turned around.

As Lena typed, the enthusiasm in her expression dimmed as if someone had snuffed out a candle. Her shoulders drooped, and she slowly walked to the door that led into the kitchen. "Maggie?"

"Yes, dear?" her mom answered from the next room.

"I'm sorry to bother you, but could you assist me with a massage client tonight at seven?"

"Sure."

"No, wait. Don't you and Ella have plans with Clarissa?" Jess asked, knowing her mother was looking forward to showing off her grandchild. "I can do it."

From her position at the door, Lena looked at Jess with wide eyes. To make matters worse, her mom appeared behind Lena, mirroring her expression.

Why were they staring? She was offering because her mom hadn't seen her friend in a while. Resisting the urge to squirm, Jess squared her shoulders. "It's not as if I haven't done it before. It's just a massage."

As soon as she said it, a wave of heat slapped her in the face as if she left an air-conditioned hotel in the middle of a southern summer. It wasn't just a massage. Maybe for Lena, who was doing her job. But for Jess it would be an exercise in self-control. Lena's touch had excited her even before they had kissed. Maybe this was a bad idea. Maybe she should take back her offer. Maybe—

"Oh, thank you." Lena's grateful smile lit up her face, and Jess knew she was lost.

"Wonderful idea. But you need to change her diaper before I can show her off." Her mom handed Ella over with a grin.

Jess pasted a light smile on her face she didn't feel at all. "I'll let you two get back to your work, and I'll take a nap with Ella."

Not that she would be able to relax for a second, but at least she could work out a strategy. She worked in a profession that included touching semi-naked people all the time, and she'd never once felt even a twinge of arousal. So if she was assisting Lena at her work, she'd approach it exactly the way she approached her own work.

And she had only three hours to get in the right frame of mind.

Chapter Eighteen

LENA TRAILED BOTH HANDS DOWN Jess's back, then pulled up the towel to cover her. After an hour of oiling skin, kneading muscles, and pressing trigger points, Jess was still as stiff and full of knots as the pines at the beach house. Lena had tried every trick in her book, but it still hadn't been enough to get Jess to relax. She would never have accepted Jess's offer if she had known how uncomfortable the experience would be for her.

Remembering her client, she suppressed a sigh and pasted on a smile. "Never forget a sheet or towel after the massage. Unless you find another method of keeping warm together."

Patty giggled, as she'd been doing all evening. Maybe Jess hadn't been able to relax with that sound. "Thank you, Lena. And you too." She awkwardly patted Jess's back. "I'll go and wash my hands and change."

Lena's fingers itched to stroke through Jess's ruffled hair, but that would be highly inappropriate. She went to the head of the table and squatted down to eye level instead. "Thank you. Everything okay?"

Jess lifted her head out of the headrest and met Lena's gaze. "Sure. Everything is perfect." But her eyes were the color of a stormy sea, and tiny lines showing her tension belied the tone.

Patty's giggles announced she finished dressing, and Lena rose to show her out. She couldn't wait to return to Jess and see if she could help her lose some of that tension.

When she came back into the room, Jess had crossed her arms under her head to raise her upper body a little. "Your patience is amazing."

"Just because I showed her the same techniques about a million times? Was it too uncomfortable?" She picked up a towel that had fallen to the floor and folded it. Not that it needed folding since it was going to be washed, but at least it kept her gaze off Jess's shoulders. Her toned, bare shoulders that gleamed golden in the candlelight.

"No, it was okay. But I hope for the sake of her partner she'll be a bit more active when she massages them. Sometimes her touch didn't even register with me." She snorted. "And the constant giggling."

"She was nervous. It's not every day you get to touch a naked stranger."

Jess smiled. "You're too nice. Are you nervous when you teach these courses?"

"Nope." That wasn't a lie. Normally, she wasn't. But today she had been nervous, just not for the reasons Jess suggested. It had thrown her that Jess *wasn't* a stranger. She could handle touching random people; that did nothing to her. But knowing the woman on the table was the woman who had kissed her passionately three nights ago was something completely different. And that was why she should go get the towels from the bathroom and start the washing machine to give Jess time to get up and get dressed.

Instead, she placed the folded towel on the small table and stepped closer. "I'm sorry the massage wasn't relaxing. Let me make it up to you." She held up the bottle of massage oil and raised her eyebrows.

Something flickered in Jess's eyes. Hesitation? Attraction? The reflection of the candlelight?

Whatever it was, it captivated Lena and filled her with sparkling energy she couldn't wait to share with Jess.

With a decisive nod, Jess lowered her head and returned her arms to her sides under the towel covering her.

Lena took her position at Jess's side and slowly removed the towel. Flawless skin hid the coiled muscles she knew she'd find. "Whenever you want me to stop, tell me." She poured a generous portion of the massage oil into her left hand and put the bottle away.

Then, as the oil warmed in her hand and the scent of jasmine and orange rose, she trickled it onto Jess's spine. Drop by drop, she moved from between her shoulder blades to the slight dip in her lower back. Goosebumps followed.

"Too cold?" Lena placed her free hand on Jess's lower back. The skin was warm beneath her palm. And incredibly soft. But she didn't want to think about that now.

"No." Jess's voice was muffled by the headrest, and the muscles vibrated beneath Lena's touch.

With long strokes along Jess's spine, over her shoulder blades, and back down again, Lena distributed the oil and warmed both her hands and Jess's skin.

The muscles stiffened under her fingers, but after a few repetitions, Jess let go and Lena was able to separate the problematic areas from the general tension. The area between her shoulder blades and neck called for Lena's attention. Her focus was on the tight cords and hard knots beneath her fingers as she called up every technique she'd ever learned to soften them.

Whenever an area turned from rocks to butter, she moved on to the next and the next. With every passing minute, pride in her accomplishments rose. She could do this, absolutely professionally, just to help Jess relax. Skin was just skin, and the woman under her fingertips was just muscles and tendons.

She stroked the thumb and forefinger of her right hand upward, one on each side of the spine, along Jess's slender neck until she reached the hairline. The short hair had darkened and curled in the warm room. Lena spread her hand and slipped it into those silky strands. Her fingertips scratched along Jess's scalp.

Jess moaned, and the vibration sent tingles up Lena's arm.

Biting her lip to stifle her own sounds, Lena moved her hand through the hair again. Her knees weakened when Jess reacted. It wasn't professional in the least, but she couldn't resist. She added her other hand and gently massaged Jess's scalp, eliciting even more sounds and vibrations.

The skin behind Jess's ear was deliciously soft. Lena caressed the area with the tip of her forefinger, then moved to her earlobe. Barely palpable indentations hinted at old piercings.

Jess slightly tilted her head as if offering herself. So sexy.

And Lena wanted to continue her exploration, add lips to fingers, press herself to Jess's back, and get lost in the sensual gliding of her body over Jess's.

And that's why she didn't. Jess had consented to a massage, not to a seduction. She'd made it clear that no matter the attraction that flared between them, she wasn't interested in pursuing anything physical.

Neither was Lena—that much she knew intellectually. But right now, with the scent of jasmine, orange, and Jess tingling in her nose, with one hand curled in Jess's hair and the other playing with her ear, she couldn't remember why.

With her last reserve of willpower and reason, she pulled back. "I'm sorry." She straightened and pulled up the towel, careful not to touch Jess again. "I'll let you get dressed."

She fled to the bathroom and washed her hands in cold water, as cold as it could get. And washed her face. And wished she could douse her head in it too.

What the fuck had just happened? During the first massage, Jess had controlled her reactions. Not that the feeble touch of what's-her-name had done anything for her. But now?

Now she had melted right through the table under Lena's skilled hands. Not only had her muscles lost the tension they'd been carrying for days, but other parts of her body had reacted too. A totally inappropriate burning sensation had started low in her middle, and every stroke had fanned the flames. And when Lena had touched her hair, her ear... Had that been part of a regular massage? It had felt more like a caress. She shivered at the thought.

She wasn't used to being on the receiving end of such affection. Or seduction? In the past she'd more often than not been the one to initiate physical contact. And often it had been enough to please her partner, to know she was giving something special—she hadn't needed anything in return.

She rolled to her side on the narrow table and sat up. Her feet got tangled in the towel as she tried to remain covered, and she quickly sorted her legs and pulled the white cotton over her chest before Lena returned. Lena didn't need to see her soft belly and breasts that still felt a size or two too large. Not that she herself wasn't able to appreciate the attraction of large breasts or the feminine swell of a belly—but preferably on other women. It just didn't feel like her body anymore.

Who cares? Get a grip and get dressed. She stood, expecting her knees to buckle. But they held, and the energy running through her was more than enough to keep her upright and help her move to the bathroom, where she'd left her clothes. The towel tucked tightly around her, she opened the door and froze.

Lena was in the bathroom, clutching the sink. She looked at Jess with wide eyes, and her hair was tousled as if she'd been running her hands through it.

Another wave of energy ran through Jess, and her fingertips itched with the urge to bury her hands in Lena's hair, doing what Lena had done to her. She wanted to take charge, to hear Lena moan and whimper, see her squirm, affect her the way she had affected Jess.

Wordlessly, she stepped into the bathroom and cupped Lena's face with one hand, holding her gaze. Slowly she moved forward, inch by inch, until their breaths mingled, giving Lena time to protest or draw back.

But she didn't. Lena's eyelids fluttered, but she didn't close them. Her pupils dilated and her breathing quickened.

With a smile, Jess leaned in to kiss her, to overwhelm her with every skill she had, to show Lena she wasn't the one in charge.

Their lips met in a hard kiss, all passion and heat and tongues. For a fleeting moment, Jess wondered why their teeth didn't clash. But they fit perfectly, kissing as if they'd done it a thousand times before.

Soon, it wasn't enough. She needed to get closer and stepped between Lena's legs, pushing her back against the sink. One hand cradled Lena's head, and the other found its way around Lena's waist to the small of her back, pressing her even closer. Sneaked under her skintight T-shirt. Stroked silken skin.

A loud moan resonated through their kiss.

Jess tore back, gasping for air. Had she moaned? Or Lena?

Who the fuck cared?

She leaned in again, this time kissing and licking her way in a line from Lena's mouth to her neck.

Lena's pulse raced under her lips, and her skin burned as if with fever. Her hands clutched Jess's shoulders and pulled her even tighter.

Through the thin layers of towel and T-shirt, their breasts touched. Jess's nipples hardened at the friction. Her legs shook as arousal shot from the hard points directly to her clit.

It had been so long, so damned fucking long since she'd felt this way.

And she wanted more. More friction, more closeness, more skin. More Lena.

She kissed her way along the line of Lena's jaw to her earlobe.

Tilting her head to the side, Lena offered herself for easy access.

How was it even possible skin was so soft? Jess nibbled on the earlobe, and when Lena moaned, she sucked it into her mouth.

Lena's fingers dug into Jess's shoulders as if they were the only thing holding her up. She squirmed, and their bodies touched all along their lengths.

"I want to…" Unsure what she really wanted, Jess kissed the area behind Lena's ear to buy time. She searched for the spot that had melted her insides into puddles when Lena had caressed her.

When she found it, Lena sucked in a deep breath. "Yes." Her voice was husky and low.

Jess leaned back to look into her eyes. As much as she wanted this, she needed to know they were on the same page. "I can't offer you anything but sex."

She found nothing but arousal and honesty in Lena's gaze. Her eyes were clear and had taken on the shade of fresh leaves in spring.

"Sex." Lena nodded, and an impish grin spread on her lips. "And fun. I want that too. I'm not expecting anything else, and I can't offer more myself."

"Fun. Perfect." And it would have been but for the tiny seed of disappointment that stirred in Jess's belly. She stomped on it before it could take root. Sex, fun, no strings—that was what she wanted. And tonight, she'd take it. "Bedroom?"

Lena trailed her hand down Jess's left arm and took her hand. "Shouldn't we talk about risks?"

Oh. As a doctor, this should have probably occurred to her without prompting. "Sorry, yeah. It's been a while since…" Jess swallowed. Lena didn't need to know that right now. "I was tested for everything under the sun during my pregnancy."

"I've been tested too. It's been a while too for me." Lena's hand was warm and steady in hers. "Anything else we need to talk about?"

When Jess shook her head, Lena led her the few steps to the small bedroom, still holding her hand. It was oddly intimate, and the flickering candlelight in the living room enhanced the impression.

The queen-size bed was neatly made, and the nightstand held only a notebook, a few pens, and a small lamp. Lena reached for it.

Before she could switch it on, Jess pressed her hand. "Don't." She closed the door with a kick of her foot. In the sudden darkness, all she could use for orientation was their joined hands.

Jess stepped closer until she stood in front of Lena. Hot air caressed her lips. She leaned in but held herself back before they touched. It wasn't time for a kiss.

A moan escaped Lena, and she reached with both hands for Jess's waist.

Oh, no, not yet. Jess caught her hands and led them back to Lena's side, then reached for the hem of her T-shirt. Lena didn't protest as Jess pulled it up inch by inch. Jess brushed against the bare skin of her abdomen with the heels of both hands, eliciting a gasp from Lena. As she reached Lena's bra, Jess steered her hands outward, skimming the soft cotton. She so wanted to explore the tantalizing curves. *Patience.*

Lena gasped and squirmed. Did she press closer?

"Patience," Jess repeated aloud. She almost didn't understand her own hoarse whisper.

But Lena stilled and took a deep breath, offering herself to Jess's exploration.

Suppressing a groan, Jess swiftly pulled Lena's shirt over her head and dropped it on the floor. The next thing that needed to go was her yoga pants. Jess hooked both thumbs into the waistband and pulled. She followed them downward and helped to free first one foot, then the other from the tight cuffs around the ankles. On her way up, she ran both her hands along the outside of Lena's legs.

The lean muscles were full of tension. The power in those legs was so sexy. The vision of them wrapped around Jess's waist flashed through her mind, and she lost her balance. Her grip tightened around Lena's ass to steady herself before she fell with her face in Lena's lap.

The musky scent of Lena's arousal shot directly to some primal part of her brain. Jess groaned and pulled down Lena's panties, not even caring what fabric or cut they were. They needed to be gone.

Jess stood again, this time fast and with a goal in mind. She reached with both hands behind Lena's back, unhooked her bra with only minimal fumbling, and removed it.

"Lie down." She swallowed twice, then removed the towel that was still tucked around her.

Her eyes had adjusted to the darkness, and the minimal light of the moon through the window was enough to see gray shapes.

Lena was sprawled on the bed on her back, her upper body raised on her elbows. Could she see Jess's body? Or her silhouette? She pushed the thought away. That didn't matter. It was only sex, and she was in charge.

She sat next to Lena on the bed. With her right hand, she trailed the feminine curve of waist to abdomen. Muscles tightened beneath her fingers, and for a second, she regretted she couldn't see details. She stopped the journey of her hand on Lena's sternum. "Lie down." This time she whispered.

When Lena lowered her upper body to the mattress, Jess continued her exploration. Up, past the sexy indentation of her collarbone to her neck. Lena tipped her head back and offered everything to Jess.

The show of trust made Jess's head swim. She stretched out on her side, one arm still free to move, to touch, to finally reach for Lena's curves.

"Yes." Lena arched into her touch as Jess cupped her breast. "More."

Oh, yes. Jess completely agreed. She wanted more too, and now was the time to take it. She explored the pliable flesh with her fingers, and as she grazed the areola, Lena's nipple hardened. Jess flicked her thumb over it.

Lena moaned and shifted onto her side, pressing her breast against Jess's hand.

Lowering her head, Jess kissed the other breast and licked until that nipple hardened too. She loved the swift reaction and rained kisses on the swell of the breast while she kneaded the tip between her thumb and forefinger. She got lost in the sensual feel of the soft tissue beneath her fingers and the salty taste of Lena's skin on her tongue. Shivers ran up and down her spine.

Wait. She stiffened. Not shivers. Lena's hand.

Lena's hand that should have been on the mattress and not on her.

Obviously, her discomfort showed because Lena stopped. "What's wrong?"

To her surprise, everything felt very right, even Lena's unplanned touch. At least on her back; she still wasn't so sure if she'd trust her with other areas of her body. "Nothing."

She relaxed, and it must have worked because Lena continued her caress with one hand. Unlike the massage earlier, her touch was light, like a breeze cooling sun-kissed skin. Her other hand wandered higher and tangled in Jess's hair, pressing Jess's head back to her breast.

It was as if those fingers were charged with electricity. Sparks ran down Jess's scalp to her neck. She didn't resist the directions but only because she wanted it too. Not because she melted again, this time not into the massage table but into Lena. Into her body, soft and firm, curvy and lean, and perfectly responsive beneath Jess.

Jess continued to kiss and suck and nibble and lick every inch of Lena's breasts until they were both out of breath. Then she kissed her way down, over her flat abdomen, and let her hands explore the shape of Lena's hips.

"Jess..." Lena's hands gripped her head, either in encouragement or restraint.

The tug wasn't painful, but it was enough to stop her. She looked up, even though she couldn't make out Lena's face. "Let me taste you." Jess's mouth watered at the thought.

Lena moaned, and the sound vibrated in her belly underneath Jess. "But I haven't prepared. I didn't expect..."

"Nothing to prepare. At least not for me." Slowly, Jess stroked with one finger from the curve of Lena's hipbone to her middle until she reached curls already softened by wetness. "Please."

"Oh, yes." Lena released the hold on her head but kept her fingers loosely tangled in Jess's hair.

That was all the encouragement Jess needed. She swiftly slid downward, ignoring the sensual glide of smooth skin against her own. If she gave in and explored the sensation, she'd lose her grip on her own arousal and give up control.

The musky scent of Lena's excitement flooded her nostrils, and she breathed in deeply. It had been so very long, but had it ever been so amazing? She couldn't remember and didn't care. The desire to taste overwhelmed her, and she inserted herself between Lena's legs and gently pushed them farther apart with her shoulders. She parted the silky curls and slid her tongue all along Lena's folds to her opening.

Heart Failure

Again, Lena moaned deeply, and the muscles in her thighs tensed. Feeling their power up close, around her shoulders, was even better than the fantasy Jess had of them wrapping around her waist.

With the next swipe of her tongue, Jess explored the hard bud of Lena's clit, and she stopped thinking and analyzing. Lena's sounds and movements and the renewed grip in Jess's hair were enough to guide her. For once, she didn't need a plan. She just followed her instincts. Her only goal was to heighten Lena's pleasure until she panted and squirmed and pressed herself against Jess's mouth with one last, drawn-out moan.

Afterward, Jess rested her head on Lena's abdomen to catch her breath and gather her wits. Only now did she become aware of the aching pulse between her own legs. She reached down with her hand to take care of her need. Already close to the edge, it just took a couple of strokes to climax. She bit her lip to contain a moan.

The fingers running lazily through her hair stilled. "Jess?" The question behind the whispered word was painfully obvious.

Don't you want me to touch you? Lena's voice echoed in her mind as if she had spoken aloud.

Jess's cheeks burned, and she was glad of the darkness to hide her blush. As she had never been one to play dumb, she rolled onto her side with a sigh and scooted upward until she lay next to Lena, facing her. "I... Usually..." She valued directness and honesty, but this wasn't something she had much experience in talking about. The last few women had been only too happy to follow Jess's lead. "You don't need to... It's better this way. I love giving pleasure." That wasn't the whole truth, of course. With the right partner, Jess enjoyed being touched and giving up control. But it had been ages since she'd known someone so well to trust her. And she wouldn't enjoy it tonight, with her soft body that had lost all attractiveness.

A featherlight touch on her cheek took Jess by surprise, but she managed not to flinch.

"Thank you for explaining. I enjoy giving too, very much so, but this is supposed to be fun for both of us. If you don't want to, I respect that." Lena brushed a strand of Jess's hair behind her ear.

What was it with Lena and her hair? The touch drove Jess crazy, and she almost regretted the conversation they'd had. She'd better leave now

177

before the combination of great sex and continued caresses further addled her brain and transformed her into a purring cat.

"Thank you. For everything." She kissed Lena's lips one last time, lightly to avoid further temptation, and rolled over to stand up. "See you tomorrow."

She left the room quickly and closed the door before Lena could catch more than a glimpse of her in the light from the main room.

After she'd dressed, she looked at the closed door of the bedroom with a sigh. The urge to go back and snuggle up next to Lena was strong, chipping away her resolution. Since when did she feel like this after sex?

She blew out the flickering candles and left the garden house.

Now she had to figure out how to sneak in past her mother to shower and change before she retrieved the baby monitor for the night.

For the first time in years, Lena wanted to pull the sheets over her head when her internal alarm clock woke her. Not because the bed was so comfortable, and especially not because it still smelled like sex, but because she didn't want to face Jess.

With a sigh, she stood and went for a quick shower. The massage table and the pile of used towels in the bathroom were visible reminders of yesterday evening's events. Not that she needed any. The pleasant relaxation of her body hadn't yet left her.

The sex had been great. Jess had seemed to know exactly what she liked, and the orgasm had been amazing. But afterward, she'd tossed and turned in her bed. Her mind had been too keyed up to sleep and had run in circles, while her body had wanted nothing more than to bask in the afterglow. And when she'd forced herself to get up to at least blow out the candles, she'd been touched Jess had been so thoughtful as to extinguish them. She'd gone back to bed and thought some more about what had happened—and what hadn't.

She'd have preferred to look at Jess and to touch her, but she'd sensed Jess had her reasons, and that was okay. If they were in a relationship, she'd like to work on that with Jess—if she wanted to—but they weren't. And that was fine. Not only fine, that was what she wanted too. Wasn't it?

Lena wasn't a dreamer who believed in happily ever after just because the princess had tumbled with the maid in the hay. She snorted. Jess would make such a bad princess.

But she'd grown to like Jess as she'd gained a glimpse of the complex and often sweet woman beneath the rough surface. And she wasn't sure in which direction their budding friendship would develop now. Would they awkwardly drift apart, or would they grow even closer? Maybe they'd repeat the sex in a sort of friends-with-benefits arrangement. If that happened, would Lena be able to draw the necessary barrier between friendship and relationship?

She'd had a couple of friends like that before, but never someone who was so linked to all aspects of her life, from her morning tai chi, to her new job with Jess's mother, to her living arrangements. Did she trust Jess not to hurt her? And even worse, for a chance to repeat their evening, did she even care about getting hurt?

She turned the shower to cold and rinsed off the soap. Now wasn't the time for reveries.

The morning was pleasantly mild, even though the sun had just grazed the horizon. A smiling Jess was waiting for her at the edge of the clearing. She greeted Lena as if she didn't have a care in the world, but dark circles under her eyes suggested Lena hadn't been the only one to lose sleep last night.

Ella could have been the reason, but Lena suspected otherwise. She was a little ashamed of how much she enjoyed not being the only one affected. Even though she wanted to talk about the consequences of last night, Lena decided it could wait until after tai chi. They could both use some routine and time to center their thoughts and emotions. She answered the greeting with an easy smile of her own and started her warm-up.

After the session, Jess was the first to speak. "Could we talk for a moment?"

Though the words were a stereotypical introduction to a brush off, Lena didn't get any negative vibes from her. "Sure. Do you want to join me for tea on the porch?" The porch of the garden house was tiny compared to the main house, but they'd have privacy.

Jess nodded and quietly followed Lena. She sat on one of the old Adirondack chairs Lena had found in Maggie's storage shed and stretched out her legs.

Preparing two mugs of green tea didn't take much effort, but Lena kept her thoughts on her actions in the kitchen instead of on the woman waiting outside. When she carried the steaming mugs out, Jess had closed her eyes and tilted her head up toward the morning sun.

Her mouth held a soft half smile, and the usual lines around her eyes and between her brows had vanished.

Lena put the mugs on the small table between the chairs and sat. She twirled the string of the tea bag around her finger, and the bag bobbed up and down in the mug.

Jess opened her eyes before Lena could think of something to say. Today, they shone in the bright blue of the morning sky.

For a second, Lena regretted not negotiating for at least some light last night. She'd have loved to study Jess's expressive eyes during the lovemaking—wait. Sex. She meant during sex. She sat up straighter. "What do you want to talk about?"

Jess mirrored her posture. "I'm sorry I left so abruptly last night, and I wanted to see if we're still okay. I know I said it before…but…" She blushed but didn't look away. The fine lines around her eyes had deepened. "I enjoyed last night, but it can't develop into a relationship. My life is focused on Ella at the moment, on getting my health back, and on going back to work. A relationship isn't in the plan, and I don't want to lead you on." She groaned and rubbed her eyes with both hands. "I'm sorry. This is presumptuous. You haven't given the slightest indication you would expect more, and why would you? I have nothing to offer."

Lena's first instinct was to comfort. She wanted to reach over, hold Jess's hand, and tell her how much she could offer, if she'd give herself permission to. Instead, she pulled the teabag from her mug and squeezed it. The hot liquid stung enough to curb her impulse. "It's okay, Jess. I enjoyed last night too, but I have my own reasons why I can't commit to a relationship."

"Really?" Jess studied her with a questioning gaze.

Lena didn't know what the unspoken question was. Did Jess want to know her reasons? She wasn't sure if she wanted to say out loud what scared her most, so she only answered the verbal part. "Really. But I hope we can still be friends. I've come to value our friendship, and I'd hate for it to be awkward when we see each other in your mother's house. Plus, I need our walks to stay fit since I quit my waitressing job."

"Nah, you're plenty fit. I can vouch for that." Jess grinned and winked.

"Ah, we've overcome the awkward morning-after phase and reached the teasing stage? That was quick." Lena leaned back as the last bit of tension drained from her. Maybe last night hadn't ruined their friendship after all.

Chapter Nineteen

Jess sat at the small table beneath the walnut tree while Ella slept in the stroller next to her. She skimmed through the *Journal of Cardiology*, but nothing caught her interest for long. She wasn't in work mode at the moment. The sun shone, bees buzzed, and the flowers scented the warm air with late summer fragrances.

The last week had flown by. During the first weeks of what Jess had thought of as exile at her mom's house, she'd expected to go mad watching the grass grow. Now she had her routine—tai chi, midday and evening walks, and enjoying every precious moment with Ella, who had grown so much and was already developing the first signs of a personality. Jess couldn't believe she'd go back to work soon and leave Ella behind.

No, that wasn't true. She wouldn't leave her behind. Millions of parents went to work every day and came home to enjoy their time with their kids even more. Work wasn't just a means of earning money for her; it was her calling, her vocation. Something she'd always wanted and needed to do. And she was still on track with her plans. Pregnancy and illness might have put her out of the race for most of the year, but she had lost neither the knowledge nor the skill to be on top of her profession.

Now she needed to go back to the city and prepare the condo. The cleaning service had been through this week, but she needed to restock the fridge and pack up her maternity clothes. She wanted to start with a clean slate.

"Hey, why are you frowning?" Lena carried two glasses with ice and a pale-green liquid that was probably one of the herbal tea mixtures her mom and Lena loved to create. "Here, Maggie decided we were done for today and sent me to find you."

With a grateful smile, Jess accepted the cool drink and sipped it carefully. Mmh, they had added lemon, and the herbal taste wasn't too overpowering. "I need to drive into the city tonight to get the condo ready for my move back on Sunday."

Lena settled on the chair next to her. "Are you taking Ella with you?"

"No, my mom is going to watch her. Maybe I'll use this last opportunity for freedom to go out to a nice restaurant. Not something I can do much when I'm alone with Ella."

"That sounds like a plan. Are you meeting friends?"

"No." How could she explain she'd grown distant from the circle of friends she had before? In recent weeks, she hadn't missed anyone and wouldn't know what to talk about with them anyway. She sighed. "I'm not in the mood for any of them. But...would you like to come with me?"

"Do you need help with moving your stuff and cleaning?" Lena fished a small ice cube from her glass and crunched on it.

"That's not why I'm asking. I thought you might like an evening off too. Going out, having some fun."

"I haven't done anything like that for ages." Lena smiled wistfully. "I used to be too tired to even miss it, but since I started working for Maggie, I don't feel like dropping into bed at nine dead to the world anymore." She brushed a strand of her curls behind her ear and nodded. "I'm game. But not too nice of a restaurant. I'm still on a limited budget."

With the promise of Lena's company, the prospect of driving to the city didn't faze Jess anymore. She drained the glass. "Don't worry about that. It's my treat."

"No, we're not dating. And even then, I'd like to be able to pay my own way."

Jess laid a hand on Lena's thigh before she could think about whether it was a good idea. But removing it now would be weird. Friends could touch like this, right? "And I respect that attitude. But I'd love to go to my favorite place and enjoy your company. It's not super elegant, but..." How did she politely say it was out of Lena's budget? She tried a different approach. "They're big on local, organic ingredients, and more than half of the menu is vegetarian or vegan. I'm sure you'd love it. Plus, I still owe you dinner. Let me take you, please."

"You do?" Lena frowned, but then her expression morphed into a smile, and she playfully hit Jess's hand still resting on her. "Oh, right, you do. You lost the blackberry competition because you wanted to play doctor."

Jess snorted and removed her hand after a light squeeze. "That's what you think playing doctor is about? Maybe I need to show you another meaning of the expression." Her mouth was dry, and she wished she hadn't finished her drink.

"Right." Laughing, Lena reached for Jess's glass and stood. "Okay, if you're going to take me out for dinner in the city, invite me to your place, and show me all about playing doctor, I should shower and change."

She was teasing, but Jess's body hadn't gotten the memo. A simmering heat burned in her middle that had nothing to do with the sunny afternoon and everything to do with the woman who walked away with gently swaying hips. It looked nothing like the high-heeled walk previous dates had used to gain her attention. No, Lena was absolutely more attractive because she moved her curves in a natural and unpretentious way.

Jess tore her gaze away and stood. She needed to get ready too, preferably with a cold shower.

††††††††

Lena licked the last of the raspberry sorbet from her spoon and gazed at the empty bowl with regret. Sharing the dessert had sounded like a great idea when Tyler, their waiter with a man bun, had suggested it. She could have devoured twice as much and was more than happy to admit Jess had been right; she loved the restaurant. Not only was the food amazing, but the wine was so good she had a hard time deciding if it was better than the one they'd had at the beach house. And the atmosphere was surprisingly relaxed. Yes, the table had a finer white cloth than she'd ever eaten from, and all the guests and staff were dressed up, but a colorful mixture of wildflowers and herbs in intentionally mismatched tiny glass vases brightened up the otherwise minimalistic decor.

"Thank you for the invitation. But how will we get home now? I'm so stuffed." Lena patted her belly. Fortunately, her dress was loose enough that she didn't feel restricted after the three-course meal.

Jess laughed. "You know, I'm so happy you came with me. This is the first time on a date I didn't feel like a pig because I wanted to have an appetizer and dessert too." Her smile faltered. "Um…not that we're on a date, but…"

Lena loved it when Jess got flustered, but the evening had been so amazing she decided to let her off the hook. "Don't worry. I know what you mean." She grinned. "You need better dates. Or to go out with friends instead."

"You can say that again. Apart from the food issue, you're much better company in all respects. Intelligent conversation, no whining about unimportant details, and best of all, no selfies." She put down her spoon and pushed the bowl to the side. "But I don't want to talk about former dates. Have I told you that you look lovely? And I mean that in a totally non-datey way."

A tingle spread through Lena's chest. The dress, Jess's attentiveness, the excellent restaurant—the evening did feel too much like a date. At first, the admiration in Jess's eyes when they'd met at the car had reassured her she wasn't underdressed in her teal sundress and dark-brown leather sandals that had way too many tiny straps to be called practical. But now it confused the hell out of her.

"Are you flirting?" Lena batted her eyelashes exaggeratedly. "Is flirting allowed when two friends go out to collect a bet on a non-date?" Light teasing and humor was always a good shield to hide behind.

"Don't we make our own rules?" Jess sipped from her wine glass, and a lovely drop of red stained her lips.

"Good question. I have another one: Do we even need rules?" She reached for her own glass, only to find it empty.

Jess held up the bottle, but Lena placed her open hand over the glass.

"I'm already a little bit tipsy. And I need my wits if we're negotiating rules of conduct."

"No." Jess put down the wine and played with the saltshaker.

"No?" Maybe she was more than tipsy because Lena didn't follow.

"No, you don't need your wits. I wouldn't want to take advantage of you. But I also don't think we need rules. We're both adults and can have a little fun flirting." Jess raised her eyebrows and flashed a smile that made sure Lena would agree to anything she asked. "Don't you think?"

"Okay." Lena placed a finger on Jess's hand, drawing spirals outward and inward and back again. Two could play this game.

The goosebumps on Jess's skin could be because Lena's finger was cool from holding the bowl of sorbet. Lena grinned. Or maybe she was enjoying their evening as much as Lena was. The twinkling in her gaze suggested the latter, and Lena couldn't look away as the cornflower blue of her eyes slowly darkened to the color of a summer evening sky.

"More wine?" Tyler appeared out of nowhere and picked up the bottle without waiting for a reply. With an exaggerated flourish, he poured in a wide arc into Jess's glass.

Just as the glass was full, the bottle slipped from his grip and hit the rim of the wine glass. It swayed precariously.

Jess reached out to steady it at the same moment as he tried to grab it.

Their hands met, and the glass toppled over. Dark-red wine splashed over Jess's shirt and face, then spilled all over the table cloth like an angry modern painting.

For a moment, nobody moved until Jess picked up her napkin and wiped her face. She lowered the linen and studied the stains for a second with a frown.

Tyler stared at her, open-mouthed, his face almost as white as the tablecloth. "Oh my God, I'm so sorry. I'll get you another napkin, and…I'm so sorry I ruined your evening."

"I'm fine. We were about to leave anyway." Jess's voice was calmer than Lena had expected. "Could you bring us the check please?"

"Check?" Tyler swallowed visibly. "Um…the meal is on the house."

Oh no. Lena had waited in enough cafés and restaurants to know *on the house* meant it would probably be deducted from his pay. And by the glimpse on the prices, it was quite possibly more than he would make this evening. If Jess accepted his offer, Lena would leave a tip on the table, everything she had with her, which, unfortunately, wasn't all that much.

"No, absolutely not." Jess smiled at him. "We had a great meal and will pay for it. And I won't even leave a bad review online."

"Thank you. I'll be back in a second." With a relieved sigh, Tyler hurried off.

"Are you okay?" Lena studied Jess for signs of distress or anger.

But Jess's shoulders were relaxed, a smile played around her lips, and her eyes shone with amusement. "It's only wine. Either the stains will get out of my shirt, or they won't." She shrugged and dabbed the napkin against her chest.

"Um, yeah, maybe." Lena had difficulty focusing on the conversation. Her mind was on the light-blue shirt with the burgundy stain that molded itself perfectly to Jess's right breast. She tore her gaze away when the waiter returned, and Jess handed him her credit card.

Lucky for them, the restaurant was only a couple of blocks from Jess's condo in Belltown. Jess phoned her mother for an update on Ella during the short walk, and Lena had time to study the area.

Everything was shiny and oozed money. Maggie lived in a well-to-do neighborhood too, but the contrast between the busy city and her serene gardens couldn't be more pronounced. Lena couldn't see Jess taking her evening walks with Ella here. But she hadn't accompanied Jess to question her. Jess had asked for support, and she would offer that. Just because she wouldn't prefer to live here herself wasn't a good enough reason to doubt Jess would be happy here.

"Give Ella a kiss from me, and tell her I love her. Sleep well, Mom." Jess hung up as they reached the high-rise.

They detoured to the garage to pick up their bags from Jess's car. Afterward, the elevator to the thirty-fourth floor didn't take long. In fact, it was so fast Lena's stomach dropped. Or maybe it was nerves because she would be alone with Jess and her wet shirt in her home.

Jess opened the door by entering a combination on a keypad and stretched her arm invitingly. "Welcome. Make yourself at home while I change." She switched on the lights.

Wow. After a few steps, Lena froze. The apartment was gigantic, with an open floor plan. A monstrous white couch and a couple of sleek white-and-chrome chairs dominated the left side of the room. They were placed around an area rug in several shades of cream, which sat next to a gas fireplace. An enormous abstract painting in pale blue and cream hung on the side wall. On the other end was a dining area with a glass-topped table made of an intentionally rusty metal structure that looked like something you'd either find in a museum or a junkyard. Eight modern chairs with high backs surrounded it. A breakfast bar was the only separation from a kitchen that seemed larger than Lena's whole house. Stainless steel appliances gleamed as if they'd been polished recently.

They probably had been. Someone who owned such a condo would hire a cleaning crew. And that explained why everything looked as if she'd opened an architectural magazine. No chair stood out of line, no cushion showed an imprint of a head, no mug sat forgotten on the bar. The closed blinds added to the eerie feeling she was on a staged set, not in a home.

Especially not in a home with a kid. Lena couldn't picture someone playing in this room. Would Ella be allowed to use crayons while lying on the cream-colored rug or play hide-and-seek under a table that looked as if it would crush a kid's skull like a snowball when it toppled over?

What had Jess said? *Make yourself at home?* Lena wouldn't even know how to begin here. A corridor on her left caught her interest. Maybe she'd find Ella's room there.

The first door opened into a bathroom. It seemed small compared to the main room and uncluttered. Maybe it was for guests? Lena didn't bother to switch on the light and moved on. Jess could have all the bathrooms she wanted; it wasn't any of her business. Next door was a guest room that looked like a hotel in even more shades of cream and gray—not that interesting either. Since she'd probably be staying there overnight, she didn't bother exploring and closed the door again.

The next door stood open. Bingo. Ella's room. The walls were painted in a soft buttery yellow with a wide border running all the way around, depicting cartoon animals playing with toys. The furniture looked brand new, but for the first time Lena detected a hint of personality. An old, handmade blanket in the same warm yellow covered a bed. Someone had stitched the silhouettes of animals, flowers, and trees on it, and it seemed the colors of the room were chosen to match it. The bed was too big for Ella, and Lena didn't see a cradle. Next to the bed, a mixture of old and new plush toys sat in a neat row on one side of the changing table. Bottles of lotion, baby powder, piles of diapers, and boxes of wipes were stacked on a board above it.

This was the first room Lena could see herself spending time in. If she was honest with herself, the rest of the apartment intimidated her. It hadn't been furnished for comfort but to impress. She shrugged. Or maybe Jess did feel comfortable here.

She left the nursery but didn't turn back to the main room. The next and last room at the end of the corridor must be Jess's bedroom. The half-open door hid most of the inside from curious gazes.

Without conscious decision, Lena stepped closer, about to enter. No, it wasn't right. She stopped with her hand on the door frame. Snooping around Jess's bedroom without invitation was too personal.

From her position, she could see a small part of the room between the bed and the window. The cradle she'd missed stood directly adjacent to Jess's bed, close enough to reach inside without getting up. Right next to the window sat a stuffed armchair with a matching footstool. The warm brown leather was crinkled and faded in places, bearing scuff marks like badges of honor. A wooden side table held a couple of books and a neat stack of magazines. The table looked as old and weathered as the chair and didn't match anything Lena had seen so far in the apartment.

Had she found where the real Jess lived? Or maybe this was wishful and romantic thinking. The real Jess might be the one who thought raising a kid on a white couch would be a good idea, for all she knew.

Without warning, Jess stepped into view. Her wet hair seemed even darker than usual and was tousled as if she had just run her fingers through it. She had wrapped a dark-blue towel around her chest. It reached to mid-thigh, leaving more than enough smooth skin visible and showcasing legs that were toned by frequent walks. Lena could very well remember the feel of those legs next to hers, but she'd never gotten to touch them.

She moaned, belatedly stifling the sound with a hand over her mouth.

Jess swiveled around and clutched the towel with one hand. She frowned, and the skin of her cheeks flushed. Her wide eyes held no anger, though, only surprise and...embarrassment?

Lena wanted to leave, she really did, but somehow her legs didn't comply. Every nerve ending tingled with the desire to get closer, to touch and be touched, to explore. But that wasn't what Jess wanted.

Lena clutched the doorframe and forced herself to keep her gaze on Jess's face.

Jess stepped closer as if reeled in by an invisible line. She stopped only inches from Lena, her eyes searching for an answer to a question she hadn't voiced.

The clean scent of aloe and something warmer, more sensual, flooded Lena's nostrils. She shivered as a wave of arousal swept through her. She balled her free hand into a fist to keep from reaching out. "I…I'm sorry. I'll wait for you in the living room." She licked her dry lips.

Jess touched her fist with a finger and slowly stroked over her knuckles. As Lena opened her hand, Jess clasped it in hers and pulled her closer. So close her breath caressed Lena's lips. "Would you…?" She rapidly blinked, then cleared her throat. "Would you like to stay?"

"Oh yeah." Lena grinned at the huskiness of her own voice. She wasn't good at hiding her desire, and why should she? Jess was a desirable woman. She leaned in and kissed her with all the fire Jess's question had ignited in her.

Still kissing, they stumbled toward the bed, both fumbling with Lena's clothes, and Lena neither knew nor cared who pushed and who pulled what. All she wanted, no, needed, was to feel Jess's skin against hers.

Finally naked, Lena tumbled backward on the bed, expecting Jess to follow. She pushed the comforter to one side of the king-size mattress. The smooth sheet beneath her was cool, and she couldn't wait to feel Jess's skin on hers.

But Jess hesitated. One hand still clutched the towel like a shield in front of her, and her eyes were fixed on something on the other side of the room.

Lena followed her gaze. The light switch. How important was darkness to Jess? Even if talking was the last thing on her mind, she was too much Jess's friend to ignore her uneasiness. "Jess? Whatever you want is okay."

Jess exhaled and looked at Lena. Her gaze was like a caress as she swept it up and down Lena's body. "I want you."

"And I want you. Very much. That's all that matters." Lena grinned. "Glad we're on the same page here. It would be super awkward to lie in your bed naked if all you wanted to do was show me your stamp collection or something."

Laughing, Jess released the iron grip on her towel and hastened to switch off the light.

It wasn't completely dark, as the city lights bathed the room in hues of gold and cast long shadows, but it was dark enough to blur the details as Jess dropped her towel and crawled onto the bed.

They both lay on their sides, facing each other. Lena's skin tingled with anticipation. She leaned in for a kiss, just to connect, to tell Jess they were here for fun. It quickly escalated from affirmation to something more and seemed to last for hours.

Breathing heavily, Jess broke the kiss but remained close enough that the warmth of her mouth still heated Lena's lips. Somehow, Jess's arm had found its way around Lena's middle without her noticing. With a decisive tug, Jess pulled Lena half on top of her as she rolled onto her back.

Lena's leg came to rest between Jess's, and it was her turn to gasp. Perfect. She could think of no other description for their position. All along her length, her skin warmed at the contact as if she was basking in the sunlight, naked. With a groan, she kissed Jess again, nibbling at her lower lip until she opened her mouth.

Jess used the advantage of having both hands free to roam all over Lena's back until she reached her ass. Her hands dug into Lena with the perfect pressure to pull her core closer to Jess.

Moans tore apart their kiss, and Lena couldn't say if they'd been hers or Jess's or if they'd both reacted at the same time to the increased friction.

Jess used Lena's distraction to reverse their positions. With a hungry gaze, she hovered over Lena for a second, then kissed her with even more passion than before. Jess's hand found Lena's breast, and her nipples hardened instantly. And then her mouth and hands were all over Lena—stroking, caressing, demanding attention.

All Lena could do was encourage and enjoy. She wouldn't fight for the lead in this dance, not when Jess so desperately needed it.

Besides, enjoy was an understatement. Jess was not only passionate but skilled, and she seemed to have remembered all of Lena's sensitive spots. And found some more that even Lena hadn't been aware of.

Almost too fast, Lena couldn't wait any longer and squirmed beneath Jess's touch. "Jess, please."

Jess slipped her hand into Lena's wetness.

Both moaned as Jess entered her, first with one finger, then with two.

"Yes." Lena moved her hips rhythmically to meet her.

When Jess added her thumb to stroke her clit, Lena couldn't hold back any longer. Her orgasm tore through her with the delicious force of a summer storm, depleting all her energy. Lena clutched Jess against her side. She wasn't ready to give up contact yet.

After a few minutes, Jess's hand left its resting place between Lena's breasts. This time, she knew what Jess's intention was. Lena caught the hand in her own, not stopping it but joining Jess in her journey.

Jess blinked a few times, and her eyes roamed Lena's face as if she was searching for something.

Even if Lena's eyes had adapted to the low light, it was still too dark to read Jess's emotions.

Finally, Jess nodded and slipped her hand out of Lena's grasp. She rolled on her back and lay her arm on the bed, opening herself to Lena.

The trust in that gesture filled Lena's heart with warmth. She wanted to devour Jess, but she hadn't forgotten Jess's hesitation the last time.

Taking her time, she stroked up and down Jess's side, never taking her gaze from Jess's face. She lingered at the side of Jess's breast, waiting for a cue. Her fingers itched to find the areola, feel it tightening beneath her fingertip, but this wasn't just about her.

Jess's breath hitched, and she shifted a little. Just enough to turn slightly into Lena's touch. "More."

Nothing could excite Lena more at this moment than to comply with Jess's wish. She turned on her side until she could bury her face in Jess's neck to nuzzle her and brush her fingers all around her breast. Under her lips, Jess's pulse soared. When Lena found her nipple, a moan tore through Jess and vibrated in her throat. It took only two soft strokes to harden the nipples to perfect points. Jess's responsiveness was a huge turn-on. Lena could have spent an eternity exploring the different textures.

But much too soon, Jess's hand grasped hers and stilled it. "Sorry." She groaned. "Too sensitive."

Lena leaned back to look at Jess. "No, I'm sorry." She studied her for signs of reluctance but found none. "Tell me if anything is off limits."

"Your touch wasn't off limits, only too much right now. There must be some kind of direct connection between my nipple and my clit they forgot to mention in my anatomy class." The corner of her mouth rose in a half grin. After a second, she steered their still clasped hands lower, never touching her abdomen, to her patch of short, curly hair.

Lena kept her gaze on Jess's face, and when Jess let go of her hand, she trailed her fingers through the short hair until she reached the smooth skin on the inside of Jess's thigh.

Jess opened her legs and tried to shift her middle toward Lena's hand. "Please."

Usually, Lena liked to play and tease, but today she didn't want to make Jess beg in earnest. Jess had trusted her, and she wouldn't let her regret it. She parted Jess's lips with one finger and slid into the waiting wetness. With a happy sigh, she stroked back and forth once. Nothing compared to this wonderful silkiness. Lena circled her clit once, twice, then dipped her finger slowly into Jess's opening to see if she liked it.

The answer was unmistakably yes. Jess tried to push closer and groaned in frustration as Lena pulled back.

This time she slipped two fingers in, just as slow.

"Faster." Jess moved with her, and Lena complied. The muscles in Jess's thighs tensed as she arched her back to get even closer to Lena's touch. One of her hands clutched Lena's shoulder.

With her thumb, Lena found Jess's clit and skimmed over it. She didn't know yet if it was as sensitive as her nipple.

"More." The word tore out of Jess with a pain-filled groan.

Lena increased the pressure, and Jess's whole body tensed. Her legs nearly crushed Lena's hand, but even in the dim light, her expression of bliss was unmistakable.

When Jess's head fell back on the pillow, Lena stilled the movements of her hand but left her fingers where they were. Jess didn't seem in a hurry to let go and neither was she.

Jess slung her arms around Lena and cradled her against her chest.

Scents of sweat, arousal, and Jess engulfed her. Lena closed her eyes and hummed contentedly. She could stay here forever. It felt like home.

She blinked. *No, no, forget that. Now!* This was all about sex, not love. About fun, not feeling at a home. This was why she didn't do flings; she couldn't trust her nesting instinct not to wake up and roar to the forefront.

"Sleep with me?" Jess's whisper caressed Lena's cheek like the touch of a butterfly wing.

Bad, bad idea. But nothing short of an earthquake or fire could chase her out of Jess's bed right now. Lena nodded, not trusting her voice.

Jess pulled the comforter over them and tightened her arms around Lena underneath the blanket.

Enveloped in a cocoon of warmth and safety, Lena closed her eyes and allowed weariness to settle.

Jess stuffed the last carton of formula into the pantry, next to the whole grain muesli. She shuddered. If anyone had told her last year she'd end up with bird food for breakfast, she'd have thrown her grilled cheese sandwich at them. But she wasn't running around, doing fourteen-hour shifts without lunch breaks anymore, so she'd had to adapt. Now that her groceries were stored and Ella's room was restocked with the right size of diapers and clothes, not much more needed to be done.

Jess pulled her crinkled to-do list from her pocket to see what came next. Her bedroom closet still needed to be cleaned out, but that would have to wait until Lena woke. Jess leaned on the wall of the hallway. The door at the far end was closed, and the apartment was silent in the early morning. Was Lena still sleeping? Or was she awake, tossing and turning, unwilling to get up? Was she regretting staying over? Or was she waiting for Jess to return? Now?

An hour before dawn, Jess had woken and been unable to return to sleep. Lena had been snuggled to her back, warm and soft, her arm holding Jess around her middle. Lena's naked front had been next to her naked back. Skin on skin. Lena's hand on her abdomen, on the ugly stretch marks, burning like a branding iron. She'd needed to get up before someone got hurt by all the heat.

Writing to-do lists for the upcoming week over her first and only cup of coffee, shopping for groceries online, and cleaning out her pantry had been great distractions. But just for a while.

Jess took a couple of steps toward her bedroom. *What are you doing?*

Lena had said she wasn't in it for a relationship either. She'd probably stayed because of the neediness Jess had shown last night and might even be glad to wake up alone.

She rubbed her temples. Why had she asked Lena to stay? What had she been thinking? Obviously, not much.

She squared her shoulders, strode into the kitchen, and opened the fridge. It was stocked with more healthy stuff than she was used to, and choosing something not only for her but for Lena seemed too complicated. She closed it again with a sigh. She wasn't hungry anyway.

"Morning." Lena's voice was still a little rough with sleep.

Jess swiveled around and smiled at the sight of Lena dressed in the bathrobe Jess had used during pregnancy. She'd had to sling the belt around herself twice. Lena's hair was damp at the tips and even curlier than usual, and the urge to bury her hands in the gleaming strands was hard to resist.

"Morning." Jess couldn't blame the roughness in her own voice on sleepiness, but maybe Lena wouldn't notice. "You want some breakfast?"

"Not yet. But I'd like something like that." With a smile, she pointed at Jess.

Instant heat hit her right in the middle like lightning, and the electric discharge raced through the length of her, leaving Jess tingling everywhere. Had she just suggested…? "What?" And now her voice was an octave too high. *Smooth, Jess, very smooth.*

Laughing, Lena tugged at Jess's T-shirt, sadly without touching her skin, then pointed at her sweatpants. "Something to wear for tai chi. I forgot to pack mine. I think we can both fit in front of the window if we move the chairs a bit." She waved her hand at the empty space between the sitting and dining area.

The last trace of electricity fled, leaving Jess empty. "Um…sure. Follow me."

With a specific mission in mind, it was easy to return to the bedroom and ignore the bed. Jess opened her closet and picked some of her prepregnancy sportswear. "I'll move the chairs." She thrust the bundle into Lena's hands and left the room. No way could she watch her change right now.

In the living room, Jess opened the blinds to let some natural light in. The windows were positioned to capture the setting sun over the water, but the view was still amazing in the morning. The first rays of sunshine painted the few clouds orange and pink on the canvas of an indigo sky.

"Beautiful." The voice came from directly behind her. Again, Lena had managed to sneak up on her. "Now I know why you chose this apartment."

"Yes, very beautiful." Jess agreed, but at that moment she could only focus on Lena's reflection in the floor-to-ceiling windows.

The running tights and T-shirt fit Lena like a second skin and were far more revealing than the loose yoga pants she usually wore.

Not that Jess needed the reminder of how perfectly the slight curve of Lena's hip fit into her hand. The memory of last night would stay with her for a while.

On the window's surface, Mirror-Lena tilted her head and focused on Jess's reflection. Their gazes met, and, for a second, Lena's gaze sliced through all the protective layers Jess had wrapped around herself. She was laid as bare as she'd been last night, and it was even more terrifying than stripping naked.

Jess broke the connection. "The view was a great selling point." And a safe topic. "Let's start."

As soon as Jess started the morning ritual, her thoughts settled like a wind chime after a storm, leaving her with a clear and calming note. When they finished, the magical predawn sky had transformed into a muted gray-blue morning. It was time to return to reality.

"I need a shower. Help yourself to anything you need—coffee, tea, cereal. I have bagels in the freezer, or…" Jess stared at the kitchen. She should prepare breakfast for Lena or at least show her where things were. She was being rude, but she needed a moment to herself.

"I'll be okay. Take your time." Lena squeezed her arm, then walked past her to the kitchen.

Jess allowed herself the pleasure of watching her walk in the workout tights for exactly three seconds before she hurried to the bedroom. She quickly made the bed, then carried her change of clothes into the bathroom so she wouldn't risk running around in a towel again.

When she emerged, Lena had curled up in her reading chair in the bedroom. She'd pulled her legs up underneath herself and had both hands wrapped around a steaming mug. One of Jess's old children's books lay open on the wide arm of the chair. Lena looked so at home as if she'd always used this chair.

A strange sense of familiarity swept over Jess, making her dizzy. She shook her head to clear it.

"Hey." Lena looked up with a tentative smile. "Join me for a minute?"

Join? On the chair? It was oversized but not that big, at least not for two people who weren't in an intimate relationship. Jess pushed the image of snuggling from her mind as fast as it had sprung up. Her gaze went to the bed. She swallowed. Even though she'd erased all visible traces of their night together, it still held the memory of waking up in Lena's embrace and everything else they'd done last night.

With one bare foot, Lena pushed the leather ottoman in her direction. It was big enough to sit one or two people and as plush as the chair.

She should know; it had been her favorite place in the world when the chair still belonged to her dad. He had read to her from the very book Lena was reading, sitting in the same spot. Just as she planned to read the same book to Ella one day.

Jess sat facing Lena, so close her knees almost brushed Lena's bare feet. Taking her old place eased some of the tension from Jess's shoulders. Years ago, she'd been more carefree, with an innate trust everything would be okay. Instead of planning every detail, she'd dreamed of the future.

Lena handed her another mug from the side table. "I made you tea. I wasn't sure if you're back to coffee yet."

"Thanks. I had my one cup per day already." Jess cradled the cup with a sigh. It looked awfully pale. "I hope that'll be enough when I get back to work."

"Are you happy to return? You sound a bit... I don't know...sad? Reluctant?"

Jess blew on the hot liquid, then took a sip. Mint. Not as good as from her mom's garden, but it was the only herbal tea she had besides some maternity anti-bloating stuff that tasted horrible. Even more shopping was needed, yet another thing for her ever-growing to-do list. She grimaced. She hadn't answered Lena's question. That was answer enough in itself.

"Yes and no. I'm looking forward to getting out of my mom's house and back to work. I love my job, and it's not only a means to earn money. But..." She sighed and took another sip. "I'll miss Ella during the day, when she's most active. And to be honest, I'll miss our morning tai chi and evening walks and talks."

A sad smile tugged at Lena's lips. "I'll miss it too. But I understand the feeling of wanting to be in your own space. You must be happy to be home again." Lena gestured to the chair and the bed, but the swipe of her hand seemed to encompass the whole apartment or even the whole city, all of which was so unlike her mom's home.

Jess wouldn't go as far as describing the fluttery feeling in her chest as happiness. It was more positive than negative, sure, but her decision was based on her mind, not her gut. And home? "I'm not so sure this is my home."

"No?" Lena rested her hand on Jess's knee; it was still warm from the tea she'd held.

"A home needs more than walls and furniture. Happy memories, personal attachment. If everything in here burned down, I wouldn't miss a thing except for this chair and some of the old children's books I saved for Ella. The rest is replaceable. Hell, most of the interior decoration wouldn't have been my first choice. And I wasn't home that much to create memories. I was either at work or out."

"So the living room…you didn't pick the furniture?" Lena was trying for a neutral expression and tone, but she failed miserably.

Jess laughed. "God, no. All that white and cream. In the beginning, I was afraid to sit on the couch. When I bought the condo, it was already furnished, and I never took the time to replace the stuff."

A real smile broke through Lena's polite facade. "I'm so glad to hear that. Yesterday I couldn't feel your energy flowing anywhere in the apartment, and that's why I ended up in your bedroom. I was looking for traces of the real Jess. I found some in Ella's room, but here, in this chair, I sense you the most. This is you."

"Yeah. This is as close as it gets at the moment." *Flowing energy.* Jess wasn't so sure she'd word it the same, but Lena was spot-on in her observation. She looked at Lena's hand, which still rested on her knee. Was the heat and tingling spreading from her hand the same kind of energy, only Lena's? Or was it plain lust and attraction? Whatever it was, she liked this connection. If her life wasn't so complicated, she'd love to explore it again, see if she could find her old self or even discover a new and improved version of herself.

"What part of yourself are you missing the most?" Lena leaned back to take another sip of tea and gave her an encouraging smile.

The urge to confess her insecurities rose to the surface like a bear stumbling out of its cave after a long sleep in winter. She wanted to tell

Lena all about how she felt soft and weak in her body, old and no longer attractive.

Maybe it was the seat. She'd had hundreds of personal talks with her dad in the same position. Only Lena didn't feel at all like a parental figure, and Jess didn't expect her to solve all her problems or give absolution for the things she'd messed up. If it wasn't the seat, maybe it was the woman. The thought sent shivers down her spine like an ice shower after the promise of spring—a warning not to trust too soon.

Instead of answering the question, Jess rose, and her thigh cooled as Lena's hand dropped away. "I need to work on my to-do list. It's getting late."

"Sure." If Lena was fazed by the change of topic, she didn't let on. "Can I help in any way?"

Even that innocent question seemed layered with a promise to listen and to encourage. But probably this extra meaning only existed in Jess's head. She just needed a little time for herself to get back on track. "No, thanks. Stay here. Enjoy your tea and the book a little longer."

Chapter Twenty

For a second, Jess hesitated at the door to the cath lab. The last time she'd been here, she'd seen the floor up close. And Kayla and Scott had needed to shock her to treat her arrhythmia. Coincidentally, those two were working together again.

Jess squared her shoulders. "Someone called for backup?"

"Sorry?" Scott did his trademark impression of a puppy, looking as if she'd yelled at him.

Which she hadn't. All day she had kept her temper at bay and reminded herself she'd be back at Ella's side soon. *Only seventeen minutes until my shift ends.* And Scott was wasting precious seconds of it. "And?"

"The patient had episodes of mild angina, and we suspected a routine case. But the stenosis of his left main coronary is ninety-nine percent." He swallowed. "I want to attempt PCI but thought I should clear it with a senior attending. Or do you think I need to call cardiac surgery?"

"Let me see the films."

Scott pressed a few buttons on the tableside control panel to call up the X-rays on the monitor.

Jess studied the anatomy of the coronaries and grinned. Definitely a problem she could solve. "Let's do PCI. I'll scrub in."

"Oh. Do you want to take over?" The sad puppy look was back. Scott had still been a cardiology fellow during Jess's pregnancy, but he'd started his interventional cardiology fellowship weeks ago and was eager to snatch up as many interventions as possible.

Kayla, who stood half a step behind him, tapped her gloved index finger to her left wrist with a grimace.

Mentally, Jess agreed. It would be so much faster if Jess did it herself. Then she could be home on time. She sighed. But that wouldn't be fair. "I'll talk you through it."

For the next fifty minutes, Jess put all thoughts of Ella from her mind. As they were finishing up, her work phone rang beneath her sterile paper gown. "Can you two manage the rest on your own?"

When Scott nodded and Kayla gave her a thumbs-up, Jess quickly pulled off her gown and gloves and left the room.

She opened her lead vest to fish the phone from her scrub pocket. "Riley."

"We need to talk about the TAVR schedules." Dr. Huong had never been one for small talk. "Do you have a few minutes?"

As he was Jess's boss, the question was entirely rhetorical. "Yes. Do you want me to come up now?"

"No. In thirty minutes." He hung up before she could answer, as usual.

Jess sighed. No way would she make it home in time to give Ella her dinner. In her experience, a thirty-minute wait would turn into forty or fifty. But getting back on the schedule to perform the most complex procedure in the cardiology department was worth any waiting time.

She slipped off the lead vest and skirt and hung them up. She hadn't noticed it during the intervention, but her prepregnancy set had fit without chafing. When had she lost weight?

To walk off some of her frustration about the delay, Jess went downstairs to slip out back. Calling the small patch of grass with a handful of trees and shrubs a garden was an insult to her mom's, but the scent of something blooming in the late evening air calmed her somewhat. As she reached the bench where she'd given birth to Ella, someone was already sitting on it. Jess was about to leave when the woman turned her head. Diana, of course.

She greeted her with a smile. "Hey, Jess. Back at work already?"

"It's my second day, but it feels as if I've been back for a month." Jess rounded the bench and sat. "And what are you doing here, Dr. Rock Chick? Shirking your duties?"

"Nah. I'm on the night shift and got here early. I tried to sneak in a visit with Emily, but she's busy." Diana sighed. "I haven't seen much of her the last couple of days."

A few months ago, Jess would have reacted to the lovesick expression on Diana's face with a smirk and a sarcastic comment, but today she felt with her. "I'm sorry."

Diana shrugged. "It is what it is. I knew what I was getting into. And when I finish my residency next year, I'll have better control over my schedule, and then we can sync our shifts. Are you on call tonight?"

"No, I'm waiting for a meeting with my boss." Jess looked at her watch. "I hope it doesn't take too long. I still have to pick up Ella from my mom's before I go home." She yawned. "Sorry. Driving back and forth to my mom's place takes a couple of hours from my day I'd rather invest in sleep."

"Is Ella sleeping through the night?"

"You're joking, right?" Jess snorted. Diana clearly didn't have much experience with babies.

"I guess that means no." Diana grinned.

"Honestly, I'm pretty lucky from what I've heard. But you can't plan on it."

Jess's phone rang. Huong again. She groaned.

"Give me another hour. Budget meeting." He hung up before she could protest.

Jess clenched the phone in her hand. "Does he think I have nothing to do but wait? Fucking idiot."

Diana looked at her with a raised eyebrow, so Jess explained.

"I need to let my mom know." She picked up her private phone.

Her mom answered after the first ring. "Jess, are you okay?"

"Yeah, sorry I didn't call earlier. I'm stuck at work and was hoping for some good news before I called. But it seems I can't make it to your place at a decent time. It could get late." Jess yawned.

"Oh, I'm sorry. Why don't you head home to sleep, and we'll take good care of Ella. She'll be sleeping anyway and won't notice you're gone."

Sleep. That was really, really tempting. "Are you sure?"

"I'm sure. Come by tomorrow after work. Or should I bring her to you?"

"No, I'll come get her." But twenty-four hours more without Ella seemed like an eternity. "Is she asleep already?"

"No, Lena is giving her a bottle. Do you want to talk to her?"

Jess didn't know who her mother was referring to, but she did want to talk with both. She wanted to listen to Ella coo nonsensical sounds and to Lena whisper her name. Loneliness grabbed her heart with icy fingers. She swallowed to keep the pain from her voice. "No, no, that's fine. Just tell her I love her."

"I will. Bye." Her mom hung up.

Jess lowered the phone and stared at the black screen. The truth of what she'd said resonated through her like a shock wave. Love. She had meant Ella, of course. Not Lena. That would be absurd.

Yes, she had spent two nights with Lena and countless evenings talking and walking. But love? What she was feeling toward Lena wasn't like the feeling she had for Ella—the unstoppable force of a waterfall taking everything that got in its wake with it without a chance of escape, frightening and exhilarating and unmistakable. No, her feelings for Lena were completely different, more like a wide river, calm on the surface but still deep and powerful enough to move its boundaries or dig canyons. Was this love too?

Yes. "Fuck, fuck, fuck."

"Everything okay?" Diana's gentle question reminded Jess she wasn't alone.

She blinked. Okay? A warm glow somewhere in her middle told her it might be okay to love Lena. What would she do with this knowledge? Could she, would she be brave enough to tell Lena? But she wasn't ready to talk about it yet. "Yeah, I won't see Ella for the next twenty-four hours." She exaggeratedly rolled her eyes. "Who would have thought I'd end up such a sappy fool?"

"I'm sorry. That sucks." Diana chuckled. "I shouldn't laugh, but your cursing reminds me of the day Ella was born."

After a second, Jess laughed with her. "I can only remember half of it, but we went through quite a collection of four-letter words between us."

┼┼┼┼┼┼┼

Lena placed the baby monitor on the table and opened the fridge to get some tea. Maggie's muted voice was getting closer, and when she entered the kitchen, her expression and the tight set of her shoulders said it all. Jess must have called to say she'd be late again, for the third time. And it had only been a week since she'd gone back to work.

Wordlessly, Lena handed Maggie the glass of tea and filled another one, then picked up the baby monitor to go outside.

Having tea together on the patio had become their new evening ritual after Lena's short walks with Ella. It wasn't much compared to the hours she and Jess had spent wandering the park, but it helped to settle Ella after her evening meal. Today she'd fallen asleep on the way back and hadn't woken when Lena transferred her to her crib.

If she was honest, the walks helped to settle Lena too. The work with Maggie was less demanding on her feet and more on her brain, so she needed the balance. But if she'd known Jess would be late again, she'd have taken a longer route.

"Did she say when she'll be here?" Lena gritted her teeth as she sat on her favorite chair next to the bench Maggie had settled on.

"She didn't know yet." Maggie yawned and rubbed her eyes. "That girl is working herself to her grave. She's barely recovered from her heart scare. Didn't she learn anything?" It was rare for Maggie to criticize Jess aloud. Either she was getting more comfortable with Lena or more frustrated with her daughter. Or both.

"If you want to go to bed, I can wait up for her." Lena wasn't tired yet, and Maggie looked ready to call it a day.

"No, this is supposed to be your free time." The care in Maggie's voice was like a hug and helped her to let go of her tension for the moment.

"I don't mind. I want to work on my sketch, and I can do that here as well as at home." That was the truth. Since she'd given up her waitressing job and most of the massage lessons, she had much more energy to be creative.

Maggie studied her for a moment and seemed pleased with whatever she saw. "Thanks. If she isn't here in half an hour, I might take you up on it."

Before the thirty minutes were up, Lena went to the garden house to get her sketching supplies and a sweater. It wasn't too cold to stay outside yet, but the warmth of the day had faded with the setting sun.

The light on the patio bathed the sitting area in an inviting glow, and Lena placed a vase with the handful of wildflowers and herbs she'd picked earlier in the middle of the wooden table.

Maggie rubbed the leaves of the pineapple mint and smelled her fingers as she stood. "That looks lovely. Will you show me the sketch tomorrow?"

"Sure." Two weeks ago, Lena might have doubted the sincerity of the question and dismissed it as politeness. But Maggie was persistent. "Sleep well."

Lena had completed the sketch and was halfway through coloring it with watercolors when steps crunched on the gravel leading to the patio. She cleaned the paintbrush in the glass of water and waited. It was later than she'd thought Jess would come, and the simmering anger flared again.

How could Jess do this to her mother? She was fit for her age, but grandmothers shouldn't do the work of mothers. It had aged her grandma before her time to raise a child again. Lena still hadn't forgiven her mother for the way she'd trampled all over her family.

Jess was pale, and even the soft light couldn't hide the dark smudges under her eyes. "Hey." She paused at the table next to Lena's chair and smiled. Only the smile didn't erase the lines around her eyes but deepened them.

Lena's anger evaporated like mist in the morning sun. Jess hadn't been out to party but to work, taking care of others. The least Lena could do was offer some care herself. "Sit down. Do you want a drink? Did you have dinner?"

"No, thanks. I better take Ella and get going. It's late. Where's Mom?"

"She already went to bed." Lena pointed to the monitor. "Ella is fine, but you look as if you need a moment to regroup before you drive back."

Jess regarded the bench next to Lena with a longing expression. "Maybe five minutes." She sat down and rested her head against the wall behind her. She wore a dark pant suit with a light-blue collared shirt. The elegant look was hot as hell but couldn't be comfortable. Jess didn't seem to mind and closed her eyes.

"I'll get you a drink and the rest of our dinner." Lena pushed her chair back to get up.

"No, please stay." Jess stopped her with a hand on her arm. "I'm not hungry. I had a sandwich on my way. But I could use some company." She pulled back her hand to stifle a yawn. "Sorry."

"Okay. But scoot over." Lena rose and made a shooing motion with both hands. "Let me sit here."

Jess arched her eyebrows but didn't ask why as she moved to the middle of the bench.

"Thanks." Lena sat and patted her lap. "Head or feet?"

"What?" Jess blinked, and her confused expression was adorable.

"Do you want to put your head or your feet in my lap for a massage? You look awful." Lena softened the last comment with a smile, but she did mean it.

For a few seconds, Jess resisted, but then she slipped out of her suit jacket and seemed to fold into herself. She carefully positioned her head in Lena's lap and stretched her legs on the bench that was just long enough to fit them both. Her body was still stiff, though, and her eyes were open and wide.

Lena couldn't read the emotion that lurked behind the blue irises. She trailed her hand through Jess's hair, gently massaging her scalp.

"Oh." The soft sigh was halfway between surprise and pleasure. Jess's eyes fluttered shut. After a minute, her features softened.

"Do you want to talk about your day?" Lena smoothed a persistent line between her brows. "Why are you so tired?"

"Nothing special." Jess sighed. "A few emergencies messed up the schedule in the cath lab, so my regular program was bumped to the end and I didn't have time for lunch. And Ella kept me awake half the night with colic." Her eyes opened again, and she looked at Lena. "Was she okay today? Mom said she was, but I know she downplays everything so I don't worry at work."

"She was fine. Maybe a bit restless in the early morning, so I kept her in the wrap for a couple of hours. Afterward she was her old self."

"Oh." Jess frowned. "I'm sorry you had to take care of her."

"Don't be. I'm happy to do it. I love babies, and Ella is special. I guess she stole a piece of my heart." A pain twisted in her chest where her heart should be. Ella hadn't stolen a piece; she had cut Lena wide open until she was bleeding. Even though she had promised herself to take better care of her heart, another part was missing, and she wasn't sure how much was left. And here she was, juggling with knives as she played with Jess's hair. The effort to keep all that from showing in her expression was almost too much, but she dug out her best smiling mask from somewhere deep inside.

"Yeah, she's like that. The little thief has a nice collection of hearts. Mine too." Jess closed her eyes again, and some of the lines around her eyes eased as she relaxed. "Thank you."

Lena concentrated on the slow scalp massage to calm her own racing pulse.

"Lena?" Jess's voice was slow and dipped in honey, on the brink of sleep.

"Yeah?"

"You would be a great mom. And partner."

"Mhm." She couldn't manage a real answer, but it wasn't necessary. Jess's breathing had evened out, and the residual tension left her body as she melted right into the bench.

Lena's heart bled a little more as she continued to caress Jess. It would keep the wound open, but she couldn't resist, like a bee drawn to sweetened water only to drown in the drink. She would give Jess twenty minutes to nap and herself twenty minutes to bathe in the illusion of having someone to share her life with. Then she'd wake Jess to let her go to her own condo, with her own kid, and leave Lena behind, alone.

━━━━━━━

Tuesday evening, Jess parked her car in the usual spot next to Lena's rusty Ford. She patted the old car with a fond smile as she walked past it. When had it ceased to be an eyesore and turned into a welcome sign of coming home?

With a lightness she'd lacked all day, Jess hurried around the garage and nearly collided with Ella's stroller. She was only able to stop in time because she wasn't dead tired for once.

Lena gasped and clutched the bar of the stroller with both hands. "Jess! What are you doing here?"

"I live here." Jess laughed. She'd never been happier she left the bitter version of herself so far behind that Lena would joke with her about it.

"Nuh-uh. I live here." Lena was teasing, but the message hit home.

Jess's laughter died. Lena was right. She didn't live here anymore. She lived thirty fucking minutes away, alone. She swallowed her disappointment and stepped to the side of the stroller to look at Ella.

She was awake, smiling and oblivious to her mother's inner turmoil. As always, her daughter's innocence set everything in the right perspective.

Jess leaned forward to reach in and caress Ella. "Hi, sweetie." She breathed in the scent of lotion and milk and let the tension drain from her shoulders. She kissed Ella's belly through the layers of clothing and blanket, straightened again, and smiled at Lena. "Where are you two going?"

"Around the block. Do you have time for a walk before you head back?"

Not only did Jess have the time for once, but she had been hoping they'd get the chance to talk again. But now that she had Lena's company, words failed her. She didn't want to talk about work or the logistics of driving back and forth. Most of all, she wanted to hear Lena's voice.

"How is working with my mom? Do you still like it?"

"Like? That doesn't do it justice. I love it. I'm learning so much. And do you know what I love best?" In her enthusiasm, Lena pushed the stroller faster up the hill.

"No?" To her surprise, Jess wasn't out of breath—yet.

"Maggie's work approach. She can't stay too long on one task and switches between outlining, writing, and editing all the time. It's wonderfully chaotic."

"Really? I take after my dad in that regard and plan everything meticulously, then stick to the plan."

"But we made a plan too and are still on schedule, just not in such a linear fashion. She takes a lot of breaks to tend to her garden, and I use those to work on my sketches. At the end of the day, we've worked way more than eight hours, but it doesn't feel that way because of all the little breaks. And that schedule works really well to take care of Ella."

"Wait, are you taking care of Ella too? I thought Mom was doing that?" Jess ran her hand through her hair and rubbed her neck.

"Isn't that okay? Don't you trust me to?" Lena whispered the last question.

"Oh, no, not at all. It's just... Mom is family, and she offered, but I feel bad for foisting this babysitting job on you." Jess opened a couple of buttons on the top of her shirt. She was warm but still not short of breath.

"You didn't foist anything on me. I only help Maggie. She loves taking care of Ella, but I think she prefers the spoiling part, and I don't mind changing diapers."

Jess stared at Lena. Did she really mean it? "Thank you." What else was there to say?

When they reached the entrance to the park, Jess stopped Lena with a hand on her arm. "I don't think my shoes are up to it. Sorry, I had an office day and needed to dress the part." She pointed to the muddy path that was strewn with red and brown leaves.

Lena's eyes twinkled. "I noticed. Very impressive, *Doctor* Riley."

Jess groaned. "You'll never let me forget that, right?"

When Lena laughed, Jess nudged her with an elbow. "Can I push the stroller for a while? I kind of missed this the last couple of weeks."

They switched sides and walked on in silence. Lena broke it first. "I miss my sister."

"You've never really told me about her. How old is she now?"

"Twelve. She was born when I was a senior in high school."

"Oh, that's a big age difference. Was she a surprise?"

"No, my mother... Actually, my mother was really, really young when she had me, so when she had Tammy, she was in her early thirties." Lena shrugged as if it wasn't important, but she kept her gaze on the ground.

That explained a lot. "Is that why you lived with your grandma for so long?"

"Yeah."

When it was clear nothing more was coming, Jess looked at Lena. Her head hung down, and she walked more mechanically, all the earlier enthusiasm drained from her. Maybe talking about her sister would bring a smile back to her face. The love in her voice was unmistakable, even if it was tinged with pain.

"And you helped take care of Tammy?"

Lena snorted. "You could say so. About a month before Tammy was born, my mother asked me to move in with her. At first, I only took care of Tammy in the evenings when my mother was sleeping, but later I skipped school a lot to be there for her. Some days it felt as if I was raising her on my own. My mother...she didn't really cope very well with noise and demands. She got migraines and..." Lena kicked at a stone on the sidewalk. "I don't need to sugarcoat it anymore." Her voice hardened like ice. "My mother wasn't fit to raise a child. She let Tammy cry in her room for hours, closed the door, and turned up the TV. She drank a lot and took pills. I think painkillers, but I'm not sure. Tammy's dad was in the military and was away for most of the first year. When he came back and realized what was going on, he tried to help her, get her in rehab, but in the end, he gave up. He divorced my mother and took Tammy away. He severed all contact. I tried to reach out later, but he wouldn't budge. I haven't heard from Tammy in nearly ten years."

"That's terrible. I'm so sorry." Jess stopped walking and reached for Lena's arm, but she shook it off.

"Nothing to be sorry about. What's done is done." Lena smiled, but it was as if she'd slipped on a mask. "He was a nice enough guy. I'm sure Tammy is better off with him."

"Didn't he want to take you with them?" Jess wasn't sure she understood the family dynamic.

"He wasn't my father. He…we didn't really have a relationship." Lena's voice held no bitterness or frustration. "I met him for the first time when my mother was eight months pregnant and I moved in with them, just before he was deployed. They'd been married for a couple of years without him even knowing about my existence. I'm not blaming him."

Jess admired her for that. "I don't know if I would be as forgiving. I'm sorry I brought up these memories for you."

"No, it's okay. They've been close to the surface lately because of Ella." Lena's mask slipped as she glanced at the sleeping baby. A genuine smile tugged at the corner of her mouth, and she let out a heavy sigh. "It's good to say it out loud. I haven't talked to anyone about it before."

Tentatively, Jess reached for Lena's arm again. This time, Lena didn't flinch or draw back. "You can talk to me anytime." Jess drew circles with her thumb on Lena's skin, not knowing if she wanted to soothe Lena or herself. "What about your mother? Did you stay with her?"

Lena looked down, and her curls fell in her face, obscuring her eyes. "I'll get sick if I remember what I did for her and how it all turned out."

"You don't need to talk about her. Never. But if you want to, I'm here to listen. And nothing you could say will diminish my opinion of you." Jess meant every word. All she knew about Lena's mother was that she was currently in prison, but it was Lena's story to tell and had absolutely no impact on Jess's feelings or the relationship between them.

"Another day, okay? But thank you." Lena slid her arm beneath Jess's fingers until their palms met, then let go before Jess had a chance to enjoy it.

┼┼┼┼┼┼┼

The next day, Jess was clever enough to bring a change of clothes to work, so she arrived at her Mom's place in jeans and a sweatshirt, a far better outfit for an evening walk than her pantsuit. She had returned to her condo late the night before, but every minute had been worth it. She'd fallen asleep with memories of Lena's trust and the touch of her hand.

Lena waited for her on the patio, gently moving the stroller back and forth with one hand. Her smile held none of yesterday's sadness as her gaze wandered over Jess's outfit. "We're going to the park today?"

Jess grinned and pointed at her sneakers. "Let's hurry so we have more daylight left."

They walked to the park in record time. Jess didn't have enough breath for talking, but she was proud to reach the entrance without panting. Right after Ella's birth, or even a month ago, she wouldn't have made it.

Jess took a deep breath of the fresh air, not because she needed to but because she'd missed it. Why had she been so stubborn last weekend and stayed in her condo? "Have I told you I got rid of my living room stuff the other day?"

"Really? What did you do with it?" Curiosity lightened Lena's tone.

"The weekend was too long. After napping with Ella on and off all day, I was still too tired to do anything on Saturday evening, so I opened a bottle of too-expensive Pinot and tried to veg on that much-too-white couch. I was so tempted to pour the glass all over it, so Ella wouldn't be the first to spoil it. But then I took some pictures of my stuff and put it online for a ridiculous price. I guess I lost my tolerance for even one glass of wine during the pregnancy."

"And?"

"When I woke up the next morning, I had tons of notifications on my phone. I sold everything to a nice gay couple. Couch, chairs, dining room set, even the rug. They picked it up the next day. It was all very cliché—one of them couldn't stop crying. He was so happy to get the table of his dreams."

"I guess they don't have kids yet." Lena snorted. "And now?"

"Now I have a new, colorful rug and half a dozen oversized pillows. I spread them in front of the windows, and Ella and I have been enjoying the view. I have no idea what kind of furniture I need or want. I'll take it day by day."

Lena studied her for a moment. The hazel eyes reflected the green of the trees around them and seemed to peel through the layers of humor Jess had wrapped around her story. "That doesn't sound like you, to be so spontaneous without a plan. Was it difficult?"

Jess didn't know what frightened her more, to act spontaneously or to be seen, really seen, by someone she cared for. "Yeah. I freaked myself out a little."

"You'll know soon enough what you want. I'm sure your gut will tell you sooner or later. Sometimes it's necessary to tear everything down before you know how you want to rebuild."

"Hmm. Maybe." The notion of her internal organs making a decision without the involvement of her brain scared her a little, and she wasn't in the right frame of mind to take care of such details as living room furniture. How could she take on the bigger decisions of her life if the idea of choosing a couch freaked her out that much?

With that uncanny ability to read her, Lena reached out to lightly touch her arm. "Jess, give yourself time. The answers to the important questions will come."

"What questions?" Jess swallowed. They were still talking about the fucking furniture, right?

"What do you want out of your life? What are your priorities?"

"I do have a plan, just not for my furniture." That sounded too defensive, and maybe it was. She couldn't face this tonight. She was tired and afraid. What if Lena was wrong and she didn't find the answers after all?

They continued walking for a few minutes until they reached the crossing where they usually turned around. Jess looked at Lena and raised her eyebrow. With a nod, Lena took a new path. The terrain was a bit rougher but nothing they couldn't handle.

Lena bent down to pick up a pinecone that lay in her way. "When my mother had me, she was fifteen." Her voice was quiet and calm, like a summer evening before a storm, when the birds stopped singing and the air compressed into a tight fist. "She hung around for a few months but then took off and disappeared for the next five or so years. After that, she sometimes visited, brought cheap presents like candy, and disappeared again. I thought she was cool, edgy, had important stuff to do, places to be, but I didn't like that she made my grandma cry. I tried to impress her. I wanted her to smile at me, notice me, when she visited." Lena twisted the pinecone around in her hands, picking off the scales one by one.

Jess wanted to hug her, but Lena walked a few steps to the side as if she needed a safe distance. "Were you angry with her or your grandparents?"

"When I fully realized it wasn't a normal thing to do for a mother, I was maybe twelve or thirteen. By then, it was only Grandma and me at home. My grandpa had died a couple of years earlier. He was older." A muscle in Lena's cheek twitched. Tears rolled down her cheeks, but she made no move to stop them. "Yeah, I was angry and disappointed and confused, and I felt adrift as if I didn't belong anywhere. I had no one to talk to. I had withdrawn from my best friend a few months earlier because I'd started to struggle with my sexuality. I was in the middle of puberty and was having crazy mood swings." She threw the rest of pinecone away. It ricocheted from a tree and almost hit Lena before it fell to the ground. She stared at the mangled seed for a moment, then laughed. "What a perfect lesson for anger management."

Maybe it was inappropriate, but Jess couldn't help but laugh with her. "True. I'll keep it in mind."

Lena picked up the pinecone and laid it to rest next to a tree. She whispered something Jess couldn't quite make out, but it sounded as if she apologized. She wiped her eyes and returned to Jess's side.

Admiration filled Jess with warmth. She could learn a life lesson or two from her. "How did you get out of your anger and mood swings? I don't remember all of puberty, but I think I picked fights with nearly everyone who crossed my path."

"Oh, that was your puberty persona? I guess I met her a couple of months ago." Lena's tone was teasing and light.

Jess chuckled. "You're right. Let's blame my hormones. Better than to admit I was an ass." She sobered and looked in Lena's eyes. "But seriously, I was an ass. I'm sorry."

"It's okay. You already apologized, and I meant it when I said I accepted it." And Lena's eyes confirmed it.

"Thank you." It was remarkable to Jess how Lena didn't hold on to anger. "So what did you do? Drink and cry?"

"I wasn't the type to do something rash or take up drinking and drugs like my mother did when she was young. I hid in the old tree house in the small backyard and poured all my conflicting emotions into my sketches. Most of it was awful teenage stuff, but some of it must have been good. I caught the attention of the art teacher, and she helped me to focus on that. Later, that led to my application for art school and even got me a scholarship. So something good did come out of all that mess after all."

"You had a scholarship to art school? Where did you go?"

"I didn't." Lena looked away and shrugged.

"Oh. Why?"

"Life. Difficult decisions. As I said, I moved in with my mother. My grades suffered, and I lost the scholarship. Then my mother needed my college fund more than I did, and I had to work to pay the bills. No time for college anymore."

"Ah." Jess couldn't find anything appropriate to say. How could a mother rob her daughter of her savings, her education, her future? Anger boiled under the surface, like an earthquake about to tear open a chasm. She clenched the bar of the stroller until her knuckles shone stark white next to the black.

"Hey." Lena's hand stroked over Jess's knuckles. "It was a long time ago. I'm over it."

How could she be? But it wasn't Jess's fight. She eased her grip and relaxed her shoulders. "You're a more forgiving person than I am."

"I'm not so sure." As if talking to herself, Lena's voice was low. She didn't elaborate.

Silence enveloped them as Jess replayed the conversation in her mind. Lena's inner strength was amazing, but it had come at a difficult price.

With her privileged background, Jess had never lacked for a home, parents, funds for college. She'd grown up in the insurmountable security of who she was and where she belonged, believing she could do everything she set her mind to. And the first time something hadn't gone as planned, she'd completely dissolved in anger and insecurity.

Jess stopped and looked at Lena. "Do you want to go back or walk a bit more?"

"You want to drive home?" Lena's eyes were red-rimmed but free of tears for now. Her lips lifted in a serene half smile, and her gaze moved over Jess as if searching for something.

Home? Jess had no idea where her home was anymore. She should turn around and leave, drive to her condo like the independent adult she pretended to be. But she wasn't in the mood to face the emptiness tonight. It was getting late, and it would be much better for Ella if she let her sleep here. Her mom wouldn't mind, and she'd save an hour tomorrow morning. And she could prolong her walk with Lena. But that wasn't why she was staying. Walking was healthy for her since she'd spent all day sitting behind her desk talking to patients and scheduling interventions. Staying was the responsible thing to do. "No. I thought... It's better for Ella to stay here tonight instead of driving back."

Lena tilted her head to the side and did that thing again where Jess felt as if she read her mind. Whatever she found in there, it made her smile.

Chapter Twenty-One

THE PARKING SPOT NEXT TO her Ford was still empty, like a half-finished picture. With a sigh, Lena pushed the stroller past her car. The automatic solar lights flared one by one as she passed them on her way to the patio. This was the third day in a row Jess had missed their walk.

Maggie was waiting with her cell phone in hand. She looked up when Lena approached, and a deep line creased her brow.

Lena parked the stroller next to the table and checked Ella was still sleeping. "Did Jess say when she was coming? Should I take Ella upstairs or leave her here?"

"I haven't heard from her yet." When Maggie shook her head, her impeccable gray updo barely moved. That was different from her usual loose bun that defied gravity with a couple of pencils and luck.

Lena gave her a second look. Maggie's outfit was different too—a neatly pressed dress. No grass stains or wrinkles. "You look great. Are you meeting someone? A date?"

"What has happened to feminism that you assume I'd only dress up if I had a date?" Maggie tutted.

"You're right." Lena sat down, stretched out her legs, and looked at her own loose linen pants, crinkled after a day of wear. Comfortable but far from elegant. "And what do I know about dates or dressing up anyway? It's been ages for me."

"Really? I thought…" Maggie studied Lena like one of her rare plants. "What about you and Jess?"

"Jess?" Her voice came out shrill, and she swallowed to get it back under control. "Why would you think that? We're just friends." With benefits, but she didn't need to say that out loud. To Jess's mother. Heat shot to her cheeks, and she bent down to adjust the closures of her sandals that didn't need adjusting.

"I might be old, but I'm not blind. Wasn't that a date three weeks ago, when you both dressed up? You two weren't wearing that nice dress and that suit to clean her apartment."

Reluctantly, Lena sat up again. Maggie's voice was still friendly, but would she approve of Lena dating her daughter? She had too much debt, no education, nothing to offer. Not that they were dating. They were friends who'd had fun—twice. How could she explain their non-relationship to Jess's mother? She wasn't sure she understood the rules and boundaries herself. "Um… We… It's not…"

Maggie reached over and lightly squeezed Lena's knee. "It's okay. You don't have to explain. You're both adults."

Lena sank back in her chair. "It's complicated. We're friends, but the rest is still…open." And whatever it was, it didn't seem to be a priority for Jess, as they'd barely spent any time together.

Again, that intense gaze held hers. But Maggie's smile was far from judgmental. The acceptance and affection reminded her of her grandma. "Whenever you want to talk about it, you can come to me. I might be Jess's mother, but I cherish you as a friend too and won't automatically take her side."

Lena blinked as tears rose. Luck and a random chat with a stranger at the market had led her to this wonderful place, and hearing their friendship was mutual warmed her more than she could say. "Thank you."

The vibration of an incoming message rattled Maggie's phone. She looked at it and sighed. "I better call my friends and cancel dinner. Jess is running late again."

"Wait, don't cancel your plans. I can watch Ella until she gets here."

"It might be late, and you're already doing so much for her."

"It's no problem. I'll put Ella to bed, and then sit here and sketch a bit."

"Thank you." Maggie stood and hugged her, then leaned in the stroller to whisper a goodbye to Ella.

Darkness had settled around the cocoon of light on the patio when steps on the gravel announced Jess's arrival.

"Oh, hi, Lena. Where's Mom?" Jess's grin was unapologetic. Did she really think this behavior was acceptable?

"She's out."

"Out? What about Ella?"

"What do you think? I didn't have anything better to do with my evening." Lena pushed the baby monitor toward her.

It tumbled over and nearly slid off the table. Jess caught it at the last moment and carefully placed it back on the table.

Oops. That hadn't been intentional, but Lena wasn't in the mood to apologize. She raised her chin.

"You didn't need to sacrifice your evening to watch her. My mom said she would do it."

"And she would have. But she had plans, and I didn't."

"She didn't say anything about plans."

"Did you even ask? It's Friday evening, and your mother has friends. Have you even considered the possibility Maggie is giving up much of her well-earned rest and plans for you?"

"Don't you think this conversation should be between her and me? You're not her daughter."

Lena flinched. That was true. She wasn't Maggie's daughter, but she still cared about her. Right now, she seemed to care more than Jess did. "Yes, you should absolutely have this conversation with your mother, but I see a side of her that you can't." She stood with the intention to leave.

"What makes you think that?" Jess's question stopped Lena before she'd gone more than a couple of steps.

She faced Jess. "Because you're never here. And when you are, you're too self-absorbed to see. You don't see how she always prepares an extra portion of dinner in case you're hungry when you come in the evening. You don't see her tired in the morning because she took care of Ella during the night when you were on call or couldn't make it. She's retired, and you're making her work twenty-four-seven."

"I'm not making her do anything. She offered, and I accepted. She loves her granddaughter." The lack of remorse in Jess's voice was maddening.

"Of course she loves her, and she loves you too. That's why she's doing it. Like my grandma took care of me without a second thought." Anger at her own mother rose like a badly buried fire in the wind. "But it aged her to have a baby again when she had already raised one difficult daughter. I'm sure that's why she had a stroke in her early sixties." Jess's shaking of her head only fanned the flames. "If you continue like this, you could kill your mom."

"You accuse me of killing my mother?" Jess recoiled as if she'd been slapped, then she squared her shoulders and took a step forward, right in Lena's personal space. "Just because you think you killed your grandmother doesn't make it true," Jess said slowly. "That's not what causes a stroke."

The easy dismissal of Lena's concerns broke her last restraints. "I'm not accusing you of anything. I'm warning you. Everything revolves around you and your work. You think you can do your thing, and everyone has to jump and cover for you. It's not fair to Ella and Maggie." *And not to me.* Lena shoved the last thought back in the recess of her mind where it belonged. She had no claim on Jess's time.

"My work is important. I can't float along and hope for the best. I made plans, and I need to stick to them. My mother gets it; that's why she supports me while I get back on track. You can't get ahead in the cardiology department if you run home at five every day."

Lena gasped as the meaning of Jess's words hit her like a kick to the gut. "And you think because I don't have a detailed plan for the rest of my life, because my work isn't important, I can't understand you? Who do you think you are, Doctor Riley? Do you think because you're a cardiologist you're the only one who knows what breaks people's hearts?"

"What? No. I haven't said that. I haven't been talking about you at all." Jess raised her hands, palms outward. "I thought we were discussing my relationship with my mom. Which is none of your business."

"Maggie is my friend, and that makes it my business." Why couldn't Jess see Lena loved Maggie almost like a mother? She tried to put all her feelings into her voice to reach Jess. "If I had a family like yours, I would do everything to show my mom how much I value her. I wouldn't disregard her feelings to follow a plan."

"So that's it? You want a substitute mom and suddenly you're an expert on our family?" Jess towered over her like the statue of an avenging goddess.

"I won't apologize for taking my work seriously and having a solid plan for my future. That's what got me this far."

Lena's head swam from the backlash. She couldn't focus on everything Jess had said and latched onto the last statement. "Forget your plan for a second! If it's so perfect, why are you so unhappy about it all? You've followed your plan and have all you need for a perfect life: a healthy daughter, your own condo, a job you love, a supportive mother, probably more money than you need—and you don't value any of it." Lena had had enough. Jess opened her mouth to reply, but she wasn't finished yet. All these weeks she'd stuffed her frustration in a locked box, and now that she'd lifted the lid a little, everything spilled out. "Yes, you had a shitty year. Your health failed you. But what did you learn from it? Your heart has recovered, but your ego is still bleeding."

Jess paled and took a step back. "Ego? You have no idea about my feelings."

"How can I? You close yourself off emotionally. We've talked and shared quite a bit over the last few weeks, but whenever we scratch the surface, you retreat. And that's why we're just friends with benefits or fuck buddies or whatever you want to call it."

"Friends? You call this friendship?" Jess gestured between them.

"Yes. I wouldn't care what a stranger or even an acquaintance thinks of me. If you weren't a friend, it wouldn't hurt that you believe I only cared about Maggie because I want a substitute mother." Lena wiped her eyes with one hand, then jerked it away and balled her hands into fists. She wouldn't give Jess the satisfaction of seeing her cry, damn it. "And if we weren't friends, I wouldn't care about you. About how your work affects you and your relationships with Maggie and Ella. How it affects your health."

Jess stared at her, lips pressed together in a thin line. Her face was flushed, but her expression didn't give away any of her thoughts or emotions. Only her expressive eyes revealed the storm brewing inside.

She reminded Lena of the Jess she'd first met. She'd been as full of anger then as she was today and had lashed out like a trapped animal.

Lena's own irritation and frustration urged her to do the same. But she wouldn't. She wanted to reach Jess, not drive her away. She deliberately opened her fists and loosened her shoulders. They weren't in a fighting match, no matter how much Jess's punches hurt. Or how much her own punches had hit Jess already. "I'm sorry for throwing it all at you when you came home after a long day."

A muscle twitched in Jess's jaw, and moisture pooled in her eyes, but she didn't say anything.

"Jess?" Lena touched her arm. The hard muscles under her fingertips vibrated.

That broke the spell. Jess grabbed the baby monitor and turned on her heel. Without another word, she stalked into the house.

Lena wanted to follow her, but instead, she packed away her sketching supplies. She cleaned the fine brushes with a bit of water, then dried them with a cloth. Meticulously, she placed each brush, pen, and pencil into its slot in her roll. The leather was worn to a perfect suppleness and frayed around the edges. Her grandma had given it to her the day she'd moved to her mother's, and it was the only personal possession, apart from a backpack of clothes, that she'd taken with her when she'd had to leave the house because her mother hadn't paid the bills.

Was she looking for another mother? She hadn't thought so, but that didn't make Jess's statement less true. Sometimes other people could see your motives more clearly. And why had she acted so out of character? She needed to do some work unpacking her emotions and examining her motives. And then she would have to make some decisions on how far she was willing to involve herself in Jess's life. If she even let her after her tirade.

++++++++

Jess had planned to get Ella and drive home, away from Lena and her accusations. But when she saw her daughter sleeping peacefully, she changed her mind. It was late anyway. And driving while angry was dangerous. She was no trauma surgeon, but she'd seen her share of unnecessary accidents during her career. And if she was honest, she hated her empty condo. So she flung herself into her old bed and tossed and turned until she passed out from sheer exhaustion in a fitful sleep. An hour before dawn, Ella's cries had woken her.

Now Jess rested on a deck chair, with a sated and clean Ella on her chest, both of them covered by a cozy blanket. She waited for dawn, the universal signal of a new day, a new start.

Last night's restlessness hadn't been conducive to logical thinking, but a realization had formed like a tiny flame growing into a signal fire. Lena was right; something had to give. She couldn't continue with her life the way she'd planned it, driving back and forth with an unreliable work schedule.

Jess considered the problem again, and this morning the solution was obvious. She had several options: She could leave Ella with her mother permanently during the week, she could take her to daycare, or she could hire a nanny.

The first option wasn't fair to her mom. Lena's accusations had been over the top, but there was a kernel of truth in them. Daycare was an option, but each and every one she'd visited had lacked something. If she was honest with herself, she didn't like the impersonal aspect of it while Ella was still so young. So number three it was.

The thought of letting a stranger into her home was disconcerting, and not only during the day but twenty-four-seven. How else would they handle the long hours or, even worse, the times she was on call? She needed someone to live with her. Someone trustworthy, reliable, honest—someone who loved Ella and whom she could stand to be around all the time. Apart from her mother, only one other person came to mind. Lena.

It was perfect. Ella sleeping on top of her stopped Jess from jumping up and pacing excitedly. Ella would get the care she needed. Lena would get a real job doing something she loved and would have enough time to sketch. Maybe she could even still work a few hours for Jess's mom if she wanted to. She could even make a career out of nannying when Ella was older and didn't need her anymore. Money wasn't an issue for Jess, so she would work out a fair wage, health insurance, and maybe even send her to a few qualification courses or something. The more she thought about the plan, the more it appealed to her.

At a quarter to six, she carried the still sleeping Ella to her room and picked up the baby monitor. Hoping Ella would give her at least a couple of hours to talk to Lena, she tiptoed to her room to change for tai chi.

With her stomach in knots, Jess crossed the lawn.

Lena had already started the greeting ritual. When Jess approached, she froze for a second, then finished the movement. Without meeting Jess's gaze, she nodded once.

It took nearly a minute for Jess to find the right stance. Wherever she put her feet, the balance was off somehow, and it was more difficult than even the first time to quell her urge to move. She'd rather talk, but she respected Lena's need for a morning routine.

Maybe they could decorate the living room together to create a training space for both of them. For the first time in weeks, a spark of enthusiasm flickered when she thought about her condo and her life there.

The hour seemed endless. As soon as Lena bowed to the ground, words spilled from Jess like an overflowing dam. "I thought a lot last night. You were right. At least partly."

"Good morning to you too." Lena's smile was more teasing than mocking and couldn't dampen Jess's eagerness.

"Sorry, good morning. Do you have some time?"

"Twenty minutes, then I need to get ready for the market. Tea on the porch?"

Jess had forgotten Lena still sold preserves. She would be able to give that up too. "Um, okay." She didn't need tea, but Lena would be more comfortable with a hot drink.

In the few minutes the water needed to boil, Jess went over her arguments again and was ready to spill the moment Lena placed two mugs between them and sat down.

But Lena beat her to it. "I'm sorry for yelling at you yesterday. I wasn't fair. That's not how I want to communicate. Or how I want to be." She shifted in her seat, but her gaze never left Jess's eyes.

"Thank you. I want to apologize too." The uneasiness in Jess's stomach dissolved. They were both ready to find a solution. "You were right about some things, and I needed to hear them. I need to change something with Ella's care, and I came up with a great solution that will solve both our problems. I need someone to take care of Ella full-time, and it can't be my mother. I still don't think it would age or even kill her, but you're right. She has her own life."

Lena opened her mouth to say something, but Jess couldn't wait. She had only twenty minutes, and she wanted to lay out every positive argument before Lena could doubt the idea. Jess reached over the small table and took Lena's hand. "Hear me out, please. I need someone who stays at my place, who adjusts to Ella's rhythm, who can even take care of her when I'm on call and need to go to the hospital in the middle of the night. And I would pay, of course, a generous wage and provide a room and all the groceries. What do you think?"

Lena's brow furrowed, and her hand was shaking. "I'm not sure what you're saying. You want to hire a nanny?"

"Exactly! I want to hire a nanny. But not anyone. You." Jess beamed, expecting Lena to smile back.

But she didn't. Lena showed no reaction, not even the tiniest smile. It was as if her face had been frozen. Maybe she hadn't understood what Jess was saying.

"It would be perfect." Jess squeezed her hand. "You could do a job you cared about instead of being my mom's assistant. And you would save on living expenses. You'd be out of debt in no time. And you could make a career out of it, attend some courses on the weekend, get a certification or something. I would pay for it."

Lena blinked, but her frown didn't lessen. "You want me to be Ella's nanny? You came up with this brilliant plan, and now you thrust it on me?" Lena's voice got louder with each word. She jumped up and shook off Jess's hand. "Without asking for my opinion, you plan out my life, my career? And why? Because it would make your life so much easier." Her eyes blazed. "I'm not obligated to make your life less complicated."

No, Lena had it all wrong. This was the perfect solution for both of them. Why couldn't she see it? "It's not for me. Well, not just for me. We would both profit from it. And we could live together. Wouldn't it be great to spend more time together?" Jess hadn't even considered the last part before she spoke it out loud, but as she said it, she knew it was important. Maybe as important as the rest.

"I won't be Ella's nanny. Been there, done that. And my career and debt aren't your business. Where I work, what I earn, and how I pay for my life might not be up to your standards, but I'm in control. It's my life, my decision. And Jess…" Lena looked her up and down with an expression as if she'd stepped into a pile of shit. "Don't ever again suggest paying me to spend time with you."

Lena strode away and closed the door behind her. The lock snapped into place like a slap.

"Fuck!" How could everything have gone so wrong so fast?

Jess rose and picked up the baby monitor with trembling hands. Should she follow, talk this out? No. She wasn't quite sure what she'd done this time to fuck it all up, and she needed to give Lena's words some serious thought. That would leave Lena some time to cool down, and then she'd talk to her again.

Chapter Twenty-Two

LENA'S CAR GROANED AS IT fought with the last steep stretch of road and sighed as they reached Maggie's driveway as if it knew it would now be able to rest after the hard labor. Lena sighed with it. The driveway was empty. Not that unusual for Monday morning, but all weekend she'd been dreading seeing Jess again. It was a relief to know she had at least a ten-hour respite until she came to pick up Ella.

Lena got out of the car and stretched her back and neck. She wished she had time for tai chi, but she was running late for work with Maggie.

The old couch had been uncomfortable but good enough. Lena had forgotten Rachel lived with her mother when she'd asked for a place to stay. But Rachel had invited her without question when Lena had told her she needed some time and space to think. Running away wasn't Lena's usual solution, but she hadn't wanted to face Jess while she was still angry and hurt. And the distance had helped. All weekend she'd gone through the things they'd said to each other. With each statement, she'd examined the emotions rising in her and had tugged and prodded at them to see if they were hiding even deeper emotions, buried beneath the fear of getting hurt again.

Jess had made a few good points. Lena was in search of a family of her own, but that wasn't so wrong. Didn't everyone look for similar things? She wasn't trying to find a replacement for her grandma and mother. She was trying to follow her own path, wherever it may lead.

Usually, it didn't lead to deeper connections to people. Even her many friendships were mostly superficial. She steered clear of commitment because she always expected rejection. She had moved from town to town, house to house, without putting down roots. Until recently. Here, in Maggie's garden, with her solid friendship, Lena wanted to stay.

That was the reason she had hesitated to get involved with Jess. Everything was too connected: her home, her job, her friendship with Maggie. She cared for Maggie and valued her opinion, she adored Ella, and Jess... It would be too easy to fall in love with her if Jess continued to be charming and attentive. But Jess had made it clear she didn't think of Lena as equal. She'd mapped out Lena's life without consulting her as if Lena wasn't able to do it herself.

Halfway to the main house, Lena's steps faltered as if she was wading through knee deep mud. What if Jess had talked with her mother and Maggie supported the plan? Lena couldn't get between mother and daughter and expect to have Maggie on her side.

She let herself fall on the bench next to the path and buried her head in her hands. What had she been thinking? Tears wet her palms, and she rubbed her eyes as if that would stop them leaking.

Jess's suggestion had been too much. It had been the situation with her mother all over again, only now Lena could see the hurt that would be in front of her. Jess wanted her as a nanny, like her mother had wanted her as a free babysitter. And Lena knew how this would end. She'd fall hopelessly in love with Ella and probably Jess as well, and then Ella would grow up, or Jess would find a partner to be the second mother, or anything else could happen, and Lena would have to go, leaving pieces of her heart behind once again.

Her heart had been pushed around so often she still felt the bruises. She hadn't wanted to make herself so vulnerable again, but it was too late. All the women in the Riley family had found their way around her protective walls.

And now the walls crumbled all around her, burying her alive. She fought to take a calming breath, but her chest was tight as if stones crushed her. A sound, half wail, half sob, escaped her, and she pressed her hand over her mouth. She couldn't cry now. She couldn't break down. *Stop it! Get up!* But her limbs didn't obey, their heaviness binding them to the bench like lead chains.

"Lena, honey." Maggie slid onto the bench next to her and slung one arm around her.

Too tired to fight for composure anymore, Lena let herself be pulled into the embrace. Her tears continued to fall, streaking in hot rivulets down her face.

Maggie held her, stroking her back.

After what felt an eternity, Lena had no tears left, and numbness had replaced the pain. She freed herself from Maggie's arms and rubbed her eyes. Her nose was stuffy, and she searched her pockets for a tissue.

"Here." Maggie held out a handkerchief—white, with a sprig of lavender stitched on it.

Lena circled the stitching with the tip of her finger. "That's too precious."

"Here," Maggie repeated and pushed it into her hand. "You're precious too."

That caused more tears, but Lena pressed her eyes closed to hold them back. "Thank you." She wiped her face, blew her nose, and carefully folded the tissue to put it in her pocket. She'd wash it later. "I'm so sorry."

Maggie shook her head. "It's okay. Come with me. I might have what you need." She stood and offered her hand.

Even though she didn't want to appear needy, Lena grasped her hand like a lifeline and let Maggie lead her to the patio. The table was set for two with a stack of cinnamon buns.

"Have you had breakfast yet? I had the urge to bake this morning." She held up the plate.

"Thank you." Lena took the offered roll even though her stomach was too tight to eat. The warm scents of cinnamon and sugar filled the air with memories of her grandma. Instead of following her first instinct to push the memory away, Lena let it soothe her like a hug. She needed it today.

Maggie poured coffee and placed a cup and a plate in front of Lena. "I haven't seen you this weekend."

"I, um, I was with Rachel." Even though she wasn't sure her stomach was up for it, she took a bite of the cinnamon roll to gain some time.

"You don't have to explain, but... Did Rachel make you cry, or has something else happened? Can I help?"

So Jess hadn't talked to her mom after all. Lena wasn't sure if she was relieved or disappointed. She put the roll on her plate, took a sip of coffee, and grimaced. It was too bitter after the intense sweetness. "I had to think about a few things and…I think I should move out." Now that she had said the thing she'd been dreading all weekend, she didn't feel the expected relief. Shouldn't things be easier once you said them aloud?

"What? Why?" Maggie seemed shocked. "Has something happened?"

"Jess and I had a couple of discussions on Friday and Saturday, and we both said some hurtful things. But some of what she said had a bit of truth in it."

"Oh no!" Maggie grimaced. "I'm so sorry you have problems. But that's no reason to move out. Can't you work it out? Let me talk to her."

Lena blinked as tears threatened to fall again. She shouldn't burden Maggie with her mess. "No, no. It's my problem. I got too tangled up with all of you, especially Ella. It's better if I keep a little distance."

"Did Jess say that?" Maggie almost growled.

"I don't want to involve you."

"I'm already involved." Maggie pointed at her tear-stained blouse and sighed. "What has happened?"

"She has this plan where I should come and live at her place as a full-time nanny." Lena tried her best to sound neutral, but she couldn't hold Maggie's gaze.

"Is that something you two have talked about before? Something you might want to do?"

Lena pushed the last bit of the cinnamon roll from one side of her plate to the other. There was no room in her stomach beside the rising dread. "No. I mean, I love Ella, but working for Jess, living with her as an employee? That feels completely wrong."

"I'd say so. Not when you're dating."

"We're not dating." How could they date if they both wanted and needed different things?

"Well, whatever you call it, it's not a work relationship, is it?"

Lena snorted. "No, not at all."

"And let me guess, this arrangement is solving all of Jess's time management problems? My girl is nothing but efficient."

Despite her predicament, Lena had to smile. "The way you say *girl*… She would hate it."

"She isn't behaving like an adult recently. But I should not call her that to her face." Maggie's dry tone was so much like Jess's that it left no doubt where her daughter had got it from.

"Probably not."

"But back to your problem. What you said so far was she offered you a job and you declined. That's hardly a reason to despair and move out. So what else has happened?"

"You're her mother. Shouldn't you be on her side?"

"I am, but you're my friend too, and I always want to hear both sides. I hate to see you hurting." The sincerity in her voice was Lena's undoing.

She couldn't hold back anymore, and she didn't want to anyway. She trusted Maggie. "It's just…a couple of days ago, I told her about my complicated relationship with my mother. I didn't grow up with her and when she took me to live with her, I was so happy…" Her eyes started to burn again, and Lena pressed them shut. She had wasted too many tears on her mother already. "I found out too late that she only wanted me as a cheap babysitter. I thought I was over it, but obviously I wasn't. Jess opened an old wound."

"Jess asked you to be her babysitter even after you told her about your mother?" Maggie growled. "That girl!"

Lena flinched. "She didn't know about my mother using me, at least not all of it." Because she had done herself what she accused Jess of: stayed on the surface and not opened deeply enough. "And I hurt her too. I said things she didn't want to hear. That her way of handling Ella's care wasn't working out. And I accused her of…" Lena buried her face in her hands and rubbed her eyes.

"But maybe she needed to hear that." Maggie sighed. "Jess brooded and sulked around all weekend, and she wouldn't have done that if you didn't hit a nerve. The truth can be hurtful, but ultimately she'll benefit from it."

She'd accused Jess of killing her mother. That wasn't only hurtful and wrong, but uncalled for. Did Maggie know? She swallowed and let her hands drop to face Maggie. "Did she talk to you?"

"Not yet. It usually takes a while." Maggie smiled ruefully.

Relief flooded Lena, immediately followed by another wave of guilt.

Maggie didn't seem to notice either. "Why don't you wait a few days before you decide whether you move out or not? And talk to Jess again after you two have cooled down. Maybe this argument between you two will work itself out. Jess won't be here that much this week because she has two nights on call."

Yesterday, moving out had seemed the best solution, but maybe Maggie was right. The garden house had become her home. Running away wasn't a solution but a childish way of avoiding her problems. She shouldn't let her fear of getting hurt direct her life. "Okay. I'll stay and see how it is."

Maggie sipped her coffee and studied Lena for a moment. "Tell me if I can do anything for you. Do you want to take the day off?"

"No, I'd rather work and get my mind on other things." The next couple of evenings and nights would be enough time to reflect on her behavior. "If that's okay with you?"

"Sure. If you want to get your mind on something completely different, I have a proposal for you. Friday evening, I had dinner with some former colleagues from the university. I was showing them pictures of Ella on my phone and some pictures of your sketches were between them. My friend Joanne loved them."

"Thank you." Lena had long ago given up her dream of sharing her art with other people but that didn't meant she couldn't appreciate compliments. "That really brightens up my day."

"You haven't heard the proposal yet. Joanne is an art professor at the University of Washington, and she's teaching a course on botanical illustration this year. She's offered to let you take the course if that's something you'd be interested in."

"Art professor? At the university?" Lena's voice was shaking, and she resisted the urge to pinch herself. "But I don't have any qualifications or formal training."

"But you have talent and an eye for details." Maggie shrugged. "Joanne loved what she saw and thinks you're more than qualified."

For a moment, Lena let herself dream. She'd take the course, meet other art students, learn about the craft. But then reality snatched her out of her vision, and she slumped down in her seat. "Thank you. But I can't afford it, and I won't have the time to spare because I'm working."

"You don't need to pay. You can sit in on the class for free. And we'll make time for it. Providing you want to continue working with me?"

"Yes, of course. Even if Jess can't forgive me, I would still like to work with you." A load lifted from Lena's shoulder. Maggie wouldn't let her go because of Jess. "But the other offer, I'm overwhelmed. I need to think about it."

"Take your time. She won't take it back. If you want to, I can invite her over and you two can talk informally. Let me know what you prefer."

"Thanks." Lena took the last bite of her cinnamon roll. The offer was tempting, but she needed to sleep on it. Today she was too emotionally drained to make a decision. With a look at Maggie's plate and cup, she confirmed that she had finished her breakfast too. "Can we start work now? I think I need to do something that is absolutely not related to any of my emotional problems."

Maggie laughed. "How about sorting my stack of handwritten notes? That might be problematic but at least not emotionally."

At the sight of Lena's car, Jess's heartbeat quickened. Not in anger but with relief and anticipation. Not knowing where Lena was the last couple of days had been exhausting. Jess had no right to know about Lena's comings and goings, but the possibility she had chased Lena away had filled her stomach with lead.

Jess wasn't up to facing her yet. She had given their discussion more than enough thought but still wasn't sure she had a good grip on the problems that had come up during their arguments. That was why she had finished work extra early today and intended to talk to her mom.

The patio was empty, but the doors to the kitchen stood wide open. Jess followed the scent of fresh vegetables and herbs. Her mom was cooking, and Ella lay in her carrier on the table, staring at the colorful chain of fish Lena had given her. Even though Jess always insisted this was her mother's house and not her own, right now the warm and fuzzy feeling in her middle told her she was coming home.

"Hi, Mom."

"Jess, you're here already." Her tone held no accusation, but it still felt like one.

Maybe because the topic had been on Jess's mind all day. "Yeah, not much going on at work." Only because she had pushed everything from her schedule that wasn't time sensitive. Her residents and fellows were annoyed, but Jess had never attempted to win the most-likable competition and wouldn't start now.

"Hi, honey. Did you have fun today?" Jess went to Ella and picked her up. She kissed the smooth cheek, inhaling her scent. Home.

Ella opened her hands and reached out, and Jess gave her a finger to cling to.

With Ella on her arm, she wandered over to the stove. "What are you cooking?" The pot was enormous as if her mom planned to feed her high school track team.

"Vegetable soup. The garden is overflowing, so I thought I'd freeze a few batches for winter. It's almost ready. Do you want to join me for dinner?"

That would be the perfect opportunity to ask her mom a few questions. At least if they were alone. "Won't Lena eat with you?"

"No, she wanted to eat alone tonight." Her mom gave her *the* look. The look prompting her to spill her guts.

Jess flashed back to her teenage years when she had done something stupid or tried to hide anything. She refrained from rolling her eyes, but it was difficult.

"I'll set the table." She switched Ella to her hip and gathered the cutlery, water glasses, and napkins one handed. Another throwback to her teenage years, but now she did the job without sulking because she was grateful someone had cooked and she didn't need to. Maybe it was time to say things like that out loud. "Thanks for cooking, Mom. I really appreciate your homemade meals."

Her mom carried two ceramic bowls filled with steaming soup to the table. She sat down with a wide smile. "I can't remember hearing that from you before. You're welcome."

They both dug in, and for a few minutes, the sounds of spoons dipping and contented sighs transported Jess to her childhood years.

"Mom, how did you do it? Balance your career and motherhood?" Jess held the spoon out of Ella's reach to let it cool.

"Mmh, I guess I was lucky. I had just gotten a secure position at the university and took a year off. You were an easy baby, and your dad worked long hours, so I had time to write my first book. That sold well, not only in academia, and the university was more than happy to get me back afterward.

Later I scheduled my lectures and office hours around your daycare and school. But we were a very privileged family. Money was never a problem for us, and we could hire people to clean, cook, and run errands."

"It all sounds so easy."

"Well, I glossed over the exhausting details." Her mom smiled and took a sip of water. "You never asked me that before."

"I always took everything for granted. Hot meals when I arrived home, clean laundry, help with my homework. I never wondered how you fit in everything with a career."

"And now you're looking for a way to handle it yourself?"

"Yes. I'm tired all the time, and I don't know if it's remnants of my illness or everything else."

"I was constantly tired for five or six years. It got better once you started school."

Jess grimaced. That wasn't an enticing prospect. "What else did you gloss over?"

"I often felt alone. I loved your dad, but he was focused on his work and we barely saw each other, mostly just on weekends. I don't know if you remember, but in the early years, he worked on Saturdays too."

Those Saturdays had been the highlight of Jess's week. "I remember he took me with him sometimes. He always told me to stay in his office and paint something, but I snuck into the exam rooms and hid while he talked to patients. He had such a calming presence. I loved to listen to him."

Her mom shook her head with an indulgent smile. "I'm glad I only learned about that years later."

"You know, when I was a teenager, I always wanted to be a parent like Dad. Relaxed, fun on the weekends, always patient. He always had time for me in the evenings." With the eyes of a single mother, these memories took on another shape as if someone had removed the colorful filter. "But he was home less than I remember, right? Did he help you with the day to day stuff?"

"Your question says it all. He was always there for you, and he helped some. But if you want to know if it was an equal partnership, no. I did most of the mundane work, and he did the fun parts. I'm not hung up about it, but maybe you shouldn't look at your dad or me as examples. Different times, different circumstances. What do you want? What kind of parent do you want to be?"

That question left her speechless for a moment. Jess ate a few more bites of soup to gain time, then put the spoon down. "I thought I knew, but...I really have no clue."

"Jess, honey, before your first day at school, you showed me a list of things you needed to learn in order to become a doctor. Before you started college, you had all your coursework mapped out for the next four years. Why do you have plans and contingency plans for everything but didn't think about this before you got pregnant? Or during your pregnancy?"

"I wish I knew. I always thought I had more time, and everything would fall into place naturally." Jess ran her hand through her hair. Her mom was right. This lack of solid plans and preparations had been so unlike her she couldn't understand it herself. "Or maybe I didn't want to admit to myself I couldn't do it alone. I had such an easy and happy childhood. I never saw you or Dad struggle."

"I think I should apologize." Her mom's sad smile underscored the realization that Jess had misinterpreted a major part of her childhood. "We always tried to keep our problems away from you."

"And I'm grateful for that. But if I had opened my eyes, I could have seen all the work it took. I guess I was blind and naive. And this might sound conceited, but I always achieved everything I set out to do. Track team, med school, getting the dates everyone else was envious of. I was the youngest cardiologist in our hospital to specialize in the TAVR technique. I thought I could do everything." Heat rose into Jess's cheeks. Yes, that did sound conceited, privileged, and terribly shallow. When had she turned into a woman she couldn't respect anymore?

"And you can do everything, but maybe not in the exact way you imagined. Change is a part of life. It's not too late to ask yourself where your priorities in life are and how you want to proceed."

That was frighteningly close to what Lena had said to her. Jess nodded. "And I need to look at how my decisions impact others. Mom, is taking care of Ella too much for you during the day?"

"At the moment, no."

Jess could leave it at that. She had an answer that could quiet her guilty conscience, but she owed it to her mom to dig deeper. "But for how long? What about in a few months or a year?"

"That's a long time from now, but you're right. We need to talk about it. I'm tapping into my energy reserves. It's not a problem for now, but I can't say how long they'll last. But you know I'm happy to take care of Ella anytime. I love her as much as I love you and would do anything for my girls."

Tears pooled in Jess's eyes, and she blinked them away. "Thank you, but I don't think it's a great idea we're both running around depleting our reserves. I have to find an alternative. I thought I had, but..." She grimaced. She didn't want to go into her discussion with Lena with her mom. She wasn't sure she understood enough of what had happened.

"I'll support you, whatever you do. This alternative... Are you talking about the offer you made Lena?"

"She told you?" Jess froze with her spoon halfway to her mouth. "What did she say?"

"Not much. She told me you offered her a job as a nanny. Why did you do that?"

"I thought she'd love working with Ella. And I trust her, more than anyone but you." Jess sighed. "I offended her, but I'm not sure why. How is she?"

"When I saw her this morning, she was hurt and confused. She's even thinking about moving."

"What? Why?" The spoon fell into the bowl, and hot soup splashed on Jess's hand. She couldn't care less about that.

"So she can avoid you. Or so she said."

"But...she loves the garden house and the work with you. Why would she give all that up to avoid me?" Jess's heart clenched. Had she driven Lena away?

"You need to ask her that, not me."

"Do you think she'd talk to me?" The thought that she wouldn't, that it was too late, hurt as if a knife twisted in Jess's stomach.

"Yes of course. Lena needs a little time. And unlike you, she likes to talk through her problems, not stew over them silently."

Since when did her mom know Lena so well? But she was right. Time was something she could give, even if it would take all her resolve not to run to Lena right now. "I'll give her time, and then I'll apologize. Maybe we can get our friendship back."

"Is friendship all there is between you?"

The memory of waking in Lena's arms flashed in her mind, followed by the picture of sitting at her feet on the ottoman in her bedroom. Jess couldn't remember the last time she'd felt so seen and cared for, but she'd fled like a coward. She'd feared she was getting in too deep, too fast. "Maybe not. But I don't know if I can offer her more. I'm not the best I can be at the moment."

"But maybe you don't need to be more now. She seems to like you as you are. You can always grow together."

Jess leaned back in her chair. "Maybe." Another thing to put on her mental list of things to consider. Even if she wasn't her best self, would she have something to offer Lena might want? Would Lena be able to see past her failings and weaknesses, or would she reject what little Jess had to offer? And where could she find the time for a relationship when she wasn't even able to care for her child alone?

Lena ripped open the large envelope and poured out the contents on the kitchen table. Her former roommate had forwarded anything in her letterbox indiscriminately. She could imagine far better plans for the evening than sorting mail, but she had learned the hard way that procrastination didn't help paying her bills.

Junk, Chinese takeout menu, junk, a bill she already had paid, junk, pizza menu. Lena sighed in relief. For once, she seemed to be on top of things. She picked up the pizza menu to add it to the recycling stack and recoiled as if she'd uncovered a snake about to bite.

The white envelope with her typed name and address looked like nothing special. But one glance at the sender was all it took to freeze her with panic.

Her mother had written her. Again. Hadn't she understood Lena didn't want to keep in contact? She'd never replied to any of the letters and had ignored all phone calls. What more could she do?

You could act like an adult and tell her. The voice of reason sounded suspiciously like her grandma. Lena put down the crinkled pizza menu and held up the letter instead.

Before she could change her mind, she tore it open and shook out the single sheet, ripped from a legal pad. Her mother's uneven handwriting covered most of it. The words tumbled over the page like drunken dancers, and the trembling of Lena's fingers didn't help to decipher the text.

Lena took a deep breath and pressed the page to the table. She could do this. She scanned the page.

Nothing new. Only the regular reminder her mother suffered in prison because she hadn't the money to buy the daily necessities.

Like painkillers and drugs. Not that her mother would spell it out for the guards to read.

It continued with the accusation that Lena owed her because she'd been the sole heir of Grandma.

Yeah, right. As if she'd seen a penny of her inheritance after she'd paid off her mother's bills.

The letter ended with a plea to pick up the phone the next time she called.

Not one question about Lena, about her life or health or financial struggle.

Not one word of affection.

She crumpled the paper into a tight ball and flung it into the recycling bin. It bounced out of the woven basket and rolled over the floor until it ended up at her feet. Like the pinecone she'd mangled on her walk with Jess.

A strangled laugh escaped Lena, halfway to a sob.

Why did she let her mother get to her like that? She'd prided herself in being over her, but that wasn't true. She'd allowed her unresolved anger at her mother to color her interaction with Jess. That wasn't fair, neither to Jess nor to herself. She needed to work on getting over her pain.

Lena jumped up and paced from the kitchen to the living room and back, picking up the discarded letter. Her mother was right even if Lena hated to admit it. They needed to talk.

Before she could change her mind, she dug her old cell phone from the desk drawer and plugged it to the charger in her kitchen. After a moment, it sprang to life with a series of loud beeps. Ten missed calls. Lena didn't need to check the numbers, only one person ever tried to reach her on this phone. Her mother must be desperate to talk to her. How long would it take until she tried again?

Please let it be soon. Dread churned in her stomach at the thought of waiting for days, always on edge. If only Lena could control the timing of the talk, but calling the prison wasn't possible and traveling all the way to Illinois for a face-to-face meeting wasn't in her budget.

As if the universe had heard her plea, the phone started to ring. The shrill tone sent shivers down her spine. She hadn't prepared, she wasn't ready, she wanted to shut it off and crawl into her bed.

Oh, no. You don't. Lena stabbed the button to answer the call. "Walker."

A mechanical voice advised her where the call came from and that it would be recorded, followed by her mother. "Lena? Is that really you?"

"Um, hi, Caroline."

"Why didn't you take any of my calls? Do you have any idea what it takes for me to get in line here?" Her mother snorted, a sound so familiar that Lena could almost see the accompanying eye-rolling. "Of course not. You're free to come and go as you please."

"I'm sorry." Lena leaned against the kitchen counter. The wood was solid behind her back.

"Yeah, yeah. I'm calling because you need to make a deposit in my account. Did you get my letter?"

Lena twisted the cable of the charger around her index finger until the blood flow was cut off. The sharp pain was a welcome distraction. This wasn't what they needed to talk about. "I did, but—"

"And why didn't you send me money already?" Her mother's voice sounded harsher than the last time they talked. Did she smoke more?

"I can't." Lena whispered the words but that wouldn't do. She swallowed and tried again, louder this time. "I can't send you money."

"Can't or won't? You don't realize how it's inside. If you hadn't bailed on me, I wouldn't be here. You owe me because you're my daughter and—"

"Stop it." Lena had enough. She let the cable twist off her finger and stood straighter even though her mother couldn't see her. "You're in prison because you decided to scam people instead of working an honest job or two. I'm in debt because I decided to trust you and support you. We're both paying for our decisions. I can't give you any money, and even if I could, I wouldn't. I'm your daughter, but I don't owe you anything."

Her mother didn't answer. Had she hung up? No. Static crackled and the faint sound of breathing proved she was still there.

Lena clutched the kitchen counter with one hand. "Caroline?"

"Don't call me Caroline, I'm your mom."

"Really? You want to go there now?" Lena clenched her teeth. "I'm not a kid anymore, waiting for you to come home. Waiting for attention and approval. I had to grow up fast when I had to pick up the slack for you."

Again, only static answered her.

Lena used the pause to regroup. She'd never before spoken to Caroline like that. Her anger diminished with every word as if voicing it gave her the chance to let it go.

"Are you talking about Tammy?" Caroline sighed, but this time the overly dramatic way didn't tug at Lena's heart. "You know I had migraines. I have them still, that's why I need medication. That's expensive. That's why I'm calling, honey. You're the only one who can help me."

Twenty years ago, Lena would have given anything to hear her mother call her honey. Even ten years ago she'd been elated. Now only sadness filled her. Sadness for the lost chances and for the woman who had never learned to take on the responsibility for her own life. Migraines weren't the problem. They never had been. But Lena didn't want to go there either. "No, I can't help you. You have to help yourself first. Please don't contact me again if all you want is money."

"You're like your grandma, always thinking you know better." Caroline's voice lost all pretense of warmth. "Ungrateful bitch." She hung up.

The last words should have stung like a slap in the face, but they buzzed right past Lena. She could see now where they came from, and she wouldn't be sucked into her mother's spiral of anger again. Sadness had replaced the hurt and anger, and that was something she could deal with. Her problem with her mother was far from over, but at least she was on the right path to begin healing.

┼┼┼┼┼┼

Jess ripped off the sterile paper gown together with her gloves and threw everything in the trash. She listened for a moment as the resident explained everything they'd done to the patient. This new guy, Marc, had a decent enough bedside manner, even if he talked too much for her taste. Especially in the middle of the night.

Jess exchanged an amused gaze with Kayla at Marc's promise to personally escort the patient to his room.

"Are you heading home?" Kayla yawned.

Jess glanced at the wall clock. It would be reasonable to head to her condo and try to grab another two hours of sleep. She shrugged. "Nah. I'm wide awake. I caught a good six hours before the call came because Ella's staying with my mom. A shower, some coffee, and I'm good to go." She could get some tedious paperwork done so she could be out of here on time this afternoon. "Do you want to join me for a coffee?"

Kayla shook her head, grinning. "I'll finish the clean up, and then I'm heading to bed in the on-call room. I've got a date later."

"Congratulations. Do I know them?" Jess opened her lead apron and leaned against the door frame. Kayla was famous for falling in love with colleagues in the blink of an eye.

"No. She's got nothing to do with medicine. She's a cop." Kayla's smiled was dreamy. "But it's the first date. Too soon to tell anything."

"Okay. Have fun." Jess waved goodbye.

On her way to the locker room, she detoured to the emergency department to see if she would be needed again anytime soon. Diana sat at the nurses' station, rapidly typing something on the computer. Her head bobbed in rhythm to a song only she could hear.

Jess leaned on the other side of the counter and waited until she finished typing. "Hi, did you catch any more cardiology cases tonight?"

With a grin, Diana looked up. "Not yet. Let me save my report, and I'll check if anyone else has a patient for you." She clicked a few times with her mouse as her eyes moved over the monitor. Finally, she gave her a thumbs-up. "All clear. Are you going home now?"

"It's not worth it. I'll get some coffee and power through."

"Do you want to run over to the coffee shop? I could use some too."

"Sure." Jess waited while Diana told one of her colleagues where she was going.

The woman's gaze followed them through the doors to the main hall. Jess snorted. "Wasn't that the resident who almost fell over her feet after I had Ella?"

Grinning, Diana held open the door to the coffee shop. "Yeah, Courtney. I'd guess she's starting another rumor as we speak."

"Oh, we're having an affair now? Does Emily know?" Jess laughed. It was great to joke around with a friend. Her human interactions recently had been either strictly professional at work or laced with tension at home.

"She'll find out soon enough." Diana winked, then addressed the guy at the counter, who seemed barely old enough to be working the night shift. "Morning, Kevin. Flat white, please."

The guy grunted and looked expectantly at Jess.

"For me too. And a bottle of water." A double shot of espresso sounded like exactly what she needed right now. Technically, it wouldn't break the one-cup-a-day rule she'd inflicted on herself. She reached into her scrub pockets for her wallet, but Diana was quicker and waved her off.

"You can pay next time." Diana looked from her to the empty coffee shop. "Is it okay if we sit here for a while? I'm not in the mood to chat with Courtney tonight."

Jess nodded, and they sat in a pair of overstuffed armchairs at the end of the shop. Quiet music was playing, something with a lot of guitars she didn't recognize, and the light wasn't too bright. Not too bad for a hospital in the middle of the night. She opened her water and drained it in one go.

When the guy brought their coffees to the table, Diana thanked him. "Cool music." She bumped his fist when he held it out to her, and he left again.

"Not very talkative?" Jess sipped her coffee and moaned. Still too hot but exactly what she needed.

"Shy. At least he has a good taste in music. He reminds me of my youngest brother when he was that age. Now James is married to a super extroverted woman and has three kids. Never a quiet moment in his house, but he loves it."

"Three kids!" Jess nearly spewed out her coffee. "How can you balance work with three kids?

"He's in IT and works from home. For a time, he barely worked. Now that the kids are all in school, he's taking on more projects. And three kids isn't too bad. I grew up with five brothers."

"Five!" The thought alone robbed Jess of all energy. "How did your parents manage?"

"They had a traditional work distribution. My mom stayed at home for fifteen years and worked part time in my father's family practice afterward. I guess she considered medicine more as a hobby and being a mother as her main profession."

Jess stirred her coffee to cool it a little. Neither option would work for her. She couldn't work from home, nor would she consider staying home full-time. There must be other alternatives.

"Is everything okay? You're frowning," Diana said in a soft voice.

"I have trouble balancing my work life with Ella's care. At the moment, I'm relying on my mom, but I can't do that indefinitely."

"What options are there?"

Holding up her hand, Jess ticked off what she had considered so far. "Daycare—haven't found the right one yet; I want to wait until she's a bit older. My hours are too long. Nanny—how do you find someone you can trust? And I don't know if I could live with a stranger. My mom—as I said, I don't want to stress her too much. And driving back and forth between my place and my mother's in addition to the long hours isn't ideal either."

"What about cutting your hours?"

"Yeah, right." Jess didn't know if she should laugh or groan. "Do you know what would happen to my standing in the department?"

"I don't know much about your department, but this is the twenty-first century. What's the worst that could happen?"

"I wouldn't get scheduled for my favorite procedures anymore." This was a fact. One of Jess's colleagues had insisted on getting a few days off to teach at the university and that had been the retaliation.

"Maybe. But haven't you told me your boss was desperate to get you back early? So he values your skills and might be willing to negotiate a schedule that's better for you. You could always threaten to leave for a private practice. I'm sure there are enough that would snatch you up in a heartbeat."

"Hm. Hadn't thought of that." Jess pondered for a moment as she sipped her coffee. With the loss of her self-worth during her illness, she had forgotten how much she was wanted for her skills.

"And another thing. I might be wrong here, but I suppose you've reached most of the professional goals you've set for yourself, or are you aiming for chief of cardiology?"

"No, way too much paperwork. I'd rather stay in the middle of things, doing actual work with my patients."

"So you have a board certification in a difficult specialty, have mastered all the advanced procedures, and even specialize in a field where only a few interventional cardiologists ever succeed, right?"

"Right."

"And you're what, thirty-seven?"

Jess nodded, still unsure where Diana was going with this.

"Have you ever considered how little time it took to get to this position as opposed to how many more years you'll still work until retirement?"

"Um, no." Jess frowned.

"I'm guessing here, but it took you maybe eleven, twelve years to get where you are now after finishing med school. And you have maybe twenty-five, thirty years still to go."

"That's a long time." Jess blinked. She'd never done the math before.

"Right. And what if you worked part time a few of those years? Will it really matter when you're sixty and look back on your career? It's not the same, but I took nine years out of my medical career to play in a band. Today I might be an old resident in my late thirties. But in a couple of years, I'll be a full-fledged emergency physician with an added bonus of some great memories. No one can take those away from me."

Could it be that easy? Why hadn't she ever considered that? And wasn't it the same with her mother? The few years in the middle where she'd stayed at home hadn't affected her career in the end.

Diana's phone interrupted Jess's musings with a series of urgent beeps.

"I'm sorry. I need to go. Are you okay?"

"No." Jess grinned, feeling lighter than she had in days. The weight that had been crushing her since she'd started juggling her life as a single mother had lifted a tiny bit. "But I will be. Thanks for the talk."

"Anytime." Diana hurried away.

Forcing herself not to run, Jess followed. She didn't know if the caffeine or adrenaline loosened her stride, but she was buzzing with energy. It was still early in the morning, and it would be hours until her boss came to work. Enough time to make a list and plan the conversation.

Chapter Twenty-Three

LENA SAT ON HER PORCH with a glass of water she wished was wine and her sketching supplies next to her on the table. But for the moment, she ignored both. The sun was setting, and the last rays intensified the colors of the garden as if it were a fairy kingdom. Birds used the last minutes of daylight to sing or chat about their days or flirt. Whatever they were doing, it was soothing, and she wanted to soak up every second of it.

And why not? She had nothing else to do but put her feet up and enjoy. Not something she had done much in her adult life.

The last week had been an emotional roller coaster. It had started low and tumultuous with her argument with Jess, reached a high with her talk with Maggie, then another low as she confronted her anger at her mother. Or had that been a high? Maybe just a bumpy stretch that rattled her until she was sick.

Her attempt to wean herself from Ella's company had been a definite low. She missed their evening walks, giving Ella the bottle during the day, or her snuggles and smiles. Instead she had improved her sketching since that had been the only distraction that had held her attention.

And that had led to the next high, her meeting with Joanne. She was friendly and down to earth, which was no surprise since she was Maggie's friend. And she had seemed interested in Lena's sketches, admiring the botanical details and her use of color. In the short couple of hours they'd spent together, she'd already provided Lena with more advice and helpful guidance than she'd ever received from anyone else. And Joanne had repeated the invitation to join her course for free.

So here she was at the end of the week, hoping her future could hold something besides work, even though her private life was bleaker than ever. She hadn't seen Jess since their second argument and even though she wanted to talk, it wasn't a conversation she could have on the phone.

Steps on the path announced a visitor. Lena rose to greet Maggie.

Only, it wasn't Maggie.

Jess approached, one hand around a bottle of wine, the other carrying two glasses. She stopped in front of the porch. "Um, hi."

Her tentative smile was difficult to resist, but Lena had spent all week hardening her heart against the impact of Ella's gaze, so she was trained to ignore the charm of the Riley women. They needed to talk first. "Hi."

Jess's smile faltered, but her eye contact didn't waver. "I hoped you'd let me apologize. Again. And I come bearing gifts." She held up the bottle.

It was the wine they'd drunk at the beach house together. That Jess had remembered and made the effort to find it charmed Lena more than she cared to admit. She took a step back from the railing and invited Jess to join her with a sweep of her arm. "The wine is a good argument." She sat again with a sigh.

Jess placed the two glasses on the table and retrieved a Swiss army knife from her pocket. The bottle was open in no time, and she poured both glasses. "May I sit?"

"Of course." The formality was cute and annoying at the same time. Even if Lena was mostly annoyed at herself for finding it cute. "You're sure about red wine? You could end up with another ruined shirt."

Jess had picked up her glass and swirled the dark-red liquid around. "I trust you not to abuse your power."

"Okay." Lena sipped her water. She needed a clear head for this conversation.

Jess took a big gulp of the wine, placed her glass on the table, and wiped her hands on her shorts. "I'm sorry for what I said and how I handled our talk last week."

The words were rushed, and the signs of nervousness tugged at Lena's determination to keep her distance. She didn't trust her voice to remain neutral, so she said nothing and waited.

Leaning forward, Jess put her hands on the table, palms up. "I was an arrogant ass. I accused you of selfishness, but it was all on me. Instead of really apologizing to you, I tried to push *my* solution to *my* problems on you. And I'm sorry I said you only cared for Maggie because you want a substitute mom." She grimaced. "That was uncalled for."

"Why did you say it?"

"Mostly selfish reasons." Jess cringed but held her gaze. "I wanted to hurt you because you said a truth I didn't want to hear. You challenged me and held me accountable. That hasn't happened in a long time, and I needed it. Without you, I wouldn't have changed. Thank you." Something new resonated in Jess's voice. Respect.

Until this second, Lena hadn't known she needed to hear this. It soothed her frayed senses better than any birds, sunset, or wine ever could. Before she could find her voice, Jess continued.

"You were right. I was asking too much of my mom. Then I arrogantly thought I could solve all our problems by foisting a solution on you that you neither wanted nor needed. And when you told me to stop, I didn't listen. I'm sorry for that as well." Jess's eyes were filled with a myriad of emotions like the shades of a stormy sky by a master painter. Remorse. Self-deprecation. Fear. Trust. And respect again.

Lena considered the right wording for her answer. The apology seemed genuine and was different from last week. Jess had given it some thought.

The want to forgive Jess warred with the instinct to protect her own heart from pain. For that she had to keep her distance. To gain some time, she took a small sip of the wine. It was as good as she remembered and conjured memories of their first kiss. That wasn't helping in the least. She scowled at the wine and her traitorous brain.

"Okay. I've said what I needed to say, and I'll leave you in peace." With a sigh, Jess rose and picked up her wine glass. "Tonight, I'll stay in my room, and tomorrow I'm going to my condo. I'll keep out of your way."

Oh no. Jess thought Lena was still angry at her. "No, wait. I wasn't scowling because of you, just at myself, and... Stay, please?"

Jess sat again, waiting.

"I accept your apology, and I owe you one too. I..." Lena swallowed against her sudden dry throat. All week she had thought about the apology and now that she faced Jess the right words eluded her. "When you offered me the position as a nanny, some of my baggage surfaced and I saw red. You couldn't have known what you really asked of me because I hadn't trusted you with all of my past. Instead of explaining, I mixed all my emotions from the past and present and overreacted. And what I said about you killing your mother... I'm sorry, that was horrible." She blinked to keep her tears from falling.

"Thank you. So we're okay?" Jess's voice hitched.

"We're getting there." Lena held up her wine glass in a peace offering.

Jess clinked hers against it, and the bright note made Lena smile.

For a moment, it was enough to drink the wine in silence as the apology settled around her. The evening sky faded from pink to dark purple, and the darkness gave her the courage to open up. To honor Jess's respect with trust.

"I've told you about Tammy but not the whole story. I was overjoyed when I moved in with my mother and when my baby sister was born. She was adorable. It was like a dream come true, playing happy family. But then things started to slide. I was afraid to tell my grandma because she had warned me about my mother, and I had ignored her." Lena sipped her wine and sighed. She was glad she couldn't see Jess's face. She didn't want to see the pity.

"I told you her husband came home, found out about her addiction, and divorced her. He took Tammy. What I haven't told you before was that he wouldn't let me near her, even though I loved her so much. He said I was as untrustworthy as my mother because I had covered for her instead of telling him. That wasn't fair, I was just a teenager who spread herself too thin, but he didn't see it that way. My mother convinced me that the only way to see Tammy again was to support her fight for custody. I gave her all my savings and the small college fund from my grandparents to help pay for a divorce lawyer. I worked to pay the bills for both of us. And when that money was gone, she tried to get me to help her with a scam to get more. I refused because I didn't want to be mixed up in illegal stuff, and she kicked me out. Now that the baby was gone, and I refused to help with her schemes, I was worthless to her. A burden." She gritted her teeth. "She told me she had only needed a babysitter, a nanny."

"I'm so sorry." Jess reached for her, and in the darkness, it took a few fumbling tries until she held Lena's hand.

"It was a long time ago. I'm over it." If she repeated it often enough, maybe one day Lena would believe it and the pain would recede. Today wasn't that day.

"It's a cruel thing to say, and I'm still sorry your mother hurt you like that." Jess's fingers traced Lena's knuckles. The touch was soft and mesmerizing. "Do you still see her?"

"No, she's tried to reestablish contact a few times over the last ten years, but it always turned out she needed something. Money or a place to stay. The first few times, I was stupid and believed her apologies until I learned my lesson not to trust her. That's the main reason for my debt problem. She writes sometimes from prison, but I ignored her letters." Lena could have stopped here but she wanted to be honest with Jess. "I ignored her because I was still angry and couldn't deal with it. Last week, I accepted a call for the first time in years. After freaking out on you, I realized I had to learn to let go of the anger and forgive her."

"How was the call? Did it help?" Jess's grip never wavered.

"I think so, yes. I'm more sad than angry now. But it'll be a long way. And I don't think I'll ever fully trust her again." As she said it out loud, something clicked.

Lena had taken the lesson to heart and stopped trusting everyone. At least with her financial security and her heart. First Maggie had broken through her safety wall and then Ella and now Jess... Jess wanted her trust, but she wasn't sure she could give her heart again.

"And here I am, thinking saying I'm sorry will magically make everything right again." Jess snorted. "Don't get me wrong, I'm still sorry, but I understand if you can't trust my apology. I basically asked you the same thing as your mother did."

True, Lena had reacted as if it was the same, but really, it wasn't. "You couldn't know."

"No." Jess's voice was hoarse, and she cleared her throat. "But I still didn't listen to what you wanted."

"It's not the same. You were honest. You offered me a job—without hidden motives—and she ensnared me with the promise of a family when she just wanted a cheap babysitter."

Jess's hand trembled in hers. "It was the right decision not to accept the job. I was thinking more about my needs than yours."

Here it was, the reason why Lena didn't trust. Everyone followed their own selfish path, and Jess had admitted she wasn't different from anyone else.

But was Lena any better? If she was being honest with herself, and this evening seemed to be all about honesty, she didn't live here for the convenience of a nice house. She enjoyed Maggie's friendship because she took Lena seriously and accepted her as she was. Ella was healing the hole in her heart Tammy had torn. And Jess…they had helped each other, and both giving and receiving support had meant more to Lena than what she expressed on the surface.

Lena's actions and thoughts were laced with hidden meanings too and motives that weren't always clear to her, but that didn't mean she wanted to take advantage of others. So why should it be different with Jess and her motives?

Lena intertwined their fingers. Jess's hand was warm and soft, vibrating with strength and energy, and holding it seemed right. "Thank you for apologizing. Again. And I'm sorry for freaking out on you. That wasn't fair."

"Maybe…" Jess cleared her throat. "Maybe we could work on being more open with each other."

Here was the roller coaster again, propelling her from fear to hope and back in a matter of seconds. With all the whiplash, Lena's thoughts reeled. But there was only one answer she wanted to give. "Yes."

††††††††

If it was up to Jess, she could sit here all night holding hands, but she had promised to respect Lena's boundaries. She reluctantly removed her hand from their clasp, and the coolness of the evening descended on her. She shivered. "I'd better go and leave you to your evening. Enjoy the wine."

"Why don't you stay and share it with me?" Lena's voice was soft and welcome as a summer breeze.

"I'd love to." For a moment, they both sipped their wine wordlessly as if it really was the reason they sat together. It was excellent but not the source of the giddy feeling that bubbled inside of Jess. Lena had not only listened to her and accepted her apology but apologized and explained as well. The invitation to stay showed that Lena, too, wanted to continue their friendship. Or courtship or whatever it was that connected them.

"Let me get some light." Lena disappeared in the house and returned with two candles.

The flickering light reminded Jess of the massages, and a twinge of arousal sparked deep inside of her. *Don't go there.*

Jess searched for a topic that would distract her. "Mom said you're thinking about moving? Is it true?"

Lena sighed and swirled her wine. "No. It was a childish impulse to run away. Everything is complicated, and I'm afraid of mixing up all the aspects of my life with your family, but I'll manage. First I was Maggie's friend, but now I work for her, and she's even helping me to get into a course at the university. And for the last few months, you've taken over most of my free time. Not that I'm complaining. A lot of great things came out of it. I got to know and love your daughter, and teaching you tai chi helped me too. And now we have this friends-with-benefits thing going on…" Lena sighed again, her gaze on the red liquid. "I don't think it's working for me."

Disappointment soured the wine in her stomach. Jess put the glass on the table; it was too heavy to hold. She dropped her hands to her lap, and her gaze followed them. Not a courtship, then. "I'm sorry. We said this was about having fun, and if you aren't enjoying it anymore, I won't bother you again."

"You're not bothering me. I'm having problems maintaining my boundaries with everything else going on, and maybe some distance would help so I don't confuse all these emotions and get too attached." Lena's tone was even and light as if they were talking about her work or anything else without deeper meaning.

Jess nearly missed the slight hitch in the last word. She looked up. What was Lena saying? Had Lena just told her she was getting too attached? A lightness filled Jess's middle as if all her burdens had been removed. "Lena?"

Lena's lip trembled, and her eyes were wide with fear of something. Or someone.

The last thing Jess wanted was to be the cause of even more pain for Lena. "I will respect every boundary you set. But I have a confession to make." She swallowed and forced herself to hold Lena's gaze. Fear of making herself vulnerable rattled inside her like a coiled snake about to bite. But she trusted Lena. "I guess I'm not doing so great with the boundaries of friends-with-benefits either. I have problems staying away from you. When I'm not here, I think of you all the time. And your opinion means much more to me than it should if we were just friends. I get all warm and tingly when I see you, and when you smile at me, my knees get weak. You're the most beautiful, warm, and caring person I've ever met, and I'm already more than attached to you. I'm falling for you."

"Oh." Lena's mouth hung open, and she stared at Jess with a dazed expression as if she'd witnessed a miracle and couldn't yet decide if it was a good or bad thing.

Jess's heartbeat thundered as fast and hard as it had three months ago when she'd collapsed. But this time her heart wasn't failing but fueled by hope and anticipation. When Lena didn't answer, a hole seemed to open up beneath Jess, but she refused to let it swallow her. "As I said, I'll respect whatever you want. And I won't hang around here and stalk you or anything. If you want me to keep my distance, I'll leave this part of the garden to you. If you want us to remain just friends, I'll deal with my feelings and won't ever bring it up again. I can certainly see why you wouldn't want me as more than a friend." Jess opened her hand to tick the points off on her fingers. "I'm a single mother without much time to give. Actually, I don't know what I can give. Money, maybe, but everything else... My body isn't in the best shape after the pregnancy. I've been a selfish idiot. I'm—"

"Stop it!" Lena put her glass on the table so fast the wine nearly spilled over and jumped up. She stepped closer into Jess's personal space. Her eyes burned with fierce determination as her gaze swept all over Jess, then she cupped Jess's face and bent down to kiss her.

Before Jess could lean into the kiss, it was already over.

Lena drew back to look into her eyes but kept her hands in Jess's hair.

This assertiveness was new and totally hot. Jess licked her lips.

"You have a lot to give, and money is the least interesting part of you." Lena's hands tensed slightly. "I'm constantly fighting the feeling that I'm not worthy, that emotional attachment is always temporary and conditional, and that everyone will leave me as soon as I open up. But I don't want to fight this fight anymore."

"We both fear the same things."

"Yes. We're both afraid of rejection." Lena massaged Jess's scalp.

Her scent enveloped Jess, and she fought to keep her eyes open. She wanted to sink into Lena's embrace and let go. But it was important Lena dictated the pace.

Lena kissed her lightly on the mouth. "Do you want to be courageous together?"

"Yes." Jess kissed her back. "Yes, yes, yes." It was only a chaste and short meeting of their lips, but it was filled with reassurance and the promise of tomorrow.

††††††††

Lena gave the desk chair on her porch a fond pat on her way back inside after her morning workout. Last night, the oversized chair had been worth every hour she'd spent sanding and painting the wood. It had proven to not only be sturdy but surprisingly comfortable for two people sitting on each other's laps and making out for hours.

Jess had eventually gone back to her room after they'd agreed to slow things down a bit. This bright idea had led to a sleep-deprived night. She'd missed Jess.

At least Jess had looked as tired as Lena was this morning when she'd joined her for tai chi. But after ten minutes, Ella's crying through the baby monitor had shattered the serene atmosphere, and Jess had left to take care of her. She had promised to make breakfast for them and was probably already waiting on Maggie's patio.

Lena showered as quick as possible. As it was shaping up to be another warm October day, Lena dressed in layers. The tank top closest to her skin was silk, and even with a loose shirt over it, she felt sexy. How would it feel if Jess sank her hands underneath the shirt and caressed her skin through the silk? Lena groaned. Why had they decided to go their separate ways last evening? She couldn't come up with one good reason.

She slipped on her sandals and flew up the path to the main house.

As promised, Jess waited on the patio with breakfast for two. Ella's stroller stood to the side, but no sound came from it.

With a big smile, Jess stood and opened her arms.

Lena hugged her and sighed against her shoulder. So much better than how they'd interacted last week. She tilted her head for a kiss.

Jess's lips were as soft and tender as last night, but instead of rich wine, she tasted of peppers, tomatoes, and new beginnings.

After a while, they separated, and Lena looked in Ella's direction. "Everything okay?"

"Yeah. She was hungry. Speaking of hungry... Are you up for an omelet?"

"I'm starving."

"Take a seat and have some tea. I'll be right back."

Instead of sitting, Lena wandered over to Ella and peered inside the stroller. She was sleeping, so Lena resisted the urge to cuddle and enjoyed the view from a distance. Ella's hands opened and closed, and her eyes moved behind closed lids. Maybe she was dreaming. Different emotions flickered over her expression, none recognizable.

Jess returned and placed a covered pan on the table. As she opened it, the aroma of vegetables, cheese, and herbs wafted over.

Her grumbling stomach told Lena to hurry to the table and sit. "That smells amazing."

"I got everything from the garden except the eggs and cheese, of course. I'd never have thought fresh vegetables could make such a difference." Jess cut the omelet and placed a generous portion on Lena's plate. "Do you need anything else?"

"Mmh, no. Thanks. Where's Maggie?"

"It's a friend's birthday, and she invited a big group for breakfast. Mom went early to help her prepare."

They both dug in, and Lena moaned. The texture and seasoning were perfect. "You're a good cook."

"Um, no. Only weekend breakfast. I learned that from my dad." Jess glanced over her shoulder at Ella. "But I guess I'll have to learn the rest soon."

"Are you planning on cooking everything yourself?" Lena couldn't imagine Jess spending hours in the kitchen every day.

"God, no. I grew up with my share of takeout and precooked meals and didn't turn out too bad. When I was little, my mom didn't have time to cook everything from scratch every day, and Dad always came home late. But I think it's all about the balance."

"True. Grandma insisted on homemade cooking, and I always tried to find excuses to go to my best friend's house when they had pizza or Chinese. I think you've still got a little time to see what'll work for you. At the moment, she's only interested in one kind of food."

Jess laughed. "My luck. Was she awake just now?"

"No, dreaming. I love how her face twitches." Lena had to smile. "I wonder what she dreams about."

"Milk?" Jess shrugged. "That's the most important part of the day for her."

"Or maybe she's dreaming about you? You're very important too."

Jess's expression softened, and she blushed. "Maybe."

That blush went right to Lena's heart. "What are you dreaming about?"

"You mean at night?" Jess waggled her eyebrows. "Is this a kind of trick question to find out if I dreamed of you? Did you dream of me?"

"Wouldn't you like to know…?" As much as Lena liked the banter between them, she wanted to use the chance to deepen their relationship. "My question was more in general. What are your dreams about your future?"

"Mmh." Jess cut a piece of omelet and chewed. Her gaze was on the plate, but Lena would bet her pencil roll she wasn't really seeing her food. "My plans are changing all the time. They aren't the same as last year or even last month. I'm not sure what my future will hold."

"But what would you want for your future? What are your big dreams?"

"I already have most of what I wanted: my dream job, a big condo in the city, a healthy kid. That's how I envisioned my future when I was a senior in high school, and I planned my life accordingly."

"And is it enough?" Lena smiled and lightly squeezed Jess's arm when she tensed. "I don't want to be contrary. But you're not the same person you were when you made those plans."

Jess tilted her head to one side. She opened and closed her mouth twice before she spoke. "You're right. I have never considered that. I was a teenager." She frowned. "I had pretty detailed plans about some things, complete with timelines, but only vague ideas about other aspects."

"And what about those vague ideas? Are those dreams for your future?"

"Maybe. It's silly, but I thought I would have a wife at my side who supported me and my plans. Before I had Ella, I was lonely and didn't know how to change that. I wanted to give love and share my life… I never envisioned details. I just knew I didn't want to be alone. It was as if I saw through thick windowpanes into a landscape shrouded in mist. I didn't know where to go to get where I wanted, so I stayed on the safe side." She grimaced. "If I say it out loud, it seems childish."

"No, not at all. Just cautious. You have dreams, and the ones you can't plan for meticulously, you pushed aside, hoping the mist would clear one day."

"It sounds so obvious when you say it." Jess pushed her half-full plate to the side and picked up the tea. "You want more?"

Lena nodded. She took the opportunity to study Jess while she poured.

A hint of confusion lingered in Jess's expression, but the determination Lena had always admired rose to the surface. Finally, she leaned back in her chair. "You're good at asking questions."

"I don't know. I think you're ready to hear those questions now."

"True. I'm done with keeping my gaze glued to my checklist, following a plan I designed when I was half my age. I haven't told you yet, but I had a talk with the chief of cardiology on Friday."

"About what?" Lena had a hard time following her change of topic, but Jess didn't seem as if she was avoiding anything.

"I told him I need to cut my hours, at least for a while. A year, maybe two."

Lena blinked. She hadn't expected that. Jess had always put her work in the center of her life. "How do you feel about it?"

"Surprisingly okay. I thought I would feel more lost as if something vital was taken from me, but all I feel now is relief."

Lena smiled. "I'm happy for you. What made you do it?"

"You."

"Oh."

"You kicked my ass and asked the right questions. You made me realize Ella is more important than any job I could have. I need to spend more time with her, quality time, for both of us. And when she grows older and more independent, I can increase the hours I work again. And either I get back to my old level, or I find something else. Medicine and cardiology have so many different possibilities. I'll find something to do."

"That's wonderful. I hated to see you so tired and torn all the time."

Jess shrugged. "I will still be tired, but I guess that comes with the territory. You can't have children and expect them to be sleeping all the time."

Ella chose this moment to cry. Not a desperate wailing, more a quiet *Hey, I'm awake, where's my entertainment?*

Jess laughed and picked her up, cuddling her close.

The sight of them together melted Lena. She should look away, but the love they shared always mesmerized her.

Jess returned to the chair and sat Ella on her lap. One arm held her around the middle, while the other stroked the small head snuggled against her chest. When she looked up at Lena, a trace of that love still lingered in her gaze. "And what are you dreaming about? What are your plans for the future?"

Lena closed her eyes to concentrate. These questions were important, and she didn't want to be distracted by the twin pairs of blue eyes that knew the shortcut to her heart. "Dreams and plans? For me, those two questions are completely separate. My immediate plans are concentrating my work efforts so that I'm not spread too thin, finding odd jobs all over the place. What your mother is offering me is actually perfect. I learn a lot, and I enjoy working with her. It's more creative than I thought. And the opportunity to study botanical illustration, to improve my skills, that's a dream come true. I have always loved nature and wanted to portray it. Even when I was little, I barely sketched anything else. Maggie has mentioned she's going to suggest to her editor that we include my illustrations in the book, but I don't know if I'm good enough. Talent isn't everything. So my plan is to work with Maggie while I improve my skills and pay off my debt. Now that I don't waste so much time running around between a handful of minimum wage jobs, I'm making a lot of progress."

"And your dreams?" Jess wiggled the fingers of her free hand in front of Ella but kept her gaze on Lena. She smiled as Ella held on with both tiny hands and examined her fingers as if they were a toy.

This time, Lena didn't hesitate. She trusted Jess with her dreams. And her heart. "I want to be seen and valued for myself, my personality. Find a home. Have a family. Be loved."

A wide grin spread on Jess's face. "That's my dream too. I want a family." She looked down at Ella. "Or rather, to share my tiny two-person family with a partner, an equal. Someone I love and who loves me and who loves Ella as her own daughter."

They stared at each other, and Lena was afraid to breathe. She didn't want to break the connection and return to reality. Could it be that easy? Could they declare they wanted the same thing and then just have it? Or was that all in her mind? Did Jess even notice what was happening here?

Ella broke the spell as she started to squirm in Jess's grip and cried.

"What's up?" Jess picked her up, then grimaced. "Ah, time for a new diaper." She got up and walked a couple of steps toward the house, then turned again. "I don't want to run, but..." She gestured at Ella. "Can we talk more later?"

Lena exhaled and nodded. "Later. We have time." Yes, they needed to talk. But they needed some time to process their revelations too and some time to connect again. Physically and emotionally.

They had been in a relationship for less than twenty-four hours. They had all the time in the world to enjoy each other and explore their romance. But knowing they shared the same dreams helped. They were walking in the same direction to a shared goal, so not only the journey mattered but the destination too.

Chapter Twenty-Four

A DOOR CREAKED AND WOKE Jess from her sleep. She blinked, but daylight forced her eyes closed again. Since when did anything creak in her condo? Everything was as good as new.

Wait. How had a door creaked? Was someone here with her? She opened her eyes again, ignoring the brightness this time. For a second, she didn't know where she was. The window was on the wrong side of the bed and much too close. The bed was different too—not uncomfortable, just not hers.

"Oh, sorry, I didn't mean to wake you. Go back to sleep," a voice whispered from behind her. Lena's voice.

Jess relaxed. There wasn't an intruder in her home; she was the intruder. She rolled onto her other side and smiled at the sight of Lena. Her skin glistened pink from hours outside, and her hair was in a loose bun. Strands of light-brown curls had escaped and stuck to her temples. Her clothes were rumpled, and she looked so lovely Jess couldn't keep her hands off her. She reached for Lena's hand and tugged her down for a kiss.

"Hey, back already? Sorry, I didn't mean to fall asleep here."

Lena pecked her on the lips but resisted being pulled onto the bed. "I'm sweaty and need a shower. It'll only take a minute. And you're welcome to stay here anytime."

Jess rolled onto her back and crossed her arms behind her head. If it were up to her, she would tell Lena to stop selling preserves at the market and make up the loss of money herself. But it wasn't up to her, and she admired Lena for her independence. The women she'd dated previously had never hesitated to let her pay for everything, and Jess had expected and accepted it but never respected them for it.

And that's why she was here—to show her support for Lena, not to nap. She got up and went to the kitchen, stretching her arms over her head as she walked.

She had barely seen Lena in the last two weeks since they'd become a couple. The first week she'd worked her ass off to organize everything for her reduced schedule, and last week Ella had fought her first of presumably many viral infections with a high fever and relentless crying. And then she'd caught the virus herself as Ella was on the mend. She'd had to call in sick to work, and they'd hunkered down in the condo despite her mom and Lena's insistence they should come to the house. The last thing she wanted was to infect even more people, especially people she cared for. People she loved.

A quick glance confirmed Ella was still enjoying her midday nap in her baby carrier in the living room. She was sleeping even more than usual after last week.

Yesterday had been Jess's first day back at work, and she'd put in long hours to catch up on all her paperwork. But now everything would be different. Her new schedule started tomorrow. Only two full and one half day a week, and half the number of nights on call. Some colleagues would hate her for the increased workload, but others would be glad for their chance to shine. She shrugged. Not her problem.

Jess poured two glasses of the herbal iced tea Lena enjoyed so much and she'd grudgingly come to like and placed them in the bedroom. Then she fetched three of the little bottles of massage oil from Lena's collection along with the colorful sheet that covered the massage table. She spread the sheet over Lena's bed and sat down to wait. It didn't take long for Lena to return from her shower, clad in a towel that ended mid-thigh.

Valiantly ignoring the beautiful skin on display, Jess stood and offered Lena a glass. "How was your day?"

"The wind was relentless at the market today." Lena drained the glass in one go and placed it on the nightstand. "The rest was fine. I've nearly sold out." She glanced at the bed and raised her eyebrows.

With an innocent grin, Jess offered her the other glass too, but Lena declined with a shake of her head, so she placed it on the nightstand without drinking from it herself.

She was thirsty too but not for tea. She stepped closer until she brushed against Lena's towel.

As if she could read Jess's mind, Lena leaned in and kissed her with all the pent-up passion that had been building between them for the last two weeks.

Texts and calls weren't enough. Jess reached for Lena's hips and pulled her closer. The towel was warm and damp against her skin, and the knowledge Lena was naked underneath it drove her crazy.

She trailed her hand up Lena's bare arm to her shoulder and her collarbone. A sexy white line crossed it, where the tank tops she often wore had protected her skin from the sun. Jess kissed it softly, then blew on the damp skin.

Goosebumps erupted, and Lena's breath caught. "More." Her whisper was barely audible.

Jess obliged all too willingly, showering Lena's shoulders and cleavage with soft kisses, edging closer to the towel hiding her breasts with each pass but never dipping beneath it. After two weeks apart, she was torn between worshipping Lena for hours and ripping the towel off to show how desperately she'd missed her. But this wasn't about passion alone. She'd missed Lena's gentle smile, her insights, and her soothing calmness, and she wanted Lena to know that too. "I missed you."

"I missed you too." Lena's hands played with Jess's hair, running to the back of her head and down her neck, stopping at the T-shirt. One finger slipped inside the collar.

Jess lost her balance. How could the simple touch of one finger be so powerful? "Wait."

Lena's fingers stilled. "Not good?"

"Very, very good. But I wanted to show you some support after a long day working at the market." Jess leaned back to look at her. "I would love to massage you."

"That's dangerous. I might fall asleep." Lena grinned.

"I doubt that." Jess traced her hands up and down Lena's arms. "And if you do, I'd be honored I could help you relax that much."

"Okay." Lena used her grip on Jess's neck to pull her in for another kiss. Then she walked forward one step, two steps, and gently pushed Jess backward.

When Jess's knees touched the bed, she let herself fall without loosening her hold on Lena.

Laughing, they tumbled onto the bed, and after a swift shuffling around, they ended up next to each other. Jess rolled onto her side and lifted onto her elbow. Lying next to Lena, being close enough to touch, to kiss, Jess almost regretted her idea of a massage. She forced her gaze upward. "Turn around."

Never taking her gaze from Jess's eyes, Lena untucked the towel and let it slip open. With a provocative smile, she stretched out on her belly.

Jess suppressed a moan. She'd only glimpsed what the towel had hidden, but it was enough to turn up the temperature in the room a notch. She rolled off the bed to get the oils and gather some control. She wasn't a hormonal teenager and could take her time to pamper her girlfriend.

The three bottles all looked the same apart from the handwritten labels with names that didn't mean much to her and the decorative drawings Jess recognized as Lena's work. "Do you have any preferences?"

Lena turned her head in Jess's direction. "See if you like the scent of the left one. It's stimulating rather than relaxing."

Jess opened the bottle to sniff it. Hmm, lavender and a hint of spiciness. "That's certainly different from the ones you used on me."

"I was aiming for a different effect. More relaxation, zen, you know. Even if it worked contrary last time." She grinned and looked Jess up and down. "How about you lose your clothes before you start? You wouldn't want oil on them. The stains are difficult to remove."

Jess laughed. "Sure. All you're thinking about is my laundry."

"No." Lena's eyes blazed with a heat that made Jess's knees weak. "I want to feel your skin on my skin when you sit beside me. When you touch me. Everywhere. I need that now."

Jess moaned. She put the bottle of oil on the nightstand and grabbed her belt buckle. Her need was the same and turned her mind hazy with anticipation. She quickly shed her jeans and underwear, kicking them off. As her hands grabbed the hem of her shirt, she froze.

Lena's gaze had tracked the movement of Jess's hands, and she smiled as if she'd been served a mouthwatering dish.

Here it was, the moment Jess had been dreading. But she didn't want to hide her body or her emotions from Lena anymore. "I'm not…" Heat rose to her cheeks. "My body changed during pregnancy."

Lena sat up at the edge of the bed as if being naked was the most natural thing in the world. And maybe it was. A year ago, Jess had thought so, but now she was blushing like a teenager, for fuck's sake.

"Of course it did." Lena reached out to take Jess's hands and tugged her closer. "But believe me, nothing on your body is a turn off for me. I love you, and I think you're hot as you are."

Love. Hearing that word from Lena filled Jess with a happiness she couldn't compare to anything else. Her heart swelled with her own love that multiplied under Lena's adoring gaze. Jess pushed her doubts into the back of her mind where they belonged. "Is it that easy?"

"It's just you and me. We can make it as easy as we want to."

"Okay." Jess took a deep breath and pulled off her T-shirt and sports bra. She flung the garments in the corner of the room, too far away to get them back.

Lena held her gaze for moment until Jess nodded, then let her eyes roam.

Jess managed not to flinch as she studied Lena's expression for any sign of distaste. Nothing but love and arousal shone in those hazel eyes. Lena pulled Jess's hand to her mouth and kissed her knuckles.

"Forget the massage." Her voice was hoarse, and the warm air tickled the skin on Jess's hand. Lena lay back on the bed.

Pulled to her as if they were bound by an invisible line, Jess followed. She did what she had wanted to do all along and kissed Lena. An odd mixture of gratitude, adoration, and love filled her heart until she thought it might burst. She tried to pour a little bit of that into the kiss as she claimed Lena's lips. They slowly rolled around until Jess was on her back and Lena rested on top, one leg between hers.

Their bodies touched all along their lengths. Lena had been right. Skin on skin was what they needed to reconnect. Her hands glided up and down Lena's back. The contrast between the softness of her curves and the subtle strength of her muscles was so hot and addictive, she couldn't stop touching.

Not that Lena seemed to mind. Her hands seemed to be everywhere at once, and her mouth rained kisses on every part she could reach. Each touch of hands and lips burned a path through Jess's skin into her heart.

She gripped Lena's ass to pull her even closer, and Lena's leg pressed against her clit. She tilted her hips upward to increase the friction and moaned. It wouldn't take long.

Lena's moan cut through the hazy fog of arousal. Jess opened her eyes and slowed the movement of her hips. As much as she wanted to let go, today was about more than a quick orgasm. She rolled them over and straddled Lena's hips.

With a sensual smile, Lena looked up at her. Jess leaned down and kissed her, let her tongue express what she couldn't say. How sexy Lena was, how much she cherished her kindness, her patience. How much she loved her.

Panting, Jess broke the kiss and nibbled along Lena's jaw, down her neck.

"Sit up." Lena's mouth was at her ear, and warm air tickled the sensitive skin of her earlobe. "Let me touch you."

Jess did as she was asked, fighting the urge to suck in her belly as Lena's hands stroked over it. As the hands moved upward to Jess's breasts, she forgot all about her belly. Her mind filled with the sensation of Lena's hands squeezing gently, thumbs flicking over her nipples. Tendrils of pleasure ran through Jess.

Without conscious thought, her hips started to move rhythmically, and her clit glided over Lena's mound, again and again and again. The delicious friction stoked a fire that melted her inside. Jess moaned and fell forward, resting her weight on shaking hands on both sides of Lena's head.

Lena's right hand left her breast, but before Jess could protest, she had worked it between them and teased Jess's opening with the tip of her finger.

"I love you." There wasn't anything else to say. Jess searched Lena's eyes, almost green with desire.

Their gazes locked, and Jess drowned in the love shining in Lena's eyes. Her world narrowed to the movement that connected their bodies and hearts. Lena's hands, Jess's hips, Lena's mouth on her nipple. Every movement was in perfect synchronicity until her orgasm threatened to rip her apart.

Shaking from head to toe, Jess clung to her self-control like a climber to the last bit of fraying robe.

But Lena was here to catch her, to hold her.

Jess let herself fall.

+++++++

Jess sat at the breakfast bar while her mom cut the carrots with a knife that belonged in a slasher movie. When she was growing up, she'd watched her mom cook on thousands of evenings from this same spot while she did her homework. But as a kid, she'd never been interested in the techniques. "If I tried anything like that, I'd lose my fingers."

"And we wouldn't want that," Lena whispered from behind, too low for her mom to hear. Her breath caressed the sensitive skin of Jess's neck.

Jess shivered as her earlobe seemed to melt. Recently, Lena seemed to have this effect on every part of her. She swiveled on the barstool to smile at her. Just the person she'd been waiting for. "Finished for today?"

Lena nodded. An adorable smudge of blue ink painted one corner of Lena's mouth.

That spot asked to be kissed, and Jess gave in to the impulse.

When the kiss ended, Lena leaned against Jess to look over her shoulder. "Hi, Maggie. Do you need any help?"

"No, I'm almost done. Take a seat." She swooped up the carrot slices and threw them into a big pot where even more vegetables had been simmering for some time, then closed the lid. After washing her hands, she joined them at the breakfast bar. "Jess, you remember Belinda, my friend from Santa Fe?" Her mom's tone changed, and the lines around her eyes deepened.

Jess sat up straighter. "Sure. Why?" How could she forget the eccentric artist who would give her homemade stuffed animals every time she visited? They had been creepy and looked like something Dr. Frankenstein would have done if he had used fabric scraps in clashing colors. She had never been able to sleep with them in the same room. But as they'd come with tons of chocolate and fun stories, she'd still liked it when Belinda visited.

"She called earlier. Her sister died, and she's devastated. They were close, lived together for the last ten years. I want to fly to her tomorrow for at least a week. Do you think it's possible?"

"Yes, absolutely." Of course it was possible. Why was her mom even asking? But then it dawned on her. Ella. "Oh." She quickly ran through her options. Most of the week she'd be at home, but tomorrow and next Tuesday and Wednesday she had work. Where could she find a trustworthy babysitter on short notice? Or would Lena...? But after their last discussion, she didn't want to use Lena as a crutch the first time she encountered a childcare obstacle. Maybe Diana had a day off?

"I'm so sorry for her." Lena hastened around the other side of the breakfast bar to Maggie's side and hugged her. "Don't worry about a thing at home. Jess and I will take care of everything."

Jess shook herself out of her thoughts and went to hug her mom too.

For a moment, all three of them huddled close together, then her mom stepped back and took Jess's and Lena's hands in each of hers.

"Lena is right." Jess kissed her mom's cheek. "We'll manage. You concentrate on Belinda. Please tell her I'm thinking of her."

"Thank you." Her mom's eyes were full of tears, and she squeezed both their hands. "I'll call her and book a flight. Lena, can you keep an eye on the stew?" She wiped her eyes and hurried off.

Should she follow? Jess rubbed her neck.

"Let's give her some time." Lena opened the lid and stirred the stew, then closed it again. "I know what you're thinking." Her tone was light and playful without a hint of accusation. She sat at the breakfast bar.

"Do you?" Jess pulled the stool closer so their knees were touching when she sat. "You think you know me."

"Yup." Lena placed her hand above Jess's knee. "You realized you have a problem with Ella's daycare, then thought about asking me and discarded the idea at once, and now you're running through a list of options that are all less than perfect."

"Huh, that's frighteningly accurate." Warmth spread from the hand at her leg throughout her body—not the sexual spark of arousal but something deeper, more substantial. Lena saw through her, and Jess didn't mind at all. In fact, she loved it. "Do you have an idea what I can do?"

"Sure. Let me take care of her." Lena held her gaze, and her eyes never wavered. "I would love to do it."

Jess never doubted her love for Ella, but she didn't want Lena to think she was taking advantage of those feelings. "I don't want you to feel as if you are her babysitter because you're not. You're…more." Jess bit her lip. She couldn't find the perfect term to describe what Lena was to her. Girlfriend sounded so young and superficial, and partner… Everything was still so new. She didn't want to be presumptuous and call her that.

"I know. I feel like more too, and I'm offering." Her open smile brushed Jess's hesitation away.

"Thank you." Jess leaned in for a kiss, but before their lips could meet, Lena's phone rang.

"Oh, that must be Joanne." Lena fished the phone from her pocket and answered with a wide grin.

To give her some privacy, Jess went to the stove and opened the lid on the pot. The stew looked like stew, at least to her untrained eyes. She stirred it once, and nothing stuck to the bottom, so everything must be going as planned. She should learn to cook soon before Ella outgrew the formula. She wandered out the patio doors but couldn't help sneaking glances back at Lena.

The phone call seemed to be good news. Lena enthusiastically nodded more than once and smiled widely. After she hung up, she joined Jess outside.

"Guess what? The paperwork went through. I'm officially a guest student in Joanne's class." She bounced on her toes.

Jess hugged her. Like always, the perfect feeling of having Lena in her arms eclipsed any other sensation. She leaned back a little to look into her eyes. "I'm so happy for you. When's the big day?"

"Next week, Friday. The twenty-third. She said the first day will be the foundation for the whole course."

"Friday is great, I can drive you since I have the day off. Then you don't need to use your death trap."

"Hey, it's not nice to talk about my car like that. She has feelings too, you know."

"Well, your safety is more important to me than her feelings." Jess winked. "What time?"

"Eleven, but I want to go earlier to look around campus a bit." Lena's enthusiasm was infectious.

"I'll write it down so it's official." Grinning, Jess pulled her phone from her pocket and opened the calendar app. "Uh, did she say next Friday or the twenty-third? Because the date doesn't match."

"She said the twenty-third. Isn't that Friday?" Lena's smiled dimmed.

"Wednesday." Jess swallowed and stared at the tiny screen of her phone as if it could give her a solution to the obvious problem. Most of Wednesday was marked with a red box labeled *work*. She typed the date and time of Lena's class into her calendar. A message appeared on her screen.

You seem to have a scheduling conflict. Do you want to continue?

Her finger hovered over the *yes* button.

"But...but Wednesday is your workday, and I..." Lena's shoulders hung low.

"You just agreed to take care of Ella." Jess frowned. This wasn't a difficult decision. Lena's chance to join this course was too good and important to pass up only because Jess needed help watching Ella. Joanne didn't teach every semester, and even if she did, it wasn't fair to make Lena wait for months to spare Jess some inconvenience.

Resolutely, Jess stabbed the *yes* button and showed the screen of her phone to Lena. "See, now it's official." She tried to lighten the mood with a teasing voice. "You have to go."

The corner of Lena's mouth twitched. "Just because your phone says so?"

"Yeah. Who are we to disagree with our computer overlords?"

"You're nuts." Lena chuckled, but then her mirth faded again. "I appreciate your sense of humor, but that still doesn't solve the problem. Ella is more important. I can call back and ask if I can start the class a week later."

Jess would do anything to return the smile to Lena's lips. And it was the right thing to do. "There is another solution. I'll reschedule work and take care of Ella myself if I can't find a babysitter."

"But it's your work." Lena tilted her head to one side, and her gaze flitted all over Jess's face.

"And it's your education." Jess cupped Lena's jaw and locked eyes with her. "It's more than that. It's your dream. And we're partners. That is, if you want to be." This time, she didn't hesitate. It might be soon, but that's how she felt about Lena and she wanted her to know that.

269

"Thank you," Lena whispered, and her breath tingled on Jess's lips. "Yes, I very much want to be. I love you."

"I love you too." This time, nothing stopped them from kissing, and Jess lost herself in the soft touch.

The December afternoon was sunny, but it was still too cold to be out without a coat for long. Lena jogged down the path to the garden house. The enticing scent of tomatoes and herbs welcomed her home after a long day at Maggie's desk. Amazement at someone cooking for her hadn't worn off in the last two months. Since she'd moved out of her grandma's, she'd been the one responsible for every meal and, more often than not, for everyone else's meals.

But now Jess had four days off every week and was using the time to learn to cook.

Lena quickened her steps, even though her muscles protested. She wasn't used to a desk job, as much as she liked the actual work. She needed a walk after dinner to work off the stiffness. Or a massage. The thought warmed her better than a coat would have.

Wearing a thick sweater and wrapped in a quilt, Jess sat on the porch with Ella, giving her the bottle. She smiled at Lena.

The image stirred Lena's heart, as always. Her favorite two women. She still couldn't believe how fast she'd gotten used to their daily presence in her life. "Hi, there." She kissed Jess on the mouth and Ella on her head.

"Dinner will take another ten or fifteen minutes. You want some tea?" Jess motioned with her head to the table, where a travel cup waited.

"For me? Thank you." Yawning, Lena sat in the other chair and sipped the still warm tea. Mint with ginger and a hint of honey. For someone who supposedly didn't like tea, Jess had become quite good at combining fresh ingredients. "How can I be so tired when I didn't do anything but sit all day?"

"Your brain needs fuel too. We can skip our walk later."

"No. I've looked forward to it all afternoon." Lena pretended to pout. "How was your day? Did you have time to do anything apart from watching cooking shows online all day?" She winked. "Still in your Italian phase?"

"Are you complaining?" Jess struck out her tongue. "Vegetable lasagna. And I even made the pasta myself. And cleaned up the mess afterward. You're welcome." She took the empty bottle from Ella when she stopped drinking, held her against her shoulder, and stroked her back. "And I did some paperwork today, preparing for tomorrow, so I won't need to be at the clinic for too long." She sighed. "I need to swing by my condo to get some more warm clothes after work. I wonder if I should stay the night there. It would be easier. But I'd miss you two." She glanced from Ella to Lena.

"Or I could come to your place after work and bring Ella if you don't mind me staying over."

"Really?" Jess's face lit up. "I thought you hated the place."

"Hate is such a strong word." Lena shrugged. "I didn't feel at home there, didn't feel your presence. But we're in a different phase of our relationship now. And I thought, maybe, sometime later, when we're both sure it's the right time, I could move in with you. Especially when you start working more hours again. It would make sense."

Jess's eyes widened. "You'd move in with me?"

"I mean, I would pay rent. At the end of the year, one debt will be paid off, and I can afford more rent and—"

"No, wait. I don't want money to be an issue between us."

Lena believed her, but it wasn't that easy for her. "I know you mean well, but you only say that because you have money."

"I know. And does it make me happy? It makes me well fed and clothed, and I have a roof over my head that's too large and empty and soulless."

"Soulless?" Lena wouldn't have worded it the same, but that had been her impression too.

Jess grinned. "Yeah. I'm not feeling at home there either. So let's not argue. I don't think either of us wants to move there. I had another idea. Today, I had a rather lengthy conversation with the real estate agent who sold me my condo."

"What were you talking about?"

"I wanted to know my options, how the market is for condos."

"You want to buy another condo?"

"No, actually, I was thinking about selling and moving back to my mom's." Her expression was carefully neutral.

By now, Lena had learned that this expression meant Jess was emotionally invested and even a bit insecure about Lena's reaction. Really, Jess wasn't as hard to decipher as she probably thought. "You want to live with Maggie? Full-time?"

"Or I'll search for another place nearby. I'd love to be closer to you. Every day. I love the long weekends, but the middle of the week is still empty."

"Why don't you move in with me?" Lena held her breath. She hadn't thought this through before offering. Were they ready to take the next step? Was she ready to give up her own space?

"In the garden house?" Jess trailed her fingers over the wooden wall next to her. "But you told me that it is your sanctuary. The first time you have something to yourself. I wouldn't want to take it from you."

That Jess had remembered and considered her feelings above her own was everything Lena needed to hear. "You wouldn't be taking it. I'm offering to share. You love this house as much as I do. And if you move in with me and pay half the rent, I wouldn't need to give massage classes anymore and we could make that Ella's room."

"I'd love to move in." Jess grinned, then her smile dimmed a little. "But isn't it too soon? I'm not talking about practical reasons like rent, which my mom wouldn't let me pay anyway, or driving back and forth. I'm talking about us."

"What more do you need to know about me? I've told you about all the problems in my past."

"I was thinking more about my flaws." Jess shifted Ella on her other shoulder and wrapped the quilt around her. "You're perfect the way you are—calm, tenacious, caring. I'm constantly fearing you'll wake up one morning and realize I don't deserve you and you can find someone better."

Shaking her head, Lena slid forward in her seat until their legs touched. "Why would I want to find someone better? You're the best for me." She held Jess's gaze. Lena didn't want any uncertainty to remain between them. "All these years, I was afraid I was too trusting. I wouldn't realize how people really were until I was in head over heels, so I started keeping everyone at a distance. But with you, it's the opposite. You broke through my walls and forced me to really see you. We clashed more than enough in the beginning, and I learned more about the negative and annoying character traits you have than I ever could if we met at any other time in your life. I saw you at your worst, and your good qualities still outshone the bad. You care about others, sometimes too much, so that you end up hurt and angry. You didn't give up, even when your body failed you. You never lost your sense of humor. You own your problems and work at them. When you do something, you're all in. You don't do anything halfway. I fell in love with you because of who you are, not in spite of it."

Tears glittered in Jess's eyes. She wiped at them with her sleeve, an awkward motion since she still held Ella against her shoulder. "I love you so much, and I'll never understand what you see in me."

"I'll work on showing you every day." Lena stroked with her thumb over Jess's cheeks, erasing the last traces of her tears. "So we're doing this? Moving in together?"

"Yes. The garden house might be small, but I think it'll let us grow together as a family."

"Family." Lena sank into Jess's eyes, blue like the sea, but instead of drowning, she floated in the warmth.

A shrill alarm sounded from Jess's phone on the table. Ella stirred and cried, and Lena reached for the phone to shut it off at the same time as Jess did. Their fingers collided, and for a second, Lena forgot what she had intended to do. But the annoying beeping reminded her soon enough.

"Dinner is ready." Jess looked from Ella on her shoulder to Lena.

"You want me to get dinner or try to reassure Ella?"

Without hesitation, Jess stood and handed Ella over. "My tears are not helping. She might be quieter with her other mom."

Lena wasn't sure she had heard right, but Jess left before she could ask her to clarify. She snuggled Ella against her and stood to pace. In combination with cooing noises, that seemed to do the trick to calm Ella, even if it didn't help Lena.

Family.

She had said it herself, not a minute ago. When Jess decided something, she went all in. Would Lena be able to do the same? She had always held something of herself back to protect her heart. Only it was too late. She was all in already. Her heart had committed to Jess and Ella and Maggie. To her family.

She hastened inside the house, needing to be close to Jess, who had just taken the pan from the oven. Mouthwatering steam filled the kitchen.

"Jess?" Lena stepped next to her. "Did you mean what you said? If it was just a figure of speech or…I can understand. I know you can give no guarantees for forever, but if you say this now and later leave me and take Ella…I don't think my heart could handle it." She knew she was babbling, but her fears needed to be voiced.

Jess slipped out of the oven mitts and hugged her, careful not to squeeze Ella between them. "Yes. I meant what I said. I know I offered myself to you already, but Ella is the most important part of me, and I would be honored to share her with you. I don't want a babysitter or a stepmom or anything like that. I want to be a family with you, and I would love for you to be her mom, same as me. If you want to?"

"Yes." Nothing more could be said, at least not with words. Lena leaned into a kiss that was different. Not because they were standing in the kitchen with Ella wedged between them. No. Because they were both parts of a whole and the kiss sealed them together.

If you enjoyed *Heart Failure*, you might want to check out Chris Zett's *Irregular Heartbeat*, the novel in which Diana and Emily met in the emergency department and fell in love.

About Chris Zett

Chris Zett lives in Berlin, Germany, with her wife. TV inspired her to study medicine, but she found out soon enough that real life in a hospital consists more of working long hours than performing heroic rescues. The part about finding a workplace romance turned out to be true, though.

She uses any opportunity to escape the routine by reading, writing, or traveling. Her favorite destinations include penguin colonies in Patagonia and stone circles in Scotland.

CONNECT WITH CHRIS
Website: www.chris-zett.com
Facebook: www.facebook.com/ChrisZettAuthor
Twitter: @ChrisZettAuthor
E-Mail: chris-zett@web.de

Other Books from Ylva Publishing

www.ylva-publishing.com

Irregular Heartbeat
Chris Zett

ISBN: 978-3-95533-996-8
Length: 261 pages (94,000 words)

When drummer Diana Petrell leaves her rock-star life to return to ER medicine, she won't let anything stop her—not even falling for aloof mentor, Dr. Emily Barnes.

Emily isn't happy having to babysit an intriguing resident with a ten-year gap in her résumé. But then the lines blur.

What happens to their careers when Diana's secret comes out?

A lesbian romance that asks how much we'd risk for love.

Major Surgery
Lola Keeley

ISBN: 978-3-96324-145-1
Length: 198 pages (69,000 words)

Surgeon and department head Veronica has life perfectly ordered...until the arrival of a new Head of Trauma. Cassie is a brash ex-army surgeon, all action and sharp edges, not interested in rules or playing nice with icy Veronica. However when they're forced to work together to uncover a scandal, things get a little heated in surprising ways.

A lesbian romance about cutting to the heart of matters.

L.A. Metro

(The L.A. Metro Series)
RJ Nolan

ISBN: 978-3-95533-041-5
Length: 349 pages (97,000 words)

Dr. Kimberly Donovan's life is in shambles. After her medical ethics are questioned, first her family, then her closeted lover, the Chief of the ER, betray her. Determined to make a fresh start, she flees to California and L.A. Metropolitan Hospital. When she meets Jess McKenna, L.A. Metro's Chief of the ER, the attraction is immediate. Can either woman overcome her past to make a future together?

Falling Hard

Jae

ISBN: 978-3-95533-829-9
Length: 346 pages (122,000 words)

Dr. Jordan Williams devotes her life to saving patients in the OR and pleasuring women in the bedroom.

Jordan's new neighbor, single mom Emma, is the polar opposite. Family and fidelity mean everything to her.

When Emma helps Jordan recover after a bad fall, they quickly grow closer.

But neither counted on falling hard—for each other.

Heart Failure
© 2020 by Chris Zett

ISBN: 978-3-96324-316-5

Also available as e-book.

Published by Ylva Publishing, legal entity of Ylva Verlag, e.Kfr.

Ylva Verlag, e.Kfr.
Owner: Astrid Ohletz
Am Kirschgarten 2
65830 Kriftel
Germany

www.ylva-publishing.com

First edition: 2020

Credits
Edited by Alissa McGowan, Miranda Miller, and Amber Williams
Cover Design and Print Layout by Streetlight Graphics